TOI & GEAUX

CUT & RUN SERIES BOOK 7

BY ABIGAIL ROUX

RIPTIDE PUBLISHING

Riptide Publishing
PO Box 6652
Hillsborough, NJ 08844
www.riptidepublishing.com

This is a work of fiction. Names, characters, places, and incidents are either the product of the author's imagination or are used fictitiously. Any resemblance to actual persons living or dead, business establishments, events, or locales is entirely coincidental.

Touch & Geaux (Cut & Run, #7)
Copyright © 2013 by Abigail Roux

Cover Art by L.C. Chase, lcchase.com/design.htm
Editor: Rachel Haimowitz
Layout: L.C. Chase, lcchase.com/design.htm

All rights reserved. No part of this book may be reproduced or transmitted in any form or by any means, electronic or mechanical, including photocopying, recording, or by any information storage and retrieval system without the written permission of the publisher, and where permitted by law. Reviewers may quote brief passages in a review. To request permission and all other inquiries, contact Riptide Publishing at the mailing address above, at Riptidepublishing.com, or at marketing@riptidepublishing.com.

ISBN: 978-1-937551-87-2

First edition
April, 2013

Also available in ebook:
ISBN: 978-1-937551-86-5

TOUCH & GEAUX

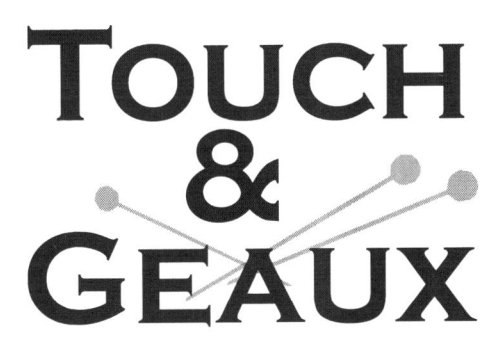

CUT & RUN SERIES BOOK 7

BY ABIGAIL ROUX

RIPTIDE PUBLISHING

To Fate. May it treat you as well as it has me.

Table of Contents

Chapter 1 1
Chapter 2 19
Chapter 3 49
Chapter 4 67
Chapter 5 89
Chapter 6 107
Chapter 7 127
Chapter 8 137
Chapter 9 155
Chapter 10 167
Chapter 11 181
Chapter 12 199
Chapter 13 211
Chapter 14 243
Chapter 15 261

Chapter 1

Zane Garrett glanced up in time to see Alston toss a balled-up scrap of paper across the pod of desks where their team of six sat. Ty Grady threw up his arms, signaling a touchdown as the paper skidded across his desk and into his lap.

"Garrett, Grady, in my office," McCoy called from his door. He disappeared inside.

"What'd you guys do now?" Alston asked.

Zane rolled his eyes. "Wasn't me."

"This time," Clancy chimed in.

"I hope it was me," Ty said with relish. He stood and buttoned his suit, leaving a half-finished firearms discharge form open on his computer.

"Sometimes I wonder how far you'd go to get out of paperwork," Alston said.

"Watch old episodes of *Pinky and the Brain* and you might get close," Zane muttered, drawing snorts of laughter from their other two teammates.

"Before everything went digital, I had the Bureau docs convinced I was allergic to paper pulp," Ty told them, dead serious. His hazel eyes were shining. "It was beautiful."

"You're allergic to everything else," Zane said as he pushed out of his chair. "Come on. You know what he did to us the last time we made him wait."

"Salon appointments," Lassiter mused.

"PR lectures," Alston said.

"Enforced vacation?" Clancy added.

"Christ, I don't know which of those is worse," Zane said. It was all part and parcel of being Ty Grady's partner. And, Zane had to be honest, some of it was his own fault too.

Ty pointed around at each of his teammates, playfully threatening them as he trailed after Zane. He knocked on the doorjamb, peering into the Special Agent in Charge's office. McCoy looked up from his computer screen and smirked.

A cold chill ran through Zane's body. "Oh hell."

"What now?" Ty blurted. They both knew that the look on McCoy's face was a harbinger of doom.

McCoy shook his head and motioned for them to come in and close the door. Once Ty had pushed it shut, McCoy waved two sheets of paper at them. "Several weeks ago, we had a request put in. An unusual one, but it's a reasonable step toward keeping our noses clean in the press."

"Is this more PR bullshit?" Ty asked.

"It's not bullshit," McCoy had the gall to say with a straight face.

Zane sat with a deep sigh. "You've still got me giving a community lecture once a month as it is. The last one? The deputy mayor asked me if I'd speak to the Chamber of Commerce. How am I supposed to be a discreet, undercover criminal investigator when everyone knows who I am?"

"That's a very good point," Ty said.

"That's one of the things I need to speak to you both about. Individually. Later," McCoy added with a more somber cast to his face. "But for now we'll deal with this one—very reasonable—request."

"Which is?" Ty asked.

"There's a fundraising calendar being put together by a local first responder organization."

Ty stood up, holding his hand out toward McCoy as if to ward off evil. "Hell no!"

Zane blinked. "A calendar?"

McCoy nodded. "They're using people from state, federal, and municipal organizations, and all proceeds are going to a fund set up to aid first responders injured in the line of duty."

"Admirable," Zane said.

"You've both been requested as . . . models," McCoy managed to say without cracking a smile.

Zane looked from his partner back to McCoy. "You're joking." Ty was shaking his head, thumbing through numbers on the cell phone in his hand. Zane hadn't even seen him pull it out.

"I never joke," McCoy said with a hint of mischief. He looked to Ty. "If you're intending to call Richard Burns to get you out of this, I won't have it. The Bureau needs this and you're the ones they want."

Ty narrowed his eyes at McCoy, then turned his phone off and curled his lip at Zane. There was also a hint of apprehension in his expression, but he hid it quickly.

"We've been assured the photographs will be tastefully done," McCoy said.

"Fine," Zane said, pointing at Ty. "Send him. But why me?"

Ty shook his head and gestured toward Zane while raising one eyebrow at McCoy. "I think the real question is: Why do they need me when they have such a fine specimen right here?" he said, sounding like a used car salesman trying to sell a Pinto.

Zane reached out and whapped Ty on the back of the head.

Ty laughed and ducked away, still trying to sell Zane. "Little bit of eyeliner, some spray tan, I mean, come on! He's beautiful!"

McCoy smiled, though he looked as if he was trying not to. "Am I to assume the two of you will agree to representing the Bureau in this?"

"I think 'agree' is too strong a term," Zane said. "This is a bad idea. Remember when we were on TV?"

"Yes, Grady got fan mail for a month."

"I did?"

"We burned it, as you should all evil things," McCoy answered.

From Ty's expression, he was trying to figure out if McCoy was being facetious or serious.

Zane laughed and wiped his hand over his face.

"I'm not going to force you, Garrett. But I am going to force Grady because he owes me."

"What?" Ty shouted.

McCoy ignored him. "But I need an answer from you right now."

Zane was still laughing over the absurdity of the idea as he glanced at Ty, weighing his options and wondering just what the punishment would be if he bowed out. Because there would be retribution from his partner. For sure. Of course, if he went along of his own free will, there might be a reward involved. A hot, naked, angry reward. Not that McCoy needed to know anything about that.

Ty flopped his hands. "I mean, hell, I have about as much say in it as I usually do, so why not? I'm game."

Zane sighed. "I'll never hear the end of it if I say no, will I?" Ty jerked his head to the side, raising an eyebrow higher in warning. He was a handsome man when he was annoyed. "Yeah, that's what I thought. Fine, I'll do it."

"Good!" McCoy stood and clapped his hands together once. "Go now."

"What?" Ty asked flatly.

"The crew is in the lobby to take you to a hotel for the photo shoot. Go. Now."

Ty stood staring at him, head cocked, apparently immobilized by the prospect.

"How long have you known about this, and you're just now telling us?" Zane asked. It was classic McCoy to sit on this for a week and then spring it on them at the last minute so they couldn't wiggle out of it.

"They're in the lobby waiting for you." McCoy sat back down and waved his hand in dismissal, even picking up his pen and pretending to study a report.

Zane pushed out of his chair with an aggrieved sigh. It took two tugs to get Ty moving. As he pushed Ty out the door, Zane turned back to McCoy. "One of these days, Mac, one of these stunts is going to backfire on you in spectacular fashion."

"But not today," McCoy said, smug and smiling.

Zane growled and turned, only to bump into Ty, who had stopped right where Zane had left him. "Grady!"

"I changed my mind."

"Too late." Zane gave Ty a gentle shove toward the elevator.

Ty gave the emergency stairs a glance. He had always been an odd mix of cocksure and shy; part showman, part recluse. He loved a crowd, playing class clown or alpha dog or whatever the situation called for like a chameleon. Zane had seen videos of him from when he had been in service, dancing with other Marines, making fools of themselves to pass the time or entertain wounded companions. He was also willing to play up the sexy in person, using his good looks and charisma for any purpose he deemed fit. But as soon as someone tried to record it for posterity, Ty would freeze like he was hiding from a T. rex. He would much rather be shot at than shot with a camera.

Zane ignored the glances from their curious coworkers, focusing instead on getting Ty into the elevator. Once the doors shut, he groaned and covered his face with both hands.

"A calendar."

"This is not my fault," Ty muttered as the elevator whisked them toward the lobby.

"Of course it's your fault, Ty. Look at you." Zane dropped his hands with a huff. "And what was he talking about with the 'talk to you individually' thing?"

Ty shrugged his broad shoulders, shaking his head and then peering at his hands like he was examining his fingernails. He definitely knew something.

"Ty," Zane rumbled.

Ty glanced at Zane. "I don't know," he insisted. His eyes were wide and sincere, but he couldn't fool Zane. Not after a year of living together.

Zane took a step, intending to pin his partner to the wall to get some answers, but then the elevator pinged to signal their arrival at the first floor, forcing him to halt.

"We will be discussing this later," Zane said through gritted teeth.

Ty's lips twitched and his eyes danced, but he didn't argue.

"You know, I might not have minded this with a little forewarning," Zane muttered. "How I became anyone's idea of a goddamn pinup, I have no idea."

Ty just looked back at him, blinking innocuously. As the doors began to grind open, he smiled. "You're my idea of a pinup," he whispered.

Zane snorted, amused by how easily Ty could still charm him. He brushed his fingertips over Ty's lips before turning to lead the way out into the lobby.

They didn't even get around the corner before three women in various styles of business attire stood and hurried over to them. "Agents Garrett and Grady, thank you so much for agreeing to support our little project!"

Ty gave them a charming smile, even though his discomfort was still obvious to Zane. "We can't really take the credit," he said, voice smooth as honey.

A slim blonde in her mid-thirties, with every hair on her head perfectly in place, shook both their hands, lingering over Ty. "If you'll come with us, we have a van waiting."

"A van?" Zane asked.

"To take us to the hotel."

Zane slid his hands into his trouser pockets and gave an uncomfortable fake smile of his own. He and Ty fell into step as they trailed after the women.

"Tell me, Special Agent Garrett," asked a rather matronly looking woman with a smile on her round cheeks. "Did you happen to ride your motorcycle to work today?"

Zane steps stuttered as they reached the lobby doors. Ty stifled a snicker by pretending to cough.

"Ah, no, ma'am, I'm afraid not," Zane lied through his teeth. It'd just gotten warm enough to start riding the Valkyrie again, so of course he had.

"Oh, that's too bad."

The other woman, dressed in a dark blue pantsuit, just laughed. "Oh, come on, it'll be fun!"

Zane nodded, unconvinced.

"I'd rather chew on a lightbulb," Ty said under his breath.

"That motorcycle was my favorite idea," the short woman said from the backseat of the van as soon as they'd all piled in.

"Oh Violet, forget the bike. We want the men, after all," the lady in blue said. "I'm Cynthia, by the way." She reached over the seat and shook Zane's hand, then Ty's.

"I'm Susan," the blonde added, her voice low and pleasant. "I'm sorry, we should have introduced ourselves before. We're just so excited you agreed to do this!"

"Susan's the one who saw you both on the news," Cynthia said.

Zane smirked. "Is that so?"

"I remember watching that newscast and getting shivers," she confided, smiling at Zane and then turning her long lashes on Ty again. "The presence you both had in front of the camera? I just knew I had to have you."

Zane could see Ty tensing, growing more uncomfortable with the situation. Flirting was like Ty's natural mode of communication, but recently he had grown less likely to engage in it.

"That newscast wasn't representative of us at work," Ty finally said.

"Oh, but it was! You were at work!" Violet leaned over the backseat. "And it's exactly what everyone thinks. That's what we want on the calendar. Something dashing."

"Daring," Susan drawled.

"Dangerous," Cynthia added with relish.

"I . . ." Ty shifted closer to Zane, nodding and clearing his throat.

"Since we did the BPD officers in the jail cell, maybe we could use the cuffs in this one?" Cynthia suggested.

Zane glanced at her, wondering if he should be scandalized.

"Okay, we have that CIA analyst in the suit already, sort of spy style," Violet said, pulling out a notebook. "The bare-chested firemen. The two uniformed police officers in lockup. The EMT in the back of the ambulance. We need something different."

"So maybe it wouldn't be a bad idea to go with a roughed-up, 'not afraid to get a suit dirty in the line of duty' look. With the guns, of course, since we've not used any actual weapons in a picture yet."

Ty looked down at his suit, his favorite Tom Ford suit, and visibly balked at the mention of getting it dirty. "Maybe you could put us in civvies and have us undercover," he suggested as he smoothed a protective hand over his lapel.

Susan gasped and grabbed his arm. "Under covers!"

"No. What? No!" Ty blurted.

"That's brilliant!" Cynthia exclaimed.

Zane felt a real flash of panic. "I really don't think—"

"Oh, I like this even more than the motorcycle!"

"He'll do the motorcycle," Ty tried, but they weren't hearing him.

"Oh, this is perfect. I'll call ahead and have them set up a bed." Susan pulled out a cell phone as the ladies in the backseat chattered and jotted down notes.

Zane leaned in and hissed at Ty. "What have you done?"

Ty shrugged helplessly. "I . . . I'm . . . this is not my fault!"

Ty didn't blame Zane for the glares he received as they rode to the penthouse suite together. He gave himself the same glares in the mirror as two makeup artists scruffed his hair. He had a napkin tucked into his collar to keep the hair product from touching the white V-neck T-shirt he was wearing. They weren't putting makeup on him, thank God. Something about natural close-ups. Ty was trying to block it all out.

He stood when the man told him he was done, and the woman yanked the napkin out of his collar and nodded. Ty turned and headed for the other room in the suite where they'd set up all the cameras and flashing things and umbrellas and what the hell ever they were. In that room was also an artfully tousled bed dressed with charcoal-colored sheets, representing the gray world of undercover work.

Ty looked down at himself. It was close to what he would normally wear: tattered stonewashed jeans, thin T-shirt that stuck close to his frame, bare feet. They'd even left his accessories on him, deeming them stylish enough. A black rubber bracelet and brown leather string on one wrist, his black-banded silver dive watch on the other, his Marine Corps signet ring, and the compass rose on its leather cord. He still felt wildly out of place.

Then Zane walked in, shaking his head. He was dressed the same as Ty, only his T-shirt was black, and his dark jeans were even more threadbare. They'd mussed his hair, too, slicking it back and letting it curl around his ears.

Ty tried to fight down the gut reaction to seeing Zane like that, but it was impossible not to stare.

"You both look incredible!" Susan crooned as she came over and looked them up and down. She flipped her fingers through Zane's hair, then turned to Ty and nodded approval. "Now, if you'll both just climb into the bed, we'll get this going!"

Ty fought back a nervous flutter and moved toward the bed, trying to relax his shoulders as he rolled onto it. Zane followed, not bothering to suppress a chuckle as he sprawled back against the headboard.

They sat side by side, long legs extended, arms crossed. Ty glanced sideways at Zane, unable to suppress the smirk. There was no denying they'd be laughing about this later. When Zane turned to meet Ty's eyes, the camera popped and flashed. Zane shook his head, but he was smiling and his dark eyes reflected a spark when the flash went off.

"It appears you're the good guy in this scenario," Zane said, reaching out to pluck at the front of Ty's white shirt.

"I think we're in this one together."

Zane's jaw jumped as he fought a smile. Ty grinned and the camera went off again.

"Get it? Good and evil in bed together?" His words drew laughter, just not from Zane. "Come on, that's funny!"

Zane rolled his eyes.

"It's a pun!"

The cameras clicked away as they were instructed to move into various positions. Under the covers, on top of the covers, sitting up, stretched out flat, doing the same thing, doing different things. They were both repeatedly told to stop smiling, stop laughing, stop looking at each other. After a while, Ty began to feel disconcertingly okay with the whole thing, lying in bed with his partner in front of a dozen or so people who were snapping off pictures left and right. It was absurd.

"Okay, boys, time for something different," Susan announced after a good half hour of them posing.

"Give us some last shots to finish, and we'll have everything we need," Susan requested. "Feel free to remove the shirts."

Zane tipped his head to one side and shrugged, then gripped the hem of his shirt. Several people in the room tried hard not to stare.

Ty couldn't blame them; Zane's bare chest and muscular shoulders were definitely something to write home about. The camera continued taking pictures as Ty watched Zane strip the shirt off. Not to be outdone, Ty gave Zane a small wink and pulled his T-shirt off as well. When he tossed it toward one of the cameras on the periphery of the staged scene, Susan told the cameraman to zoom as close as he could to the scars that covered both men's torsos.

Ty met Zane's gaze. Zane's eyes were drawn to Ty's lips, and when he looked up again there was a new heat in his gaze. It stole Ty's breath and he couldn't look away.

"Gentlemen, keep looking at each other like that, please; these shots are incredible," Susan told them.

Flashes continued to pop and the camera clicked away. It all faded as Ty stared at Zane.

"Well, I think that will certainly do it," Violet finally said. Ty had to tear his eyes away before he was compelled to lean over and kiss his lover in front of all those cameras.

"Oh, definitely," Susan agreed. "Agent Grady, come and take a look."

Ty rolled out of bed and bent to pick up his discarded T-shirt, careful not to look back at Zane. He leaned next to her to look at the laptop. The photos taken were displayed in a grid on the screen, and Susan had the photographer go through them one by one, critiquing angles and posture, marking some as "no," narrowing down the choices, all the while commenting on how photogenic Ty and Zane were.

"I think we'll have to use one of the ones with the handcuffs," Cynthia said, hesitance in her voice. "They're cute and fit the tone of the rest of the calendar."

Susan nodded. She pulled up one of the favorites. The picture showed Zane stretched out on the bed in the background, hands behind his head as he leaned against the headboard. He was smirking, an almost mischievous expression that was accented by smile lines and the streaks of gray hair at his temples, bare feet crossed at the ankles, biceps displayed prominently. Ty sat at the end of the bed in the foreground, leaning toward the camera, knees apart, elbows resting on them. He held a pair of handcuffs with one finger, letting them dangle. One eyebrow was arched, a sardonic expression on his face. It would probably end up being the photo used for the calendar—for the month of July, apparently, because it rhymed with FBI.

Cynthia sighed as she flipped through the rest of the shots. "These last ones..." She shook her head. "Those are something special though."

Susan hummed as she looked at the last series of pictures. Ty leaned closer. They were more somber than he had thought they'd be, all black and white and gray. Zane looked pensive and melancholy, and even Ty's playful smile seemed world-weary through the lens of the camera. The light highlighted the white slashes of scars on both their bodies. It seemed the only color in the entire canvas was the shock of Ty's washed-out tattoo. There was nothing erotic about the picture. The sheets were barely in the frame, and it left nothing but the starkness of two warriors sharing something infinitely beyond the reach of the camera.

Ty swallowed hard, struck by the image in a way he couldn't quite explain. "Can I get a few copies of one of those?" he asked.

Susan was already nodding before his words were out. "Of course," she answered, eyes glued to the screen. "If you'll just, um . . . sign the usage waivers and . . ." she waved toward a pile of papers, her eyes still on the screen.

Zane walked up to the other side of the makeshift desk, shirt back on, weapons back in hand already. "Are we done?"

Ty looked up at him, mouth gone dry. He nodded and met Zane's eyes. "Come look at these," he requested, voice hoarse.

Zane rounded the pile of equipment as the photographer walked over to the camera. Susan followed him, still talking. Cynthia and Violet chattered off to the side. Zane stopped at Ty's side and looked down at the screen. Ty heard his sharp inhalation.

"Good, right?" Ty whispered.

"Yeah," Zane breathed. "They're not going to use . . . are they?" He pointed at the last few photos.

Ty looked over at Susan, the lines furrowing her clean brow, the look in her eyes. "No. They're going for feel-good, not . . . not that."

He studied the photos again, wondering what people would see in them. There was nothing sexual or even romantic there. But there was something.

"That's us," Zane said quietly. "Really us."

"I asked for a copy," Ty told him, watching him closely.

"Just one?" The corner of Zane's mouth quirked. Then he looked up from the photo, and Ty could read Zane loud and clear. He wanted that photo, but more importantly, he wanted Ty, and he wanted him now.

"I'll share," Ty told him under his breath. He cleared his throat, needing to look away from the expression on Zane's face before they really gave those cameras something to shoot. He picked up one of the waivers and signed it without reading over it, then handed the clipboard to Zane. "Did you get everything you needed from us?" he called to Susan.

They came over to fawn over Ty and Zane a little more, thanking them and praising the pictures they'd taken. One of the assistants took down some information and gave them both a card. Ty's had Susan's number handwritten on it. Then they were left alone to go change back into their suits.

"That was kind of fun," Ty admitted as he stripped off the jeans in the little dressing area.

"Not too bad, I guess. Depends on how cheesy of a photo they end up choosing." Zane changed jeans for suit pants and pulled his T-shirt off again. "I might have been less out of sorts with more warning. It was just . . . weird."

Ty nodded as he stepped into his trousers. He glanced toward the outer room, seeing that everyone out there was occupied, and advanced on Zane even as he buttoned up his pants. He grabbed Zane's face without warning and kissed him. Zane grunted in surprise but was quick on the uptake, hands gripping Ty's upper arms as he joined in the kiss for the few intense seconds.

"McCoy never has to know we got done early," Ty whispered as his hands dropped to Zane's shoulders.

"I don't give a shit about Mac. Let's get out of here."

Ty nodded and stooped to gather the rest of his clothes, tossing his tie around his neck and picking up his shoes and socks. Zane pulled his dress shirt on and did up three buttons, tucked it in haphazardly, just enough to get by, and gathered up the rest.

Ty jerked his head toward the door and headed for it. They weren't far from the house, but they would have to get a cab. He'd rather walk than deal with the photographers and their kidnapper van again.

As soon as the door to the hotel room closed behind them, Ty looked up and down the hallway and then back at Zane with a grin.

"Let's get a room."

Zane laughed and shrugged. "Okay? You missing hotel bathrooms that much?"

The memory of their first time together flashed through Ty's mind, and he nodded. Zane must have seen the hunger streaking through Ty's eyes, because he started hurrying Ty down the hall toward the bank of elevators. Ty grinned, not even worrying about the shoes he carried or the fact that they both looked like they'd already been at it in a janitor's closet somewhere.

Once in the elevator, everything hit the floor anyway, except for Ty, who hit the wall, pinned there by Zane's firm body and demanding mouth. Ty could do nothing but moan and wrap his arms around Zane's shoulders.

If someone had told him this morning that a surprise FBI photo shoot would end up with them making out in a hotel elevator, Ty probably wouldn't have been shocked. He found it funny, anyway.

Zane pulled back for breath and set one palm flat on Ty's chest, holding him in place while stepping backward. "Stay," Zane ordered, pulling his hand away but still pointing at Ty.

Ty nodded wordlessly, wide-eyed and unashamed. Zane did up his buttons, smoothed his sleeves, and shrugged into his jacket, somehow managing to look mostly put together, even if his face was flushed and his hair was still mussed from the shoot. He had just shoved his feet into his dress shoes when the elevator door pinged and opened. "I'll be right back," he said, looking Ty up and down deliberately before growling and striding out of the elevator.

Even after all this time, the prospect of what Zane intended to do to him made Ty's chest flutter.

The phone in his jacket began to ring. "No, no, no!" He fished it out anyway, checking he caller ID. "No!"

He looked up. Several people were backing away from the doors to find an alternate way up as he stood in the elevator shouting at his phone.

"Grady," he growled when he answered the call.

"We're ready here," Dan McCoy said without further greeting.

Ty sighed. "Yes sir."

He hung up just as Zane returned.

"No," Zane said when he saw the look on Ty's face and the phone in his hand. "No! How urgent is it?"

Ty shook his head. "It was Burns."

"Dammit, Grady!"

Traffic was minimal as they made their way toward the Bureau office. Ty either wouldn't or couldn't fill Zane in on why they were needed, and he wouldn't speculate as they walked together toward the elevators. Zane wasn't surprised. Burns was pretty closed mouthed with everything he did. It was odd that they'd come here when Burns had called them. Burns worked in DC, not Baltimore. But nothing Richard Burns did was normal.

Ty punched the button for their floor and then leaned against the elevator wall, watching Zane with sidelong glances. Zane gave him a small smile. Hopefully they'd be able to get back to that hotel suite before the night was over.

The elevator lurched to a stop and the doors shivered open. Ty didn't move. Zane stepped out of the elevator first. He looked over his shoulder at Ty, frowning.

As soon as he turned, roughly three dozen coworkers and friends jumped out of their various hiding places amidst the desks and file cabinets and cubicle dividers, all of them yelling some version of "Surprise!"

Zane's hand went to his gun, but Ty grabbed his wrist before he could pull it. Everyone was laughing and blowing on noisemakers, and for a long moment Zane just didn't understand what was going on. "What the hell? This is what the damn calendar thing was for?"

Ty laughed and wrapped his arm around Zane's shoulder. "Just an unfortunate necessity we managed to take advantage of. Happy twenty years with the Bureau, partner."

Zane groaned and rolled his eyes as people all around them started whistling and applauding. "The first eighteen were easy," he said, deadpan, drawing laughter as he jabbed Ty in the ribs with an elbow.

"But the last two were fun."

"Our definitions of 'fun' clearly vary."

"Whatever, Zane. There's cake."

Zane grinned. "You realize last month was actually twenty-one years, right?"

Ty shrugged, smiling crookedly. "Wouldn't have been a surprise if we'd done it at the right time."

Zane rolled his eyes, fighting the huge grin on his face.

"Congratulations, Garrett," Clancy said as she approached them.

Others began surrounding him, offering him words of admiration, some bringing him cake, a drink, or a present. Probably thirty minutes had passed before Zane looked up and realized Ty was nowhere to be found.

"Where's Grady?" he asked, looking over at Perrimore.

Perrimore shrugged. "Skipped out about fifteen minutes after you got here."

Zane frowned and scanned the room. Why would Ty leave in the middle of a party he'd obviously helped plan? Zane shrugged it off. Lassiter gained his attention by approaching to shake his hand and ask for advice on how to be old. He was distracted by more laughter and light ribbing, and he lost track of time again, surrounded by the men and women he'd come to call his friends.

It was Good Friday, though, so the party cleared out quickly. Some left to spend the holiday with their families. Others wandered with every intention of heading to one of the local bars to continue what they'd started here. Zane sat at his desk looking at his twenty-year certificate, which had been stolen and framed while he was gone and then presented as a gift from the rest of his team. The back of the frame was signed by everyone he worked with. In the very middle, Ty's signature stood out. Under it was written a simple note: "You're the best partner I could have asked for."

Zane smiled as he read it. It was so like Ty. Short, sweet, and with a meaning that was innocuous and yet so meaningful. He turned it over and ran his thumb across the glass. Twenty years.

He was so intent on the certificate and what it meant that he didn't realize he had company until Ty sat on the edge of his desk.

Zane smiled and gazed up at his partner. "Where'd you run off to?"

"I was here," Ty told him. "Wanted you to enjoy your day in the sun so I made myself scarce."

"Would've been just fine with you next to me," Zane said, but he smiled and shrugged. It was a sweet thought on Ty's part, and they'd been making a point not to hover over each other at work functions. "Maybe you could have kept them from ragging on me about my age. Apparently I'm the old man of the department, which I find hard to believe."

"No, I'm pretty sure you are." Ty's voice was teasing, but there wasn't much heart behind the effort. He reached behind himself and picked something up he'd been hiding with his body, setting it in front of Zane with a wistful smile.

Zane stared at the row of delicate white flowers stemming from a sleek black pot, nonplussed until he realized what it was.

"An orchid." He laughed, remembering the day Ty had suggested they cut and run to start a flower shop together and sell black-market orchids out of the back. He glanced up at Ty as warmth spread through him. Anyone who knew Ty may have said differently, but Zane knew he had a knack for sentimental gestures. Of the two of them, Ty was the real romantic.

Ty was smiling, but it didn't reach his eyes. He was fidgeting, messing with the USMC signet ring on his finger.

"Hey, what's that about?" Zane asked, keeping his voice low as he nudged Ty's knee.

Ty looked up at the ceiling and inhaled deeply. "I think you could call it melancholy," he admitted. He didn't even try to deflect it with a joke or a denial.

"About . . . me being older than you?" Zane asked.

Ty shook his head and looked back down at the ring. "It's just . . . what am I going to do when you retire?"

Zane blinked. "Retire? I . . . can't say I've ever thought about it." The words grew more painful as they came out, as it sunk in what Ty was thinking about. Them, apart. Or not together, anyway. No longer partners.

"Well, I think about it all the time." Ty reached out and ran his hand down Zane's face. "You ready to go home?"

The intimacy of both Ty's comment and touch stopped Zane's immediate reply, and he considered his lover for a long moment before nodding. "Yeah."

Ty slid off the desk. He reached across it to gather his keys and coat. Zane's mind flashed back to the photograph of them in bed together and suddenly it was important for him to say something. He stood up and stepped around the desk to stand close, catching Ty's elbow with one hand. "Hey."

They were close enough that Ty couldn't even turn to face Zane. He tried to, brushing his cheek against Zane's nose. Zane whispered in his ear. "I'm not going anywhere. Not without you."

Ty smiled, crow's feet appearing briefly. He was staring at Zane's hand on his arm. "Okay."

"Okay," Zane said, even though it didn't feel like the subject was resolved at all. He watched Ty for a moment, wondering if it was something they'd need to bring up later or if the melancholy Ty had admitted to would pass naturally. That's how Ty usually handled these things.

"C'mon. I've got a hotel room all lined up for something dirty. I also have cake," Zane growled as he stepped back to pick up the napkin-covered plate Alston had given him when he'd cleaned up. He dropped his voice to a near-whisper and grinned. "I'll feed it to you."

Ty laughed breathily and turned toward the elevators, shaking his head.

Zane glanced at the framed certificate and decided to leave it on his desk. It wasn't something he wanted to think about at home. In the reflection, he caught sight of a figure moving down the hallway. They weren't alone, after all. He turned to look over his shoulder and saw Richard Burns stepping into the stairwell. The door shut behind him, not making a sound. Zane stared for a moment, then hurried to catch up with Ty.

"I didn't see Director Burns here during the party, did you?"

Ty shook his head and pushed the button on the elevator. "No, why?"

"He was here."

Ty turned and glanced past Zane at the empty floor. "Pretty sure he wasn't."

"I'm pretty sure he was. I just saw him," Zane said with another look at the stairwell. "We can probably catch him if the elevator hurries."

But Ty shook his head. "Why would Dick be here?"

"You're the one who said he called you."

"I just used his name 'cause I knew you wouldn't argue when I said we had to come here."

Zane searched Ty's eyes for any hint of a lie, but saw nothing to indicate one. He gave the stairwell door another hard glare. He knew what he'd seen. Why the hell was Richard Burns in Baltimore on a Friday night? And why wouldn't he come say hello? What was brewing? The elevator dinged and Ty stepped in, holding the door.

"Zane?"

Zane nodded, eyes still on the stairwell as an uneasiness began to settle in his chest.

Chapter 2

Ty began to laugh when the Valkyrie turned toward the waterfront instead of the row house.

"He's actually going back to the hotel," Ty muttered, following in his old Mustang.

By the time Ty found a spot for the car, Zane had already disappeared inside. Ty gave the front of the car a pat as he walked by. He'd intended to spend the Easter weekend working on her, since he'd only managed to restore the mechanical and interior parts so far, but he had a feeling Zane had other plans. Ty strolled into the lobby, expecting Zane to be waiting for him, but he didn't catch sight of his partner anywhere.

"Special Agent Grady?" a woman asked from the front desk.

Ty walked over, still grinning.

"Your partner said to give this to you," the young woman said with a polite smile. She handed him a room key.

"Thank you." Ty turned toward the elevators as he searched for the room number on the envelope. He'd gotten a suite. "Jesus, Zane. You go all out, don't you?"

He hadn't even gotten through the door of the suite when he was grabbed and shoved against the wall. Hands found their way under his tailored suit and lips pressed against his.

"Zane," Ty gasped.

"You better hope it is," Zane growled. "You ready to be fed cake?"

Ty grinned, looking into Zane's nearly black eyes. He dragged his fingers over Zane's shoulder, tugging at his dress shirt, enjoying the way Zane's eyes were drawn to his lips when he licked them.

Zane's voice dropped. "And some cream too?"

"Bad pun penalty," Ty announced in the deep tones of a sportscaster as he held up an imaginary red card.

Zane grabbed his wrist and pressed it against the wall. "Oh, punish me," he said as he started unbuttoning his shirt with his other hand.

"I think I'm the one being punished." They both laughed.

Ty tugged Zane's shirt out of his pants and ran his hand up Zane's belly. Zane pressed against him and dragged his lips over Ty's. His grip tightened on Ty's wrist and Ty's heart sped up. This first round was going to be hard and messy, he could tell that much.

"Let's get to the bed," he managed to grumble. "Last time we did this against a wall, my calves cramped for a week. And my back has been killing me the last couple days."

Zane chuckled and nodded. He put his lips against Ty's ear, then cupped Ty through his trousers. "Tell me where you disappeared to tonight."

Ty huffed against Zane's cheek. "You think you can torture me for information?"

"Yeah I do." He nipped at Ty's ear, and a shiver ran all the way to Ty's toes.

Ty tried to laugh, but it came out as a gasp as Zane squeezed him again. "I had to get your orchid from the car."

Zane turned his head to brush his nose against Ty's cheek. He was humming, as if trying to decide whether to accept Ty's explanation. He finally chuckled, then ran his hand up and down Ty's torso and kissed him.

"You're lying." Zane's harsh whisper broke the kiss. Ty groaned. "What were you up to?"

Ty slung his free arm over Zane's shoulder, holding on tight. "You always know."

"You have a tell."

Ty laughed, then sighed. "If I tell you now, you promise to still fuck me?"

"Depends," Zane growled.

"Mac pulled me aside. He said we're going to have to start looking at options that don't involve undercover work soon."

Zane took a small step back, his grip on Ty's wrist loosening. "Well, we knew that'd be coming soon. We've had too much exposure."

Ty nodded. "He said we have until November when those calendars hit the shelves. Then we're off UC work and into strictly investigative stuff."

Zane chewed on his lower lip, a frown creasing his brow briefly before it passed and his fingers tightened against Ty's wrist again. "Maybe we can start talking about the afterlife then."

A grin stole over Ty's lips and he nodded. The afterlife. Their plans for when work no longer called them, for when they could come out and truly build a life together. That familiar warmth began to seep through Ty as he stared into Zane's eyes. It wasn't the blinding flare of consuming heat it had once been. The flash and bang were gone, but the desire had grown into something less glitzy and more intense. Ty would never get tired of feeling that way when Zane was close.

"I love you," Ty said, a hint of longing in his voice that he was surprised to hear. He didn't want to have to wait for that afterlife; he wanted it now.

Zane took Ty's face in his hands. "I'm not going anywhere."

Ty's stomach flipped at the mere thought, but he nodded.

Zane huffed, then he was against Ty again, kissing his neck, holding him against the wall and murmuring into his ear. "I have something for you. Something I need to ask you."

"Ask me anything," Ty whispered.

Zane wrapped an arm around him. Ty could feel him trembling. His hand delved into his pocket, searching for something as he gave Ty a slow, sensual kiss. The moment held a sudden weight, something intense enough to push aside Ty's odd sense of impending trouble.

His instincts were proven right when his phone began to ring.

"Don't answer it this time," Zane murmured. His lips dragged against Ty's. "Please."

Ty shook his head. They both knew he had to. He always answered his phone, no matter the time of day or what he was doing. Deuce was constantly complaining about Ty answering his calls during sex.

Zane stepped away with a growl. His hand was still in his pocket. "Better not be work."

Ty's eyes stayed on Zane as he stalked toward the large window of the suite. "Grady," he answered, voice still hoarse.

"Ty," Nick O'Flaherty said in a low voice, small and distorted over the phone.

"Nick?" Ty cleared his throat. It hadn't been one of the ring tones Ty associated with the man.

"I need your help."

The simple phrase hit Ty hard, and his stomach tumbled. "Why, what's wrong? Where are you?" Ty demanded as he trailed after Zane. Zane returned to his side and placed his hand on the small of Ty's back, leaning close to listen in.

"I'm in New Orleans," Nick answered, his voice still pitched low. "I need you to come down here."

"Why, what happened?"

"I've been arrested. They're going to charge me with murder, Ty."

Ty stood in stunned silence for a few moments before looking up and turning to meet Zane's eyes. "What?"

Zane gestured for him to hit the speaker button, and Ty did.

"I'm in jail in New Orleans," Nick said slowly, as if speaking to a child. "They think I killed somebody, Ty. You've got to help me, man."

"What do you want me to do, come bust you out?"

"Ty, you were assigned here for almost two years!" Someone yelled something unintelligible in the background, and when Nick spoke again his voice was lower. "I'm not asking you to come get me out of jail. I'm asking you to come down here and find the real killer!"

Ty looked down at the phone and shook his head.

"They're not looking for anyone else," Nick insisted.

"Who did you kill?"

"Nobody!"

Ty winced. "I mean, who do they *think* you killed?"

"I don't even know. But Digger and I have been together since I landed."

"Where's Digger?"

"He's in the fucking cell next to me, Grady!" Nick shouted. He regained control and whispered his next words. "Ty, please. They find out I'm a cop, I'm as good as dead down here."

Ty narrowed his eyes. "Is this like the time you called me from Panama and said—"

"Ty!"

"Because the 'I've been arrested for murder' gag only flies so many times," Ty warned.

"Ty."

"I mean, one day I'm going to stop coming."

"Ty!" Nick shouted, attempting to be calm and serious but clearly losing his patience. Another shout in the background caused him to hesitate. "Please. You're the only person we know to call."

Ty swallowed with difficulty and frowned at Zane. Zane nodded. "We'll be on the next flight out."

"Thank you, Six," Nick whispered, and the nickname caused the hairs on Ty's arms to rise.

Another voice told Nick that his time was up and the call ended abruptly, leaving Ty staring at his phone.

Zane had to say his name twice before Ty looked up at him. "Let's get moving. I'll go book the tickets. Should we call Mac?"

Ty shook his head. "We'll try to fix this before we go back Tuesday. Maybe we won't miss work."

Better to ask forgiveness than permission. That had become their motto.

Zane grimaced as he turned to get his phone.

"Hey, what did you want to ask me?"

Zane shrugged and gave him a small smile as they headed for the door. "It'll wait."

***

It was well past midnight when Ty and Zane walked through Louis Armstrong International Airport in New Orleans. The shops and restaurants were all closed and barred up, and very few people were walking the concourses.

Ty kept his head down, not speaking at all. He'd said maybe ten words the entire flight from Baltimore, and his barely controlled need to fidget during the 45-minute layover in Charlotte had been like watching a chimpanzee trying to figure out how to pick the lock on its cage. Zane knew all the things that had to be swirling through his partner's mind. Nick and Digger—two of his oldest, dearest friends, brothers in arms—were in trouble down here. Trouble that Ty might not be able to help them out of.

Zane also knew Ty was concerned about showing his face in New Orleans. He'd spent almost two years in a deep undercover operation down here, and he hadn't left on his own terms. Simply being seen by someone he'd known then could put him in a bad spot.

It spoke to Ty's loyalty and love of his friends that he was braving the city at all. Zane couldn't think of many people he'd head back into Miami for.

Ty was holding all of that in, though, keeping his worries to himself and storing them in the tightness of his jaw and shoulders.

They retrieved their one checked bag, which held a few changes of clothing and two hard cases with their service weapons in them, but Ty was too eager to get to the police station to take the time to get the guns out and strap them on.

"We'll get them out in the cab," Ty reasoned. Zane trailed after him, pulling the suitcase along.

When they stepped out of the glass doors and headed for the line of black and white United taxis awaiting fares, the humidity and warmth hit Zane like a physical blow after the long winter in Baltimore.

Ty mumbled under his breath as they walked toward the curb. "Ugh, late April. Never come here after May," he told Zane. "October to April. Place is uninhabitable otherwise."

"Good to know."

The sound of screeching tires drew their attention to the end of the roadway, and a white van came tearing up the loading zone lane. The few people in the crosswalk leaped out of its way as it screamed past the line of taxis.

Ty took a step toward the curb, reaching under his suit coat where his gun usually was as the van's brakes squealed. It rocked to a halt right in front of them.

Someone hit Zane from behind, wrapping his head up in a black cloth and restraining his arms as he was shoved forward. He could hear Ty shouting as he struggled with his attackers, but they were both overpowered and shoved into the back of the unmarked van.

The van pulled away from the curb as the sliding door slammed shut.

"Stop struggling," a voice ordered Zane as his hands and feet were held down against a seat that smelled like Febreze. "We'll be there soon," the kidnapper promised with a sadistic laugh.

"Garrett, don't kill anyone," Ty muttered from another row seat. He sounded calm, and Zane forced himself not to thrash and struggle. They'd have a better chance of escape once the van stopped moving.

Roughly fifteen minutes and a lot of traffic later, the van came to a jarring stop. The door opened, and Zane was dragged out and put on his feet. The hood was yanked off, and Zane blinked a few times as he found himself standing in what was unmistakably the French Quarter. He saw a lamppost with black street signs for Bourbon and St. Philip. The building in front of them was ancient, with timbers and stacked brick showing through the cracking plaster. The second story had no balcony or gallery like most of the French Quarter architecture, just a few dormer windows with light shining through their shutters.

An old wooden plank sign that said Lafitte's Blacksmith Shop was hanging over one of the many open doors. And there were people everywhere. The van pulled away, leaving them standing in the middle of St. Philip with their kidnappers and dozens of drunk revelers staring at them.

The men who'd snatched them were laughing and patting him on the shoulder. He glared at them, recognizing one of the four as he finally got a good look.

Nick O'Flaherty. "You fall for it every time, man," he said to Ty, a hand on his shoulder as Ty glared at him. If Nick was here, then Zane could only assume the identities of the other three. Their faces matched those of the photos on Ty's walls. Sidewinder.

"Asshole," Ty said, voice flat.

Nick grinned and pulled Ty into a hug. "You're an asshole too," Ty said to Digger, who gave Ty's back a pat and stepped away.

Ty was smiling, though he was trying not to, as each of the other men greeted him in turn. Kelly Abbott was there, and Zane was surprised to see Owen Johns present. The last time he'd heard anything about Owen was after Ty had come out to his recon team and Owen had stormed off.

"Zane," Nick greeted. He held his hand out to Zane. "Sorry about that," he added, smiling widely.

"You're an incredible asshole," Zane said. "What the hell is this?"

Ty glanced at him and shook his head, starting to grin wider. "I can only assume this is a birthday party."

"For a psychopath?"

Ty gave him a sad smile and nodded.

"Elias Sanchez," Nick answered, and with the name, the five Marines grew more somber.

Zane inclined his head. Sanchez had lost his life not in battle, but to a serial killer in New York City. The same killer who'd almost taken Ty from them as well, the same one Zane had killed.

"Tomorrow would have been his fortieth birthday," Kelly offered.

"No it wouldn't," Ty said.

"But tomorrow's his birthday."

"Kelly, man, he was the same age as me and Nick," Ty said with an exasperated wave of his hand. Nick covered his mouth.

Kelly frowned and glanced around. "How old are you?"

"Thirty-seven."

Digger pursed his lips. "Anyway. Tomorrow's Sanchez's birthday. Ty's always refused to come party in NOLA, so we knew we'd have to bait-and-switch you down here."

"Wow," Zane grunted. He had a feeling the Recon boys had no idea *why* Ty refused to come to New Orleans. They didn't know luring him here could have put him in danger, and knowing Ty, he wouldn't tell them now. Zane decided to keep his mouth shut.

Digger leaned toward Ty, raising his eyebrows. "And we can't celebrate anywhere else because why?"

Ty rolled his eyes and looked at his feet, shuffling. "Because Digger isn't allowed to leave the state for another year."

"Because why?"

"Because we sent a CIA kill team to his bayou and he almost blew them up."

They all snickered, little boys in the schoolyard talking about a frog they'd stuck in the teacher's drawer.

Zane looked around, his mouth hanging open. "You're all insane."

"Welcome to Recon, baby!" Digger said with a slap to Zane's back that almost knocked him over. The man gave a boisterous laugh and headed off toward a group of women who stood drinking near the entrance to Lafitte's. Owen drifted away with him, having said nothing to Zane and barely greeting Ty with a nod.

Zane looked around, still stunned by the turn of events. They weren't here for a rescue. They were here for a party.

"Life with Ty, huh?" Kelly said to him. He was smiling, his hands in his pockets, just as relaxed and laid back as he had sounded the first time Zane had met him. He was an unremarkable-looking man, with hair a shade between brown and blond and eyes that may or may not have been gray. Or blue. Or green. But Zane remembered Ty talking about how capable the team's medic had been.

Zane nodded, trying to return the smile. "You never know, I guess."

Ty and Nick were in the middle of the street bickering again. Or rather, Ty had his finger in Nick's face and Nick was laughing at him.

"Last time I fall for it, O'Flaherty, I swear to God! Next time you call and need help, you're on your own."

"Yeah, tell that to my boat!"

"*You* shot the holes in it!"

"Strategically! It still floats!"

"I coughed up glitter for a week after Panama, you prick!"

Nick put up both hands to fend off Ty's ranting, but he was laughing too hard to respond again.

"Every fucking time!" Ty shouted before he smacked Nick on the side of the head and stormed off.

Nick doubled over laughing.

"So . . . how many times has he fallen for that gag?" Zane asked.

Nick gasped and held up his hand, displaying all five fingers. "This makes five!"

Zane began to chuckle. It was Ty's one true weakness they could exploit, his loyalty to them. He had come every time they'd called, and would continue to do so no matter what.

Kelly chuckled at Zane's side as they watched Ty disappear into the bar. They followed after him, and Zane's mind immediately went to the last time he'd been in New Orleans, to the last time he'd followed someone he loved down one of these streets.

2003. New Orleans, Louisiana.

"Where are you taking us?" Zane asked as his wife led him down a series of alleys in the French Quarter that looked like they should be filled with vampires. Or prostitutes.

She looked back at him, her eyes sparkling and her hair cascading down her back in waves.

"I promise you'll love it."

Zane smiled and followed, willing to give anything a chance if it got her this excited. New Orleans was their treat to themselves for their tenth anniversary, and Becky had been looking forward to this for months.

"It's this little dive I heard about. They do a sort of comedy burlesque act. It's supposed to be one of the hidden gems of the French Quarter."

"I hate to break it to you honey, but we're not even in the French Quarter anymore."

After another thirty yards, Becky paused at a weathered, wooden door set into a stone wall. They were close to the river, heading past the Market and toward the outskirts of the French Quarter. The carved wooden sign that hung perpendicular from the wall named the pitiful little establishment as La Fée Verte.

"I think this is it."

Zane glanced around and smiled weakly. They were well off the beaten path, the noise of the main thoroughfares dulled by the thick walls and crumbling plaster. "If this isn't it, we're going to end the night in jail."

"You, hush," Becky muttered as she pushed through the door.

Within was a surprisingly large room. It was ill lit and crowded with scarred chairs and tables, most of which were full. The walls were brick stained by age, with patches covered haphazardly by aging plaster and thick baroque fabric. A long bar lined the far wall, and opposite that was a stage with a single microphone stand and heavy, wine-colored curtains.

There were no windows, and the light in the bar came from antique string lights overhead and sconces along the walls that held real candles flickering within hurricane lamps. Wax dripped onto the tables from many nights of lit candles that had never been cleaned up.

Zane let his eyes adjust to the dim light. He'd seen worse. Better too. But also worse. "Wow, sweetie, you take me to the nicest places," he drawled.

Becky laughed and led him to a table near the middle of the room. There was a folded card with the name Garrett written on it in beautiful calligraphy.

Zane pulled her chair out for her, then unbuttoned his suit coat and sat.

She leaned toward him, the firelight flickering in her eyes. "I heard the two performers are incredible. And the rumor is that every Friday and Saturday night, they pick out people from the audience to join them afterward."

"Join them?"

"You know, *join t*hem."

"Oh. Oh!" Zane laughed and looked around as Becky giggled. "What have you gotten us into?"

"Oh come on, it's just a rumor. It'll be fun," she said as she slid her hand into his and scooted her chair closer so she could settle against his shoulder.

A woman came to take their drink order just as a man stepped up onto the stage and took the old-fashioned microphone in his hand. The people around them began to applaud, some of them even whistling and hooting.

Zane smiled and sat back, willing to try to enjoy the evening for his wife's sake. The man on stage wore an old-fashioned suit and eyeliner, and his long hair was slicked back to the point that the candlelight reflected off it. He held a bowler hat in his hand, pressed to his chest. Zane cocked his head as he admired the man. He had wide shoulders and compact, hard muscles that showed through the thin, ruffled shirt he wore.

Becky whistled and began to laugh. "He's pretty."

Zane clucked his tongue, mentally echoing her.

The man welcomed them to a night of debauchery and decadence, and almost immediately he began to pick people out of the crowd and insult them. Zane was surprised at first, but the packed audience was eating it up.

The man turned his attention on them with an appreciative whistle. "Well hello, beautiful," he said in a deep voice as he took a few steps toward their table. "Where have you been all my life? Where are you from, gorgeous?"

Becky laughed and sat forward. "Austin, Texas."

"Yeah, wait your turn, honey, I'm talking to your boyfriend."

Becky cackled and covered her mouth with her hands, looking at Zane as the audience laughed.

Zane felt himself blushing. He laughed and shook his head, meeting the man's eyes with a strange rush of excitement. He realized he was enjoying the attention.

The man on stage gave him a rakish once over. "Congratulations on your face, darlin'," he said, and then moved on, addressing a few other couples.

Zane watched him, his mouth ajar. He'd rarely experienced even a passing interest in anyone but his wife. What was it about this guy that had caught his eye?

It wasn't long before a woman joined the man on stage. They made an attractive couple, with talent and chemistry. Their voices battled for supremacy at times, other times melding together smooth as silk. They sang, told jokes, and even performed some physical gags, almost like skits. And some of the sexiest costumes Zane had ever seen. He wasn't watching the sensuous curves of the woman in her corset, though, but rather the solid lines of the man's shoulders as he moved. When he offered his rendition of "House of the Rising Sun," it raised the hairs on Zane's arms. He couldn't look away.

For the last act of the show, the woman sang a rousing patriotic burlesque number as the man weaved his way through the crowd with his bowler hat, collecting tips from the tables. He would clap along with the music as he moved from table to table, egging people on and getting the crowd involved. Zane's eyes followed his movements. Over the last hour of watching him, Zane had decided that he was definitely attracted to the man. It didn't strike him as odd, but it was distracting enough that he had to sit and dwell on it.

When the performer approached their table, Zane's heart rate sped up. The man grinned at them, showing perfect teeth to go with his handsome face. He held his hat out, and Zane dug out a hundred dollar bill and tossed it in, trying to get a look at the guy's eyes. He decided they were green.

The guy watched the bill flutter into his hat, then twirled the hat around his hand and displayed the empty inside of it to them, his expression scandalized as he discovered the seemingly disappearing bill. Becky laughed and Zane grinned, impressed with the man's nimble fingers. The bill was nowhere to be found.

He bowed, then plopped the hat on his head and gave Zane a wink as he turned away.

Zane's heart gave a skip and he cleared his throat, growing more flustered and confused by his reaction.

Becky leaned closer, biting her lip on a smile. "I just want you to know that if you ever wanted to hit that, I'd totally be behind it if I could watch."

"Oh my God," Zane muttered, but he couldn't help but laugh.

"You're blushing!"

Zane laughed harder. "Let's just go."

"I told you it'd be fun," she said as she grabbed for her coat.

They were standing from their table when the woman who'd been performing came up behind them and put her hands on each of their shoulders to keep them in their seats.

"Did you enjoy the show?" she purred.

Becky beamed up at her. "Oh, it was so much fun."

The woman gave her a gracious nod. "Would the two of you be interested in joining us for an after-party?"

"Oh," Becky murmured, and Zane could see the blush creeping up her face now. She looked at Zane, her eyes wide.

Zane smiled at her, but underneath the amusement, he realized he was curious. Not necessarily tempted, but certainly curious. He shook his head though, chalking it up to too many hurricanes and too much debauched revelry for the night.

"Thank you, but . . . we'll have to pass," he said to the woman.

"Shame. Y'all come back any time."

Becky held her breath until the woman was gone, and then she gasped and hit Zane in the chest. "I can't believe that just happened!"

Zane laughed and took her elbow, helping her to her feet. "Let's get you back to the hotel so I can take advantage of you."

They were still laughing as they pushed through the heavy wooden door into the alley. Zane glanced to his right to see a dark figure leaning against the wall further down, a halo of blue smoke rising from his lips. His back was against the wall, his hips jutting out, one foot propped up against the brick. He made an enticing, sensual silhouette.

Zane nodded at him, recognizing the outline of the bowler hat. The man reached up to the bill of his hat, tipping it to them. Zane stared for another moment before he tore his eyes away and followed his wife out of the alley.

"You've never told me that story," Ty said with a frown.

Zane shrugged. He'd never had occasion to tell it, he supposed. They were huddled around a tiny bar table in one of the quieter establishments, far away from Bourbon Street. The memories had surfaced clearer than he'd expected, but he was frustrated to realize that he couldn't describe the man in the bowler hat. He only recalled the impression he'd left so many years ago, but Zane supposed that was enough.

He played with the ice in his glass of Coke, fighting the desire to pick up Kelly's drink and throw it back. His one year sober chip was heavy in his pocket. Ty wasn't drinking, putting up a united front with Zane so it wouldn't be quite so hard to fight the urge to indulge. Zane appreciated the gesture, but he hated to tell Ty that no matter what he did, Zane still suffered.

"What year was it?" Ty asked.

"2003. Our tenth anniversary."

"And you don't remember what he looked like?"

"Couldn't pick him out of a lineup."

Ty nodded, looking almost relieved. Zane studied him for a moment, wondering why. Was it possible Ty knew the man he was talking about?

"So that was your first foray into the gay, huh?" Digger asked. They were far enough into the night that Ty and Zane were the only ones who were sober.

Zane laughed. "I wouldn't call it a foray, but yeah, I guess. I didn't often notice anyone other than my wife, actually. The first actual foray didn't come until I was in Miami."

"That was after your wife passed away, right?" Owen asked. Zane nodded. The man had been making an effort, Zane would give him that. He looked supremely uncomfortable whenever Ty and Zane displayed any kind of affection, but he was keeping his mouth shut.

The conversation drifted into an awkward lull. Zane glanced at Ty and patted his back pocket. He'd stopped at one point in the night and bought a pack of cigarettes and a lighter. Ty hadn't said anything, seeming to know that giving in to this one vice would help him fight the rest.

Zane excused himself and headed outside to light up. He leaned against the old brick in an alcove off the sidewalk, trying to clear his head and enjoying the cigarette just a little too much. He could tell Ty was feeling guilty that they were here, and part of that was knowing what the atmosphere would do to Zane. Ty hadn't known what they were getting into down here, though, and none of the others knew Zane was an alcoholic. It was no one's fault, but Zane was still growing annoyed by it all.

The longer he fought the pull of all that alcohol, the meaner he would get.

A man strolling along the sidewalk bumped into him as he leaned against the wall. Zane peered around the corner of the alcove as the stranger turned. His hand reached for Zane's waist as if to steady himself.

"I'm sorry, love. I didn't see you there," he said, patting Zane's side in an overly friendly gesture. His British accent was pleasant, and it immediately reminded Zane of Ty and the Christmas cruise they'd shared. He was handsome, with blue eyes that Zane could just barely see in the dim light, scruffy blond hair, and a smattering of rakish stubble. He had full lips that Zane's eyes were immediately drawn to, and though he was half a foot shorter than Zane, he was fit and muscular.

Zane gave him a second look over, appreciating the view. He nodded. "Don't worry about it."

The man was patting his pockets, an unlit cigarette between his lips. He grinned. "I see you suffer the same vice."

Zane held up his cigarette. "Guilty. I can't say I'm suffering though."

The stranger laughed. "Filthy habit, I'm told. And the company is often lacking. I can't say that's true tonight." He stuck out his hand. "My name's Liam. Liam Bell."

Zane offered his hand and his name, finding himself growing warmer with the overt flirtation. Liam's hand was rough and strong, and Zane liked the feel of it as he gripped it.

Liam continued to pat his pockets, a frown creasing his brow. "I seem to have misplaced my lighter; you wouldn't mind if I nicked yours, would you?"

Zane placed his cigarette in his mouth and searched his pockets for his new lighter, but all he found was the pack of cigarettes and his wallet. He glanced around the brick wall to see if he'd set it down on a ledge, but it was nowhere to be found.

"Slippery buggers, aren't they?"

Zane snorted. "If I hadn't just lit up, I'd say my boyfriend stole it like he usually does."

"Oh dear, that's unfortunate."

"What is? That he disapproves of smoking?"

"To say the least, yes. That you have a boyfriend at all is distressing."

Zane choked on a laugh, growing warmer still.

"I'm sorry, I forget you Yanks are more coy than I'm accustomed to."

Zane dismissed the apology with a wave. "It's okay. I'm just sorry I don't have a light now."

Liam looked down at the cigarette in his hand and sighed. "Well. I suppose it won't hurt me to miss one."

Zane had a free pass for the weekend; he sure as hell wasn't going to miss any. He was going to have to buy another lighter. He glanced over the crestfallen look on Liam's face and shook his head. "We can't have that."

Liam arched an eyebrow, his lips curving into a smirk. He placed his cigarette in his mouth and stepped closer to Zane. Zane had to duck his head to place the tips of both cigarettes together, and Liam's hand came up to cup them, brushing Zane's face. Zane put a hand on Liam's shoulder, holding him still. He had to close his eyes, because being that close to the man made his stomach flutter, and no one had done that to him since the last time he'd kissed Ty.

He sucked on the cigarette, stoking it enough to heat Liam's and start it burning. Liam stepped away, nodding his thanks as Zane's hand dragged across his shoulder. He blew smoke away from Zane's face and winked. "Best chance encounter I've had tonight."

Zane laughed uncomfortably and licked his lips, putting the cigarette in his mouth again so he wouldn't have to say anything.

They stood together, enjoying their cigarettes and the warm night, watching the different sorts of people passing. A man in a top hat and cape strolled by, clicking a walking stick on the pavement. A woman rode the other way on a bike, fairy wings and ribbons fluttering behind her.

"It's an odd sort of place, yeah?" Liam commented. Zane laughed. "That's a big son of a bitch right there," Liam added. He nodded toward the intersection as a man walked across the street. Zane's eyes followed. It was unusual to encounter people that made Zane feel small.

"Hey Zane!" Ty called from the pool of light around the door of the tavern.

Zane glanced toward him and waved. "Be there in a minute."

"Your boyfriend?" Liam asked.

"Yeah."

Liam glanced toward the light. Ty was joined by the others and they stood around talking and laughing, waiting for Zane. It was dark enough in Zane's alcove for Liam and Zane to stare without fear of being seen ogling them.

Liam looked Zane up and down one last time. "Lucky him," he drawled.

Zane glanced at him, surprised. Typically when people saw Ty, the response Zane expected was "lucky *you*."

"Perhaps I'll see you around again. Without your boyfriend," Liam added, giving Zane another wink before he turned and made his way down the darkened sidewalk, away from the tavern.

Zane took a step to watch him walk away. He had no intention of ever being with someone else again, but he could see why Ty enjoyed a harmless flirtation now and then. It was quite the ego booster. And kind of a turn-on. He wanted to get Ty back to the hotel and into a bed now. *Thank you, stranger.* He pursed his lips, turning his back on Liam Bell's retreating form and strolling toward Ty and the others.

Ty put a hand around his waist when he joined them. "Making friends?"

Zane shook his head. "Arranging a tryst for later tonight."

"Oh yeah?" Ty asked, his tone as casual as Zane's had been. "Well, what happens in NOLA . . . goes home with an STD."

A scream tore through the night and interrupted their laughter. Zane wasn't the first to push through the door of the bar, but he could see the commotion over the shoulders of the men in front of him. A woman was in hysterics, being held in place by two men who were trying to ascertain what had frightened her so much. She finally gave up on words and pointed to the tiny bathrooms at the back of the bar.

A red stiletto sat in the doorway, blocking the door open. Beyond, Zane could see one bare foot on the floor.

Nick forced his way through the crowd, reaching the bathrooms first. "I'm a cop, I'm a cop, move aside," he kept repeating, until he'd almost cleared out the area. One look into the bathroom was all he needed. He didn't even try to step in to check the girl. He turned to them and gave a curt nod. "Call it in," he said. "And don't let anybody leave."

Owen and Digger had stayed near the entrance, and they closed in to block the doors, preventing anyone inside from exiting. The patrons began to protest, panic building as they realized they were trapped.

"Everyone stay calm," Zane called out, raising his badge so people could see it. "Remain calm until the police arrive and we'll get this sorted out. We're containing the scene and material witnesses, that's all this is. We thank you for your cooperation."

The crowd began to calm with his words. Nick nodded to him and smiled gamely. None of them were armed because neither Ty nor Zane had been given the chance to get their weapons before they'd been kidnapped. And it was merely luck that Zane still had his badge on him. He was surprised Ty hadn't flashed his as well to help him calm people. Zane took a moment to glance around the bar for his partner. But Ty was gone.

Nick knelt at the door to the tiny bathroom and peered through the crack left by the shoe wedged in it. He had no jurisdiction down here, but it was ingrained to try to preserve a crime scene and that's what he'd done. He felt someone kneel beside him, and was surprised to find Zane instead of Ty there.

Zane gave him a shrug. "I'll have to do for your sidekick this time. Ty's gone."

"What? Where'd he go?"

"I have no idea. He was right beside me one second, then he was gone. He had to have slipped out before you said to block the exits. Fire hazard, by the way."

"The cops can arrest me when they get here," Nick muttered.

Zane snorted. "Is this a murder?"

"I would say so, but I'm sure as hell not touching anything to find out. I'll fake getting pegged for a murder all day, but I don't want to do it in real life. You got a pen or something?"

Zane dug around in his pockets and pulled out a Bic. Nick took it and nudged the door open wider. It was mostly out of habit and curiosity that he was looking at the scene, because the FBI didn't have jurisdiction here, and the Boston Police Department sure as hell didn't either.

"Ligature marks," he whispered to Zane. "Definitely a crime scene."

"What is that in her hand?" Zane asked. He glanced over his shoulder at the people around them trying to peer in.

Nick waved for Kelly, and the man came over to usher people away. Nick smiled. Sidewinder had never been used to investigate crimes, but Nick had to give the boys credit for being able to handle crowd control. Except for Ty, who had bailed on them.

With a bit more privacy to work with, Nick gently lifted the girl's fingers with the tip of the pen. She was holding a small white bag in her palm. Its contents had spilled open: dried herbs of some sort. Probably drugs, but not the kind Nick usually saw at murder scenes. The fact that they were still there meant they weren't anything to write home about. In her other hand was a small strip of paper. Nick was careful not to touch it as he pushed her fingers aside.

Zane crowded closer to him, and Nick shifted to let him see. Zane reached his phone over the girl's hand and snapped a picture. They could hear the sirens drawing near, so they both stood and backed away from the door. They helped Kelly keep people away from it until the police took over.

"What's the FBI and Boston PD doing here?" one of the officers asked Zane, his shoulders squaring like he was preparing for a fight.

"Just on vacation," Zane said with a sigh.

"We didn't touch a thing, just tried to lock it down until you got here," Nick assured the man. "All we want to do is give our statements and move along."

The cop eyed him suspiciously, but he finally gave a nod and took down their accounts. Nick didn't have to tell the others not to mention Ty being there. They all knew he'd spent a few years undercover in the city. Whatever his reasons for disappearing, they were probably good ones.

It was nearly an hour after the discovery of the body before they were allowed to leave.

"Least they could have done was thank us for helping," Owen muttered as they trudged across the street into a crowd of curious onlookers.

"We're lucky they didn't arrest Nick for poking the dead girl," Digger said.

"I didn't poke her. Jesus."

"Looked like you poked her."

"Shut up."

Zane laughed ahead of them, and slowed to let Nick catch up. He glanced at Nick, smiling wryly. "I forget how much you and Ty have in common sometimes."

"Yeah, until O starts taking it up the ass, they're not as alike as you think," Owen mumbled from behind them.

Nick turned and held up his hand, stopping the group in the middle of the road. "Enough with that bullshit, hear me?" He tried to catch his breath to add more, to tell Owen that he did in fact enjoy such things, to finally put up the united front Ty deserved, but a hand on his arm stopped him. He turned to find Ty there, looking sheepish.

"Where the hell did you go, man?" Kelly demanded. "Left us there to do the dirty work."

Ty glanced around guiltily. "I didn't want the locals catching sight of me. And all those people with cameras in their phones, I had to get out."

"Why?" Owen asked. He was still scowling, transferring his irritation from Nick to Ty.

"I wasn't exactly friendly with the locals when I was undercover, okay? I don't want to spend my weekend in lockup."

"Again," Digger added.

"Yes, thank you," Ty snapped. He nodded at Nick. "Was it a murder?"

"Definitely. Looked like it might be drug related."

Zane shook his head. "I don't think so. She was strangled. Pretty efficient. The scene wasn't messy and the drugs were still there. If that's even what they were. Drug deal gone wrong would have been more spontaneous. And the bag in her hand didn't look like any drug I've ever seen."

"Wait, she had a bag in her hand? What kind?" Digger asked.

Zane and Nick shared a glance, then both shrugged. "It was just a little white bag," Nick said.

Ty held up his hand, making a circle out of his thumb and forefinger. "About this big? Full of herbs?"

"Yeah," Zane said.

"I saw you take a picture. What was that of?"

"You *saw* me? How? Where were you?"

Ty shrugged. "Around. Did you get a picture of the bag?"

"No. She had a slip of paper in her other hand," Zane said, glancing at the others as he dug out his phone. "I took a picture of it to see if we could read what was on it, but I couldn't get a good angle."

"Can I see?" Ty held his hand out for the phone. Zane handed it to him. Ty's frown deepened as he looked it over, then he glanced up to meet Digger's eyes. "It looks like a strip of parchment."

"It would have had her name on it then. It was a gris-gris bag," Digger said. Ty nodded.

"What the hell is a gris-gris bag?" Nick asked.

"Voodoo," Zane said. "Right?"

Ty nodded again and gave him his phone back. "They're usually used for good things. Luck, love, safe travel, protection. All kinds of stuff. But sometimes they can be used to bind or hex. It's rare; most voodoo practitioners don't mess with the negative outcomes."

"Too dangerous," Digger explained.

"Dangerous? What does that mean?" Owen asked.

Ty looked around the crowd that had formed. He took a deep breath, beginning to edge toward the nearest side street as he spoke. "It's like a boomerang. The evil comes back at you."

"Threefold."

Nick snorted. Between Ty, Digger, and Sanchez on missions, all the superstitions had almost killed them all. It was contagious, though, because Nick had carried his own good luck charms with him. So many that other Marines had taken to calling him Lucky. After all he'd seen and been through, he was willing to put some stock in the reality of magic.

But Zane gaped at Ty. "You actually believe in that stuff?"

"To an extent, yeah. Yeah, I do." Ty shrugged. "And you can bet people around here believe it too."

"The stronger you believe, the stronger the power of the spells," Digger added.

"Wow, D. Wow," Kelly said. He was keeping a straight face, but his mouth twitched.

"Well, the bag the girl had was white," Nick said. "What's that mean?"

Ty ran a finger over his lower lip, wincing. He walked further into the shadows, like a magnet being repelled by the crowd. "I think it's for protection. Something about protecting your home, maybe. I don't remember."

"It's for any kind of protection," Digger said.

"Well, it didn't work for her," Owen muttered.

They all stared at him for a second before Nick cleared his throat. "Anyway."

"Are we investigating a murder while we're here, or are we actually going to get to be normal tourists this time?" Kelly asked.

Zane glanced at the scowls they all gave Kelly and he laughed. "This time, huh?"

"Don't ask," Nick muttered. His theory was that it was because they were all trained to help, but even he had to admit they stumbled over crimes more often than your average bear.

Digger shrugged. "Sounds like a hoodoo thing. Turf wars. The locals can handle the weird ones like that."

Ty looked relieved.

Nick wondered just how much trouble Ty would be in if someone recognized him down here. He knew Ty would never tell them until trouble reared its ugly head, but he supposed he should have expected Ty to have left New Orleans with enemies. He was suddenly very conscious of the fact that they might have put Ty in danger by luring him here.

"Not our jurisdiction. Not our problem, right?" Ty said.

Zane's brow furrowed, but he remained silent.

Nick shrugged. "I guess not."

Kelly continued on down the street. "Kind of a buzzkill though."

The grisly crime in the middle of their revelry had indeed cast a pall over the night, but they only had the weekend to enjoy each other, so they continued on. They hopped from bar to bar for another hour, and after a quiet talk with Zane about the alcohol, Ty finally ordered himself a few oddly colored drinks to toast the memory of their fallen brother. They told stories, sharing them with Zane so he wouldn't feel left out, and reminisced about the good days they'd spent together.

Most of the tales had to do with Elias Sanchez, and Ty had to force himself to relax and enjoy it. It wasn't hard to push the murder out of mind; that was what they dealt with every day and he'd learned to compartmentalize. He ignored the fact that Owen was ignoring him. He battled the guilt that came with every sip someone took in Zane's line of sight. He tried to forget that he might be recognized by the wrong person and bring all kinds of trouble down on them.

The ambiance and good company were finally enough to filter through the worries, and the night wound down as a success. As they were strolling toward the hotel, Ty slipped his arm around Zane's shoulders. New Orleans was still one of the most romantic places Ty had ever been. He couldn't wait to get Zane alone and finish what they'd started back in Baltimore.

Nick had booked them all into the Bourbon Orleans, making a point of giving Ty and Zane their own room for the weekend. The rooms weren't together, so they said good night to the Recon boys in the elevator at the third floor, and then rode up two more to their own room.

"It was nice of him to do this," Zane said. He was working the key card to the room as Ty leaned against the wall beside the door.

"More like self-preservation. Nobody wanted to share a room with us."

Zane glanced at him with a smirk. "How drunk are you?"

Ty bit his lip against a smile. He reached out for Zane, hooking him by his belt to pull him closer, and Zane left the key in the door and reached for Ty's hips with both hands. He pressed Ty hard against the wall as they shared a languorous kiss. Ty was ever conscious of the taste of liquor on his tongue, but he supposed the cigarette taste in Zane's mouth would combat it.

Zane broke away and opened the door, shoving Ty in ahead of him. Ty chuckled as he entered the room.

Zane gave him a smack on the ass, then shrugged out of his jacket and tossed it at the chair in the corner as he headed for the balcony doors to peer at the view. Ty hung back, enjoying the roll of Zane's shoulders and the way his long body leaned to the left without him realizing it. Ty had decided it was a cowboy lean, something he'd never actually noticed until after he'd seen Zane in Texas over the summer. It probably had more to do with the gunshot he'd taken to his thigh than anything, but something about it hit Ty the right way.

"Ty."

"Huh?"

"You didn't hear a word I just said, did you?"

Ty looked into Zane's eyes and began to smile, shaking his head. Zane huffed.

"What did you say?"

"I was talking about how odd it is that we keep stumbling over these murders. It's like someone has it out for us."

"Ugh, Zane, don't think too hard about it."

"Fine. I'm too tired to shower and too dirty to go to bed," Zane said. He was stripping off the rest of his clothing, tossing them toward the chair.

"That's the beauty of a hotel."

Zane narrowed his eyes, looking Ty up and down. "You coming to bed?"

Ty nodded, but he made no move to undress. "Will you tell me a story?"

"A story? What are you, five?"

Ty grinned. He began pulling at his buttons. "Tell me about the guy in Miami."

Zane snorted. He reached to help Ty out of his shirt. "Why? Does it turn you on to hear about my past conquests?"

"A little, yeah," Ty admitted.

Zane arched an eyebrow. "Really?" He tossed Ty's shirt away and pulled him closer. "Take that shower with me first?"

Ty nudged his nose against Zane's cheek, grinning.

It didn't take much to convince Ty to shuck his clothing and climb into the shower with Zane. They went about it slowly as they let the water heat up, standing in the middle of the bathroom and kissing. Zane could see them in the mirror over Ty's shoulder. He watched his hands drag across Ty's skin, leaving red streaks behind that soon disappeared. He watched the muscles of Ty's back slide, the biceps with the bulldog on it flex.

He grabbed Ty's arm and dragged his teeth over the tattoo. "This might be my favorite part of you."

Ty turned his head to press a kiss to Zane's chin. "Why?"

"It's who you are." He kissed Ty again, holding him tighter. "It's you in meta form."

"Zane." Ty's voice was harsh in his ear. "Don't speak geek to me when you're naked. It shatters the illusion."

Zane laughed and grabbed Ty's ass, squeezing hard enough to force Ty to stand on the tips of his toes. He dragged him into the bathtub, kissing him messily as the water beat down on them both.

"I like seeing you with your team," Zane said against Ty's cheek.

"Really?"

"It's kind of hot."

Zane inhaled through his nose as he was thoroughly kissed, and he slid his arms around Ty's waist to pull his lover against his body.

When Ty ended the kiss and pressed his nose to Zane's cheek, his fingers were digging in harder, giving him an almost desperate edge.

"Sometimes I wonder who I'd be if it weren't for them," Ty said, his voice a whisper that barely rose above the sound of the water.

Zane swallowed hard. He'd played that game, and all too often it resembled Russian roulette. What if he hadn't broken with his family? What if he hadn't joined the Bureau? What if Becky hadn't died? What if he hadn't gone to Miami? But all those things had put him on the road that had led him to Ty.

And Ty's road had been just as rocky, but it had led him here.

"You," Zane said, his voice thick. "You'd still be you."

Ty shook his head in a stubborn denial, but he kissed Zane again without offering any evidence to support his belief.

When they broke apart, the bare honesty of what Zane wanted to say hurt him all over. But it was high time these things started being said. "Things have happened to us, to both of us, horrible things that changed us. If you want to tell me, I'll listen, or if . . ." Zane swallowed hard. He knew that Ty had endured worse than he had, but there were dark spots in Zane's past that he didn't want to relive, much less tell anyone about. "If you want to know, I'll tell you."

Ty's hands slid over Zane's hair and he patted him before kissing him again. The water was still pounding down on Ty's back, running in rivulets down his face. "I want to know."

Zane nodded and slid his hands down Ty's back to cup his ass, then slid one hand between them.

Ty's breath stuttered. He relaxed against Zane and kissed him again.

Zane wrapped his hand around Ty's cock, warm and wet and firm under his fingers. Zane had been hard since Ty had touched him, and he pushed against Ty's thigh, moaning as he dipped his head for another kiss.

Ty's breaths came hard against Zane's skin, gusting over his lips and warming his cheek as Ty pushed closer. Then his hands were gripping Zane's arms hard and they separated, Ty holding him at bay in the bathtub. There was a familiar light in Ty's eyes as he pushed him against the tile.

Zane lifted his chin as he hit the cool, slick wall with a muffled thump. "God I love it when you drink."

Ty took one more rough kiss before letting his hands drag down Zane's body. He sank to his knees at Zane's feet. Zane's head thudded back against the wall. His breath came out with a shudder as he watched.

Ty didn't waste time. He rarely did, not when Zane was already hard and begging for it. He gripped one of Zane's hips with one hand, taking Zane's cock in the other and pumping him as he let his lips bump against the head. He looked up, giving a teasing lick. Zane narrowed his eyes and reached for him, cupping his palm around the back of Ty's head, tugging. Ty didn't make him wait any longer, but he did force Zane to be patient as he slid his lips over Zane's cock with agonizing slowness. Ty never did anything that slow unless he was trying to drive Zane insane.

It was working.

Zane curled the fingers of his free hand into a fist and tried to breathe evenly.

Ty's free hand splayed against Zane's hip, and he finally, mercifully, dipped his head to take Zane all the way into his mouth. Zane bit his lip and squeezed his eyes shut, concentrating on Ty's tongue and the warm slide of his cock into Ty's mouth. A clicking noise from the outer room filtered through his pleasure, like someone trying to use a key that wasn't working. Zane glanced at the door to the bathroom, which they'd left wide open. Ty didn't seem to care about any noises as he worked, trying to make Zane come as quickly and messily as possible—something he was singularly good at.

Zane groaned and closed his eyes, forgetting the sounds. There was something too debauched about Ty on his knees, water streaming over hard muscle and smooth skin, Zane's hard cock sliding between his lips, forcing them apart to find his flickering tongue. To top it all off, Ty met his eyes, then ducked his head forward, taking Zane into the back of his throat, burying his nose against Zane's groin and pulling him close as if he couldn't get Zane deep enough.

Zane smothered a curse, and his gut clenched. He had no control around Ty; never had, never would. He took Ty's head in both hands and pumped his hips, feeling the head of his cock forcing its way past Ty's tongue to hit the back of his throat. He gave a plaintive grunt as Ty pulled back, tugging on Ty's head until Ty let him thrust in again. How the hell he did that without gagging, Zane would never know. He'd been practicing, but he still couldn't manage. What he did know was there was very little he enjoyed more than shooting a load into Ty's mouth and watching him swallow it down. Ty always hummed when he blew him, and he moaned when he swallowed.

He half bent over in reaction as the trembling started, and he grabbed at Ty's shoulder as he started to come, teeth gritted.

But Ty didn't swallow this time. He pulled back just enough, holding Zane's hip against the shower wall with one hand so Zane couldn't chase his mouth, and he pumped Zane dry with the other hand, letting cum spurt all over his chin and neck. It hit Ty's skin, and Zane could see it dripping down Ty's throat, sliding off his lower lip. It just made Zane's climax more intense, like he was marking his territory. He choked off a curse as the heat flooding him left him dizzy.

Ty kept at it until there was nothing left but Zane's whimpers, then he let Zane slide out of his hand and looked up at him, licking his lips and wiping his palm across his chin. Zane dragged his fingers along those lips before tapping under Ty's chin, wanting him to stand.

Ty climbed to his feet, diving into the kiss Zane had ordered with alarming obedience. He pressed against Zane, hips flexing as he delved into another, more demanding kiss. Zane could taste his cum on Ty's lips. Ty was hard against him.

"You are too fucking hot for your own good," Zane gritted out.

Ty made a frustrated sound into Zane's mouth. "God, the things I want to do to you right now."

Zane nodded, biting at Ty's full lower lip. "Do them." He reached for Ty's cock and squeezed.

Ty's hands found their way into Zane's hair, and he continued to kiss him, holding him there by his wet curls as Zane stroked him. "Next time we do this, I'm bending you over that balcony," Ty said. His voice was just as strained and taut as his body.

Ty bit Zane's lip, not hard enough to hurt, but hard enough that Zane knew he was getting worked up.

"C'mon, Ty. Let me see you come. So fucking gorgeous when you come."

"Jesus, Zane, stop talking," Ty gritted out.

Zane laughed. He heard another sound from the room and turned his head to glance out the door. "Did you hear that?"

Ty growled low in his throat. "No." He swiped at Zane's cum, still sliding down his neck and chest, gathered it all into his palm, and replaced Zane's hand on his cock with his own. Zane leaned back, expecting the kind of show that Ty was so good at, but then Ty tugged at his shoulder and turned him around. Zane's chest hit the tile as Ty pressed against him from behind.

"Fuck, Ty," Zane gasped out as he realized what he was really going to get. "God, yeah."

Ty's cock was already pushing at him, Ty's lips on his neck, his body hard and wet against Zane's. Then the head of his cock, slicked with Zane's cum, pressed against the tight muscles of Zane's ass. Zane pushed his hips back and Ty thrust up against him, the slick head sliding between Zane's legs. He didn't enter him, though he came close.

Ty smacked a hand over Zane's mouth and buried his face against Zane's shoulder. His other hand wrapped around Zane's chest. He drove his hips against Zane's ass, using Zane's own cum to slick the way, using Zane's body for the friction he needed.

Ty grunted against Zane's shoulder and dragged his teeth over Zane's skin, tightening his hold as he came. Zane could feel Ty's cum sliding over his ass even as Ty continued to thrust against him. He was making a messy job of it as the water ran over them. It stole Zane's breath and made his knees weak.

Zane reached behind him, dragging his hands along Ty's ribs. When Ty finally stopped moving, he let his hand slide from Zane's mouth and pulled Zane's head around into a slow, languid kiss.

"Now go see what the hell that noise was," Zane mumbled as soon as he was able.

"Not exactly Casanova, are you?" Ty kissed him again, licking at his lips. "But if you insist."

He pushed away and left Zane in the shower to clean up. When Zane finally joined him, he found Ty standing at the foot of the bed, still dripping wet, looking at a stack of folded towels.

"It was a maid?" Zane asked.

"Looks like. Way to ruin the post-orgasm buzz with paranoia, Garrett."

Zane laughed. He stepped behind Ty and wrapped him up in the towel he had around his shoulders, pressing against Ty's back. He kissed his neck. "Let me make it up to you then."

Chapter 3

July, 2004. Miami, Florida.

Zane hadn't heard his real name spoken in almost six months. Two weeks after his wife's funeral, Zane had begged for a new assignment, part of him hoping a change of scenery would make him want to kill himself less, and the other part hoping for an assignment so dangerous he wouldn't have to do it himself. He'd been undercover in Miami ever since, nothing but pure luck and an overdeveloped sense of justice keeping him alive. He wanted to see these bastards go down, and he'd do whatever it took.

He'd found it hard to sleep when he'd first arrived in Miami, a combination of on-the-job jitters and missing his wife so much it felt like his soul was dying. He'd begun drinking to combat the dreams.

A few weeks after that, he'd started popping uppers to combat the hangovers, and sometimes even in a bid to mimic sobriety. He found that it worked for his cover, and it simultaneously dulled and sharpened his mind to the point that all he thought of was the case at hand, like a pen light for his brain. He would do anything to get the wife he'd lost, the life he'd lost, off his mind.

His life had become a high-wire act, and every breath brought him closer to death. He had begun to place bets on what would kill him first: the drinking, the drugs, or the cartel. Tonight was a soiree, held to celebrate the success of a deal Zane had been active on closing. He'd also been active on sending the details to his handler, and he lived in fear of being found out.

The rooftop garden in downtown Miami had been commandeered by the Miami boss, and no expense had been spared to entertain their new partners from Colombia. Alcohol and heroin flowed freely, mixed with multicolored designer drugs and neon blue drinks that looked like antifreeze and kind of tasted like it too. Expensive escorts, both male and female, roamed the crowd, offering their services.

"Xander," a man said as he approached Zane. Zane smiled and turned toward his boss, accustomed to the fake name. His boss had a woman on each arm, both smiling and beautiful, eyes raking up and down Zane's frame. "I have your yearly bonus," el Jefe said with a sideways leer at one of the women.

Zane glanced at her, and his stomach turned at the thought of taking another woman to bed.

"Gracias, Jefe. But no thank you."

"What is it?" el Jefe asked. "Her tits are perfect and her ass is sublime!" He smacked the escort's ass to prove his point.

Zane laughed and nodded, though his mind was still desperately churning.

"Jefe, I think maybe I'm not his type," the woman said with a pout.

Zane was nodding before he could think twice, latching on to that excuse like a lifeline.

El Jefe began laughing and slapped Zane's shoulder. He dragged Zane along with him, taking him toward a corner where people sat drinking and laughing, some sprawled on the plush couches, others perched on the furniture, showing off their wares for anyone interested.

"You pick your own prize, Xander! Have fun tonight, you deserve it!" el Jefe said as he left Zane there and returned to the two women he would be taking for himself.

Zane watched him go, one eyebrow raised as he realized that nobody cared who he took to bed tonight as long as he didn't rain on anyone else's parade. He glanced toward the open bar, fully intending to drink himself into a stupor and pass out on one of the deck chairs around the pool.

He caught a man's profile in his peripheral vision and quickly looked back to find him. For a brief moment he would have sworn it was the man he'd seen in New Orleans all those months ago. When he caught sight of him again, he realized his mistake. The resemblance was striking, though, and as Zane stared, the escort caught his eye and gave him a slow smile.

For the first time in months, that smile stirred something in Zane. He swallowed hard, recognizing the same feeling he'd noticed in New Orleans when the singer in the bowler hat had winked at him.

The man was making his way through the crowd, eyes on Zane, smile still soft and inviting. Zane licked his lips as he drew closer, noticing the way he moved through the crowd, appreciating the roll of his muscular shoulders. Yeah, Zane was definitely attracted to him.

The man stopped in front of him, and Zane stared, unable to get his mind to push past the drugs and alcohol clouding his thoughts.

"Do I know you?" Zane finally asked.

"Would you like to?"

Zane nodded. The man reached out and took his hand.

"Wait, so you picked out the guy in Miami because a dude in New Orleans winked at you the year before?" Ty asked, incredulous and almost offended by Zane's story. They were sprawled sideways in the king-size bed, feet hanging off the edge.

Zane draped his knee over Ty's thighs, his fingers idly running through the fuzz on Ty's chest. "You have your type, I have mine."

"My type is dark hair!"

Zane barked a laugh. "Your type is a gun."

"Whatever, Zane." Ty slid his arm under Zane's neck and stretched, then pulled Zane closer to rest his head on Ty's shoulder.

Zane grinned, running his finger down the center of Ty's chest. "You remind me of him too."

"Who, the escort?"

"No. Well, yeah. A little. But I mean you kind of remind me of the guy in the bowler hat. Just about every guy I've ever been with has reminded me of him in some way."

Ty propped himself on his elbow and looked down at Zane, eyes narrowed. He seemed concerned. "Did you fuck me the first time because I reminded you of some random in a bar?"

"Sort of," Zane muttered. He reached to drag his hand up Ty's arm, appreciating the slide of his muscles. Ty frowned harder. "Do you think you knew him?"

Ty jerked. "What?"

"Is that why you're obsessing?"

"I'm not obsessing."

"You are a little bit. You know who it was, don't you?"

"No," Ty claimed as he pushed up.

Zane grabbed for him, laughing. "Okay, fine, no need to get defensive. Did you fuck me the first time because I had a gun?"

"Yes." Ty leaned over and kissed him, then slid his leg between Zane's, shifting his weight just enough to be on top of Zane again. "You had a gun. And knives. That's a better reason than yours."

"Not really." Zane pulled his knee up to knock it against Ty's hip. "Because mostly it was that you were hard and wet and begging me to."

Ty grunted in protest, but Zane grabbed him and pulled him closer before he could turn away. He rolled him, pinning Ty beneath him to look down into his changeable eyes. "My type is you."

"Well," Ty finally said with a small smile. "I guess I owe the dude from New Orleans a thank-you if he was the one that convinced you to like dick."

"I knew you'd see it my way."

Ty rolled his hips and pulled his knee up higher, pushing his hard body against Zane's. They'd already used up what little energy they had left tonight, though, and no matter how Ty moved, he wasn't going to convince Zane's cock to join the party.

Neither of them cared. They'd settled into a level of comfort with each other where simply curling up together and enjoying the warmth and familiarity was pleasurable.

Zane rested his body on Ty's. He could feel Ty relaxing under him, feel his attention wavering. He propped himself on his elbows and gazed down into Ty's eyes with a small smile.

"As soon as we're done here, you're going to go sit out on the balcony and smoke a cigar, aren't you?"

Ty blinked at him. "How'd you know that?"

Zane lowered himself and cupped Ty's cheek. "Because it's how you mourn," he whispered. "And I have a feeling that tonight you need to mourn."

Ty blinked rapidly and seemed to be fighting to swallow past a lump in his throat. "I never did say good-bye to him."

"I know." Zane gave him a chaste kiss and then rolled off him. "I'm going to have a smoke with you. Then I'll leave you to it."

Ty nodded, but he reached out to grab Zane's arm and stop him. He pushed up onto his elbow. "Zane." His voice was hushed and pensive. "Sometimes I'm not capable of expressing how grateful I am for you."

"What do you mean?"

Ty put a hand to his own chest, visibly struggling to find the right words. "For your . . . So few people have ever understood the way I work. In here." He tapped his chest. "Thank you for . . . your insight."

The words were sincere, but so unlike anything Ty usually said. Zane was struck dumb by the notion. He could only nod.

Ty rolled out of bed, breaking the spell of the moment. Zane lay stunned for another few seconds as Ty pulled on a pair of sweatpants. Then he sat on the end of the bed, watching Ty, letting his words settle somewhere deep. His fingers rested on the pile of fresh towels, and his eyes were drawn to one of them. He didn't know why it bothered him, but they were folded wrong, different from the others in the bathroom.

"Jesus," he whispered. Ty's OCD was starting to rub off on him. He forced himself to get up and pull on his boxers and follow Ty to the balcony.

"You owe me a story, you know," he said as soon as he stepped out.

"A story?"

"Yeah. I told you one of mine, you have to tell me one of yours."

"None of mine are quite as lascivious as yours," Ty mumbled as he settled into one of the chairs.

"Humor me. Tell me about the Marine you said you got involved with."

"Nope."

"Ty!"

"Nope, nope, nope."

"Come on! Please?"

A smile spread across Ty's face and he glanced sideways at Zane. He was teasing him, the bastard.

"As you wish," Ty drawled, amused.

Zane brought out his pack of cigarettes, but Ty reached and placed a hand over them. Zane met his eyes, prepared to argue for his right to smoke while they were here, but then Ty pulled one of his cigars out and handed it to Zane instead.

"Cuban?" Zane asked.

"Only if you're not a Fed."

"Deal."

"Where's your lighter?" Ty asked.

"I lost it."

Ty flopped his hands dramatically. "This is why we can't have nice things, Zane!"

The scuff of a boot heel below drew Zane's attention before he could respond. They both sat up straighter, peering at the edge of the balcony. Zane jumped when a hand reached up and grabbed onto the bottom of the railing. They were five stories high.

A second later, Nick's head appeared over the edge. All Zane could do was blink at him.

Nick grinned and pulled himself up, rolling over the railing and landing with ease and silence. The man was an impressive specimen, Zane would give him that.

"What the hell, man?" Ty said.

"Maid parked a housekeeping cart in front of our room. We couldn't get it to budge."

"So climbing the *building* was easier than climbing over the cart?"

Nick laughed, then turned to peer over the railing. "Come on, son, you're getting slow."

"I really haven't had occasion to climb buildings in the last couple years, okay?" a voice said from over the edge. "*Why* do you know how to do this so easily?"

Nick reached down and helped Kelly climb onto the balcony. Kelly leaned against the railing and took a deep breath as Nick clapped him on the shoulder. They both looked at Ty and Zane, grinning.

Ty glanced at Zane, not even trying to explain.

Nick pulled two bottles out of his pockets and offered them to Ty and Zane. The one he handed Zane was water. Zane glanced up at him, surprised. How the hell did Nick know he wouldn't drink a beer? Nick merely gave him a gentle smile. He took another beer out of somewhere and sat in the chair beside Ty, kicking his feet onto the railing. Kelly did the same, settling in the chair on Zane's other side and producing more bottles, setting them on the ground for later.

Nick took a long drink as Zane stared at his profile.

Nick smiled, not looking at them. "We knew you'd be out here eventually. After you got the knocking boots out of the way. The housekeeping around here is kind of aggressive, huh? They tried to get in our room twice after we got in."

"Yeah, we got extra towels while we were in the . . . shower," Zane said before he could think better of it.

"You dirty little bunnies," Kelly mumbled, smiling.

Ty shook his head and looked at Nick. "How many floors did you just climb up?"

"Only two, why?"

Ty laughed and touched his beer bottle to Nick's, and then Kelly's, and then Zane's water bottle before taking a drink.

"Were we interrupting?" Kelly asked.

"No, Ty was just getting ready to tell me about the Marine he was fucking back in the day," Zane answered.

"Seriously?" Nick asked, voice breaking. "Jesus, did everyone know you were queer but me?"

"Shut up!"

Zane tossed his head back and laughed.

"I want to hear it," Kelly said with obvious relish. He sat forward. "Was it someone we were stationed with?"

Nick muttered and jerked his head, but he didn't comment further. Ty just rolled his eyes. He gave the other two men a wary glance. "I don't want to hear any shit for this if you two listen in."

Nick solemnly held up a hand, but Kelly shook his head. "No promises. And don't leave out the skeevy parts."

Ty ran a hand over his face. "Oh God."

Zane tried to keep his laughter quiet. He reached out and slid his fingers into Ty's hand, squeezing.

"Okay," Ty said with a deep inhalation. "You asked for it."

1996. LOCATION CLASSIFIED.

Corporal Tyler Grady sat in his rack, reading the letter for perhaps the tenth time. He had known he'd get news like this one day, but it still hit him hard. His eyes traced over the handwriting again.

David Whitlock had written to congratulate him on making Force Recon. He'd ended the letter by telling Ty that he'd met someone in college. He was happy, and he thought he might be in love. But David was asking Ty's permission to proceed, saying that he would wait if Ty asked it, just like he'd promised when Ty left.

Ty shook his head as he read it. He wouldn't stand for that. David deserved so much more than Ty could ever have given him.

He pressed the letter to his bare chest and fell back onto his rack to stare at the canvas top of the tent above his head. After a moment he threw his arm over his eyes. He'd left for this very reason, to give David the freedom to move, to give himself options that didn't involve sharing his life with someone he couldn't commit himself to completely.

That didn't make it feel any less like heartbreak.

The rack beside him creaked as someone sat down. Ty peered out from under his arm to see dark blond hair, compelling eyes that changed from blue to gray and back, and a smirk that always looked like it needed to be slapped.

"Ugh."

Captain Chas Turner pursed his lips. "Oh, I know, it's the intelligence officer, bury your head in the sand."

Ty sat up. "Good afternoon, Captain."

"Good afternoon, Corporal." His eyes drifted to the letter Ty held in his hand. "I came to discuss the new policy I've instituted with the mail."

Ty inclined his head as a sinking feeling started in his stomach.

"Every batch, we open a letter or two at random, just to make sure nothing important is being leaked. Yours happened to be that random letter this week."

Ty held his breath and waited for the other shoe to drop.

Turner clucked his tongue and looked behind him to make sure they were alone in the barracks. The rest of the boys were outside, blowing off steam. When Ty had left them, they'd been creating a scarecrow out of munitions debris and dressing it in someone's pilfered salty cammies. Ty had received his letters before the real fun could start and chosen to retreat to read them in peace, missing the culmination of the exercise.

"I have a proposition for you," Turner said when he looked back at Ty.

Ty continued to stare at him, wary of the man no one in the group trusted. He was the very epitome of what they called a Secret Squirrel. Always running dark, always skittering here and there. He ran too many cloak-and-dagger missions, and it was like he'd forgotten how to be straightforward.

"I wish you to meet with me, privately, once or twice a week."

Ty's back stiffened. "Is that an order, Captain?"

"Not yet. And I'll make sure your mail never gets read again. So you can write back to your . . . friend and tell him what's what."

"You're blackmailing me?"

"No. Well, yes. But I'm proposing a mutually beneficial arrangement."

"Which would be what, exactly?"

Turner leaned forward, propping his elbows on his knees. Ty narrowed his eyes. "I keep your secrets. You keep mine. And we both get to blow off a little steam in a way far more interesting than creating scrap metal targets for the rocket launchers."

Ty glanced around the racks, feeling himself growing warm. He met Turner's eyes. "You're blackmailing me to have sex with you?"

"Well, when you put it that way, it sounds so crass."

"What exactly would you like me to call it?"

"Crass works, I guess."

They stared at each other as Ty mulled it over, his stomach tumbling end over end. He really didn't have much choice if he didn't want to be exposed. Ty clenched his jaw. "Fuck off, Captain."

Turner clucked his tongue, then grinned. "I was hoping you might react that way."

Ty tried not to frown, but his confusion was clear.

"You have backbone, I'll give you that. Not afraid to tell an officer to go fuck himself. Good. I have a real proposition for you now. One I think you'll want to give consideration to."

Ty shook his head and stood, growing angry enough to forget the man's rank. Turner stood with him, both of them in the tight space between the racks.

"Come with me, Corporal. There are matters we need to discuss." Turner moved away, but Ty remained rooted to the spot. Turner looked over his shoulder. "That's not a request."

Ty stood by his rack for another few seconds, stunned. This would probably end with one of them throwing a punch, or at least filing some sort of complaint, but Ty's survival instincts told him to follow and see what exactly Turner was up to. He stuffed the letter under his pillow and grabbed his shirt to pull it on as he followed Turner across the camp to the officer's quarters.

Turner glanced around as he ushered him inside, making sure no one had seen Ty go in, then latched the door behind him. Ty struggled not to fidget, feeling off-balance and a little cornered.

"There are benefits to having a private rack," Turner murmured as he circled Ty and stood to face him.

Ty's jaw clenched hard, and he had to fight not to turn around and leave.

Turner snorted. "Don't be like that. Have a seat." He went to a trunk in the corner.

Ty finally moved to sit in the field chair Turner had indicated, beside a small table made out of a metal water barrel with a bullet hole in it. The rack on the other side served as a second seat.

Ty watched out of the corner of his eye as Turner muttered to himself and rummaged through the trunk. He pulled out a wooden box and set it on the barrel between them. A fan in the corner chugged as it rotated, working to cool off the quarters. It was the only sound.

Turner sat on the end of his rack and met Ty's eyes. Ty's shoulders stiffened.

"You play chess?" Turner asked.

Ty looked down at the box. "No."

Turner pulled the lid off it, unfolding it to reveal a portable chess set. "Thinking man's checkers. I'll teach you."

"You brought me in here to beat me at chess?"

"No, Ty. But I'm not going to force you to have sex with me, either, if that's what you came in here thinking." He looked up and raised an eyebrow, smirking.

Ty glared at him. The man played mind games, and Ty had never been anything but a straight shooter. He didn't like it.

"You see, by the time I'm done with you, you're going to be making the first move. And after that, we'll be looking at quite a few sessions of what is no doubt going to be very athletic, very angry sex."

Ty gaped, but he couldn't seem to stop himself.

"You see? You're already intrigued."

Ty snorted. "Look, we just got back from a five-day hump in the desert, and all I wanted was a cool drink and an hour in my rack to sleep. If you want to play games, there are other intelligence officers around camp to play with."

"That's just the thing, Ty," Turner whispered. He leaned closer. "You offer far more to me than they do."

Ty sighed hard and ran his hand over his face.

"Why did you join the Marines and leave this David kid behind? He obviously loved you."

"None of your business."

"Sense of duty? Adventure? Fear of commitment? Fear of taking it up the ass?"

"Is your plan to make me beg for sex just to shut you up? Because it's kind of working."

Turner laughed and shook his head. "I want you. But not just because I want to see what you look like on top of me." He paused, obviously knowing that the visual had hit home with Ty. Then he continued. "I'm building a team. And I want you on it."

That brought Ty up short. He met Turner's eyes for a long minute. "What kind of team?"

"The kind that doesn't exist."

"Right."

"Look, I've seen your scores and I've seen your evals. You're smart, you're fit, you're loyal and motivated. You've got instincts most kids don't come out here with, you're already fluent in Farsi, and I understand you've been teaching yourself Dari on the side."

"How the hell do you know that?"

"Because you interest me, Grady. You're clever, you're adaptive. You've got balls the size of coconuts. Figuratively speaking, of course.

And you're pretty as hell, which actually gets you farther in these kinds of things than you'd think."

"You're talking about–"

"I'm talking about making a difference. I'm talking about files so redacted they print them on black paper. I'm talking about things you could never spill to that Boy Scout O'Flaherty unless he's in on it."

"Boy Scout."

Turner nodded. "You two are joined at the hip. I know he dragged you off the ground when you fell out of a PT run to make Recon, and I know you carried him to the end of a course when he nearly broke his ankle, giving up the course record in the process, all so you could stay together."

Ty grew warmer, realizing how much homework Turner had done on him. It was flattering, in a way.

"For a while I thought you two were an item, but seeing that letter I realized my mistake."

"What the hell does any of this have to do with your team?"

"If you say yes, you'll have to bring him with you."

"I'm not pulling O'Flaherty into anything unless I vet it first."

"Of course. Which is why you're here now and he's not."

Ty grunted, growing more frustrated.

"I don't need an answer right now," Turner said with a smirk. "To either proposition. And one is not dependent on the other. You should think it over."

Ty nodded, dazed.

"Think over it hard. Once you go down my road, you don't go back. You'll come out the other end someone else. Someone . . . you might not like. Someone this David of yours definitely won't like."

Ty looked him up and down. "That what happened to you?"

Turner shrugged.

"You seem pretty okay with yourself."

"Well, I was an asshole when I started." He handed Ty a carved white knight. Ty stared at it, spinning it between his fingers. Turner kept talking, his voice low and persuasive. "You could be some anonymous white knight, Grady. If that's the road you want to take. Loyalty and honor. A drop of decency in a bucket with a hole too large to patch. Or you could be my rook."

He slid a black playing piece across the board.

Ty looked from the rook to Turner again, fighting the magnetic pull of the man, intrigued by his offer despite the feeling of foreboding growing in the pit of his stomach.

"Say yes, Ty, and I'll teach you everything I know."

1997. LOCATION CLASSIFIED.

Ty shielded his eyes from the sun, watching the men load the deuce and a half with unmarked crates.

Turner came up to stand beside him, geared up and ready to go.

"Where's your detail?" Ty asked.

"We're going in light on this one."

"Bullshit." Ty turned to face Turner, eyes growing wider. "There's a shit storm ten klicks from here. You can't head out there without a detail."

Turner shook his head. "The major disagrees." He stepped away, heading for the heavy transport vehicle.

"Chas," Ty hissed as he lunged to grab at his elbow and stop him. They both glanced around to make sure no one was watching. "I've got a bad feeling about this. Take my boys with you. Hell, take me with you, someone that isn't a goddamn paper pusher with a toy gun."

Turner shook his head and looked away. Ty shoved his arm in frustration.

"Careful, Sergeant," Turner said in a harsh whisper. "It's not my call, okay? You're not ready for this."

"Why not?"

"I can't tell you; you haven't been read in," Turner said between gritted teeth.

"So read me in and take me with you to watch your back."

Turner narrowed his eyes. "Rook, just calm down, go inside with your boys. I'll be back tomorrow and you can take it out of my ass then."

Ty snorted through his nose like an angry bull. Turner gave him a condescending pat on the cheek before striding off.

"Hey, Captain," Ty called after him.

Turner stopped and turned, raising an eyebrow.

"Is there a reason you have to be such a dick all the time?"

Turner licked his lips and walked closer, looking all around them to ensure they were having a private discussion. "Because," he said in a low voice as he drew closer. "Being such a dick all the time lets you know that when I stand here and tell you I love you, I fucking mean it."

Ty's mouth dropped open as he stared. Turner put a finger under his chin and pushed his jaw shut.

"Now. You stay here and ponder that, and when I get back we'll discuss it."

Ty nodded and watched him walk off. "Watch your damn six," he said. Turner gave him a cocky wave over his shoulder, but didn't turn back around.

Two days later, Ty stood with Nick O'Flaherty and Elias Sanchez and watched the deuce and a half roll in. They kept their distance with the other Recon boys, silent sentinels as the men unloaded the bodies.

"I'm sorry, Grady. I know you two were close," Nick finally said.

Ty just nodded, unable to speak for the tightness in his throat.

"If they'd let us run detail," Sanchez muttered. "What a fucking waste."

They turned away and headed back for the barracks tent, but Ty remained, watching silently as they laid Chas Turner's body in a wooden coffin and closed it up.

"Jesus, Ty. I had no idea," Nick murmured. "You hid your grief well."

Zane held tighter to Ty's hand, but Ty shrugged off the sentiment. He took another swallow of beer. They'd all lost people they cared for. Chas Turner was no different, nor was Eli Sanchez. The losses never stopped hurting.

"Eli hit me harder than the captain ever did," Ty admitted. He squeezed Zane's hand, glancing at his lover and offering him a sad smile. "But when I look back and wonder what moment really made me who I am, it's him."

"He taught us just about every goddamned thing we know," Nick muttered.

Ty nodded and glanced at his lover again. Zane hadn't said anything, but Ty knew he was processing. He'd probably come up in a week or a month or a year and want to discuss it. The thought made Ty's smile grow warmer, and he brought Zane's hand up to kiss his fingers.

"Captain Turner was one badass mother, though," Nick mused. "And now I understand why they called you Rook when we ran those missions."

"What did they call you?" Zane asked.

"Ricochet."

"Why is that?"

Nick shrugged, smiling enigmatically. "Couple lucky trick shots."

"Marine nicknames usually don't have a lot of thought put into them," Ty explained. "And they change all the damn time. Nick had like five. I went through about ten."

"Huh." Zane glanced at Ty and smiled. "Rook, huh? I like that. It's sexy."

Ty winced. It wasn't a name anyone had called him in years. Possibly a decade. He liked the way it rolled off Zane's tongue, but he didn't like the echoes of the past that came with it.

Zane leaned toward him, putting his lips to Ty's ear. "I think I'll stick with Bulldog."

Ty turned his head to capture a quick kiss.

"Oh, stop," Nick drawled. "I'm going into a diabetic coma over here."

"I find myself fascinated by it," Kelly said as he stared at Ty. "I can't even come up with an appropriate comparison."

"Stop trying," Ty grunted. He brushed his thumb over Zane's palm.

They settled back to enjoy the silence of the night, something the Recon team had done so many times over the years. Silence was a commodity where they'd spent most of their time. They had learned to appreciate it. And Zane was a man who inherently knew the value of silence.

Ty's mind drifted over the many years they'd spent scratching and clawing their way through battle after battle. He and Nick had been together since the beginning, their promotions never more than a few months apart, their achievements linked in ways not many people understood.

Sanchez had come next. He'd put in for Recon at the same time as Ty and Nick, and it hadn't taken long for him to fall into step with them. The others hadn't arrived until they'd moved up to Force Recon, and then the six of them had been inseparable until the day they'd gone home.

And then Sanchez had come with Ty to the FBI.

"I miss him too," Nick said.

Ty nodded and swallowed hard. Kelly sniffed.

"It wasn't your fault, you know," Nick said.

Ty took a deep breath, not surprised that Nick had known exactly what he'd been thinking. "He called me for help," he whispered. "I didn't answer it, and two days later he was dead."

"Ty," Zane whispered. "Jesus, is that why you always answer your phone?"

Ty nodded curtly.

Zane's hand tightened in his.

"You wouldn't have saved him, Six," Nick murmured.

Ty's throat tightened and he looked away. He covered his mouth with his beer bottle and slumped further into his chair. Zane's hand in his offered more consolation than their words, though.

"Eli . . . he went out with his boots on," Kelly said. He shook his head and took a drink. "That's the only comfort there is in losing him."

"And you know what? Zane took care of it," Nick added.

Zane flinched, and he leaned forward to look at Nick. Nick raised his beer bottle in a salute.

"That's right," Kelly said. "Zane handled that shit. Like a boss."

Zane barked a laugh. "Thanks. I think."

Ty gave Kelly an incredulous glance. "How long has he been drinking?"

Nick shrugged. "Since we got here."

"He's not climbing back down there."

"I think the word you're looking for is 'falling,'" Kelly muttered. "Falling."

Nick reached across Ty's lap and tapped Zane on the knee. "We know how you handled it, Garrett. And to us, that means you're our brother too, you know?"

Ty watched Nick's profile as the man settled back in his chair, throat constricting again. Nick calling someone his brother was the ultimate in acceptance from him. There was no higher honor in Nick's mind.

"I, uh . . . thank you," Zane stuttered.

Kelly leaned forward, holding his beer up. "To Sanchez."

Ty swallowed hard and held his beer out. Zane joined with his water bottle. The glass clinked as they each said a solemn, "Oorah."

"Happy birthday, buddy," Kelly said as he stared out into the night sky and finished off his beer.

Chapter 4

It was over-warm and stuffy in their suite, and Zane woke up feeling half-suffocated. New Orleans in late April was pleasant after the chill of Baltimore, but it seemed the air conditioning was having trouble keeping up. It didn't help that he was half-draped over Ty as they slept.

He slowly extricated himself from Ty's arms and sat up, rubbing his eyes before looking down at his lover, who lay sprawled beside him. The heavy curtains blocked the morning sun, and he could barely see Ty as he tossed and turned.

Ty wasn't an unusually restless sleeper, a fact at great odds with his waking hours. But now he seemed unsettled. He tossed his head and shifted his legs, a soft groan passing his lips. He rolled onto his side, his shoulders beginning the slow, rhythmic rocking that often kept Zane awake.

Zane watched him for a few moments, wondering if it was a dream that was causing the grimace on Ty's face. He got up to head for the bathroom, only to find Kelly and Nick both tangled on the floor at the foot of the bed. He knew they hadn't made it back to their room last night, but they had both started on the pullout sofa. It must have been uncomfortable as hell to make them move to the floor.

Nick was using a pillow Ty had tossed him in the middle of the night, and Kelly was using Nick's stomach to rest his head as he snored. Zane snorted.

He rolled his eyes and stepped over them to head for the bathroom, where he took his time, brushing his teeth, shaving, savoring the silence of the early morning. He fumbled in the dark for the pile of clothing he'd left last night and grabbed his pants to hunt for his cigarettes, remembering too late that his lighter had gone missing. "Dammit."

He was surprised when his fingers brushed the tip of the lighter, though, stuck down in his jeans pocket. He dug it out, and a piece of paper came wrapped tightly around it. Zane scowled as he unrolled it and held it up to the sliver of weak light coming through the part in the curtain to read the words scrawled on it. It was a phone number and the name "Liam" in small, neat lettering.

Zane snorted. He remembered Liam's hand at his hip. Had the man pickpocketed him just to make an impression? He'd certainly forced a memorable way of lighting his cigarette. He'd stolen Zane's lighter, then put it back with the number around it. Impressive. And just a little flattering. Also creepy.

Zane glanced at Ty, smiling fondly as he thought about just how riled his lover would get if he saw that note. Ty didn't consider jealousy a part of his emotional spectrum, but it sure as hell was. Zane would always be more flattered by that than a stranger's number in his pocket. He balled it up and dropped it and his jeans back to the floor. He'd smoke later.

He had to navigate his way through the tangle of Sidewinder limbs on the floor to make it back to the bed. He was a little annoyed that he wouldn't be able to greet Ty in the way he wanted, but he supposed he could sacrifice a morning of groping for Ty to have some time with his friends. If they ever woke up.

Kelly snorted in his sleep and tried to burrow his face into Nick's stomach, causing Nick to groan and push him away. Neither man woke.

Ty tossed onto his side, echoing the groan. Zane recognized the signs of a nightmare. Sometimes Ty woke disoriented and dangerous. Other times he woke shaken and frightened. And sometimes he dreamt of pain.

Zane lay back down on his side and scooted close to Ty, hoping he might be able to get him to rest a little more without having to wake him up from the nightmare. He placed his hand on Ty's back and rubbed.

Ty groaned again, a louder, more pained sound as he rolled back toward Zane. He gasped in a breath, as if surprised that he'd woken, and blinked blearily at Zane.

Zane frowned. Ty was damp to the touch, more than he would have expected even in the warm bed. "You okay?" he whispered.

"I hurt," Ty answered, hoarse and sleepy.

"Is it your back again?"

Ty nodded. He reached down to his side, his elbow jabbing Zane in the stomach as he did so, and curled up again. "Feels like you've been sleeping on top of me."

"I *was* sleeping on top of you." Zane slid his hand against Ty's forehead, surprised by how hot Ty felt against his warm fingers.

Ty rolled onto his back again, gasping as if his pain had spiked. He kept his knees bent, curled up as if it hurt him to straighten out. He immediately rocked back to his side, not able to stay still, then mumbled something as he slid out of the bed and staggered toward the bathroom in the dark. He tripped over one of the men on the floor and stumbled, causing Nick to cry out and lurch to his feet, ready for battle. Sort of. But Ty disappeared into the bathroom before Nick had gained his bearings.

"What the hell just happened?" Nick demanded.

"What is wrong with you gay people?" Kelly moaned, still out of sight on the floor. "Why can't you just sleep in?"

Nick looked down at him. "What?"

"Where am I?"

Zane sat up, torn between being amused and concerned. He could hear Ty retching in the bathroom. He'd been with Ty through allergic reactions, hangovers, and hospital stays, but not an actual illness. Ty was too damn healthy for the flu. Maybe it was something he ate. Like alligator. Or drank. Like five hurricanes.

Zane had never seen Ty so hungover he was sick, though.

Nick ran a hand through his hair and sat on the end of the bed. They could hear Ty in the bathroom, still throwing up. "Is that Ty?" Nick asked.

Zane nodded. "He woke up sick."

"Where am I?" Kelly asked again, sitting up.

After a few torturous minutes, Ty called out to them, "Check under the pillows!"

"You okay?" Zane called back.

"No, just look under the pillows!"

"For what?" Zane asked as he glanced at Ty's side of the bed.

"Gris-gris. Hex bags," Ty answered, his voice laced with pain. "Look all over the bed. Under the mattress. Little felt bags!"

"You all right, buddy?" Nick asked. "Still drunk?"

"Shut up and help him!"

Zane snorted and shook his head. "Nutbar. I think we would have noticed a little bag of crunchy things, as much as we shook the mattress last night," he said wryly.

"Oh God, please," Kelly muttered. He raised a hand as if to ward off the images.

"Agreed," Nick grunted.

Zane laughed, but he started a slow perusal of the bed.

Ty was muttering incoherently from the bathroom when Zane found a small felt bag beneath Ty's pillow, wedged between the headboard and the mattress. He pulled it out and straightened, looking at the little bag with a frown as he reached over and flipped the lamp on.

"This isn't good," he muttered, turning it over in his hand before squeezing it to try to get an idea of the contents. It was roughly two inches by three, tied with a simple cord. It felt like a tea bag, like there was something dry and shredded inside. With a few hard chunks. It looked like the bag in the dead girl's hand from last night.

He heard Ty stumble, gasping for breath. He was silhouetted by the light from the bathroom, bent over, clutching his side. "What color is it?" He was completely serious, as if the color of the bag would tell him anything at all. He bypassed Kelly's legs and lurched toward the bed.

Zane was starting to feel a little queasy too. "It's red. Felt, I think."

"Wait, someone was in here?" Nick asked.

"Housekeeping. Had to be," Zane said grimly. "I knew those towels were folded wrong."

Ty lowered his head, biting his lip as he hunched against the wall beside the bed. "Take me to the hospital," he said. "And let me have the bag."

"You don't really think . . ." Zane let the words trail off and shook his head. It didn't matter. Ty definitely looked ill, and Zane was more convinced by that than some fantasy about voodoo curses. "All right. Can you get dressed?"

Ty nodded, but he didn't actually seem to be listening. He was still clutching his side when he snatched the bag out of Zane's hand. He fumbled with the string that bound the bag, and peered in. He didn't have a chance to examine the contents, though. He doubled over with a gasp, leaning against the mattress as his knees started to fold.

Nick rolled over the corner of the bed to come to his side, and Zane crawled over to put a hand on his shoulder.

His entire body was trembling, but he was taking deep breaths, trying to fight through the obvious pain.

"Do we need to call an ambulance?" Kelly asked. He was finally fully awake, though he looked almost as rough as Ty did.

"You're the corpsman," Nick grunted.

"Well, as a trained professional, I advise we call an ambulance."

"No," Ty gasped. "Fuck the shirt, just get me to the ER." He let the bag go, leaving it on the bed.

Zane tugged his jeans on and grabbed the first shirt his fingers touched, one of Ty's T-shirts. He pulled it on as Nick tried to help Ty into a button-up flannel. Zane grabbed his wallet and Ty's, then the felt bag, and nodded to Nick. "Time to go."

"I'll help you get him into a cab," Nick said. Ty threw an arm over his shoulders. "Then I'll get the boys and we'll meet you there."

"Feels like my insides are being torn apart," Ty groaned.

When they hit the lobby, it was relatively empty, but two of the young bellhops soon took notice of them.

"Does he need help?" one of them asked Zane as they came toward them.

"We're going to the hospital," Zane said, taking a lot of Ty's weight onto himself as Ty bent in pain. "We need a cab or the hotel shuttle."

One of them turned to jog for the entryway and hail a cab.

"Too many hurricanes?" the younger man asked with a knowing smile.

"Bad gris-gris," Ty muttered to him. The man hopped away from him as if he'd said he had the plague.

"It's just food poisoning," Zane insisted.

Ty growled, pulling away from Zane and Nick to stand on his own and pace several steps. He held to his side. He couldn't seem to stay still. He would stalk back and forth and then curl as pain overtook him, then start the whole thing again.

In a matter of minutes, the hotel's courtesy shuttle was pulling up outside and they were on their way to the hospital. Ty rocked in the backseat, fumbling with the little red bag he'd snatched from Zane's hand as he tried to get it open.

"Give me that," Zane said, taking it out of Ty's hand and putting it in his pocket. "Let's not scare the locals any more than we have to until we find out what's wrong." When the van pulled up to the emergency entrance, he climbed out of the van and reached back in to help Ty out.

Ty gripped his hand hard and practically fell out of the van. Someone called to them, asking if he needed a wheelchair. Ty nodded wordlessly. It seemed he wasn't going another step.

"I know what it is, Zane," he gasped. He looked up at Zane, and Zane could have sworn that he was smiling. "Fucking kidney stone."

Zane groaned and covered his face with his hands for a moment, ashamed to be relieved by Ty's self-diagnosis. "And you know this from experience, I take it?"

Ty practically fell into the wheelchair that was brought to him, and he leaned over and began the incessant rocking again. "Last time was like the most pain I've ever been in . . . in my life," he told Zane haltingly. His eyes were watering; he was very nearly in tears. He was smiling, though.

Zane leaned over and put one hand on each of the arms of the wheelchair so he could look Ty in the eyes. "Considering I know what sort of injuries you've had, that doesn't make me feel better. At all." He stood up and gestured for the orderly to push Ty inside.

"At least it won't kill me," Ty replied as he was pushed away.

Ty stared at the ceiling tile and the block of light above him. The nurse had put something he couldn't pronounce into the IV in his arm about two minutes ago, and the space-time continuum had opened up shortly thereafter. His ears buzzed, his eyes wouldn't blink, he couldn't feel his extremities, and there was a low sound in the distance that might have been his own breathing.

But he no longer hurt.

The lady who'd taken his insurance information had promised to go retrieve Zane, and Ty was simply reminding himself to continue breathing until he got there.

"Hey, how are you doing?" It was Zane, finally. Nick and Digger were with him, looking more bemused than worried.

Ty turned his head slowly, his eyes focusing on Zane with what he could only consider utter contentment. "Better," he managed to answer. "Kidney stone."

"Yeah, *somebody's* stoned," Digger said with a laugh.

Zane stopped at the bedside, hands in his pockets. "Did they give you something for the pain?"

"Oh yeah," Ty practically crooned. He shifted on the narrow hospital bed, pulling the blankets around him to ward off the chill caused by the saline being pumped into him. There was still discomfort all through his lower half, but it was dull enough that he didn't care. He had even welcomed the catheter they put in because it had been less painful than what he'd been going through. "They took a CT and said it should pass soon." He held out his hand. "Can I have the bag?"

"What bag?" Digger asked. He and Nick still hung back by the door.

Zane looked reluctant to hand it over as he pulled it out of his pocket, pinched between two fingers.

"Oh, son of a bitch," Digger said, and he shifted his weight from one foot to the other as he dug around in a pocket.

Nick held out one hand, and Digger slapped a twenty dollar bill onto his palm. "Never bet against the crazy hoodoo ex," Nick said as he folded the money into his own pocket.

"You're both assholes," Ty told them.

Zane turned to look at them, and he was still glaring when he met Ty's eyes again. He held the bag up. "Don't scare the doctors with this voodoo stuff, huh?" he said after too long of a pause. "I don't want you hurting."

"What are you talking about?" Ty asked as he took the bag with clumsy fingers.

73

Zane motioned to the bag. "This superstition stuff. The doctors might take you seriously and kick you out of here. That nurse has voodoo dolls at her station out there." He sounded a little unnerved, which was unusual.

"Voodoo dolls are usually used for good things, you know," Ty said. He frowned as his fingers began working on the string of the bag. "It's a religion, Zane. Nothing sinister."

"Sure."

Digger grunted. "You sound like a skeptic."

"I *am* a skeptic," Zane confirmed.

"Well," Ty murmured as he tried to find a more comfortable position. He settled on instructing Zane to lift the head of his bed so he could recline and still inspect the gris-gris bag without too much discomfort. "You might think it's just fairy-tale stuff, but this is serious. Serious business."

Zane frowned. "So what is that thing?"

"It's gris-gris," Ty answered slowly. He was probably slurring, but as far as he knew he was still making sense.

"Yes, dear, we got that part," Nick said. He and Digger came closer, and Digger sat on the end of Ty's bed, jarring it. Ty didn't care.

Zane nodded, glancing at the others again. "You asked specifically about the color," Zane prompted.

Ty gazed up at him, wishing he had the ability to convince Zane to take him seriously. He knew Nick, and probably Zane, thought all of it was stupid. A least Digger believed.

"He's so fucking stoned," Digger said, laughing as he patted Ty's leg.

"His mind is processing at turtle speed," Nick added, snickering behind his hand.

Zane placed a hand on Ty's forehead, and Ty's eyes fell shut. The warmth of Zane's palm was like heaven.

"You know about this voodoo stuff, right?" Zane asked.

"Yeah," Digger answered. Ty felt him shift on the bed. "The color and material of the bag are just as important to its purpose as the contents. I'm not an expert, but I'm betting if we get it open, Grady and I can tell you what it was meant to do."

Ty opened his eyes at the sound of his name.

"You want me to open it?" Ty asked. Zane and Nick both nodded. "Are y'all going to freak out if I open it?" He held up the bag gingerly. He wasn't an expert by any means, but he knew enough about the purposes and the ingredients to get a good idea of what the bag had been intended to do. And what he didn't know, Digger probably did.

"Why would we freak out?" Zane pulled the little rolling table over to the bedside and turned it so Ty had a flat surface in front of him.

"You freak out over things like that," Ty mumbled. He pulled at the opening to the bag but couldn't get the string loose. His fingers weren't working. Digger finally took it from him and carefully poured the contents onto the shiny surface of the table.

Ty looked up and around the room, his mind chugging to work. Finally he pointed at the boxes of sterile gloves that were attached to the wall. "Hand me some of those, please."

Zane amiably nabbed a couple of pairs and brought them back. "Things like that," he repeated.

"What?"

"You said I freak out over things like that."

Ty pulled on one of the gloves. "You just . . . don't believe in them."

"You're right," Zane said with a shrug.

"Ty don't touch home plate before the first pitch," Digger added. "He believes in *everything*."

"Shut up," Ty muttered. He poked through the contents as Digger and Nick laughed at him. He began to separate the different things, making little piles, forgetting what he was doing.

"Hey Ty? Buddy?" Nick finally said gently. "Time to stop organizing and get back on task."

Ty looked up at him. Nick was smiling fondly.

"Sorry."

"It's okay. You can straighten them later."

Ty nodded. He knew they were humoring him, but he also didn't give a fuck. He bent his attention back to the gris-gris bag. There was a small roll of parchment, a sprig of crushed juniper, a mossy substance he couldn't identify, a root of some sort, what appeared to be iron shavings, and two large teeth. Ty pushed them around the table, tidying up his little piles.

"How do you connect not believing in something with freaking out about it?" Zane asked. He'd pulled one of the chairs over to the side of the bed and was now sitting at Ty's side.

"I meant, are you going to make me feel stupid for believing this was put under my mattress to kill me?"

"Is that what you believe?" Zane sat and leaned back in the chair, right ankle propped on his left knee.

Ty narrowed his eyes, recognizing Zane's interrogation posture.

Nick leaned forward. "Is that what he does when he's questioning suspects?"

"Yes," Ty groused.

"Well hello, Agent Garrett," Nick said, laughing.

"Behave yourself," Zane grumbled. He looked back to Ty. "Is that what you believe?"

"Yes," Ty answered after a moment of thought.

Zane was watching him intently despite his casual pose. "Can you explain to me why?"

Ty looked back down at the assortment of items that had been in the gris-gris bag. He was blushing, but during the course of his time in New Orleans, he'd seen and learned things that made it impossible to dismiss the power of simple faith.

"Ty?" Zane sounded more curious than anything. Not amused, and certainly not angry or frustrated like he got when he couldn't figure out a puzzle by logical means. He was probably still humoring Ty, but hopefully he wouldn't dismiss any of this, thinking the drugs were making Ty goofy.

"It's about faith," Ty finally said, looking first at Zane and then at Nick and Digger. Nick was frowning now, and Digger was nodding. Ty met Zane's eyes again. "I've seen things I can't explain. And I believe in things I can't see. I believe in fate and luck and curses."

Zane crossed his arms. "Really?"

Nick nodded. "Really."

Digger was nodding too. "So do I. I also know that people around here don't take this stuff lightly. And this bag here is quality work; it's no tourist prank."

Ty took a deep breath. "It's a murder weapon. Just like a gun or knife. It's poison. It was put in our room by someone with knowledge and belief in the power to cause us harm."

Nick turned to whisper into Digger's ear, but Ty heard his words anyway. "Goddamn, I hate it when he uses real logic."

Digger made a dismissive noise and shivered.

Zane didn't speak for a long moment as he studied Ty, and then he abruptly nodded. "All right."

Ty watched him with narrowed eyes. Zane never agreed with him that easily. Maybe he was just taking pity on him since he was in pain and medicated and planned to continue the conversation later. Ty nodded, though, willing to accept it for now.

Nick stood again and leaned over him, studying the contents on the metal table. "Can you tell what's in it? What's it meant to do?"

"I'm not sure what this moss is, but the rest . . . This is juniper, and I think this root is High John the Conqueror root."

"What do those things do?"

Ty shrugged one shoulder. "I don't know."

"Dammit, Ty," Nick grunted.

"The red felt bag is usually used to attract a lover, but the contents aren't consistent with that purpose," Digger offered. "They're meant to draw something. Like those iron fillings."

Ty sighed. "Yeah. So basically . . ."

"The whole bag is one big-ass hoodoo magnet."

Nick rolled his eyes. "Thank you, Digger, as always, for your contribution to the sanity of the group."

"So it's a magnet," Zane said.

Ty nodded. "A bad one."

"A magnet to draw something bad to us," Zane concluded.

"A big bad magnet."

Digger snorted. "That's where the teeth come in."

Ty held one up and looked at it critically. "Gator teeth?"

Digger nodded. "They look it. They good luck, though."

"Not for the gator we ate last night," Nick said.

Digger waved him off.

"They are good luck," Ty said.

"But gris-gris bags are only supposed to have one," Digger told them. "And they're supposed to have an odd number of ingredients. So throwing in an extra tooth to make it even, I'm assuming, is bad."

"Or whoever put it together just tossed some things in," Zane suggested. "And then planted it to scare us."

Ty nodded and lowered the tooth.

"The fact they planted it at all scares me," Digger added. He looked at Nick critically. "You didn't hear 'em? See 'em?"

"I . . . I may have climbed a building last night. I don't remember a lot."

"We think they came in as housekeeping. I heard them from the shower but didn't think anything of it."

"Makes sense," Digger said. "We had a fuckton of fresh towels in our room when we got back. Then we had someone knock again trying to clean the room."

Nick frowned. "If that's the case, whoever it was went to all our rooms, hunting for Ty. That's a lot of trouble to go to for a scare."

Ty bit his lip, wondering if he should even be pondering this while the cold buzz was still running through his system. He looked up and winced. "It wasn't meant to scare us because it was too well hidden. A tiny bag behind your mattress can only scare you if you know it's there. If I hadn't woke up like I did, we never would have looked for it, we never would have found it."

"A fair point," Zane said. "I may not believe in this, but I do believe in you. If you say we should take it seriously, then we will."

"I think we should," Ty said. "I mean, shit, if this can shake loose a kidney stone, I don't want to see what else this guy knows how to do."

Zane laughed and scooted his chair a little closer so he could lean sideways against the bed. "First Edgar Allan Poe, now voodoo. Great."

"I'm never inviting you two to a party again," Nick grumbled.

"You and your goddamn coconuts," Digger added. He shifted on the edge of Ty's bed, jostling him and making a full-body shiver run through Ty.

"Did you call that detective from last night?" Ty asked as he continued to push around the little bit of moss.

"No, why?"

"Girl dies with a gris-gris bag in her hand. Next morning . . ."

Zane hesitated, sharing a glance with Nick. "You want to call the police and report this?"

"Maybe you two can sniff around. See if it's connected. But you can't bring me into it."

"They'll boot us out as soon as we show our creds," Nick argued. "They were already all over us just for being there last night."

"Can you try?" Ty asked.

Nick sighed loudly and looked away.

Ty carefully put everything back into the bag. He picked up the roll of parchment and pulled it apart, cold settling in him when he saw "Tyler Beaumont" written in beautiful calligraphy.

"Wait, is that like the paper Garrett took a picture of?" Nick asked, sounding shocked.

Ty nodded.

Zane craned his neck to look at the parchment. His face clouded over. "Yeah, okay, that's enough connection for me," he admitted. "Was that your alias while you were here?"

Ty nodded, rolling the parchment up as it had been.

"If that's bat's blood ink, you're fucked," Digger drawled with all seriousness.

Ty shot him a glare, careful to leave out the roll of parchment and one of the alligator teeth as he put the bag back together. It wouldn't make it a good luck charm, but it would lose most of its power. In theory.

He cleared his throat uncomfortably. He wasn't ashamed of the fact that he put stock in this, but he still felt a little silly.

Ty pushed the bag away and began plucking at the fingertips of his gloves. His fingers trembled and he couldn't seem to grab the purple glove to get it off.

Zane reached out to still his hands and took over peeling them off.

"We could just go home," Ty said. "But now I'm hexed. It'll just follow."

"Ty, you're not hexed," Nick said.

"Disagreed," Digger grunted.

Zane sighed. "We can't go home. One, you're in the hospital with a kidney stone. Two, there is a murderer out there and we have possible evidence in the case, and I don't think any of us could just walk away with a clear conscience. And three, you really believe in that gris-gris stuff, so there's no point in trying to run. Every little paper cut and stubbed toe you get will be the bag's fault until we fix this."

Zane dropped the gloves onto the table and then pushed it out from between them and away, keeping Ty's hand in his.

Ty relaxed back into the bed, holding Zane's hand. He watched him in open admiration. Not many people would so easily accept that he was cursed after one little trip to the ER and because he said so. He was, but not many people would believe him. Or pretend to believe him. Except Digger, but fuck, Digger was certifiable so that didn't make Ty feel better.

"Thanks, Zane," he whispered.

Zane pulled Ty's hand to his lips and kissed his knuckles.

"Ugh, gross," Digger said with a laugh.

"And we're leaving," Nick added. They headed for the door, but Ty knew they wouldn't go far. They could smell trouble just like he could. The door closed and Ty returned his gaze to Zane.

"I hate seeing you like this," Zane whispered.

Ty laughed. Hard. He was folded up in a rolling hospital bed with an IV in his arm and a catheter in a less pleasant place, wearing hospital-issue socks with little rubber paws on the bottoms and a gown that didn't close all the way in the back. And Zane hated seeing him like this?

"I hope so!" he said. He covered his mouth to stop the snickering, but his eyes watered as he watched Zane. His partner did offer him a weak smile, but he wasn't hiding the worry in his eyes.

"Oh come on, Zane!" Ty said as he squeezed his hand. "Enjoy it while my meds last."

"I'm not enjoying anything until you're healthy and out of here."

Ty sobered and looked at him apologetically. He patted his hand. "Last time it only took a few hours from start to finish. I just didn't have any drugs, so I was begging O and Eli to kill me the whole time. This time is much more fun so far."

Zane moved his other hand so both of them closed around Ty's. "Maybe some of it will be lingering when I get to take you out of here. You can be a lot of fun when you're so open to suggestion," he drawled, making a visible effort to relax.

That got another round of laughter out of Ty, and he had to be careful not to move his legs or roll as he cackled at his lover. "Because nothing says sexy like a catheter."

Zane finally laughed with him. "Not my kink, but okay."

Ty was still laughing when a nurse poked her head into the room to check on them. "I see he's feeling better."

"Don't let it fool you," Zane said, turning his head to look at her. He didn't let go of Ty's hand. "He's got the good drugs."

"Oh I know it, honey, I gave them to him."

Ty was still laughing. The nurse came into the room and changed his saline bag, telling him the more he got in him, the easier the stone would pass. She checked his vitals, then moved on, leaving them alone again.

"I almost think I'd rather be gut shot than have to pass a kidney stone, from the sound of it," Zane said once she disappeared.

"Same here," Ty muttered. Suddenly, nothing was all that funny anymore.

Nick and the others were in the waiting room, sprawled among the sick and injured, when Zane joined them. Zane had no idea how to proceed. He didn't want to be around Ty's Recon team without Ty there as a buffer, and he certainly didn't want to go to the New Orleans PD and tell them his lover had been cursed by voodoo and wanted them to investigate. He wished Ty had never answered that phone call in Baltimore right now.

"How's he doing?" Kelly asked.

Zane winced and shrugged. "He'll be fine. They've got him drugged up. Now he just has to wait it out, I guess."

"The one thing Ty hates doing most," Digger mused. "Waiting. So poetic."

"You're a sick man, D."

"He ruins every trip," Nick muttered. He smiled at Zane. "What do we do about the hoodoo thing?"

"What hoodoo thing?" Owen asked.

Digger poked at him. "That voodoo you do, baby!"

Owen batted Digger's hands away. "Stop it, what is wrong with you?"

"Ty found one of those gris-gris bag things under his pillow this morning," Nick explained.

"Like the one with the dead girl?" Owen asked.

"He thinks he's cursed."

"He wants us to report it to the police," Zane said with a grimace. The bag was in his pocket, and he pulled it out to look at it.

"He wants to report being cursed to the police?" Owen's voice had gone flat.

Nick stood and stretched. "I'm going out on a limb and guessing they get that a lot down here."

"So what do we do? Are we really going to call the police?" Kelly asked, smirking. They were all looking to Nick to make the decision. Zane supposed that was their habit, since Nick had been the team's second-in-command.

"He does have a point. The dead girl had a hoodoo bag, and whoever put that shit in Ty's room was slick enough to get in and out without either him or Zane noticing."

"Did you two stumble into the room groping each other?" Owen asked Zane.

Zane glared at him for a second before deciding it didn't warrant a response.

"Anyway," Nick said loudly. "I'll call the number they left me when I gave my statement last night. Let them decide if they want to pursue it as a lead."

"What are you going to do about Ty?" Zane asked.

"What about him?"

"You can't let the cops come here and interview him. They might recognize him."

Nick glanced toward the doors, chewing on his lip. "We can't report it without him."

"Do we have to report it at all?" Kelly asked.

"Ty is drugged up to his asshole right now; can't we just *tell* him we called it in and let it drop?" Digger said.

Nick stared at him for a long moment, then met Zane's eyes with a shrug. "Works for me."

Zane rolled his eyes. "We'd be withholding evidence in a homicide investigation."

"It's either that or run Ty right into a whole load of questions with no answers."

"How do we know this bag thing is even connected?" Owen asked. "Are we going on Ty's assessment? Because he didn't even see the other one."

"A valid point," Kelly said. "He's also high. I mean . . . y'all remember the last time he was high?" He began to laugh, then cut himself short and schooled his expression when no one else laughed with him.

Nick had his hands stuffed in his pockets, not reacting as each man offered up his opinion. He glanced to Zane again. Zane found himself nodding. He was tired of finding himself embroiled in problems that weren't his.

He immediately chastised himself. Truth and justice were part of his job. What the hell was he thinking? If that bag had any possibility of being linked to the murder of that girl, they had a responsibility, not only as officers of the law, but also as human beings, to report it.

Nick seemed to read his expression, and it wasn't the first time Nick had done so since Zane had met him. The man was perceptive as hell. "Okay. You and I will go down there and turn this thing in. If we can keep his name out of it, we will. If not . . . maybe we can use the FBI thing to slip past it. You have your badge?"

"Yeah. What about Ty?"

"We'll stay here. Make sure he doesn't die," Kelly offered, smiling widely.

"That's . . . that's comforting, thank you," Zane drawled.

Kelly shrugged. "I do what I can."

Ty faded in and out of sleep after Zane left him. It was easier to let whatever was in that IV do its work than to fight it trying to stay lucid. He dozed, never quite sure when he was asleep and dreaming, or when he was awake staring at the ceiling and listening to the beeps and thrums of the busy emergency department.

At times he dreamed of visitors coming to see him. Zane holding his hand. Nick sitting on his bed to laugh at him. Kelly bending over him to check his vitals. Sanchez begging him to wake up and move before they were blown up. Deuce sitting by his bed with his brand new baby girl in his arms. Chester waving a shovel at a nurse.

He would sort out the reality from the hallucinations later.

Something jostled the bed and Ty forced his eyes to open. There was a man sitting on the side of the hospital bed, dressed in blue scrubs and sunglasses.

"Hello, Tyler," he said, British accent steeped in sarcasm. "Fancy meeting you here."

Ty jolted in bed, adrenaline racing through him when he recognized his visitor.

"Liam."

Liam Bell's lips curved into an evil smirk. Ty tried to sit up, but Liam put a hand on his sternum and shoved him back to the mattress.

"Don't make a fuss, love, I won't be long."

Ty reached to grab at the front of his scrubs, but Liam gripped his wrist, twisting Ty's arm away and pinning it to the hospital bed.

"You never did handle the hard stuff well," Liam said as he peered at the little machine that registered Ty's heart rate. "Calm down, I'm not here to hurt you. Yet."

Ty's other hand grasped at him. "Why are you here? How?"

"Haven't you heard? Revenge is all the rage this season." He leaned closer to Ty's face, using his elbow to push into Ty's chest. "I'm so glad you're here."

"Where have you been?"

Liam smiled crookedly and peered over the tops of his sunglasses, blue eyes shining. "The same place you have, Ty. Hell."

Ty gasped for air. He couldn't understand why he couldn't defend himself, why his breath was so hard to catch. "Did you leave the bag?"

"I don't intend to kill you when you can't fight back." Liam leaned closer, close enough for his breath to gust across Ty's face. "We shall meet again, Tyler. When you're well. Until then."

He pulled away from Ty's grasp, which was easier than it should have been. Ty struggled to sit up, but Liam was gone.

They went a few blocks before Nick worked up the nerve to broach the subject with his companion, but he took a deep breath and cleared his throat. "Hey, Zane, I need to apologize to you. For the others."

Zane glanced at him as they walked, eyebrows raised. "What for?"

"They're assholes."

Zane laughed, shaking his head. "They haven't done anything."

"Yeah, maybe not. It's just . . . Ty and I have always been sort of responsible for them, you know?" Nick reached out to stop Zane so he could face him as they spoke. "Look, the guys, they judge pretty harshly. They think you have something to prove."

Zane's smile fell. He glanced away, nodding and pressing his lips tightly together.

"They're wrong, you know."

Zane looked back at him sharply.

"I've seen how you handle yourself. Give it some time; they'll realize Ty trusts you with his life. They'll come around."

He waited for Zane to say something, but the man remained silent, his dark eyes unreadable. At last, Zane licked his lips and smiled weakly. "Thanks," he said before he started walking again.

They were stepping through the iron gate surrounding the coral-colored 8th district police station on Royal Street when Nick's phone rang. He dug it out and called for Zane to hold up when he saw it was Kelly.

"Hey," he answered, giving Zane a shrug when the man made an inquiring gesture with his hands.

"You guys gotta come back here," Kelly said in a rush. "Ty's freaking the fuck out, he's trying to take out his IV and they're talking about sedating him."

"What? What happened?"

"He keeps saying he's *not* hallucinating and you two can't go to the police. I don't know, that's all I can get out of him."

"What's going on?" Zane asked.

"I have no idea," Nick mouthed.

"Just come back here," Kelly said on the phone. "Maybe Zane can get him calm, because I sure as hell can't."

"Okay, we're on our way." Nick ended the call and waved at Zane. "Kelly says Ty's losing it, they need us back there."

It was almost eight blocks from the station to Tulane Medical Center, but Zane didn't even hesitate. He took off at a run, and Nick sprinted after him. Taxis in the French Quarter were few and far between, but by the time they crossed Rampart and got to the emergency department doors, Nick was pretty sure they could have carjacked someone and gotten there with less trouble. He had a hard time keeping up with Zane's long strides.

When they were let into the room, they found Ty sleeping. Owen and Digger were leaning against the supply cabinet on one wall, and Kelly was sitting on Ty's bed, arms crossed. Everything was calm, except for Nick and Zane gasping as they both tried to catch their breath.

"What the hell, man?" Nick blurted.

Kelly shrugged. "They had to sedate him."

Nick leaned against the wall, panting.

Zane moved closer, taking Ty's hand. "What triggered him? What happened?"

"No clue," Kelly answered. "We barely got any sense out of him."

"We were in the lobby when a nurse came running out begging for our help," Owen explained. "When we got back here, three orderlies were holding him down. We tried to tell them he didn't like being restrained, but they said he'd tried to attack a male nurse who came to take his vitals."

Zane looked momentarily horrified, but he hid it quickly and gripped Ty's limp hand tighter.

"When he saw us, he calmed a little, but not enough. The good news, though," Kelly added, keeping his voice bright. "He passed the stone."

"Great," Nick huffed. "Now we just have to wait for him to fucking wake up. How long will that take?"

"Judging by the amount of sedative they gave him and the way Ty reacts to medications?" Kelly looked at the watch on his wrist. He shrugged. "I don't have a fucking clue."

Nick glared at him. "I hate you. We ran here. Sprinted."

Kelly looked him up and down appraisingly. "Good job."

Digger clucked his tongue and smacked a hand against Nick's arm. "The only sense we could make out of what he was saying was to get you two the fuck away from the police."

Nick nodded, looking from Digger to Ty, who lay peacefully now. Zane sat on the chair beside the bed, holding Ty's hand in both of his. He was staring at Ty's face, seemingly oblivious to the rest of them.

"Well," Nick said, at a loss. "Why don't we, uh . . . we'll go get some breakfast and . . ." He gestured at Zane, and the others filtered toward the door with him. They left Ty to his sedation and Zane to his vigil.

Chapter 5

Ty moved gingerly as Zane walked with him to the hotel room. Zane had never passed a kidney stone, but he'd heard the horror stories. All he knew was that Ty had been lucky to be drugged and having a minor meltdown to distract him during the process.

As they made their way down the hall, Ty reached out to steady himself on Zane's arm. The medicine he'd been given was still in effect, and he was wobbly and uncertain of his footing.

"Need help?"

Ty shook his head. "No, I'm good." But he didn't let go of Zane's arm. He kept his other hand on his side. Zane wasn't sure if he was hurting there, or it just made him feel better to hold it.

When they reached their room, Zane wasn't surprised to see the other men already there. He'd called ahead to let them know Ty was being released, and Nick had a key. They all stood when Ty stepped into the room.

"You okay, Six?" Digger asked.

Ty nodded curtly.

"So," Kelly said with a smirk. "Psychotic episode is the new prescribed treatment for passing one of these things?"

Ty cleared his throat, his cheeks coloring. "Hallucinations are a bitch when they talk back."

Zane put his hand on Ty's arm, offering a modicum of support. Ty's hand trembled as it hung between them. He clenched it to make it stop.

"I need a cigarette or something," Ty mumbled.

"My pack's in my jeans," Zane offered.

Ty headed for the pile of clothing Zane had discarded the night before. Zane recognized it as more of a distraction than the actual need for a cigarette. It was something for Ty to do with himself, with his hands and his mind, so he had a little bit more time to figure out how to explain his behavior to the rest of them.

He bent gingerly, holding his side as he dug through Zane's pockets. Everyone else was quiet, waiting, knowing the silence itself would do more to force Ty to talk than any pointed queries. Zane smiled. He kind of liked watching the dynamic of Sidewinder, because even though he still felt like a bit of an outcast, he also knew he was in a room with some of the people who knew Ty best. He was no longer the only one present who would call Ty on his bullshit.

Ty straightened with a grimace once he found the pack and the lighter. He was frowning, holding the piece of paper Zane had wadded up this morning. It took a moment for Zane to remember what it was. He was pretty sure Ty was too high to be bothered by it. He might even find it funny. Ty tapped one of the cigarettes out of the pack and put it in his mouth, then dropped the pack and idly flattened the paper to read.

Zane was expecting him to make a joke or a lewd comment about someone slipping Zane a phone number in a bar, so he was shocked by the change that came over Ty's face. He took the cigarette out of his mouth and dropped it to the floor. His jaw tightened and his hard eyes darted to Zane.

"What?" Zane asked.

Ty held up the paper and crumpled it in his fist. "Where'd you get this?"

"Last night, some guy slipped it into my pocket."

"What guy?" Ty demanded. His voice had gone low and dangerous, and he advanced on Zane from across the room, heedless of the other men, no longer slow or shaky.

"I don't know, Ty, some guy who wanted a light." Zane peered over Ty's shoulder at the others. They were all growing uneasy, sharing wide-eyed glances and shifting where they sat. Even Ty wasn't usually this overtly possessive or combative.

Ty was oblivious to the discomfort in the room as he stalked up to Zane, cornering him in the little entryway. He held the paper up. "What did he look like?"

"Ty," Zane said gently. "It's a piece of trash in my pocket. He pickpocketed my lighter and slipped it back in with that note. It's not a big deal, okay? Maybe we can talk about it once the meds wear off."

Ty's eyes flashed and he struck out at the wall next to Zane, slapping his palm and the piece of paper against it. Zane flinched away, eyes going wider.

"What did he look like?" Ty shouted.

"Grady!" Kelly called. "You need to sit down before the morphine gets the better of you."

Zane's eyes stayed on Ty's. He shook his head. He knew Ty wasn't going to hurt him, but it was growing embarrassing. He just wanted to keep Ty calm until the drugs could wear off. "He was . . . blond. British. Blue eyes. I don't know, it was dark."

"Was his name Liam Bell?" Ty growled.

Zane heard a sharp inhalation from one of the others, and it distracted him enough to glance at them and see Nick and Kelly both standing. He met Ty's eyes again and nodded. "Yeah. I think that was his name. How'd you know that?"

Ty took a step back, releasing the paper. It fluttered to the ground at Zane's feet. Ty put a hand over his mouth and turned away.

"Liam Bell?" Nick asked, aghast. "How is that possible?"

"Who is Liam Bell?" Zane asked. "How do you know him?"

"How did you know it was him, Ty?" Owen demanded.

Ty still had a hand over his mouth. He closed his eyes.

"You saw him, didn't you?" Nick said. "In the ER. That's why you freaked out. You saw him there."

Ty nodded, eyes still closed. "I thought I was hallucinating."

"Who is Liam Bell?" Zane asked again.

Kelly took a deep breath, looking between Ty and Zane. "He was . . . uh."

"He's a ghost," Digger answered. "He's dead."

"We have to get out of here," Ty muttered. "We have to leave town."

Zane barked a laugh. "Are you serious?"

Ty turned on him. "What else did he say to you?"

Zane sighed, far too aware of all the eyes on him. He shrugged it off. "He wanted a light. He sort of flirted with me. There was nothing."

Ty gritted his teeth, stepping closer. "Zane, the words he used. What did he *say*?"

Zane's brow furrowed as he fought past the sense of urgency and confusion to remember exactly what the man had said to him. He shook his head, distracted by the look of near panic on Ty's face. "He said something about looking forward to seeing me again." He paused, taking a deep breath to steel himself for Ty's reaction. "Without my boyfriend around."

Ty's shoulders straightened and his features grew harder, more dangerous. He glanced over his shoulder. "He told me he wanted revenge." He looked back at Zane, fear skittering through his eyes. "He's coming after you."

"What the hell are you talking about, Ty?"

Ty backed away, covering his face like he was trying to block out everything so he could think clearly. Those meds were still doing a number on him, and Zane wasn't quite sure what to do. He wasn't even sure if this warranted the kind of panic Ty had spiraled into, but the rest of them looked shocked as well.

"Why is this guy so scary?" Zane asked, growing frustrated. He needed details, not more rambling hoodoo ghost talk.

Ty sat down hard on the end of the bed and swiped a hand over his eyes. He glanced up at Zane, his head resting on his hand. "You remember me telling you about training with an SAS team?"

Zane nodded, even as he tried to think back. It had been before they'd left for the cruise ship assignment and Ty had explained where he'd picked up the British accent he'd been forced to use.

"Liam was the leader of the group we were assigned with. It was an advanced Coalition team."

"Okay," Zane said, still confused. He sat in one of the chairs near the bed, watching Ty's body language more than anything else. His knee was bouncing, he couldn't stop fidgeting with his hands, and he wouldn't meet anyone's eyes.

"We were each buddied to our counterpart of the SAS team for the duration," Nick explained when Ty remained silent. "We lived together, ate together, went on missions together. They said it was a test to see how it would work, Spec Ops integration or some shit. They were trying to form an international first-strike team."

Zane glanced around the room at the five men. "With the SAS?"

Nick nodded. "There were others. SEALs and Aussies, Green Berets and Canadians. Two months in, we discovered a mole. We hunted him as a team. For months."

"Canadians are shifty, man," Digger muttered.

Zane rolled his eyes. "So, if Liam Bell was the team leader, he was buddied with Ty."

"Yes," Ty answered curtly. His knee was bouncing faster, and he had his hands clasped between his thighs, trying not to fidget.

Zane stared at him, waiting for him to make eye contact. When the silence began to stretch too thin and Ty was still staring at the floor, Zane sighed. He knew Ty's M.O. "Were you involved with him?"

Ty finally looked up and met his eyes. He nodded jerkily. Zane wasn't surprised, but the other four men burst into a chorus of shock and anger. Ty winced as they each expressed themselves.

Kelly and Digger both shouted, "What?"

Nick ran a hand through his hair and turned away.

Zane raised his voice to be heard. "Why is that a problem?"

"Because Ty's the one who fucking shot him!" Owen blurted.

Zane's eyes widened and he gaped at Ty, unable to conceal his surprise. Ty had his hand over his mouth and his eyes were closed again.

"Ty?" Zane whispered. "Was he the mole?"

Ty ran his fingers over his lips and took a deep breath, his eyes still closed. He finally opened them as he nodded.

"You fucking shot a guy you were sleeping with?" Owen asked, and it was hard to tell which part scandalized him more.

"It's not what you think it was," Ty explained, voice hoarse.

"Jesus," Kelly whispered. He sank to a chair, brow furrowed.

"That's cold, man. Even for you, that's some shit," Digger muttered. He paced toward the balcony, shaking his head.

Nick was still standing in the little entryway near the bathroom with his back to them. His head was down and he had one hand on his hip. Zane's eyes were drawn to him. Why did he seem so betrayed by the knowledge? What Ty had done was harsh, Zane had no illusions about it. But it didn't necessarily bother him. He knew how Ty felt about treachery, and he was a dangerous man, quick to action and rarely looking back. Nick and the others had to know that too. Once you turned on Ty, your time was up.

Nick finally raised his head, but he didn't turn around. "You hit center mass," he said, his voice low.

Ty turned, but Zane couldn't see his expression as he stared at Nick's back. His entire body trembled, and Zane wondered if it was the meds, the nerves, or both.

Nick turned to face him, looking grim. "You fired at center mass from seven yards away, but you missed almost every vital organ."

"How do you know that?" Kelly asked.

"Because I wrote up the report," Nick snarled. He pointed a finger at Ty. "You missed on purpose."

Ty stared at him, unmoving. The trembling had stopped almost as if Ty had shut it off with a switch.

Nick took a step. "You helped him escape. Didn't you? That's why you know he's alive."

Ty hesitated before giving a curt nod.

The group erupted in another round of protests.

Nick dragged both hands through his hair and turned around again. "You missed center mass to help him escape, and you're the one who covered it up!"

Zane stood, intending to try to calm the emotions he could see brewing, but the movement stirred the room instead. Ty stood with him, stepping toward Nick. But Nick whirled around when he felt Ty behind him, grabbed Ty by his shirt front, and slammed him into the wall.

"Hey!" Zane called, taking a step to intercede. Kelly grabbed his arm and held him off, patting him on the chest like he would to calm a dog.

Nick snarled in Ty's face. "I swore under oath you had nothing to do with it, Ty!"

"So did I," Ty gritted out. He shoved at Nick's chest, forcing him to loosen his hold.

Kelly let Zane go. His voice was grim. "You helped a traitor escape."

Ty glanced around at everyone before meeting Nick's eyes again. He squared his shoulders and raised his head, preparing for the worst. "Yeah. Yeah, I did."

2000. Location classified.

"All this time!" Ty shouted as he stalked around the room. He was too angry to be still. He gripped his gun so hard that his knuckles were turning white.

"Tyler, I know you're angry, but—"

"Angry? Liam! This is beyond angry!"

Liam nodded and took a step to the side.

"Stop moving!" Ty shouted. He raised his gun and pointed it at Liam's head.

Liam stopped and stared, meeting Ty's eyes without flinching. "Do you intend to shoot me, Ty?"

"We've been looking for this mole for months," Ty said through gritted teeth.

"I've been right by your side."

"You're a traitor!"

"No, I'm not. Not to you," Liam said, remaining calm in the face of Ty's growing rage. "And not to them."

Ty shook his head.

"I've never betrayed you, mate. I'm just doing my job."

"So am I."

"If you'll let me explain."

Ty growled, his grip tightening on the gun. "I don't want to fucking hear it, I'm tired of spy games."

"That's funny, Ty, because you're one of the best players I've ever seen."

"Likewise," Ty snarled.

Liam nodded, taking a harsh breath.

Ty could barely look the man in the eye, and he lowered his gun for fear of shooting him in the face just to wipe that wounded look off it. "Fine. Explain. Do it quickly."

"I was planted here by the NIA."

"The NIA? Do you think I'm stupid?"

"Tyler, I think you're anything but."

"NIA is a toothless old aunt in the CIA's basement. They don't get involved in this shit."

"They didn't. They're being militarized. Dipping into military personnel who already have the access to build their stable. The NIA pulled me from SAS and recruited me for military ops they couldn't get their own people into. I know you know about this, because they tried to pull you too."

Ty gritted his teeth, fighting not to react to that knowledge. Chas Turner had tried for months to recruit him for the National Intelligence Agency's first wave of dark military ops, but Ty never bit. He'd worked a few missions and become a valuable piece of artillery, but he took his orders from the Marine Corps, not suits at the NIA.

"They put me here to feed false information to the opposition."

"Why you?" Ty demanded.

Liam licked his lips. "I have family in Russia. They created a KGB past that could be exploited, and waited for someone to find it and contact me."

"That's weak, Liam."

"It worked nonetheless. I've been transmitting false information for months. I'm not your enemy."

The gun lowered as Ty stared at the SAS sergeant he'd called his friend and lover for the past few months.

"Every day you've looked me in the fucking eye and lied to me."

"I never lied."

"Bullshit!" Ty raised the gun again and jabbed it at Liam in utter frustration.

"Stubborn wanker! Listen to me. Life isn't black and white! You know that better than anyone. I'm not the bad guy here."

Ty realized he was nearly hyperventilating. He was so livid the edges of his vision were beginning to blur.

Liam continued talking, voice soft and low, like a man trying to calm a wild animal. He'd done it before to Ty, soothing him and coaxing him back to sanity.

"Now listen, I need your help. Word has to get out the spy's been rooted out and eliminated, or the insurgent forces will try to extract me. I don't know about you, but I don't fancy that sort of homecoming. If they can't extract me and they don't hear of my death, they'll know all those messages were fake. It will cost lives. Many lives."

"You're asking me not to turn you in?"

"No. I'm asking you to come with me."

"Come with you?"

"I have to fake my death, I've known that all along. It was always the only exit strategy. But then you came along and . . ." He licked his lips, wincing. He sighed and flopped his hands. "I'm in love with you, Ty."

Ty took an involuntary step back, gaping and grasping for words, and nearly tripped over a pair of boots. Liam followed and Ty raised the gun again in unsteady hands.

Liam noticed the tremble and shook his head. "I need you steady tonight, darling."

"No."

"Help me die tonight. Then you can come with me, we'll start over somewhere."

Ty shook his head, at a loss for words.

"I'm offering you a chance at a life without orders, without rules, without being a pawn in someone else's game."

"We've never been pawns."

"No? Your code name is Rook. Make no mistake, you are just a player in a game. As am I."

Ty stared, fighting to calm himself. Liam stood with his hands at his sides, nonthreatening and earnest.

"Let's run, Ty. Come with me. We'll bury ourselves and start over. With nothing to do but lie on a beach all day and drink and fuck."

Ty couldn't answer, still torn between shock and anger. "Yeah," he finally sneered. "Drink and fuck and run from the NIA."

"You bloody stubborn bastard!" Liam shouted, his façade finally cracking. "I'm telling you right here, I love you! We have a chance to cut and run, and I want you to come with me!"

"Liam," Ty said as despair and uncertainty began to seep in.

"Fine. You still want to serve? I'm game. Come with me to the NIA," Liam tried. "We'd be unstoppable."

"How?"

"We'll shoot it out. You take me down, I'll clip you in a leg, make you unfit for service in the Corps."

"I'm not going to shoot you! And you're sure as shit not shooting me!"

"I'll get you with a knife then! Come with me, Ty."

Ty took in a shaky breath, not allowing himself to ponder the possibility or even be tempted to desert. "I can't."

Liam's mask broke, and Ty could see the pain in his clear blue eyes. He recognized it well because he'd been feeling it ever since he'd discovered that Liam had been using his clearance to transmit on the CB frequency the rebels were monitoring. Ty gritted his teeth. He'd thought Liam a traitor, and though he was relieved to be wrong, it seemed he would lose him anyway. For the first time, uncertainty began to gnaw its way into him.

Liam shook it off, rallying faster than Ty had been able to. "If you don't intend to go with me, will you still help me? Will you join me later?"

"How?"

Liam shook his head sadly, his hands still held out to his sides. "You have to shoot me. And it has to be out there, in the common areas, to make sure you're not at risk and to get scuttlebutt going."

Ty shook his head, his voice harsh. "I can't do that."

"You can."

"I can't let you go like that."

Liam gave him a weak smile. "Oh, how I wish you meant that like it sounds, darling." He took a step toward the door.

"Stop moving."

"Make me, Ty." Liam took another backward step and put his hand on the doorknob. "You and I both know you can't take me down without a gun, and you won't even shoot me when I ask you to."

Ty drew in a deep breath. "Liam. We'll figure something else out. Please don't go."

"Why not? Would you miss me?"

Ty looked into his eyes and nodded jerkily. "Yes, I would."

"So tell me why I shouldn't go." They stared at each other. Liam took a step back. "Or better yet, come with me and tell me every night."

Ty's heart pounded, the blood rushing through him and making him light-headed.

"If you don't follow and shoot me somewhere that looks like a kill shot, I'm going to go find someone else who will. Someone without your aim."

Ty narrowed his eyes.

"You could be killing me if they miss." Liam turned and disappeared around the corner.

Ty holstered his gun and darted after the man, knowing Liam would do exactly what he'd threatened. He caught up to him in the canteen. It was crowded with troops, laughing and eating, playing pool and darts, relaxing after a long, trying day.

"Sergeant Bell!" Ty shouted.

Liam stopped on the other side of the room, turning to meet his eyes.

The room gradually quieted, confused by their combative stances.

Liam glanced around at their comrades in arms. Ty understood now that Liam had always intended to leave them, known forever to them as the spy among them who was shot and killed. They would never know what he'd done for their safety, what he'd sacrificed, and Liam had known that all along.

Ty grew angrier as the confusion ebbed. Who the hell had the right to ask them to be like this? Who decided it was their job to sacrifice their lives?

Liam looked at him expectantly, silently begging him to announce he was a traitor, to draw on him. A low murmur of confusion and amusement began to rumble through the room.

Ty couldn't get the words out. They stuck in his throat. His hand wouldn't reach for his gun. He shook his head, unable to come through for Liam when he needed him most.

Liam mouthed the word, "Please."

Ty's hand settled on his gun. His body was cold all over and his hand shook. There was no way he could take that shot. He'd miss the target and kill him.

Liam sneered and peered at Ty with icy blue eyes. He drew his gun. Shock and alarm rippled through the soldiers and Marines as Liam aimed at Ty. "I'll shoot you, Tyler," Liam murmured.

Ty went cold, seeing the truth in the man's eyes, and yet he still couldn't pull his own weapon. If he had to die, he wanted someone worthy to take the kill shot.

Liam fired and the bullet caught Ty in the left shoulder. He cried out and stumbled back, fighting past the shock to realize that if he didn't shoot Liam, someone else in the room would. He pulled his service pistol, not taking the time to think, not letting his nerves overtake his hands, and put two rounds in Liam's chest.

"You shot him because he *asked* you to?" Zane asked.

Nick released Ty's shirt and backed away. They all gaped at Ty.

"Technically, I shot him because he shot me." Ty pressed his back against the wall. He was breathing hard, like he expected one of them to come at him again. He looked cornered.

Zane knew what happened to Ty, and to the people around him, when he was cornered. He moved forward, brushing past Nick. "You need to sit down," he said under his breath.

Ty nodded, taking a deep breath. He locked eyes with Zane, refusing to look away as Zane placed a hand on his shoulder.

"If he asked you to shoot him, why would he be here for revenge? Why are you scared?" Owen asked.

Ty cleared his throat, taking a step toward the bed and then reversing and pacing past Zane. He met Zane's eyes again briefly, then turned back to the bed.

Nick caught him by the arm to stop him. "Answer him."

Ty took another deep breath. "I'm sorry," he whispered.

"For what?" Nick demanded.

Ty cleared his throat and glanced around the room. He gently pulled his arm out of Nick's grasp. He sat down hard. "Liam is the reason Sidewinder was discharged."

A chorus of questions and complaints arose, but all Zane could do was watch the line of Ty's shoulders as he leaned forward and rested his face in his hands. He suddenly looked like a man who'd been carrying a great weight, and Zane knew there were other secrets Ty carried, secrets as big as this one. Secrets that weighed on him in ways no one could understand by merely looking at his façade.

Nick took a step into the center of the room, raising his hands to calm the other three. He turned to Ty and knelt in front of him. "Tell us what happened. Please, Ty. You've obviously been keeping this on yourself, it's time to trust us."

Ty straightened, both hands on his knees. He looked down at Nick. "Once they had him declared dead and he'd recovered enough to move, I think Liam pulled strings with NIA. He convinced them we'd make a good asset, the whole team, that we could be military assets for NIA just like he'd been."

"NIA made a deal with the Marine Corps?" Kelly asked.

Ty nodded, looking sick. "They tried to, from what I was able to gather. I was never given the full briefing, but I do know we were to be released into the umbrella of the National Intelligence Agency to be used as part of a new ultra-militarized arm of the CIA. We'd have had to jump whenever they called. We wouldn't have been real Marines anymore, we would have been spooks in Marine uniforms. When I was informed of the orders, I . . . I refused them."

"You spoke for the whole team?" Zane asked.

"Yes, I did."

"You're telling me I got kicked out of the Corps because you had a lover's spat?" Owen growled.

Ty stood, baring his teeth like an animal. Nick stood with him, just managing to stop him from advancing. He shoved him back to the bed. Ty bounced on the mattress, grabbing his side and grunting.

"Shit, sorry!" Nick said. He patted Ty's head but kept his body between him and Owen. "Why would Bell be back here for revenge?"

"I don't know, but that's what he told me in the hospital. His plan all along was for me to join him. I chose the Corps, all of you, over him. I can only assume."

"And now you're here with Zane," Nick added. "Who is the partner you never let Liam be."

Zane's stomach flipped to hear someone say that. He probably should have been ashamed to be thrilled by the words, but he wasn't.

"So you think he's here in New Orleans, murdering people because he's pissed at you?" Kelly asked. "Why?"

Ty shook his head.

Digger stood and ambled toward the balcony. "This explains so much. I feel like I've just finished a crossword puzzle."

"How do you know what that feels like?" Kelly asked.

"I don't."

Kelly sniffed.

"This is why they paid us off, to keep quiet about the NIA. And why they gave us those release terms," Owen said. "Good God, Ty, why didn't you tell us any of this?"

"It was top secret," Ty answered. He sounded and looked exhausted. "I couldn't."

Zane stepped forward, frowning. "What terms?"

They all turned to look at him, as if they'd forgotten he was there.

"Are you serious?" Owen blurted. He looked from Zane to Ty. "You talk about how much you love this guy and you haven't even told him?"

Ty pointed a finger at him and snarled, "Shut up."

"Told me what?" Zane asked cautiously.

Owen glanced at him, curling his lip. "Ask your boyfriend. He's the one with all the secrets."

Nick strode toward Owen, giving his shoulder a shove. "Johns, shut your fucking mouth."

But Zane turned his attention to Ty. The look on his lover's face didn't do much to dispel the sudden bout of nerves. "Ty?"

Ty stood. His hands balled into fists as he glanced from Zane to Nick. Nick nodded.

"Tell him, Grady!" Owen shouted. Nick shoved Owen into the wall and pointed a finger in his face, hissing.

"Get him out of here," Ty growled. Nick grabbed Owen's shoulder, but the man shrugged him off.

"Don't have to tell me twice. I'm fucking out of here." He stormed out, letting the door slam behind him.

Nick squared his shoulders, regaining his calming demeanor with impressive speed. He gave them one last glance, then headed for the door. Kelly and Digger followed, murmuring good-byes to Zane as they passed.

As soon as the door closed, Zane heard Owen shouting in the hallway. He turned to Ty, though. "What the hell is going on?"

"Zane," Ty said, his voice hoarse. He cleared his throat. He seemed to be fighting to meet Zane's eyes. "There's something . . . something I've been keeping from you."

Zane's stomach flipped. "I thought we got all the secrets out."

Ty shook his head, looking sick. "Not this one."

Zane took a deep breath, trying to come to terms with the flicker of fear in Ty's eyes. "So tell me."

Ty struggled to meet Zane's eyes as he began to speak. "I was never completely discharged from the Marines."

Zane barked a laugh. "You're so full of shit."

"I'm not joking, Zane."

Zane's smile fell and he took a step toward Ty. "What are you talking about?"

Ty glanced at the door. "The boys and me ... the team. We're still obligated to the Marines."

Zane stared, mouth hanging open. "What?"

Ty ran a hand through his hair. "It happens with a lot of Special Ops crews; the military never really lets us go. We're too highly trained, too much money and time has been put into us. And the terms we signed when they released us compel us to go back if they order it. If they want us back ..."

"What the hell are you talking about?"

"Zane."

"No, Ty, I mean ... what the hell are you talking about?"

"I was never discharged from the Marines. Sidewinder wasn't disbanded, even though the official paperwork cited disobedience as the reason for leaving. We were just ... put on reserve because of the fuss the NIA made. They took my refusal of the orders and used it as the excuse to put us all into cold storage."

Ty looked both riddled with nerves and relieved to have said the words. Zane tried to speak, but nothing would come out. He took a staggering step back and pressed his hand to his stomach, feeling sick and dizzy.

After a few moments of tense silence, Ty leaned closer. "Zane?"

"You're saying you're still a Marine."

"Not technically. Sort of."

"You can't be sort of technically a Marine, Ty. You either are or you aren't!"

Ty put a hand up to calm him, but Zane batted it away. "You're still a Marine! You're telling me that any day, you could be called back into service and you'd have to prance off with your little go bag and be gone for months on the front line?"

"You're upset."

"You're damn right I'm upset!" Zane roared. "This is something you stay prepared for, isn't it? The bag in the closet, never missing a morning run. When the fuck were you planning on telling me this?"

"I was . . . I was hoping I wouldn't need to. The contracts expire in December."

Zane sniffed in disgust. "Jesus Christ, Ty."

Ty raised both hands. "It's not like it's something I can just go around telling everyone."

"I'm not everyone!"

"I know that! But Zane, there's nothing we can do about it."

"And that makes it okay not to tell me?"

Ty shook his head.

"Give me details," Zane demanded.

"I can't tell you more. I wasn't supposed to tell you that much."

"The fuck you can't. You're standing here telling me you're still a fucking Marine, that you and your team are still on some sort of long-term fucking—"

"Zane, calm down."

Zane slammed his fist into the wall. Blood was roaring through his ears and he had to shout to hear himself. "I've been living with you for a year and you can't tell me more?"

"I'm—"

"Bullshit!"

"I can't tell you, Zane!" Ty shouted. "God! What I've said already could get me thrown in the Disciplinary Barracks at Leavenworth! Do you understand? I am still subject to USMC laws and codes of conduct!"

Zane ran his hands through his hair.

"And frankly, Liam Bell scares me more right now than any secrets I've been keeping from you."

"Are there more?" Zane asked sarcastically.

Ty hesitated, and Zane caught a flicker of guilt in his eyes.

"Oh my God," Zane whispered. "There's more. There's something worse than this?"

"Zane."

"Tell me what else you're hiding."

Ty raised his head and squared his shoulders, his nostrils flaring. "No."

Zane stared. His heart was pounding. He'd known they had secrets between them, things they weren't ready to share. They'd discussed these things, shady parts of their pasts they'd rather not take out of the box. But Zane had never expected Ty's secrets to be something that could hurt him. Hurt them.

Zane studied his lover, letting that truth settle somewhere deep inside him.

"Tell me now, tell me everything I need to know."

Ty's jaw muscles jumped, but he stayed straight and tall, matching Zane's glare with his own. When he spoke, though, it came out broken. "No."

Zane gritted his teeth and slammed his palm against the wall. "Tell me the truth or I walk!"

Ty swallowed hard, but it was obvious that he was weighing whether or not he should speak.

"You really have to think about it?" Zane shoved away from Ty, unable to tear his eyes from him even as the pain twisted in his chest like a knife. "I guess we finally found the one thing more important to you than I am."

Ty's face hardened. "You know that's not true."

"Fuck you, Ty! I feel like I don't know a goddamned thing now!" Zane jabbed his finger toward Ty. "I tell you I'm going to walk and you have to fucking think about it? Just fuck you!"

Ty took a deep breath, but it didn't help the strength of his words when he tried to speak. "If I told you . . . I'm afraid you'd walk anyway."

Zane threw his hands out. "What have you got to lose?"

Ty's jaw tightened. Zane held his breath, waiting, giving him a last chance to come clean, unable to imagine what Ty could have been keeping from him that he was so afraid to admit to.

Ty shook his head, his jaw set.

Zane took a step back. He was devastated to have been backed down, called on his bluff. He had no idea where to go from here.

Only one place came to mind, one place to retreat from the stone wall Ty had just raised. It wasn't just a wall to protect Ty or his secrets. It was a wall to protect Ty's secrets *from Zane*.

He turned on his heel and grabbed up his cigarettes and lighter from the floor. He brushed past Ty as he headed for the door.

"Zane."

Zane turned.

"There's a man out there who wants to hurt you. And he's good. Please don't go off alone."

"Go to Hell, Ty," Zane grunted, and he wrenched the door open and stalked out.

Chapter 6

Nick was waiting when the door opened, but Zane brushed past him when he tried to stop him. He had to jog to catch up with Zane's angry strides, and he felt like a puppy hopping along with its master as he tried to keep abreast of the man stalking down the hall.

"I know you're pissed, man, I am too. But Ty keeps secrets, that's what he does. That's what he's trained to do."

"You don't have to defend him," Zane snarled. "Is that what you've done for twenty years? Defend Ty? You must be goddamned exhausted."

"Yeah, pretty much." Nick reached out and took Zane's arm. "Would you slow down? Jesus."

Zane stopped and turned to face him. Nick could tell he had about two seconds to make his case. "Look, I'm not stepping into this, okay? Whatever he said in there, it's between you and him. But I knew Liam Bell. And if Ty says he's out to get you, I believe him. Don't go out there alone just because you're pissed."

Zane rolled his eyes and huffed. Nick tightened his grip on Zane's arm, hard enough that Zane looked down at it pointedly.

"Imagine that you're out there in this city, and *Ty* is hunting you down," Nick said.

Zane's nostrils flared and his eyes darkened.

"Now imagine him smarter. Faster. Imagine him more ruthless and with less to lose. Now imagine *that* Ty, and he wants revenge. I don't know about you, man, but that scares the living hell out of me."

Zane swallowed hard. He looked mutinous for a moment, but then nodded. "I see your point."

"Will you let me go with you?"

Zane grumbled and glanced down the hall at the door to their room.

"Let me tail you, then," Nick tried. "You'll never know I was there and I'll watch your six while you do whatever it is you need to do to cool down."

Zane laughed and finally wrenched his arm out of Nick's grasp. "Just leave me alone, all right?"

He stalked away before Nick could argue. Nick stood and watched Zane's retreat for a few seconds, torn. He trusted Ty when he said Zane was the target, but he couldn't and wouldn't tag along with the man if Zane refused to let him. Zane would shake him easily, and in the end Zane was responsible for his own safety.

He turned and headed back down the hall to knock on Ty's door.

Ty opened it almost immediately. Nick shook his head in answer to Ty's questioning look.

"Goddammit," Ty spat. He ran his hands through his hair and paced into the room.

Nick held the door open for Kelly and Digger, who'd been standing by, waiting to see what would happen next. Owen was long gone. They filed into Ty's room, gathering around him.

"What do we do?" Digger asked.

Ty had his hands on his hips and his head lowered. He looked pale and drawn, and Nick could see he wasn't running on all cylinders yet. But years of training forced them to look to him first.

Ty shook his head. "I . . . I don't know."

Nick watched him for a long moment, and when it became obvious Ty wasn't pulling it together, Nick cleared his throat. "We can leave town. But I got a feeling Bell isn't here 'cause he can't find us at home. He's here because he wants us all together. He wants us here. And he knew we'd be here."

Kelly shrugged. "I agree, but how?"

"Sanchez," Digger said. "He knew we'd get together for Sanchez's birthday."

"Which means he also has the resources to know Eli is dead, and that Digger is confined to the state," Ty murmured. "He's either here on company business, or he's using those resources and gone off the reservation."

"What does he have to do with the gris-gris bag?" Digger asked. "You really think he killed that girl last night?"

Nick's brow furrowed. Ty grimaced and shrugged.

"Sneaking in as a maid and leaving towels on the bed is a little sloppy for Bell," Kelly said.

Ty held up a hand. "We're running off the rails here." He rubbed at his face, massaging between his eyes.

"Why would he approach Zane first?" Digger asked. "He couldn't know you'd find that note, or that Zane would tell you about meeting him. What's his game?"

"Everything is a game to him. It's like chess."

"You don't play chess," Nick said.

"Yes, thank you!" Ty barked.

Nick shrugged.

"We need to take care of this, right here, right now," Ty said. "While we're all together."

Nick nodded. He knew he wouldn't feel safe heading back to Boston with a man like Liam holding a grudge. "What about Zane?"

Ty hesitated, breathing faster. "I'll send him home."

"Will he listen?" Kelly asked, looking dubious. "He's pretty understandably pissed."

Nick snorted. "Ty. He's not going to leave you here, in danger, even if he is pissed at you. Even I know him better than that."

Ty ran a hand over his eyes again. "You're right."

"We have to get him back here," Nick said. "Use him as our sixth."

"Is he up for that?" Digger asked.

Ty straightened and shot Digger a look. "I trust my life to him every day. He's up for anything we throw at him."

Digger pursed his lips. "Okay. So go fetch him."

Ty growled. "And you two go find Owen and drag his ass back here."

Kelly and Digger nodded and turned, almost synchronized in their movements. There was something comfortable about sinking back into that uniformity, into that chain of leadership and trust.

Nick watched Ty rummage through Zane's jeans, looking for something. "What about me?"

"Stay here. If someone's not back in an hour you're the cavalry. Turn on the GPS tracking on the phones."

"Great."

Ty stood, holding a bronze sobriety chip. Nick's father had dozens of them in a drawer at home.

"Zane's?"

Ty nodded, looking grim and distressed. "He might need it."

"Really? Is he that easy to knock off the wagon?"

Ty glared at him for a moment, but then he swallowed hard. "No," he whispered. "No, he's not." He headed for the door and was almost out of the room before Nick called after him.

"Take your piece!"

Ty cursed and went back to his suitcase to rummage through it.

"Are you sure you're okay to do this? I can go out there and bring him back. I wasn't on a morphine drip all day and he's not *quite* as pissed at me as he is at you."

Ty checked the clip of his service weapon and jammed the magazine home, then stuffed it in the back of his jeans and covered it with his flannel shirt.

Nick watched him with a growing sense of unease. His movements weren't measured, his mind was all over the place. "Ty," he whispered.

Ty just shook his head.

"Ty, you're not up to this."

"I will be," Ty growled. "A few hours for the drugs to clear, I'll be fine."

"Ty, I'm telling you as a friend. You're not up to this, drugs or not."

Ty turned to meet his eyes.

"Liam Bell. He's the only person I know who was ever as good as you. And right now, he's better than you are."

Ty breathed out harshly and looked away. "I know," he said, heading for the door. "He always was."

***

There was no finding a quiet spot in the French Quarter, especially when half the revelers were wearing huge Easter hats, bunny ears, and layers of beads.

Zane had wandered toward the outskirts of the Quarter, looking for familiar ground. His steps tried to follow in those of the past, trying to find that little bar he and Becky had visited so long ago. His memory wouldn't lead him there, though, so he settled for a little tavern on a side street with empty tables.

His mind was roiling, seething, replaying the look in Ty's eyes when he'd refused to tell Zane what he was holding back. They had been living together for a year. Lovers for almost two. Partners for longer than that. The idea that Ty had been able to keep something from him, with so little effort, was staggering. And he could feel there was worse, lying in wait.

This Liam Bell business was only the half of it.

By the time he reached the bar, his entire body was shaking with anger and adrenaline. He ordered a whiskey straight and took the glass to sit at the corner table.

He placed it in front of him. A challenge. A test of how far he'd come. He'd done everything in the last year for Ty, trying to be worthy, trying to make himself a better, healthier man. He'd fought the withdrawal that had wracked his body and the cloying need that filled his mind every morning when he woke, all to prove to himself that he deserved to be happy, that he deserved Ty's love.

Had Ty even been worth it?

He stared at the whiskey glass, letting the pull envelop him just to see how strong he was to fight it now.

Ty thumped into the empty chair across from him, rattling the table. The whiskey in Zane's glass sloshed. He stared at it, not looking up to meet Ty's eyes.

"Please don't do this, Zane."

"Go away, Ty," Zane said without looking up from the glass.

"You've worked so hard to get past this, don't do this now. Not like this."

Zane glowered at him. "Who the hell are you to tell me anything?"

Ty recoiled like Zane had slapped him, but he jutted his chin out and squared his shoulders. "I'm your partner. And I'm your friend. And I love you."

"You're a liar."

"You're right. And you can hate me if you want to, but that doesn't change the fact that I love you. And I'm not going to sit idly by while you do this to yourself because of me."

Zane glared, but the pain in the pit of his stomach was overpowering the anger. He looked back to the glass, still full of whiskey.

Ty reached out and slammed something onto the table. When he moved his hand, Zane's one year sobriety chip remained.

Zane stared at it, then transferred his glare to Ty. "You think I need that?"

Ty shrugged, looking pointedly at the glass.

"I really am that weak to you, aren't I?"

Ty's eyes were steady and dark as they stared at each other, neither man flinching. "You're not weak, Zane," Ty said. "But we all need help sometimes."

"And now you need *my* help, right? To deal with this Liam Bell guy, this guy from your past you were never going to tell me about. It's okay to lie to me, keep things from me, but when you need a spare gun, oh, go pick Zane up at the bar."

"Don't sulk, it doesn't suit you."

"Fuck you, Ty."

Ty snorted and finally looked away. "Will you come back with me? Help us figure this shit out?"

"You're not on the first plane home anymore?" Ty shook his head. "You're going to make a stand here?"

"Here we're all together. We know where he is. He's lost the element of surprise and we have the stronger force."

Zane nodded. "Fine."

Ty gave a curt nod and pushed his chair back to stand.

"On one condition," Zane added.

Ty sat back, resigned.

"Tell me everything. You're hiding something, something big, and I want to know what it is. And if you tell me it's classified, I will smash this glass into your face. And then I'll be on the first plane home."

Ty remained motionless, not even blinking. Zane had to fight to meet his stare. He rarely saw Ty so still. The last time had been in a blizzard, when Ty had denied ever being in Paris when he damn well had been.

It was Ty's only tell. He stopped moving when he lied.

"You're really going to force this out of me?" Ty snarled after a few more seconds.

Zane gave a single nod.

Ty sat forward, staring at the tabletop. He took a long, deep breath. "Okay," he whispered, losing the hard edge to his voice. He looked up at Zane, his eyes dark in the low light. His nerves must've been contagious, because Zane's stomach was churning. "After the Tri-State case, after you were pulled from Miami, Richard Burns assigned me as your partner so I could protect you."

Zane narrowed his eyes. "What?"

Ty rolled his shoulders, pulling one hand below the table. Zane knew he was rubbing his palm across his thigh to dispel the urge to fidget, but he also knew Ty had a gun under there, and Ty's hand always hovered near his gun when he was scared.

"The Vega cartel," Ty said.

Zane straightened. "How did you know I was under with them? Have you read my file?"

"No. It was given to me as part of my briefing, but I didn't read it."

"Your briefing. What are you talking about?"

"Zane . . . for the last year and a half, *you* have been my assignment."

The world seemed to slow around them. Sounds faded. The pangs in Zane's chest were the labored beating of his heart as he tried to absorb what Ty was telling him.

"You're . . . you're, what, on guard duty? You're my personal protection detail, complete with free blowjobs?"

"Stop it," Ty snarled. "The Vega cartel found out they had a UC working within them. You got pulled before they could get to you. They've had feelers out all over the agency ever since. They know what you looked like. If they found out your identity or location, they'd come for you, and they'd come hard. Almost every time Burns has called me for a job, it's been to head them off."

"Oh my God," Zane gasped. "You're the one who's been wreaking havoc in Miami."

Ty lifted his head, his expression guarded.

Zane couldn't breathe. "I've been following the reports. Someone's taking out Vega people left and right, no one knows who it is or why. Even the Bureau is after this guy. But it's you."

"Yeah," Ty whispered.

"Jesus."

Zane tried to get a handle on that, the image of Ty sneaking off to Miami, hunting people down, terrorizing the lower rungs of the cartel, leaving mangled bodies behind, forcing men on their knees and putting bullets in their heads to leave dread and suspicion in his wake. The man Zane crawled into bed with every night, the man who held him, the man he talked down from nightmares, was the same man doing that.

"Don't look at me like that, Zane," Ty begged.

Zane struggled to reconcile it with the man he knew. "You're saying you've done all that to cover my ass."

"Yes."

"That's why Burns let you run off to Texas so fast, wasn't it? He thought it was related."

Ty nodded.

Zane gaped. "You . . . I've been your mark."

"No, Zane."

Zane brought his hand to his mouth because he couldn't seem to force it to close on his own. His fingers trembled against his face.

"Zane," Ty said harshly.

"Has this all been some sort of long con?" he choked out. "An easy way to get close to me and watch me?"

"You know that's not true! Will you let me explain without getting dramatic?"

"Dramatic? You're telling me everything our relationship is based on came out of some assignment briefing, and I'm being *dramatic*?"

Ty raised a hand to calm him, which only served to make Zane angrier. Ty had no right to try to calm him now.

"You've had damn near two years to explain, Ty! But you didn't say a fucking word, just kept on like it wouldn't destroy us when that came out."

"I couldn't tell you!"

Zane banged his fist on the table. Whiskey sloshed across the scarred top. "Bullshit! Why the hell would Dick make you protect me from something and not *tell* me I was in danger? It makes no sense!"

Ty flinched and lowered his head, then brought both hands up and placed them on the table, twining his fingers. Zane had seen him do it plenty of times when he was nervous. But Zane didn't care that

Ty was nervous right now. He wanted him nervous. He wanted the bastard squirming in his seat because Zane's world had suddenly fallen away to reveal nothing but a glass floor beneath him.

When Ty spoke, his voice was quiet, but Zane could hear the tremor in it. "I couldn't tell you because my second objective was to make sure you hadn't been turned." He looked up to meet Zane's eyes.

The implications stole Zane's breath, making him light-headed. Burns had put Ty on him to make sure he hadn't become a cartel mole, to make sure he hadn't betrayed the agency. All those years, Richard Burns had suspected him of being a traitor, of working for the very cartel he'd almost killed himself to bring down. The man he'd thought had battled for his career, who'd saved him and shoved him through rehab to get him clean, had merely been waiting for him to prove himself the enemy. And the instrument of that betrayal was the only man in the world Zane had ever trusted implicitly. Ty.

The anger and pain were so sharp and sudden that Zane brought a hand to his chest to combat the tightness.

"Zane," Ty whispered.

Zane swallowed past the knot in his throat and met Ty's eyes again. It was hard to breathe. "You thought I was a traitor?"

Ty shook his head and reached across the table for Zane's hand. "I know you, Zane, I know what you are."

Zane pushed his hand away and stood. "Then why the hell would you let it go on? He would listen to you if you told him!"

Ty stood with him, reaching out to put a hand on his shoulder. Zane swatted it away, balling his fist. Ty put up both hands to calm him. "It was the only way to—"

"Bullshit!"

Heads began to turn, people staring at them, but Zane didn't give a fuck. Ty glanced over his shoulder. "Can we please sit down?" he asked. The tone of voice was the same one Ty used when he was trying to coerce someone into being calm. Zane had always found it amusing and oddly comforting. Now, he recognized it as just another of the many ways Ty could manipulate and hurt someone. He'd used that voice to smooth over too many lies, too many half-truths, and too many indiscretions.

Zane took a shaky breath and sat on the edge of his seat, willing to listen but also ready to bolt if the pain in his chest grew any sharper. Ty sat with him, maintaining eye contact. He scooted his chair closer so their knees were touching, and leaned on his elbows so he was as close to Zane as possible. Zane's heart sped up, and he fought not to reach out and touch Ty's face.

Ty cleared his throat, struggling to start. "I couldn't . . . I couldn't tell Burns you were clean."

Zane gritted his teeth and gripped the edge of the table.

Ty spoke faster. "As soon as he knew, he could have reassigned me. He might have moved me on to the next job, and I wasn't ready to risk that. What we have, Zane, it is the best thing in my life. And I know you feel that way too, because we both fought hard for it."

"I fought hard for *you*, Ty. I loved you, how could you keep this from me?"

Ty put a hand over his mouth. His fingers were trembling, but he grabbed Zane's hand, holding it hard. Zane tried to yank it away, but Ty held on. "Because I knew it would hurt you. I didn't want to hurt you, I didn't want you to ever know Dick questioned your loyalty. I was hoping to wait it out, hoping I could hand in my final report when you retired and be done with it."

Zane shook his head. He'd never realized it was possible for a heart to break for so many reasons at the same time. "You didn't want to hurt me? Well you failed that mission miserably. That's really the only thing you care about, right? Mission accomplished?"

Ty's grip tightened and he lowered his head. He was holding onto Zane as if he'd fall if he let go. Zane recalled the last time they'd both fallen; Ty'd begged him to trust him, and then thrown him off a building. Literally. And Zane *had* trusted him, with his life, with his happiness, and finally with his heart.

During all that, though, Ty hadn't trusted Zane with one simple secret.

Their entire time together flashed through his mind as the pressure in his chest grew. He ran his thumb over Ty's finger, trying to understand Ty's reasoning, desperately trying to believe him.

Ty's eyes were drawn to the movement, to the finger that would wear a ring if their plans went the way Zane wanted them to. "Nothing about us was a lie," Ty whispered brokenly.

Zane had heard that before. *Nothing else was a lie, Zane.* Except all of it had been a lie. "Fool me once, Ty, shame on you."

Ty raised his head, his eyes pleading.

"Fool me twice . . ." Zane shook his head. He let go of Ty's hand.

"Zane, please."

Zane shut his eyes as he stood. "I need some time, okay? I just need . . . I need to think."

"You shouldn't go anywhere alone."

Zane turned and kicked the closest empty chair, sending it clattering to the floor. "I've always been alone!" he shouted.

He stalked away before Ty could say anything more. Zane knew how good Ty was with words, how easily he could manipulate someone into doing what he wanted. He knew Ty's weapons, and he would be damned if he let himself be susceptible to any of them now.

Ty called his name as Zane walked away, but Zane knew that if he turned around, he'd be lost in Ty's labyrinth again. He deserved to be angry. He deserved to be hurt. He wouldn't give Ty a chance to slither his way out of a betrayal like this until he'd had time to think. He desperately needed to think.

He made it all the way out the door and around the corner before he leaned against the brick façade of the building and took a deep, shaky breath.

"Just walk away," he whispered. He couldn't turn around. His resolve would crumble.

But how could he walk away? He'd never seen Ty's fingers tremble like that. He'd never heard Ty plead with anyone like that. Perhaps if he looked back, he'd be able to hold onto the anger long enough to keep a clear head.

When he craned his head to look through the window, Ty was still sitting where he'd left him, the toppled chair next to him, his head bowed, his hand covering his mouth.

"That looked rough," a man said at Zane's shoulder.

Zane glanced at him, not really seeing him. He nodded, and looked through the window again. His heart was breaking and the only person he could think to go to for comfort was still sitting at that goddamned table. "I, uh, I need to go back in there," he stuttered, taking a step past the man.

The muzzle of a gun shoved into his side stopped him in his tracks.

"Not so fast, love. We have some catching up to do," Liam Bell purred against Zane's ear.

Pain blossomed at Zane's temple, and the lights flickered out.

Ty had his phone to his ear, calling Zane's number for the tenth time as he stepped out of the elevator. It clicked over to voice mail again, and Ty left another message. He was sounding more and more pissed and panicked with each one, but he didn't care.

It took him three tries to get his key card to work, and he shoved his shoulder into the door to push it open.

When he stalked into the room, Nick was perched on the end of the bed. Kelly and Digger were sitting opposite him, all of them looking grim.

"No Zane?" Nick asked.

Ty shook his head, fighting past the wave of nausea, grief, and panic. "No Owen?" He asked in return, surprised when his voice cracked.

"He left the hotel," Kelly explained. "He'll come back, no need to track him down."

"Yeah, unless Bell gets to him first," Digger muttered.

Nick rolled his eyes. "Okay, this isn't some horror movie. He's not going to pick us off one by one when we venture out."

"I don't know, Irish," Digger said. "I remember Liam being pretty gleeful about hunting people down."

"Yeah, well, he's not after all of you," Ty said. "He wants *me* to suffer."

Nick lifted his head. "Killing off the people you love is the way I'd go."

"Dude, you're getting creepier since you came out," Kelly muttered. Nick winked at him.

"And if Bell's not behind the gris-gris, who is?" Digger added.

Ty ran his hand through his hair. He dialed Zane's number again.

"Who are you calling?" Kelly asked.

"Zane. I can't reach him."

"Man down," Digger whispered.

"Shut up," Nick hissed. He looked at Ty, frowning deeply. "Would he really disappear on you knowing what's going down? That doesn't seem like Garrett's style."

"It's not," Ty said as he listened to Zane's voice mail message again. He ended the call and stuffed the phone into his pocket, staring at the floor as waves of prickling cold hit him. "He's got him."

"You can't know that," Nick tried.

Ty shook his head. "He's got him, Nick." He looked around his feet, searching for the crumpled piece of paper he'd found in Zane's pocket.

"What are you doing?" Nick asked.

"Where's the paper?"

"I put it on the counter in the bathroom."

Ty stalked into the bathroom and grabbed it off the vanity. There was a phone number with the name. He dug his phone back out and dialed it, forcing his fingers to work.

After two rings a recording answered, a voice that had haunted his dreams for years.

"Wait your turn," it said.

Ty gritted his teeth and forced himself not to leave a message that would have come out seething and incoherent and panicked. Instead he ended the call and stared at the phone, his world reeling. He had to think clearly, he had to get to Zane and do it now.

He slammed the paper back onto the counter and fought hard not to toss his phone. He hung his head, taking deep, calming gulps of air. His breath slid the scrap of paper across the marble, and Ty looked closer at it. Now he saw more on the scrap of paper. Streaks of yellowish stains.

"Irish!" he called. Nick appeared in the doorway. Ty picked up the paper, glancing up at the glaring vanity lights overhead. "Did something spill on it?"

"Not that I know of," Nick said. He peered over Ty's shoulder, then up at the hot light bulbs. "What's it smell like?"

Ty sniffed the paper. "Citrus. Lemon maybe."

Nick stepped closer and grabbed the hairdryer off its dock on the side wall. Ty flattened the paper out and Nick turned the hairdryer on the paper. The yellow streaks began to form words.

"Ugh, I knew I hated him when we were stationed together," Nick grumbled. The words became clearer as the heat brought out the acid in the lemon juice. "He probably sat in a bar somewhere and used the damn lemon from his water. I hate him!"

Ty just shook his head, heart hammering as the words became clear. Liam Bell had slipped this piece of paper into Zane's pocket, knowing it would make its way to Ty, believing Ty would keep a level enough head to find the message written here.

Liam was already outthinking him and Ty was already relying on luck.

2 AM. Jackson Square. Be there or your partner dies.

"I'm gonna kill him," Ty growled.

Nick put a hand on his shoulder, squeezing gently. "Easy, Ty."

Ty slammed his hand against the paper. "I'll kill him!"

He turned, but Nick grabbed him by both shoulders, holding him there and forcing Ty to meet his eyes. "Think, okay? Breathe."

Ty lowered his head like a bull preparing to charge, but Nick faced him down, waiting for him to calm himself. Ty took a deep breath and nodded.

"Okay," Nick whispered. He released Ty.

Nick's phone began to ring from his back pocket, breaking the spell. Ty was shaking when Nick pulled the phone out and turned away from him. He glanced up, trying to stay calm, trying not to think of the things that could happen to Zane between now and 2 AM.

Nick cursed as he checked the caller ID, walking away. "Good afternoon, Detective," he answered with a wince. He turned to Ty. "Of course, any way we can help. When would you like us to come in?" His eyes widened and he waved at Ty. "You're coming to the hotel?"

He pointed to the phone and then to his feet. The detective was coming here to interview them again. "No, no, that's fine. But I'm afraid Agent Garrett isn't here right now, maybe we can delay it until he is."

Ty shoved his phone in his pocket and rushed to the bed to grab his jacket. He couldn't be caught in the room. He glanced at the others, and they both waved him toward the door. Nick tapped his watch and held up five fingers: *five minutes to get clear.*

Ty made a gesture to let them know he'd find them, then wrenched the door open, only to stop short when he found himself face-to-face with a man holding a phone to his ear and a badge, two uniformed policemen flanking him.

"Son of a bitch," Ty grunted.

"Well, Tyler Beaumont," the detective drawled. He shut his phone, and Nick cursed behind Ty. "I should have known you'd show up with a load of trouble and a couple fake badges."

"Wake up, darling, we're wasting time here," a voice said in the darkness.

It was the same name Ty called him sometimes, but it wasn't the same word. There was no drawl to it, no affectionate smirk in the voice. It was British, said with sarcasm and disdain.

Zane forced his eyes open, wincing as light lanced through his brain. A blond man came into focus. He leaned over Zane, holding a penlight. He shined it in Zane's eyes, and Zane groaned and turned his head away.

"Wakey wakey," Liam crooned.

"Go to Hell," Zane grunted.

"No need to be testy, Zane. I'm here to help you."

Zane ignored the throbbing in the back of his head to glare at the man. "By bashing me in the head?"

"Nothing less would have stopped you from going back in that pub and making a huge mistake."

Ty. Zane tried to sit up, but his hands and arms were tied down. He was stretched out on a concrete floor, trussed up with ropes around his ankles, knees, and wrists. Liam sat beside him on the ground. "What is this?" Zane growled.

"Merely precautionary," Liam said. Zane was already tired of the way he talked, all dark threat laced with that cheerful British accent. "Hear me out, and then I'll let you go."

Zane didn't trust that for a second, but as long as Liam was talking, Zane had a chance of slipping his ties and escaping.

"You see, I know Tyler Grady. Quite well, to be frank, and he's a danger to you. To everyone, really, but we can't all be perfect."

"Tyler who?" Zane mumbled as he stared up at the ceiling.

"Oh, that's sweet. Still protecting him even after what he's done."

Zane cut his eyes sideways.

"That's right, Zane. I know what happened. I knew before you did. And I know more. Do you care to hear?"

"No." He couldn't stand the thought of hearing more of Ty's sins, not from this source.

Liam leaned closer, casually resting his elbow on Zane's chest so he could look down into his eyes. "It's okay. I understand. Ty broke my heart too. It's a small but spectacular club. Welcome."

Zane licked his lips, trying to regulate his breathing, desperate to slow his heartbeat so the man wouldn't feel it banging against his chest.

"It's not really his fault, it's just how Ty works. He's easy to fall for when he's got that mask up. He makes you love him because he knows that's the easiest way to get what he wants from you. You trust him, you see something worthwhile, something vulnerable in him, and you think you can help. Six months later, he has all your secrets, and he's gone."

Zane was shaking his head as Liam spoke.

Liam reached to pop the button on his shirt. "You're lucky your heart was merely broken."

Zane's eyes darted between Liam's hand and his face, his mind whirring. Liam yanked another button loose, then another. He pulled his collar down to reveal two circular scars on his chest. Bullet wounds. He tapped one with a finger. "Courtesy of the love of your life."

Zane stared at the scar.

"A .45 caliber MEUSOC pistol. Standard for Force Recon, you know. Back in the day."

"You're SAS?"

"I was. I see he's told you the story."

Zane was silent. This really was the man Ty had been talking about. The man he'd been involved with in the service, the man he'd shot. He was handsome and charismatic, exactly the type Ty would be drawn to. Zane could see that much. That, and he carried a gun.

Zane wanted to question him further, but doing so would reveal how much he already knew. He wanted Liam to keep talking.

"No matter. I've always said the past is the past for a reason, yeah? Although it does occasionally come back to bite you in the arse. Do you remember a man named Antonio de la Vega?" Liam asked, his blue eyes narrowing.

Zane's breath caught. "Name's familiar. Zorro, right?"

"Oh come now, Zane, don't be coy with me. We're all friends here. We can share."

"Friends don't tie friends up."

"Oh, you've got the wrong sort of friends then," Liam purred. He laughed, a surprisingly warm, pleasant sound. "I quite like you. You're fun. Listen, Ty's already called me once so he knows I have you. I'm not going to harm you, I promise. And I keep my promises, unlike some of us. But I need to lay some groundwork before I call him back, so do me a favor and indulge me. Antonio de la Vega?"

Zane gritted his teeth, but he supposed he didn't have much to lose. "I heard he was dead."

"That doesn't answer my question. Nor is it news."

Zane groaned. "I remember him. Head of the Vega cartel, out of the Republic of Colombia. Feeds into the larger set of Gulf cartels."

"Excellent. He is indeed very dead. You were one of the FBI agents to infiltrate them. The last one left alive, to be exact. You lot almost took him down, from what I understand. Quite a nice body of work." He paused to glance down the long line of Zane's body.

"Eyes are up here," Zane grunted.

Liam was smirking when he looked back at Zane's face. "There's a bit of a price on your head." He paused, waiting for a response. When Zane merely stared at him, he nodded. "When that plane crashed with Antonio de la Vega in it, his brother took over. You remember his brother?"

Zane did. Antonio de la Vega had been smart and controlled, stingy and almost surgical with his use of violence. He'd lived by a certain code of loyalty and honor. He hadn't been a bad man to work for, and illegalities aside, Zane had quite liked the man. He'd been saddened when he'd heard of his death. But the younger de la Vega was a different animal altogether. He had a temper. Zane nodded curtly.

"Well. He believes the FBI agent who helped destroy part of his operation is the very same agent who killed his brother. He's out for blood."

"I didn't kill Antonio."

"We know."

"We? You went from SAS to being a cartel henchman?"

"No, darling, I went from SAS to NIA."

Zane rested his aching head on the cold floor. It seemed that what Ty had told him was at least partially true. "NIA."

"Your very own National Intelligence Agency."

"I know what it fucking stands for. What are they doing involved with this?"

"They're not."

Zane closed his eyes. "You're freelancing."

"Hmm. Juan Carlos de la Vega was contacted earlier this week and told the FBI agent who killed his brother would be here in New Orleans this weekend."

"By who?"

"Whom." Liam shrugged, pursing his lips. "I was merely contracted to take care of it."

That got Zane's attention, and fast. He raised his head. "I told you, I didn't kill his brother."

"No. But Tyler did." Liam nodded condescendingly. "Don't look surprised. It's what he does, Zane."

"So, what, you're here to kill him for a paycheck?"

Liam quirked an eyebrow. "Does this low opinion of me come from Tyler, or from my actions, I wonder?"

Zane could only assume that was a rhetorical question, since he could feel where the blood had caked on the back of his head.

"I didn't know who my target was until I got here, so you can stow the attitude. I can only stall for so long, however. When the job doesn't get done, more will come. And you know what will happen then."

Zane clenched his jaw and nodded.

"Now, you're a smart boy, so I assume you've already detected the real problem. For you, that is. It's not that someone wants to kill Ty."

"That seems like a real problem to me."

Liam waved that off. "As you like. The real issue, of course, is de la Vega's henchmen don't know what *Ty* looks like. They will, however, spot *your* beautiful face from a mile away. And I'm pretty sure they don't believe in coincidences."

Zane was silent.

"I'm going to untie you now," Liam said. He leaned over Zane, still smirking. "You must promise not to try to maim me, because I will put you down."

Zane snorted. Liam was at least six inches shorter than Zane, with compact, wiry muscles and very little bulk to him. "You'll put me down?" he repeated, incredulous. Liam nodded. "You and what army?"

Liam grinned wider. He pulled a knife from a sheath in his boot and cut through the zip tie that held Zane's feet together. As soon as Zane was free, he kicked up, aiming for Liam's head. Liam blocked the blow with his forearm, then rolled over his own shoulder to crouch several feet away. He was still grinning.

Zane arched his back, pushing himself off the floor so he could pull his tied hands under his body and over his legs, bringing them in front of him as he rolled to his feet. He faced Liam, bent low, ready for an attack.

Liam shook his head. "I'm not here to fight you, love. I do enjoy the feisty ones, so if you're willing, I'm ready to go. That being said, I'd rather not make you bleed anymore today. I'll even hand you the phone so you can call Tyler yourself." He pulled a cell phone from his back pocket and waved it enticingly.

Zane nodded. The man was convincing, but Zane couldn't help but expect a trap. No one so calm and soothing could be up to any good. "Slide it over."

Liam placed it on the floor and pushed it. Zane stopped it with his foot, not taking his eyes off Liam.

Liam held up the knife as well. "A peace offering, yes?" He placed it on the ground and shoved it toward Zane too.

Zane bent slowly, not taking his eyes from his opponent as he grasped the knife. He cut the tie on his wrists and then whirled the handle of the knife around his fingers, gripping it so the blade rested along his wrist, ready to fight.

Liam propped his elbow on his knee, resting his chin in his hand. "Feel better now?"

"A little."

"You're armed. Go ahead and give Tyler a call. I'm sure he's burning down the Quarter looking for you by now."

Zane fumbled with the cell phone, using his free hand without moving his eyes from Liam's. He hit send twice, assuming it would be Ty's number. Nerves skittered through him as the phone rang. Liam remained in a crouch. His composure and reassurance were infuriating.

When Ty's voice mail picked up, Zane frowned harder. "Ty," he gritted out. "You answer your goddamned phone in the middle of sex but you can't pick up now?" He jabbed the phone off, cursing.

Liam's brow creased. "He didn't answer?"

Zane shook his head.

Liam ran one finger along his lower lip, frowning harder. "Odd, that."

Zane took deep, calming breaths and tried to push past his whirlwind of thoughts to find a point of clarity. It all boiled down to whether to trust Liam Bell's word right here and now. And it was hard to a trust a man who'd smashed your skull in and then tied you up.

"Don't get me wrong, Zane, it's been a while since I knew him. But with all his faults, he always made a bloody good cavalry. If he's not answering, he's in trouble."

"You're right," Zane whispered, hating to agree with the man. If Liam had said the sky was blue right now, Zane would have felt compelled to argue that it was in fact merely refracting light.

"I'll help you, if you'll let me."

Zane shifted from foot to foot, as if the battle in his mind was taking place in his body as well. He finally held up the knife. "I want another one of these. Then we'll talk."

Chapter 7

Ty sat on the wrong side of a battered wooden table in a small interrogation room with no air conditioning. He wasn't handcuffed, not yet, and they'd yet to read him his rights. But he had no illusions about being able to get up and walk out. The easiest way out of this would be to identify himself as an FBI agent and be done with it. But there were too many risks, too many loose threads left over from his days undercover, and he'd have to play the part he'd once played down here until he had more information.

He had some time if Liam intended to meet him at 2 AM.

The door creaked as it opened, and the same detective from the hotel sauntered in and tossed a heavy file on the table. An officer pulled the door closed behind him. Ty's eyes strayed to the door as it clicked shut. They had him under guard. His knee began to bounce and he forced himself to stop.

He met the detective's eyes, sprawling in his chair in a casual, insolent pose.

"Surprised to see you crawling to town," the detective said.

Ty clucked his tongue. When he spoke, it was with the same affected drawl he'd perfected while undercover years ago. "Detective Poirot, wasn't it?"

"Poirier. But you can call me Sir. It'll be Boss here soon. Soon as we get you in chains."

Ty narrowed his eyes. "And what is it I've done to deserve being chained up?"

"Did you kill that girl, Tyler Beaumont?"

"I did not."

"Your crew we have in the lobby? Witnesses say they saw a man with them the night of the murder. Description fits you to a T. They say you ducked out, then your buddies closed up shop, wouldn't let anyone leave. Smart. Make the police think the scene's pure while you slip out the hole you crawled in through."

Ty sighed and sat forward. "There's a real killer out there somewhere. And you're wasting your time here with me."

"How do you figure?"

"I'm just in town on a jaunt, Detective. Little harmless fun."

"You suppose Ava Gaudet would think your little jaunt is harmless?"

Ty cocked his head, trying hard not to react. Ava had been his main contact here during his undercover days. Another few months in town and he probably would have married her. "We made our peace. What's she got to do with a murdered girl?"

"That murdered girl calls her to mind. Dark hair. Dark eyes. Tattoos. Even had one of them cute little feathers tucked behind her ear."

"I wouldn't know."

Poirier laughed. He tapped the file on the table between them. "I have you here for half a dozen offenses in the two years you were on our radar. Breaking and entering. Money laundering. Racketeering. Assault and battery. Did you beat your girl too? Her daddy sure thinks you did."

Ty remained motionless. He had to keep his cover if Ava Gaudet's father had Poirier's ear. He was the precinct commander. And he was dirty as hell. Only two people in town had known Ty was FBI at the time Katrina hit, and Ty knew neither of them would have given up that information, and certainly not to Louis Gaudet. It would have cast doubt on them by association.

Poirier wasn't deterred by Ty's silence. He continued flipping through the file. "All that, not to mention over a dozen drunk and disorderlies. You were in the tank more often than not every Thursday night. Like clockwork." They stared at each other, each waiting for the other to flinch. Finally Poirier leaned his elbows on the table. "You ever get a little too drunk, Tyler Beaumont? Get a little too angry? A little too out of control?"

Ty crossed his arms, inclining his head. He'd met his handler in the drunk tank every three or four weeks. But he couldn't tell Poirier that.

"You ever put your hands around a girl's neck and squeezed? Watch the life drain from her?"

Ty didn't rise to the bait, but he was beginning to question the wisdom of not identifying himself. He couldn't, though. If he did and Gaudet got a hold of him, he'd never make it out of the police station alive.

Poirier narrowed his eyes, moving his tongue around inside his mouth like he was chewing on something. He picked up the folder and tapped it on its side, then opened it.

"I'd like to make a phone call."

"Answer my questions first. Why are you here? You left under cover of water six years ago, why come back? Why now?"

Ty's knee began to bounce again as he fought to concentrate on the interrogation and not worry himself into a fit about Zane.

"Was it Arthur Murdoch? He owned the tavern you worked for. You come for his funeral?"

Ty's knee stopped. "Murdoch's dead?"

Poirier nodded solemnly. "Gris-gris bag in his hand. Your name written on that little piece of parchment."

Ty's jaw tightened and he fought a wave of nausea. Murdoch had owned the dive where Ty had worked and lived. He'd been almost like a father to Ty, and he and his beloved mongrel had taken seats on the helicopter Ty had pulled every string to get before Katrina made landfall. He had known Ty was an FBI agent, and he'd sworn to take that secret to the grave. Now someone had killed him, pointing his fingers at Ty in the end.

"Either read me my rights, or I'm walking."

"I'll do that, right after you give me one last answer." Poirier pulled an evidence bag out of his pocket and plopped it on the table. Inside was the gris-gris bag Ty had kept in his pocket. They'd taken it along with all his other belongings when they'd brought him in. "It matches the one the girl was holding. And the one Murdoch was found with."

Ty could feel the blood draining from his face as he stared at the bag.

Poirier leaned forward, lowering his voice. "Tell me, Tyler Beaumont. Who was your next victim going to be?"

It was under an uneasy peace that Zane and Liam rode the elevator of the Bourbon Orleans to the fifth floor. Zane stood far enough away to be able to maneuver, keeping an eye on Liam even though the man had proved true to his word thus far.

Liam shook his head, smiling as he stared at the doors. "Are you always this paranoid?"

"When I'm still bleeding from our introduction, yeah."

"Fair enough." Liam glanced at him and winked.

Zane rolled his eyes. The man was insufferable. No wonder he and Ty had been an item. He forced Liam to move ahead of him as they made their way down the hall, and he hung back out of reach. He'd seen the fear in Ty's eyes when he'd said Liam was here for trouble. And men like Ty didn't scare easily.

Liam held up the room key Zane had given him and slid it in, stepping back as the little light flicked green. Zane pushed the door open and called out, "Coming in with company!"

No one responded, and Zane nodded for Liam to go in. Liam put both hands behind his head and strolled into the room, Zane moving behind with one of the borrowed knives in his hand.

As soon as Liam cleared the entryway, a gun appeared from behind the corner, pressing to Liam's temple. "Oh dear," Liam drawled.

Owen Johns stepped away from his hiding spot and out of Liam's reach with practiced speed, keeping the gun trained on him.

Zane groaned. The one man here who wouldn't listen to a word either of them said.

"It's okay," he tried anyway. He held up his knife. "I'm fifty percent sure he's on our side."

Owen's lip curled and he grunted. "Last time I saw him, he was dead, so forgive me for being a little wary." He narrowed his eyes at Liam. "Get on your knees."

"This isn't that sort of game." Liam sighed. "Go fetch me your master and we'll discuss it together."

Owen bristled at the condescension, but he began to relax his stance. "The others have been arrested."

"What?" Zane blurted.

"I watched from across the street. Took all of them."

"Would it be possible to dispense with some weaponry here?" Liam drawled. "My fingers are going numb."

"Not a unicorn's chance in Hell," Owen grunted.

"Now, what would a unicorn be doing in Hell?" Liam asked.

"You can ask him when you get there."

Zane slid his knife back into the sheath Liam had given him for it. "What else do we know? Why were they all taken?"

"I can only assume someone figured out who Ty was," Owen answered grudgingly. "Someone fingered him for the murder."

"What murder?" Liam asked. For the first time, he sounded genuinely confused.

"The one you committed," Owen snarled. "Killed a girl, left a hoodoo curse bag behind. The same one you stuffed in Ty's bed."

"I've not stuffed anything in Ty's bed in some years. And I didn't kill anyone last night, certainly not some girl with a voodoo curse. Are you all still this insane? I thought that faded with time."

Zane pointedly cleared his throat. "You think someone saw him and recognized him from when he was undercover?"

Owen nodded.

"Or someone's setting him up," Liam offered, turning to meet Zane's eyes for emphasis. "Someone who knew he'd be here."

Zane gritted his teeth. If that were the case, the cartel merely had to get to Ty in jail and he was done. They had him cornered already and Ty didn't even know they were after him. "What do you know?"

Liam shrugged. "He went by the name Tyler Beaumont while here. Not exactly original, but one shouldn't stray too far, am I right?" Liam winked at Owen.

"Oh God, I forgot how annoying you are," Owen grumbled. He still had his gun up. Where had the man gotten it? Zane remembered someone saying Owen was a head of security at some big corporation, so he might carry all the time. But knowing what he did now, Zane could only assume Sidewinder carried all the time no matter what, in case they were called to action. The thought made Zane both sad and exceptionally angry.

Liam shrugged and finally lowered his hands. He edged toward the interior of the room and sat in one of the chairs, smirking at Owen as the man followed him with his gun.

"Garrett, what the fuck is going on?" Owen growled.

"Let's just say, Mr. Bell was persuasive in getting an audience with me. There's some stuff in play that's going to get ugly."

"What kind of stuff?"

"Bloody stuff," Liam answered.

"We need to get to Ty and the others," Zane said. "I'll go down there, identify myself. We'll clear this up and get to work."

Liam tutted and shook his head.

"What?" Zane demanded, already exasperated by the man.

"Identifying yourself will leave you wide open. The New Orleans Police Department is a sieve, it always has been. If the cartel lads don't already know Ty's there, when word gets out that a Fed was in there throwing weight around? You'll be dead before Ty's out of his cell and Ty will soon follow."

"Why? What cartel guys? What the fuck are you talking about?" Owen asked. He was growing more agitated, and he was still holding the gun.

Zane took him by the shoulders so the gun was no longer trained on Liam, and he forced Owen to meet his eyes. "Listen carefully, because I'm only going to say this once. Liam is with the NIA, but he's undercover taking jobs as a paid assassin. He was hired by a cartel in Miami to come here and kill me and/or Ty, but he's trying to help us."

"Why?" Owen asked.

"I . . . I don't really know."

Owen glared at Liam. "So you're really NIA like Ty said." He slid his gun into the holster under his arm, but advanced on the man, pointing his finger. "You're the one got us tossed?"

"That was not my intention," Liam said, cool as ever as Owen seethed over him. "What the Marines did to you lot after was unconscionable and had nothing to do with me. I am sorry it happened, but I am no longer officially affiliated with the NIA."

"You told me you *were* NIA," Zane said in exasperation.

"I lied. I tend to do that. Sorry."

Owen shook his head.

Zane waved a hand. "If you're not really NIA, that just makes you a paid assassin!"

Liam shrugged.

Zane had to take a moment to calm his thoughts before he spoke again. "Ty thinks you're here for revenge."

Liam laughed. It was a deep, rich sound. "I suppose he would. Guilt does odd things to an already unstable mind. Now! Shall we discuss how we're going to break him out of jail?"

"First we grab all our stuff," Zane said, fighting back his misgivings. "We probably won't be able to come back for it after this."

Liam chuckled. "This should be fun!"

"Shut up," Owen grumbled before turning away.

"I am a Boston Police Detective," Nick hissed to the officer manning the front desk. He was sitting between Kelly and Digger, all of them handcuffed to a bench as they waited to be processed. It was humiliating, to say the least. "My name is Nicholas O'Flaherty, my badge is in my luggage. All you have to do is give my captain a call and we'll clear this up!"

The woman at the desk continued to ignore him.

"Wasting your breath, man," Digger grumbled.

Nick thumped his head against the wall. People came and went through the ornate lobby of the old building even though it was now after midnight. Tourists walked in off the street to buy T-shirts out of a vending machine. Some of them stopped to gawk at the three of them sitting there. Digger had taken to waving at them to show his handcuffs.

Kelly leaned against Nick, his head on Nick's shoulder as he drowsed. "This is not the way I saw this weekend going."

"Really?" Digger asked. "Because I figured it was sixty/forty we'd end up just like this. Again."

Nick rolled his eyes.

The most frustrating part of it was knowing all three of them could have picked the locks on the handcuffs in the blink of an eye. But what were they supposed to do? Storm the police station and bust Ty out of some cell or interrogation room? Go on the lam in NOLA? And for what?

"Which one was the sixty?" Kelly asked after a few minutes.

Digger pointed to the floor.

Kelly nodded. "Yeah."

The door opened again and a rush of air blew through the lobby. Nick jerked to attention. He recognized the line of Owen Johns's shoulders as the man slunk into the station and loitered near the T-shirt machine. Trailing in behind him was another man, and Nick belatedly realized it was Zane.

"It's the cavalry," Digger said.

"Thank Christ," Kelly grumbled. He raised his hands, rubbing at one wrist and dropping his handcuffs to the floor.

"What the hell, man?" Nick whispered.

"What? They were too tight."

Digger dropped his cuffs to the floor with a clank that echoed through the station. "If he's not wearing his, neither am I."

When Nick looked back, Zane was at the desk speaking to the officer. Nick's fingers began to work at the lock of his handcuffs. Owen was sauntering toward them, a smirk on his face. "We're busting you out."

Nick stood and yanked his handcuffs off his wrists, then tossed them at Owen with a curse. "You should be sitting here with us."

Owen caught the cuffs, but he was laughing. "And if I was? Who'd be saving your ass then?"

"What about Ty?"

"We've got it covered."

"We can't just leave him in here," Kelly said.

Nick scowled. Cold settled in the pit of his stomach. "Garrett's not flashing a badge over there. This isn't official, is it?"

"Nope."

"How are you getting us out?"

Owen glanced casually over his shoulder and reached under his jacket. "Plan B."

"Plan B? What's Plan B?"

Owen clucked his tongue, held up a small canister, and grinned.

"That's mine!" Digger hissed. "You went through my stuff?"

"You travel with smoke grenades?" Nick blurted.

"Boys," Owen said. He flicked the starter ring of the grenade and tossed it over his shoulder. Violet smoke began to billow from it as it spiraled through the air. "Run like hell."

Ty had been read his rights, handcuffed to the table, and then left alone once he'd refused to say more. He tended to carry a key in the lining of all his shoes, so dealing with the lock on his handcuffs was simply a matter of getting his foot high enough to dig the key out. When he got them off, he wrapped them around his fingers to use like brass knuckles. He was taking down whoever stepped through that door next. He refused to sit here while Zane was in danger, and if that meant breaking out of jail and becoming a fugitive for the duration, then so be it.

He also knew he was in quite a bit of trouble here himself. Part of his work while in New Orleans had been tracking the activities of one seriously scary bad cop. That cop was now the commander for the Royal Street station. And he'd be coming for Ty.

He stood beside the door, waiting to pounce on the next man who came through it.

He didn't understand what the gris-gris had to do with Liam Bell. Was Liam really just here for revenge? It didn't make sense, and he was beginning to suspect his own guilt and feelings over how that had ended were clouding his assessment. Why here? Why now? If the plan was to set Ty up for the murders of that girl and Arthur Murdoch, then it was a piss-poor plan. And if the intention hadn't been to peg Ty as the murderer, that meant the gris-gris bag in his hotel room was a promise. He was the next victim.

And what in the hell did Liam grabbing Zane have to do with any of it?

The doorknob rattled beside him, and then the door cracked open. Ty tensed, preparing to launch himself. Then the heavy metal door was shoved open as if someone had thrown all their weight into it. It slammed into Ty, knocking him against the cinderblock wall. He staggered as the door swung away, regaining his bearings only to find a gun trained on him.

"So predictable," Liam said with a shake of his head. "Hello, love."

He was standing far enough away that Ty wouldn't be able to reach him without lunging past the barrel of that gun. Ty leaned against the wall, breathing hard. "Where is Zane?"

"He's fine. Out in the lobby acting as a distraction. It's sweet he's the first thing you think of, though."

Ty lunged at him, and Liam brought up the gun, shaking his head.

"If you've hurt him, I swear to God I'll make you bleed."

"I have no intention of hurting anyone, Tyler, I merely needed your full attention."

"2 AM or your partner dies? *That's* how you get my attention?"

"It worked, didn't it? But things have changed. We're in a bit of a hurry here, so..."

"What are you doing here?"

Liam tossed him his jacket and his gun. "I'm the rescue party."

Chapter 8

It was the middle of the night, but the French Quarter didn't seem to realize it. Zane and the others had escaped the police station in a whirl of purple smoke and chaos, and each man had darted off in a different direction. The crowded streets helped to hide them. They were supposed to scramble for fifteen minutes, then make their way to a rendezvous point once they were sure they were clear.

Any man who couldn't shake the police was going to have to take one for the team.

Zane had easily evaded any pursuit, using the crowds as cover. After darting down a few side roads, he wandered along Bourbon Street for ten minutes, the dancing crowd full of Easter revelers guiding him like a ship on a river.

He tried not to contemplate his predicament, but it was hard to keep it out of mind. They were now wanted by the police. He and Nick had both given their identification to the detective when they'd given their accounts of the murder scene, so eventually they'd be connected to the breakout. His real name would come out of this and the Bureau would get involved. They would have a lot of explaining to do, but he felt certain he and Ty could talk their way out of it.

And then there was Ty. It seemed like Zane kept forgetting what Ty had admitted to, like his mind was actively trying to block it out. Ty had essentially spent the last two years spying on him. How was Zane supposed to know what was real and what had been another of Ty's clever tricks to glean information from him?

How much of Ty had he really seen? How well did he know Ty at all?

When he reached Jackson Square, Kelly was the only one there. He was loitering near the iron fence that surrounded the raised, grassy park area. During the day, people used the fence to hang artwork and sell their wares, but at night it was all cleared away. People sat on the concrete ledge or leaned against the fence, smoking, drinking, laughing. Several of them played music with tip jars in front of them.

Kelly was lingering near a man with a guitar. When he spotted Zane, he pushed away from the wall and grinned lopsidedly. "Not exactly a discreet meeting place."

Zane shrugged. "It was the only place we all knew how to get to. And it's crowded."

"Fair enough. What the hell is going on?"

Zane winced and glanced around the throng. He didn't want to go through this more than once, and he knew the others would have the same question. "It's complicated."

"I'm fairly intelligent," Kelly said with a laugh. "I can usually follow."

Zane snorted.

"Garrett, the others will be here soon, and then we're dealing with the whole group dynamic and accusations and serious ADD, so . . . you want to let me know what's going on now so I can help you?"

Zane stared at the man for a long moment, then nodded. "You were the group's corpsman, right? So you can deal with . . . any injuries that come from this?"

"Yeah," Kelly said warily. "Why?"

"I ran into Liam Bell," Zane said, and hurried to explain faster as Kelly's eyes widened. "He claims he was hired by a Miami cartel to come here and kill Ty."

"What? Why?"

"It's a really long story."

"How'd you get away from him?"

"I didn't."

Kelly narrowed his eyes, looking off into the distance over Zane's shoulder. "I don't understand," he finally said.

Zane couldn't help but laugh. A hand touched his back and he jerked, reaching for the knife in his pocket.

"Easy, tiger," Nick said as he stepped around Zane and patted him on the back. "Someone want to tell me why I just made myself a fugitive?"

"It's complicated," Kelly answered.

"I'm not doing this again," Zane grumbled.

Nick stood on his tip toes and looked around the crowd. Several uniformed policemen were walking along the edges of the crowd. Others rode horses. The way they were scanning faces made it obvious they were looking for someone. "We should start moving," Nick whispered. "We're too conspicuous standing like this."

Kelly grabbed Nick's arm and stopped him.

Nick and Zane both turned to see what had caught Kelly's attention. Zane spotted Ty immediately. He was still moving slowly, obviously still in some pain and fighting off the remainder of the sedative the hospital had given him. He was keeping his head down and his face in shadow, but Zane knew the roll of his shoulders. Trailing behind Ty, looking far less conspicuous, was Liam Bell. Ty's eyes locked on Zane's, and relief flooded through his entire body. Ty took a hasty step forward, but a hand appeared on his shoulder, jerking him back. He went rigid again, putting his hands to his sides.

Zane would recognize that posture anywhere. Ty had a gun at his back.

Ty's eyes stayed on Zane's, and Liam used Ty's body to cover himself. "Let's all be calm now," Liam said when they got close. "Who's armed?"

Zane pulled his jacket away to reveal the knife there. Nick and Kelly both shook their heads.

Liam eased his grip on Ty's shoulder, then gave him a pat on the back. He slid the gun under his coat and grinned. "Just making sure."

"What the fuck is going on?" Nick demanded. "Why is he here and am I allowed to hurt him?"

"Not yet," Ty answered.

"Where are the others?" Liam asked.

Zane glanced at his watch. "They haven't shown yet. They've got two more minutes."

They remained in an uneasy standoff as the bells of the cathedral rang out the hour. Liam still lingered behind Ty's shoulder for cover. No one spoke. No one moved, save for Zane periodically checking the time.

Digger eventually materialized from the crowd, Owen on his heels. They'd apparently met up somewhere and made their way here together. They approached warily, sensing the tension in the group. Neither man said a word when they joined them.

"Okay then," Zane finally said, relieved everyone had made it out. "We have all our stuff stashed, we'll go get it. But where to after that?"

"We can't break town," Nick grunted. He had yet to take his eyes off Liam. "We need somewhere to lay low, regroup."

"And then you can tell us what the fuck is going on," Kelly added. Zane nodded.

"Where do we go?" Liam asked. "My safe house is blown."

"How?" Zane demanded.

"Too much activity, I don't trust it."

Ty glanced over his shoulder at the man, then back at Zane. His mouth was set in a grim line. "I might know the perfect place."

"Ava?" Zane asked. Ty nodded.

Nick snorted. "The girl who tried to kill you with a cleaver?"

"It's worth a shot. I think she might be in danger too; I need to warn her."

"We'll split up, then," Liam said. He gave Ty another pat. "You test the waters with cleaver girl, and we'll get our supplies."

Ty glared over his shoulder, but he nodded. "You four, go with him. Keep him in line. Zane and I will scout it out and call you in thirty."

The others nodded, albeit grudgingly as Liam led them away. Zane and Ty were left alone. Meeting Ty's eyes made Zane's stomach flutter, but the anger lingered. He clenched his teeth, trying to keep it in.

"You okay?" Ty asked.

"He didn't hurt me."

"Not yet, maybe. He's slick, Zane. Don't ever let your guard down around him."

"Really?" Zane snarled. He took a step closer, straightening to his full height so he could look down at Ty. "Because that's what people have been saying about you for two years now."

Ty flinched, but he didn't look away. He pushed his shoulders back, narrowing his eyes. It was like watching a dog bristle as it stared down a threat. Zane hadn't felt that since their first few weeks together.

He refused to back off, though. He put his finger on Ty's chest. "Don't think I've forgotten just because your ass needed saving."

It was too dark to read Ty's expression, but he finally broke eye contact to glance down at Zane's finger.

"Where is this place?" Zane asked when it became apparent that Ty wasn't going to respond.

Ty spoke through gritted teeth. "Just off Frenchmen Street. Down Decatur and across Esplanade."

"Lead the way."

Ty stared at Zane for another few breaths. Then he stepped past him, brushing his shoulder against Zane's as he set off through the carousing crowd.

Ty didn't say a word as they prowled toward the far edge of the French Quarter, heading to the little two-block area of Frenchmen Street and the adjoining Faubourg Marigny. Zane knew how Ty felt about going to see Ava again, and Zane wasn't too happy about it either. There was a good chance she'd be holding a grudge, and with good reason. Zane knew what kind of lies had to be told when you were undercover, and now, thanks to Ty, he realized how badly it hurt to be on the receiving end of them.

But their options were few and far between, and Ty seemed to think she was in danger.

At least he'd be along to make sure she didn't throw another knife at Ty. If she did, she'd have a couple to dodge herself.

So, forearmed and forewarned, Zane followed Ty out of the lively French Quarter into the more sedate residential area of Marigny.

Ty turned onto a cobblestone alley of stone walls covered with ivy and blooming flowers. It really was gorgeous down here, with the gaslights and wrought-iron gates and ambiance galore. Even the shards of glass in the concrete on top of walls and fences, meant to keep revelers out of private yards, had its own charm. New Orleans had character. Zane hadn't really appreciated it when he'd been here with Becky. He'd been more concerned with watching her, observing the joy of the experience through the way she lit up.

He often found himself doing the same thing with Ty. He enjoyed the way Ty lived through every pitch at a baseball game more than he enjoyed the game itself.

How much of his own life had he forgotten to live as he watched the people he loved?

The crowd thinned until they were the only ones on the street, offering them less cover. Ty took Zane's arm so they'd look more like a couple returning home than two fugitives skirting the shadows. He felt stiff as he did it, as if he expected Zane to rebuff him. Zane's breath was hard to catch. He had never imagined being alone with Ty feeling so awkward.

"Places this side close down at two," Ty said. He abruptly turned into a narrower, shadier alley.

Zane slowed, scowling at his surroundings. His arm slipped out of Ty's as Ty kept walking. "Hey."

Ty stopped and turned, and Zane had a flash of memory, a picture of Becky, her hair bouncing as she turned, her eyes shining.

Zane stared at Ty's hazel eyes, shocked into silence.

"You okay?" Ty asked.

Zane shook his head. "I think I've been here before."

Ty raised an eyebrow and looked down the alleyway. "Lots of these back alleys look alike. This is a local place, pretty far off the tourist path."

Zane glanced at the cobblestone and the plain stone walls. He nodded. "Yeah."

Ty continued down the alley, and after a few dozen yards he stopped at a weathered wooden door set into the crumbling stone wall. The carved sign that hung over the door read La Fée Verte.

Zane stared at it. He was almost certain that had been the name of the dive Becky had dragged him to all those years ago.

Ty pressed his shoulder against the door, and it creaked open accusingly.

Within was the same large room Zane remembered from his dreams. It was still ill-lit and crowded with tables, and the single microphone stand still stood on the stage in front of wine-colored curtains.

Candles flickered in hurricane lamps on the tables, only now it seemed they were battery powered. Years of wax drippings still decorated the tables.

Zane glanced around, stunned. He turned where he stood, staring at the stage, his mind recreating that night, the man he'd watched and found himself attracted to, the first man he'd ever realized he might want, the man he'd almost unconsciously based most of his sexual encounters on since. He could still see the man standing on that stage, wide shoulders, playful smirk, shining eyes, and a beautiful voice.

"Ty." Zane gaped at him.

"You sure you're okay?"

"It was you," Zane whispered.

Ty looked around the bar, brow furrowing.

"Ty, it was you. The man I saw singing, the one I told you about... it was you, wasn't it?"

Ty's eyes strayed to the stage, then back to Zane. He didn't look all that shocked. There was a bang from the back and a curtain behind the bar wavered.

A dark-haired woman poked her head out to call, "We're all closed up now. Try Bourbon Street." She disappeared behind the curtain again.

Ty and Zane both stared at the curtain before sharing a glance. "It was you," Zane whispered again, still rocked to his very foundations by the revelation.

"It couldn't be. You said it was your anniversary. I wasn't here yet in July."

"It was *for* our anniversary. We came in December because it was easier."

Ty stood motionless, eyes on Zane for a long moment before he glanced back at the curtain. It wasn't but a few seconds before the curtain swayed again, and the woman shoved it aside as she stepped out. She was on the shorter side, with long hair so black it was almost blue in the smoky haze. A fluffy white feather was tucked behind her ear, and on closer inspection, several more feathers of various colors appeared to be part of her hair too.

Her dark eyes were lined in kohl, masking their real color, and it was hard to tell in the dim light but she seemed exotic in a way, like there may have been Native American blood in her. She was athletic and curvy, certainly Ty's type, wearing black pants that hugged her hips and a laced corset for a top. Her body was tense as she stared at them.

Zane glanced from Ty to her and back. She was surprised, that was clear, which told Zane she wasn't behind the hex Ty was sure had been put on him.

"Tyler Beaumont," she said.

"Hello, Ava," Ty responded. Zane knew he was nowhere near as calm as he sounded.

She moved suddenly, vaulting over the bar and running toward him. Zane almost moved to block her, but Ty didn't flinch as she launched herself at him and wrapped her arms around his neck. He grunted in pain, stumbling beneath her weight as she hugged him.

She let him go and slid her feet to the floor, then smacked Ty with an oath that sounded like mangled French. When she pulled back for another smack, Zane reached out and caught her wrist midair. Ty's guilty conscience may have been willing to stand there and take it, but there was a limit to how much Zane would allow, even if he did want to do the same right now.

She yanked her hand out of Zane's grasp and drew a deep breath. "What are you doing here?" she hissed.

"I heard about Murdoch," Ty told her, remarkably calm in the face of her temper.

She glared at Zane, her eyes raking him up and down.

"This is my partner, Zane Garrett."

"You're a Fed too?" she spat at Zane.

It was sort of a bullshit question, but she was obviously rattled by Ty showing up out of thin air. Zane tipped his head and raised one eyebrow in silent confirmation, if not a subtle dare to comment about it, before looking her over in return, checking for obvious weapons.

"Zane, this is Ava Gaudet. Ava, we need your help."

"Right," she said with obvious disdain. She turned her dark eyes back to Ty. "You need my help. Like you needed my help before?"

Ty narrowed his eyes before letting them stray to meet Zane's. He shook his head. "This was a waste of time," he said to Zane. He jerked his head toward the door. "Let's go."

Zane was perfectly willing to let any of Ty's old flames carry on without them, so he nodded and took a slow step back. He didn't see any knives on Ava, but that didn't mean there wasn't one. Or more.

Ty turned to go, showing no compunctions about exposing his back to the woman.

She sighed loudly and held up her hand. "Wait. What do you want from me?"

Ty studied her briefly before digging into his pocket and pulling out the small red bag he'd been carrying. Zane didn't know how he'd retrieved it from the police station, but he'd obviously thought it a priority as he and Liam had escaped. He held it up and let it drop, holding it between two fingers by its cord.

Ava gasped and took an involuntary step back, running into Zane. He steadied her with a hand on each arm. "Well, I guess that answers that."

"Is that like the one the cops said they found on Murdoch? Where did you get that?" Ava asked Ty, sounding as if she'd forgotten how angry she was.

"It was under my mattress," Ty answered through gritted teeth.

She glanced between them. "Well, I didn't do it! I didn't even know you were in town."

"We need a place to lay low. There are seven of us. People are after us, and so are the police."

"*Feet pue tan*!" she shouted.

Ty cleared his throat, looking at Zane wryly. "She just called me a goddamned son of a bitch."

"I like her," Zane responded.

"You need my help? You don't need my help, you need an army!" She shooed Ty toward the door. "I want no part in whatever you're doing."

"A girl was murdered last night," Ty hissed.

"That is not my problem!" Ava shoved him toward the door, both hands on his chest. He didn't budge, and she couldn't make him.

"She looked like you," Ty said loudly. He held up the bag. "She had one of these."

Ava was breathing hard, but she stepped back and stared at the bag, then glanced over her shoulder at Zane. She looked genuinely frightened. "You think they meant to kill me?"

"Yes. The police think I killed her and Murdoch. My name was in these bags."

"You're being set up."

Ty nodded. "And you know the only person who could possibly have known I was in town."

Ava licked her lips. "Daddy."

Ty quirked an eyebrow.

"Whoa, wait, *Daddy*?" Zane blurted.

Ty and Ava both nodded. Ava put a hand over her mouth.

"Now," Ty said almost gently. "We need a place to stay for the night. They'll never look here. Are the rooms upstairs empty?"

"Yeah," Ava whispered. She put a hand on her hip and lowered her head like she was trying to catch her breath.

Ty met Zane's eyes. "Call them. Let them know how to get here."

Zane took out his phone, glancing between them as he dialed. He couldn't wait to hear the rest of *this* story.

"Can you tell me about this bag?" Ty asked Ava.

Ava glowered at Ty mutinously for a few moments, then dropped her hands and gave a curt nod. "Dump it on the table. I'll get some drinks."

She turned on her heel and stalked back to the curtained doorway behind the bar as Zane spoke with Owen. They were the only two who had retained their phones. Once he hung up, he stared at Ty until the man met his eyes.

"Her father was my case when I was here," Ty told him. "He's the 8th District Police Commander. He's dirty as all hell."

Zane felt his blood run cold. "When you said you left a pissed off Cajun daddy down here . . ."

"I meant it. I never knew if he figured out I was his problem or not. Now I know. He probably caught wind of me when we hit the airport. We've been dead men walking ever since we got here."

"Wow. And I thought I had a scary father-in-law."

Ty rolled his eyes. He looked around the dim tavern. "Are you sure you and Becky were here?"

"Ty, I may not remember what your face looked like, but I remember this place like it was yesterday. It was you. How long were you down here?"

"Couple years."

Zane nodded. That wasn't unusual. It had taken him several months to establish himself in Miami. And they'd both been yanked out of their assignments: Ty because of Hurricane Katrina, Zane because he'd been arrested and had to be pulled for his own safety. When he'd been put back in, he'd discovered most of the Miami cartel still thought he had done his time in prison somewhere and his cover remained intact. Ty's cover had weathered the storm too, and now he was back in the thick of it.

Ty was chewing on the inside of his lip, his eyes focused on the wall near the door, where an array of framed photographs lined the brick.

A crash and muttered curse came from the kitchen, then Ava stomped through the heavy curtain with a couple of bottles in her hand and a cloth thrown over her shoulder. Ty took a few steps and tossed the bag onto the table. She glared evilly and sat down in front of it, thumped the bottles down, and used the edge of the table to open one with the heel of her hand.

Zane snorted. He liked this one.

"So, Ty's partner, tell me why you're here." She reached for the bag and began pulling at the strings.

Zane considered truth or evasion for a few seconds before shrugging. "We're celebrating a birthday."

She laid the cloth out on the table and dumped the contents of the bag onto it. She nodded but didn't respond, fiddling with the pieces of the gris-gris bag for a few moments. "How did you find the bag?"

"I told you, it—"

"I was talking to your partner," Ava snapped.

Ty growled softly but let Zane answer, mumbling under his breath as he paced away.

Zane glanced between them. He could see the possibility of chemistry there. A lot of flash and bang . . . much like himself and Ty. Had Ty ever been in a relationship that hadn't either begun or ended with open animosity?

"We found it in a standard search," Zane said, wondering how familiar she was with law enforcement procedures.

"Bullshit." She put her nose closer to the mossy substance on the cloth. "Probably found it having sex."

Zane snorted. He wasn't getting any threatening vibe off her, and he kind of liked how direct she was.

She cocked her head at Zane as if sizing him up. Then she turned the other way, to Ty. He was watching her from several feet away, hands in his pockets.

"What was it?" she asked him. "Migraine? Stomach bug?"

"Kidney stone."

She snorted and nodded. Zane narrowed his eyes, not happy that she'd known something had been wrong with Ty. He pressed his lips together tightly. He didn't like putting any stock in this voodoo stuff, but he seemed to be the only one. And he had to admit, it was pretty coincidental that Ty had been struck down with a kidney stone on the same night he'd slept over a hoodoo bad luck magnet.

"I don't recognize the work," she said stiffly after examining the bag and its contents.

"You're lying," Ty hissed.

She smacked her hand against the table.

"Is it your father's?"

She didn't answer, still staring at the tabletop.

Ty got in her face and lowered his voice. "Is it Shine's?"

She jerked her head away and closed her eyes.

"Who is Shine?" Zane ventured to ask.

Ty straightened, looking grim. "Ava's brother."

She frowned. "It's more refined than his work usually is. And its purpose is . . ." She shook her head. "This level of skill is beyond me, and I would say it's beyond Shine, but I haven't spoken to him in a year. I don't know where he's been or what he's been into."

Ty grunted, stepped forward, and placed the second alligator tooth on the corner of the cloth, along with the roll of parchment with his alias on it. "I kept that out."

"Oh," she said quietly. She picked up the paper and studied the calligraphy. "That does make things clearer. It seems it was meant to do you great harm. How many people here want to kill you? Because with this in your pocket, they will *all* find you."

"You tell me," Ty said gruffly. He was standing at her shoulder, large and grim next to her.

She met his eyes and straightened her shoulders. "I didn't tell anyone who you really were. Not even my dad."

Ty didn't look surprised. More relieved.

But Zane wasn't all that taken aback. "If she'd told anyone, it would have cast doubt on her as well, just by association. Especially since you were . . . close."

Ty nodded and moved to sit in one of the chairs beside her. Ava was doggedly staring at the red felt bag. "So . . . my cover?"

"Is still intact," she told him grudgingly. "Although I told everyone you left me for the Russian whore, so you're still an ass."

Ty grunted at Zane. "She means she told everyone I ran from the hurricane."

Zane snorted and didn't try to hide his smile as he walked toward the wall to peer at the pictures. He supposed he ought to feel more awkward being here with Ty, who he wanted to throttle, and his former almost-fiancée, who had tried to kill him. Especially since he was now positive he had actually met them both years ago and been asked to join them after a show.

Zane grew warmer with the knowledge. The man he'd seen in New Orleans had been the little spark of interest he'd needed for his first encounter with a man. It had been Ty all along. Zane sniffed and shoved his hands in his pockets. He wasn't even sure what to do with that realization, especially since every time he thought of Ty, the anger and betrayal threatened to overwhelm him.

Ty and Ava were talking about the ingredients of the gris-gris as Zane studied the pictures. The one Ty had been staring at earlier was large, with a simple wooden frame, and beneath it the date and event were written on a piece of tape. Easter, 2004. Seven years ago. The picture was of a man sitting in a chair, tipping it back, feet on the table as he grinned. A crowd of people in festive masks danced in the small confines of the bar in the background of the photo, their motions blurred and surreal. The man sitting was the only thing in focus. He wore a bowler hat and a vest. He held a thin cigar near his face, the frozen smoke curling up over his hand.

It was the man Zane remembered, there in black and white. And after a long moment of staring, Zane knew that he was looking at a picture of a younger, wirier Ty. His hair was different, longer. He had a Van Dyke beard. His face seemed gaunt in a way. He truly was a chameleon. But it was still Ty.

"I don't know, Ty, there have to be half a dozen people who'd want to make you miserable," Ava sneered as Zane turned back to them.

Ty flopped a hand. "Can you reverse it?"

"No. Only one who can reverse it is the one who put it on you. Or you."

"Well, how do *I* reverse it, then?"

"I don't know."

Ty sat back and ran both hands over his face.

"I'll see if I can't find out, though, okay? This curse on you will spread to those around you. Anyone who comes in contact with you now is in danger, including me."

"What, like it's contagious?" Zane couldn't keep the amusement or the cynicism out of his voice. But Ty and Ava both looked grim.

"This is like a black spot on his soul," Ava whispered. "It will spread to everyone he cares for, everyone his soul has touched."

Ty slumped and banged his forehead on the table.

The three rooms above La Fée Verte had once been rented out to travelers, back in the early days of the city, and though most of the old buildings in the neighborhood had been converted into condos and apartments, the layout of La Fée Verte's rooms was very much unchanged from one hundred years ago. They all had small kitchenettes and just enough space for a double bed, a wardrobe, and a chair. They shared a washroom at the end of the hall, and adjoined a smaller room that served as an office for the bar below.

Ty knew all of the rooms well. He had lived in one of them for almost two years. They generated extra income for the bar, but Murdoch had rented mostly to employees at a ridiculously low rate. It kept someone on the premises at all times, and it kept them loyal to him. For Ty's purposes, living there had thrown him right into the middle of the world he'd needed at the time.

Ava led them up the narrow stairs. Ty let his hand caress the brocade wallpaper as he went, the texture and scent bringing back memories that were, for the most part, good ones.

His life here had been different from any other he had lived or pretended to live. But there'd been a heady seductiveness about it, something dark and rich and tempting. Ty had almost succumbed to its charms.

Ava used a key on a long purple ribbon to unlock one of the doors, and she stepped aside to let them into the room. Ty took the key from her. She met his eyes defiantly, but there was pain there too. He knew he'd hurt her. All in the name of doing his job. Just like he'd hurt Zane. He tore his eyes away from her and looked into the room.

He was stunned to find that little was different since he'd last been there.

"Murdoch didn't see any point in changing what you did to it," Ava told him.

Ty shook his head and stepped into the room. An odd sense of homesickness flooded him. He stopped in the middle of the threadbare Oriental rug as he distantly registered Ava's footsteps moving away.

Not one thing seemed different from the night he'd left.

The simple iron bed was burnished silver, the patina of age giving it a character the delicate scrollwork could not manage. The ivory quilt was plain, and the design of the cotton sheets was faded and well-worn, giving the entire bed a vintage Dust Bowl look.

The walls were covered with yellowing pages out of old books, glued haphazardly, one on top of another, onto wooden paneling that could no longer be seen. Ty had spent days doing it, trying to insulate the thin walls so no one could hear what he was up to when he was alone, but people who'd seen his work afterward had attributed it to an artistic, quirky personality instead of simple paranoia.

Along one wall sat an old stove and an antique Crosley refrigerator that occasionally needed rewiring. Beside that was a tiny table with two celery green padded chairs, and a sink below open shelves that held dishes.

In the corner of the room opposite the bed was a large wardrobe. Ty stepped toward it and opened the door on the right, almost expecting to see his clothes still hung neatly inside. It was empty, however, not even a hanger left.

He turned to face Zane, who had stopped on the threshold. "This is almost exactly how I left it."

Zane's focus was on him, though, not the room. His words were quiet, almost bitter. "I can't believe it was you."

Ty swallowed hard. He didn't know if this was promising or damning.

"You knew, didn't you?" Zane asked. "Why didn't you say something?"

Ty had to avert his eyes. "I wasn't sure. I didn't . . . I was hoping it wasn't."

"Why?"

"You and your perfect wife versus me in eyeliner and my girlfriend with feathers in her hair, asking you to play with us? Come on, man."

"That's what makes you *you*. Jackass."

"Exactly."

Zane remained silent, but the irritation and disgust in his expression hit harder than any words. It seemed all Zane could see were lies. The tension was growing heavier, pressing at Ty, making him want to fidget. "You think it was fate?"

"I don't believe in fate."

Ty nodded, pushing back the tumbling of his nerves. "It believes in you."

"I think people make their own fate."

Ty could think of nothing to say to the anger in Zane's eyes.

Zane glared at him for a moment. "This is cozy," he said, sliding his hand along the doorjamb. "Nicer than my warehouse, that's for sure." He stepped inside. "Did you do this to the walls?"

"Yeah. It's *The Three Musketeers*. Mostly."

Zane's brow furrowed as he stepped closer to the pages. "In French."

Ty shrugged. "It's better that way." Since Zane read novels in Spanish, Ty figured he'd understand.

Zane had one hand in a pocket. "This place is . . ." He shook his head. "Gothic."

Ty nodded wistfully. "That's part of what I loved about it."

"Yeah?" Zane moved a few steps closer. "Another new side to Ty Grady."

They faced each other, the silence heavy and tense.

"I wonder what other sides I don't know about," Zane finally murmured, as if talking to himself.

Ty swallowed hard. "Zane."

"What did you take with you when you left?" Zane asked. He turned away, unwilling to let Ty explain. "Anything? Or just the memories?"

Ty scowled. "Just a book I carried with me. It had a cut-out in it with my real passport."

Zane's jaw clenched, like he was physically holding back his emotions. "What did you miss most?"

Ty frowned, confused by the questions, until he finally recognized what Zane was doing. This was how his partner interrogated suspects. He would start with that intense stare and then ask mundane questions to throw the suspect off. Then he'd ease out just enough to make it seem okay before he punched through to the real queries in a quiet, frightening voice. It was quite effective, and Ty had seen Zane break people no one else could get to talk.

Ty chewed on his lip thoughtfully, trying to give Zane a real answer even as he dreaded the punch of the final question. "I missed the smell," he finally decided.

Most people would have taken that as a joke, but Zane would take it seriously. He'd been there, that somewhere you remembered by feel and scent more so than sight or sound. It was a visceral answer.

"Why?" Ty asked when Zane didn't respond.

Zane slid his other hand into his pocket and shrugged. "No one ever asked me to remember the good things."

Ty sighed. He'd done things here he hadn't necessarily been proud of. But for the most part, it had been two of the better years of his life. He remembered all of it fondly until the end. He knew Zane's experience in Miami had been vastly different.

They were still standing there, silent and uncomfortable, a few minutes later when Ava returned.

"You find what you need?" she asked, her voice breaking the spell.

Ty cleared his throat and shook his head. "Got distracted," he said, surprised when his voice came out hoarse.

"I called Shine. He wasn't home. I can go out there, snoop around."

"No, I can't let you do that," Ty said.

Ava smirked. "You won't be *letting* me do anything."

Zane snorted. Ava looked him up and down, then whistled and shook her head. "Tyler does have a type."

"Okay," Ty said loudly.

She merely smiled at him. "I'll go keep a lookout for your friends." She turned away.

Zane leaned sideways to watch her walk down the hall. "I like her."

Ty nodded, unable to say anything.

"Is there anything else you want to tell me before the others get here?"

Ty took in the rigid line of his shoulders, the tension in his jaw, and the hardness of his eyes. Zane had every right to be angry. The timing could have been better, but all of this mess was on Ty's head.

"I love you," he said quietly.

"That's it?"

Ty nodded.

Zane met his eyes for a few seconds before turning away and disappearing down the hall.

Chapter 9

"I would very much like to know what the hell is going on," Kelly said.

He was sitting across from Nick at the largest table in the place. Nick had his eyes on Liam, who was wandering around the edges of the barroom and refused to sit with the rest of them. Nick didn't trust the man one bit, but he was willing to hear an explanation from someone before punches were thrown.

The woman who'd let them in, Ava, had subsequently barred the door and disappeared behind a curtain. Nick could hear her moving back there, but he had no idea what she was doing, nor did he really care.

Ty sat to Nick's right, sedate and unusually flustered. And to Nick's left sat Zane, who seemed irritated and harsh. It wasn't difficult to deduce whatever Ty had told Zane had jammed a wedge between them. Nick hoped they could keep it together long enough to get through whatever this was and sort it out when they got home.

The floorboards above them creaked, and all of them looked up.

"Is someone else here?" Owen asked.

Zane shook his head.

"The floors do that," Ty muttered. He was rubbing the bridge of his nose with two fingers, hunched over the table.

Nick glanced at the ceiling again. The place had an eerie feeling to it, like it had been abandoned by the living but was still occupied. A shiver ran down Nick's spine. The whole city kind of felt like that, actually. All the voodoo crap was getting to him.

"Garrett, why don't you fill us in," Nick said, keeping his voice low. If Ty wasn't going to lead the discussion, someone had to.

Zane's dark eyes slid to glare at him, then he glanced up, his gaze following Liam as the man moved. He took a deep breath before speaking. "I was undercover for a while in Miami, working in the Vega cartel."

"I've heard of them," Nick said. "They reach all the way to Boston sometimes."

"And further. They got a tip that they had a mole, so they started a witch hunt. I got arrested one night on a DUI and the Bureau took the opportunity to pull me out, to save me and the information I'd stolen."

Liam drifted closer, and everyone was silent as they waited for Zane to connect the pieces.

"I thought that part of my life was history, but . . ." Zane stared at the tabletop, shaking his head.

Liam cleared his throat. "*But*. Roughly two years ago Garrett was inserted back into the cartel for a brief stay. He was pulled again, just days before Antonio de la Vega, the head asshole in charge, died in a plane crash in the Caribbean while returning to Colombia. Of course, Zane's alter ego became the prime suspect within the cartel. Juan Carlos de la Vega took over, righted the Vega ship, and went on a crusade to find the man who murdered his brother."

"How do you come into this?" Ty asked.

Liam kicked out a chair and sat, staring at Ty. His face was expressionless. "After you shot me, thank you for that by the way, I couldn't go to the NIA as planned. I had to find work somewhere."

Owen huffed and leaned away from Liam to look at him. "You're a mercenary."

"Pays the bills."

"Why not NIA?" Ty asked. His frown had deepened.

Liam's eyes narrowed and he leaned closer. He tapped his chest with one finger. "Because you missed, darling."

Ty's eyes followed Liam's hand, and Nick could see the blood draining from his friend's face.

"Clipped my heart. The right ventricle."

Ty either couldn't or wouldn't respond. He sat back in his chair, resting his chin in his hand. Nick wondered what was going on inside Ty's mind, how he would have reacted if everyone at the table weren't looking to him for leadership.

"It was repaired before I bled out, but they weren't willing to take an active field agent with a compromised heart."

"I thought you always had a compromised heart," Digger muttered.

"That's funny from you, Back Woods. How many innocent little bunnies do you have strung up in your hunting shed right now?"

"I don't eat bunny!" Digger shouted.

"Why are you here?" Kelly asked Liam.

"I was hired by de la Vega. He received an anonymous tip saying the man who killed his brother would be here Easter weekend."

All eyes shifted to Zane, but Zane's eyes were on Ty. He tore them away to glance around the table. "I didn't kill him," he said, returning his gaze to Ty.

"Tyler?" Liam drawled. "Care to share with the class?"

Ty didn't move, which was never a good sign. He looked from Zane to Liam, then spoke without removing his hand from his chin. "I tampered with the navigational equipment of his plane," he admitted. "The horizon should have read wrong and they would have flown straight into the water when the autopilot was turned on. I planted explosive charges as a backup."

Zane inhaled sharply. Nick got the feeling Zane already knew this, but hearing it straight from Ty's mouth was disconcerting, even for Nick.

"Did you go with the polymer bonded?" Digger asked.

"Slurries and gel mix."

"Oh, nice."

"Is that how you broke your finger when we were apart?" Zane demanded. Ty nodded curtly and Zane grunted, looking away with a sneer. "You deserved it, then."

Kelly cleared his throat and pointed at Liam. "So let me get this straight. You're here to kill him," he said, indicating at Ty. Then he gestured to Zane. "But you thought you were after him because he was the mole."

After a moment of contemplation, Liam nodded. "At its very basic, yes."

"So why aren't either of them dead?" Owen asked.

"Well," Liam said, drawing out the word. "Either I am the worst assassin in the world, which, if you want a hint, is not the right answer. Or . . . I realized I was after a couple of Feds and I pulled out."

"You refused the job?" Nick asked.

"Yes."

"You told me you hadn't called it in yet!" Zane shouted.

"I lied." Liam winked at Zane. "I do that, remember?"

"Are you lying now?" Nick asked.

Liam grinned as they locked eyes. "Maybe."

Nick ran a finger over the bridge of his nose. "Either way. By now they'll have sent a backup."

"Precisely!" Liam grinned. "You were always the brains of this operation, weren't you?"

"Bite me, British."

Liam shivered theatrically and grinned. "They won't have had the time to plan that I did, so they will go for something with less charisma and more brute strength."

"How many?" Ty asked.

"I would say six to eight. Just to cover their bases."

"So, we have cartel hit men after us?" Digger asked. "What the shit does that have to do with gris-gris?"

"What is a gris-gris?" Liam asked.

Liam and Digger stared at each other, eyes narrowing, lips curving into snarls.

Nick passed a hand over his eyes, groaning.

"Why did you come to the hospital?" Ty demanded of Liam.

A frown creased Liam's brow. "I haven't been to hospital."

"You didn't come to my room and threaten me?"

"Why in the hell would I go to all this trouble if I could have found you at the hospital? Why were you in hospital?"

Ty glanced at Nick and slid lower in his seat, rubbing his hand over his face.

"Does that mean you really did attack a male nurse at the ER?" Owen asked.

Ty nodded from behind his hand.

Liam shook his head, peering at Ty. "You really are off the rails, huh?"

Ty sat forward, holding out a hand. "The point is, the situation has changed. The cleanest way to handle any of this is to skip town."

"You want to run?" Zane asked, practically sneering.

Nick narrowed his eyes, trying not get defensive. "There's running and then there's strategic retreat. It's good to know the difference."

"You want to run," Zane repeated.

"Yes," Ty said. "We're not equipped to handle this here."

"We'll never have a better chance against them. There are seven of us."

"Six," Ty corrected.

Liam counted the men around the table. When he got to seven, he pointed to himself and shook his head. "This is not my fight," he said. "I don't plan on dying for any of you."

Ty and Zane locked eyes again. Nick sort of wanted to lean away from the line of fire.

"You know damn well we will never have another opportunity like this one," Zane said through gritted teeth. "We know they're coming. Even if this isn't *their* fight, it's yours and mine."

"Garrett, we are outgunned," Ty said, his voice getting louder. He pressed a finger against the table. "We know they're coming, but we don't know how or when. And in case you've forgotten, there is a city full of cops hunting us down right now. If there's trouble, we're just as likely to end up in jail as we are dead, and either way ends bloody for me."

Zane crossed his arms and huffed. "I never thought I'd see the day I wanted to call you a coward."

"Whoa," Owen whispered.

Nick sat straighter and put both hands out. "Okay, slow down."

Ty stared at Zane, not moving, not blinking. He didn't even appear to be breathing. Nick tensed, preparing to grab Ty when he lunged. Zane returned the stare, unwavering. Across the table, Liam whistled softly.

Ty stood as if the noise had propelled him, his chair scratching against the wooden floorboards. Nick stood with him, but Ty didn't attack.

"Where are you going?" Kelly asked.

"To get a drink," Ty spat. Nick sighed as Ty stalked toward the bar.

"Well that was productive," Digger muttered.

Nick sat again. Digger and Kelly were both shaking their heads, looking to Nick for guidance. Owen had his arms on the table, resting his head on them. Liam was sitting with his lips pursed, and when Nick made eye contact, Liam grinned and winked. Zane was still leaning back in his chair, but his body wasn't relaxed. He was resting his mouth against his hand, elbow propped on the arm of the chair. His hard eyes followed Ty's movements.

"Okay," Nick said. "Nothing good is going to come of us sitting here sniping at each other. We'll call it a night, come back with clearer heads at dawn. Keep watch in shifts of two. Bell doesn't take a turn."

"You're putting a guard on me?" Liam asked.

"Yes. Would you like to tell me why I shouldn't?"

"I'd like to tell you where to *go*, do I have permission to do that?" He stood, muttering under his breath as he walked away. He said something to Ty as he mounted the stairs, then ducked and covered when Ty chucked a heavy glass at him. It shattered against the wall and rained shards over Liam's shoulders.

"Excellent idea, Grady!" Liam shouted. He stood from his crouch. "Lace the steps with glass so we can hear them coming, good thinking."

"Keep running your mouth, you bastard, you'll wake up bloody!" Ty shouted.

"Yeah, in my sleep, that's the only way you'll ever get the upper hand."

Liam hustled up the steps before Ty could reply, taking them two at a time and narrowly avoiding the second glass Ty threw at him.

Nick chewed on his lip for a few seconds, then turned to glance at the others. "Who wants to volunteer for first watch with Ty?"

The bar felt heavy when it was deserted, as if the music and smoke and drink had all risen to the top and begun pressing down on everyone below. That had always been Ty's favorite time of day. The memories weren't so sweet now, though.

"Drew the short straw, huh?" Ty said as Zane came up behind him. Ty couldn't look him in the eye now, not even through the mirror that hung over the back of the bar. The last time he'd been called a coward,

Zane had been the one defending him. It was dizzying to see how all they'd built could unravel so quickly.

Zane slid onto the stool beside him. Ty doggedly stared at the bar top. He didn't want to look at Zane right now, didn't want to feel the pain that came with those dark eyes.

"I was out of line, saying that in front of everyone," Zane said. His voice was soft, but still cold.

"You wanted to take me down a peg or two in front of the boys. You did it. Congratulations."

Zane sighed, and Ty felt the gust of his breath against his cheek. "This is where you're supposed to apologize too, and we start trying to make sense of what we have left to us."

Ty glanced up sharply. "What we have *left* to us? Why are you so ready to walk, Zane? I was doing my job. You of all people should understand what that means."

Zane grunted. "Don't you dare throw that in my face. You know as well as I do that whatever you've been doing the past two years was anything but your job."

"Please," Ty sneered.

"How about apologizing for lying to me? For spying on me? Using me?"

Ty slammed his hand on the bar. "I never lied to you, Garrett, not about us! Never once did I tell you anything that wasn't true, not when it came to you and me. And I sure as hell didn't *use* you for anything."

"Well forgive me if I don't believe a goddamn word you say. The only way I hear the truth from you is when someone has a gun to your fucking head. Or mine!"

"Someone did have a gun to your head!" Zane started to get up, but Ty reached out to grab him. He didn't dare let him turn away, afraid Zane wouldn't ever turn back again. "After everything we've been through, why the hell can't you believe me?"

"Because you lie."

The words hit him in the gut, and he gasped for air.

The curtain rustled and Ava came through carrying three reservoir glasses. She set them on the bar, looking between Ty and Zane with a raised eyebrow.

"You two going to sit there glaring at each other all night?" she asked before ducking below the bar to retrieve a wooden box from underneath.

Zane didn't flinch. He continued to glower at Ty, the anger and betrayal roiling in the air between them. They were both frightened, and the only thing they knew to do when they were scared was lash out.

Ty leaned closer. "You can be angry for as long as you want, Zane. It doesn't change what's happened, and it doesn't change the way I feel about you. Remember that, if nothing else."

Ty left it at that, turning away from Zane to take one of the glasses. They were specially made for preparing absinthe; thick and heavy, with a wide mouth and a small reservoir in the stem. They were quite beautiful, as drinking glasses went. Ava pulled three ornate spoons from the wooden box and set them on the bar.

The silence stretched thin. Ty had tried every avenue. He'd explained himself, pleaded, reasoned with Zane, and professed his love over and over. None of it had made a dent in Zane's armor. Ty peered sideways at Zane. There wasn't much else he could do, and Zane seemed just as willing to toss it all away now as he had earlier. "This is the part where I drink and don't give a damn if it bothers you," he whispered. "Feel free to look away."

Zane's lip curled and he narrowed his eyes. "No need to be concerned about me. Maybe a stiff drink will settle your nerves."

"My, my," Ava said. "I see that gris-gris is working already."

Ty snorted. He didn't know if it was the gris-gris, but he and this town sure as hell were cursed.

"Thank you for throwing the cheap glasses instead of these," Ava said as she poured a reservoir full of light green liquid into each glass. The bottle was labeled Vieux Pontarlier. It was the very best absinthe you could buy, made exactly the same way it had been two hundred years before and imported from France.

He knew Zane had delved into all manner of chemicals, legal and illegal. He wasn't sure absinthe had made it to the Miami scene, though, and he wasn't sure Zane would know what Ava was doing.

Zane glanced from the spoons to the dark bottle she set on the bar, then back to Ty for a moment. He looked suspicious, as if he thought Ty was about to do something dangerous or illegal.

There was a completely mistaken aura surrounding absinthe as that of a mysterious, addictive, mind-altering substance, giving it a gothic horror sort of taboo. It was all completely unfounded, of course. It was just about the only thing Ty could drink while on the job, because while absinthe did get you drunk, it also made you unusually lucid, creating the illusion of a waking dream. He functioned well. It was all he had drunk for nearly two years while undercover.

He set the spoon on his glass, making sure the special lip underneath caught the edge of the glass to keep it in place. Then he plucked a sugar cube from the bowl Ava had set down and placed it on the center of the spoon.

Ava turned to fill a pitcher with water.

"What is this?" Zane finally asked, sounding annoyed to have to ask.

"Absinthe. The real stuff, not the tourist trade."

Zane frowned but didn't say anything. Ty didn't try to set any of his preconceptions straight.

"We'd sit and do this every night," Ava told Zane as she returned with the pitcher full of ice water. "You should try it."

"Garrett's got poor impulse control. Don't you, Garrett? Has to stay away from the cocktails." Ty poured the water out over his sugar cube. The water and dissolving sugar mixed with the green absinthe below, turning it a weak, milky green.

"That's right," Zane snarled. "Maybe you should learn a thing or two about it."

Ty removed the spoon, shaking his head.

"Every night after we sang, we'd go sit in that corner there, pour a glass of *la fée verte*, and *laissez les bon temps rouler*," Ava told Zane with a hint of bittersweet irony. She leaned her elbows on the bar and took a sip of her drink. "And every Saturday night," she continued, voice lower, growing huskier, "we would pick a plaything to join us. You would have been chosen, no doubt."

"He was," Ty muttered.

After what felt like a drawn-out moment of silence, Zane said, "Let the good times roll, huh?"

Ty focused on his drink, watching the green liquid swirl and mix. "When in Rome."

"Rome wasn't the only thing that burned in a day," Zane replied evenly.

Ty met his eyes for a long moment, for the first time seeing distrust in them. He lowered his head, closing his eyes, then took a drink.

Ava reached beneath the bar again and pulled out a little homemade voodoo doll, made with sticks and a piece of burlap. The eyes had been drawn on, and the hair was bundled sage. She set it on the bar.

"What's this?" Ty reached for it, recognizing the ring around its neck. It was his, one he'd thought he'd lost years ago. His confusion turned to outrage and he grabbed the doll. "This is me?"

Ava shrugged. "I had some free time. It's served its purpose. I guess you'll be wanting it back. I'm going to bed." She picked up her glass to take with her. "You boys play nice."

"You voodoo'd me?" Ty gaped at her as she left, the voodoo doll still in his hand. "You bitch!"

Her laughter reached them from the back.

Zane plucked the doll from his hand. "You told me voodoo dolls were good luck."

"They are," Ty answered, still scowling at the curtain.

"She's got a lot of pins in you."

Ty glanced at him and yanked the doll out of his hand. The pins were mostly in his head, blue ones, meant to draw love. But there were also white, red, and black pins scattered over the doll's torso, hands, and groin, symbolizing positivity, power, and repelling evil.

"There's one in almost every place you've been hurt the past few years."

"None of them mean bad things," Ty insisted, though he was flustered by the coincidence of the locations. He started yanking them out and tossing the pins on the bar.

"I thought you said they meant good things."

"Shut up."

The silence began to stretch, growing more unbearable by the second. Ty could feel Zane's eyes on him. He glared at the doll for a minute before taking a deep breath and looking at Zane. "What now?"

Zane still watched him intently. He shook his head. "You think you did no wrong. And I can't trust you." He shrugged. "What else is there?"

Ty held his breath for a few heartbeats, just to see if his heart was actually still beating. Zane couldn't have crushed it more completely if he'd used his boot heel. Then he took a long drink.

"What's it taste like?" Zane asked. He seemed remarkably detached for a man who was talking about ending them.

Ty pursed his lips and sighed. If Zane intended for this to be the last night they were together, then Ty was going to make the most of it. He took another sip, then spun on his stool to face Zane. He reached out for Zane's shirt and pulled him closer. Butterflies started in his stomach, like it was the first time he'd ever tried to kiss his lover. Zane stiffened but allowed Ty to draw him near, his lips parting. Ty pressed his lips to Zane's. Once his tongue slid along Zane's, Zane shuddered and gave a barely audible moan.

The kiss felt like they were back at square one trying to decide how brave they had to be to initiate something. Ty was almost light-headed with nerves.

Their lips lingered too long before Ty pulled away and met Zane's eyes. They were a little wide, but Ty suspected it had nothing to do with the kiss and everything to do with the absinthe. The taste was distinct, as were its effects. Ty could already feel it working its way through him, calming his mind and body, enhancing the sensations of touch and smell. It couldn't soothe the ache in his chest, though.

"Fuck," Zane whispered, and he licked his lower lip.

Ty eased back onto his stool and took another sip from the heavy glass. "This was my life for two years," he finally said. "I almost lost myself to it."

Zane propped his elbows on the bar and folded his hands. "I can see how you'd get lost in this lifestyle. You've never seemed to have an addictive personality, though, so I'm a little surprised."

Ty finished off the drink, shivering as it went through him. He set the glass down with a loud clunk. "You're not the only one who fights things every day, Garrett. Yours are just harder battles, closer to the surface. Mine . . ." He swallowed and peered around the bar, taking in the overwhelming mystique of something ageless in the air and in the city. It shimmered. He didn't finish what he was saying, lost in the glow until he felt the touch of warm fingers on his hand.

"Grady, come back," Zane said quietly.

Ty tore his eyes away from the shimmer and met Zane's gaze.

"That stuff must have a hell of a punch."

"Easy to get lost in," Ty murmured.

"Yes," Zane said under his breath. His façade cracked, and suddenly he looked devastated. Like he'd given up. "You are."

Ty stared hard at him. For the first time it began to sink in that Zane might truly mean to leave. There might not be anything Ty could say or do to stop it, and suddenly he couldn't sit there any longer. He pulled his hand from Zane's grasp and stepped away. "I'll take watch upstairs," he said, voice hoarse. His boots crunched on the broken glass at the base of the staircase as he walked away.

"Ty," Zane called after him. Ty paused on the bottom step. Zane hesitated long enough that Ty took another step before he spoke. "Do I really know you? Do I know Ty Grady at all?"

Ty studied him, trying to parse the anger and pain into something that didn't feel like he was dying. Zane was still sitting at the bar, his eyes dark and wounded, his shoulders slumped. One chance. That was all Zane was willing to give, even if it broke them both. Ty shook his head and started back up the steps, speaking in a low voice as he went. "If you have to ask that, I guess not."

Chapter 10

Two hours after Ty left him, Kelly joined Zane downstairs for the changing of the guard.

"Nick's got upstairs," Kelly told him.

"Great," Zane grunted. He started up the steps, each crunch of the glass bringing him closer to another confrontation with Ty, to a night of sleeping with his lover right next to him and feeling like there was a stranger in his bed.

When he reached the top of the steps, he took a deep breath to steady himself. It was harder and harder to curb the anger growing. He'd had two hours to think of nothing but all the times Ty must have lied to him to keep from being caught, all the times they'd talked about Zane's time in Miami that Ty must have been digging for information.

All the times Ty had simply looked him in the eye and lied.

His twenty-year party. He *had* seen Richard Burns there, and now he knew exactly where Ty had disappeared to. He hadn't been retrieving that damn orchid from his car. God knew what they had been discussing. Zane's hands balled into fists and he stopped on the steps. He wanted to stomp up there and clock Ty just to get the anger out, just to do *something*. And his entire body screamed for a drink. He wavered, fighting the urge to go back and pour himself a whiskey.

The familiar rumbling undertone of Ty's voice stopped him.

Ty and Nick were at the far end of the hall, standing outside the room Liam must have taken. Zane studied Ty's silhouette in the dim hallway. He seemed rigid and tense. He spoke with extensive use of his hands, but nothing of the low murmur reached Zane's ears.

Goddamn, Ty. Why couldn't he have made this easy? Why did he have to tell Zane the truth about his assignment? Why now? Why not hold onto it like he said he'd wanted to instead of breaking Zane's heart with it? Why did he have to accept the assignment at all? He should have just used some backbone and said no!

Zane would have said no, had their position been reversed. That much he knew. He would never have kept a secret that big from Ty, not after that first week in New York. Trust was all they'd had, and Ty had used it, abused it. The only thing Ty was afraid of was saying no to a set of orders.

Ty headed down the hall. Behind him, Nick rested his back against the wall and slid down to sit. Zane supposed that was where Ty had set up camp too. Right outside Liam's door, using shadow for cover, with a direct view of the only exit. He wondered what Liam thought about having an armed guard at his door, about not being trusted without a handler on top of him.

Then Zane realized he knew exactly how Liam felt.

Ty stopped in front of Zane, both of them standing in the doorway to the room Ty had once occupied. Zane gritted his teeth when he met Ty's eyes.

"You want to talk?" Ty asked. "Or are you still too mad at me?"

"You don't think I deserve to be mad for a little longer?"

Ty's eyes searched over Zane's face, then he stepped into the room. He kicked his shoes off, pulled his T-shirt over his head, and tossed it at the table.

Zane followed, pulling the door closed behind him. He made sure to lock it.

"You're seriously going to leave it at that?" Zane said, voice pitched low. They were in the room with the pages plastered to the walls. He had confidence in Ty's work, that they couldn't be overheard.

Ty faced him. He shrugged. "What do you want me to say? I told you I was sorry. I told you why I did it. And you know what, Zane? I'd do it again. In a heartbeat. Because I was protecting someone I love."

"You weren't *protecting* me, Ty, you were spying on me. The fact that you don't see that, that you'd march right down that road again without thinking twice, that scares the piss out of me. How the hell can I trust you now?"

Ty rolled his eyes.

"You were meeting with Burns in Baltimore, weren't you?" Zane growled.

"Burns wasn't in Baltimore, Zane!"

Zane took several long strides and grabbed Ty by his shoulders, shoving him up against the wall. "Stop lying to me!"

Ty's eyes flashed and he clenched his jaw, baring his teeth. "Call me a liar one more time and I'll put you down."

Zane's grip tightened. His breaths came harder and faster. Maybe a good knock-down, drag-out fight would do them both some good. Zane certainly wanted to smash his fist into Ty's teeth right now.

He pushed away instead, backing toward the door so he wouldn't be tempted to lash out. "You might want to get used to it. That's the kind of stuff you call people who lie for a living."

"Where are you going?" Ty demanded.

Zane turned his back on him. "I need a drink."

Ty had to take a few seconds to gather himself before he could follow Zane out the door. He'd be goddamned if Zane headed down there to drink, not because of him, not without a fight. He glanced down the hall as he pulled his shirt back on. Nick had come to his feet, his gun in hand.

"What's going on?"

Ty waved him off. "I got this."

He hurried down the steps and reached the barroom just in time to see Zane pouring a snifter full of whiskey.

"Zane."

Zane glared at him, and Ty had to fight every fiber of his being not to avert his eyes. He plowed on, though, stepping up behind the bar, opposite Zane.

"I'm going to give you ten seconds to get the fuck away from me," Zane snarled.

Ty's heart stuttered. He had never seen Zane like this, had never known he even had it in him to seethe like this. He squared his shoulders, though. "I'm not going to let you do this."

Zane held perfectly still. He didn't even seem to be breathing. "*You* did this, Ty," he said, then lifted the glass to his lips.

Ty grabbed his wrist. The whiskey spilled all over the bar. Zane stood so fast that his stool clattered to the floor. Ty barely managed to block Zane's arm before the glass crashed into the side of his head, then Zane reached across the bar and grabbed Ty by his shirt, lifting him off the ground and dragging him across the bar top.

Ty could do nothing but grasp Zane's forearms and hold on as Zane yanked him off the bar and threw him to the floor. He rolled and pushed to his hands and knees, then to his feet. Zane picked up the barstool beside him and swung it with one hand, as if it were nothing more than a pillow.

The stool crashed to the floor at Ty's feet as he staggered back. He was both shocked that Zane had lashed out and chastising himself for not expecting it. He knew how deeply he'd hurt Zane, and he knew what happened when Zane's anger went unchecked. He should have known. Zane's rage only served to calm Ty further.

"Everything I've done, Ty, I've done it for you!" Zane shouted.

Ty was peripherally aware of Kelly hovering near the bar and Nick and Liam standing on the stairs watching. He waved at them to make sure no one interfered. He couldn't have anyone getting hurt in a scuffle. He shook his head as Zane came at him. "Not like this, Zane," he tried.

Zane's fist flew at him. Then again. Ty was able to block the first two punches, but the third caught him in the kidney and he doubled over. Waves of pain almost brought him to his knees. He lunged forward, wrapping Zane up to try to stop him without hurting him. He refused to throw a punch in retaliation.

Zane shouted, his voice full of anger, pain, and betrayal. He picked Ty up and slammed him against the large wooden support beam in the middle of the room. The glass of a picture frame cracked against Ty's shoulders. Ty tightened his hold on Zane's arms, locking him down, trying to immobilize him before he hurt himself or Ty.

"I'm sorry, Zane," he gasped, trying to hold tight.

Zane pressed his face into Ty's neck, fighting back a sob. His entire body was trembling.

Ty dug his fingers into Zane's back, holding him close. He put his lips to Zane's ear. "I'm so sorry."

Zane's shoulders tightened under Ty's hands. "I would have chosen you over anything," Zane hissed. He pulled back, breaking Ty's hold, bunched the front of Ty's shirt in both hands, and jerked Ty forward until they were nose-to-nose, until Ty's feet weren't solidly on the floor. "My job, my family, my *wife*. I would have given my life for you! But you! You can't even give me the truth!"

Ty only had time to squeeze his eyes closed before Zane picked him up and tossed him sideways. He crashed against one of the tables and slid with it as it tumbled over amidst breaking glass and bits of splintered wood.

It took him a moment to get his wits about him. The others were wide-eyed and gaping. Ty rolled to his stomach and pushed up, accompanied by the tinkling of glass from a broken hurricane lamp as it cascaded down his arms and back.

Zane was framed by the neon light coming from the bar behind him, casting him into darkness and shadow.

"Jesus, Zane," Ty muttered.

Zane turned his back on him and went back to the bar. He pulled out a new glass and poured another whiskey, neat. "I don't know about you, but I certainly feel better," he said before throwing the whiskey back in one gulp.

Zane stood at the bar, watching the scene unfold in the mirror as the whiskey burned its way through him.

Nick and Kelly moved to help Ty out of the debris from the table and chairs they'd destroyed. Liam hung back, arms crossed, watching with one eyebrow raised. When Ty stood, his hand went immediately to his side, and he doubled over again. Zane was struck with concern, but he shrugged it off. He'd known Ty would still be tender in the kidney area. One good jab had made it almost impossible for him to defend himself. It had been unnecessary, though. Ty hadn't even tried to fight back.

Zane ducked his head when Ty's eyes found his in the mirror. Zane caught the pain and fury despite trying not to. He continued to stare at the empty glass in front of him as they helped Ty up the steps.

Zane reached for the bottle and poured himself another glass.

"Is that really the best idea?" Liam asked. He leaned against the bar beside Zane. "I've managed to deduce you might be one who imbibes a bit too much."

"Go away," Zane growled.

"An alcoholic, that's what I meant by that," Liam said. "In case that wasn't clear."

"I said go away."

"Or what? You'll toss me over a table as well?"

Zane bared his teeth at Liam.

"I'll tell you one thing, love, I wouldn't pull my punches like he did. Seems an unfair advantage, trying to hurt someone who refuses to swing back." He reached for the glass in Zane's hand and took a sip. "Might as well drink tonight, though, yeah? Tomorrow, Ty's going to get you all killed." He handed the glass back to Zane and smirked.

"What makes you say that?"

Liam tapped his temple. "He's not thinking. Neither are you, for that matter." His arm brushed Zane's as he leaned against the bar again. "These cartel hooligans. You know who they'll send, don't you?"

"I have an inkling, yes. Mateo Valencia."

"Is he good?"

Zane shrugged and took another sip. The whiskey scorched its way down his throat, lighting a fire inside him he'd been sorely missing. The world around him grew cooler compared to it.

"Is he better than you?"

Zane flexed his wrist, where a sheath and knife felt just right against his skin. He remembered a meeting in a penthouse suite when one of Antonio's pups had yapped one too many times. Zane'd slashed the man from lip to ear, just to teach him a lesson. Just to remind him he didn't speak until spoken to.

"No," he answered.

Liam cocked his head. "Good to know." He glanced at the steps. They were still alone. Kelly was probably checking Ty over to make sure he wasn't hurt. "When you've finished satisfying your need for fine whiskey, I'd like to speak with you upstairs. Privately."

Zane huffed. He took another sip, closing his eyes. He had missed the smell. The taste. He had missed the world of black and white. "Can't you say it here?"

Liam whistled low and moved closer to whisper in Zane's ear. "I'd prefer to discuss such things without clothing."

Zane turned his head sharply, but Liam didn't back away. His nose brushed Zane's, and for a few heartbeats, Zane thought he was going to kiss him. Liam didn't move though, and Zane finally backed away with a jerky nod.

"You *are* single now, Zane, in case that wasn't clear in the way he looked at you. Ty doesn't mess around with people who don't want him."

Zane's heart hammered faster.

"Take your time," Liam murmured before walking away.

Zane pushed the door open and stepped inside, closing it behind him with a click that seemed to echo through the building. He took a few tentative steps in the darkness, and set the bottle and glass on the kitchen table.

A light flipped on, and Zane looked over his shoulder at the gun pointed at him.

"Put that away," he grumbled.

Ty sat up in bed and swung his legs to the floor. He slid the gun under his pillow again. "How many have you had?"

Zane shook his head and tapped the bottle. "Not enough to make it okay."

Ty's expression remained impassive, which was singularly annoying since Zane usually read him so well. "I was doing my job," he said, his voice low and even. "I was doing what I had to do to stay with you. What's so fucking wrong with that?"

Zane sneered. "Tell me something, Ty, is there anything you won't do for a job?"

Ty didn't have an answer for that. He stood instead, crossing his arms. His breaths were harsh, like every word Zane hurled was making it harder for him to get air.

"There isn't a part of you that you haven't sold for one thing or another," Zane snarled. He advanced on Ty, giving an almost manic laugh. Ty stood his ground, merely cocking his head as Zane got in his face. "I've spent half my adult life with whores. You're just better at your job than the others were."

"You're drunk, Zane," Ty finally managed to say. The blood had drained from his face, but he was standing straight and tall. "Keep your mouth shut before you say something I won't forgive."

Zane took one more step, trying to crowd him into retreating toward the wall or the bed. But Ty still stood his ground. "God forbid you refuse an order, Ty. God forbid you choose something you love over being told what to do."

Ty rolled his shoulders and met Zane's words with a stony face. The only thing Zane wanted to see in Ty's eyes was pain. He wanted to hit him where it would hurt like nothing else, and punching him or tossing him around wouldn't hurt someone like Ty. Sticks and stones could break his bones . . .

Words were what hit Ty hardest.

Zane closed his eyes. It was hard to fight the urge to jab at that soft spot with the whiskey flowing through him. He moved away and ran his fingers through his hair. "Jesus Christ, Ty, I thought I was going to marry you. Did you know that? I've been trying to decide how to ask you for months! I was trying to fucking ask you when Nick fucking O'Flaherty called you for help! You just had to answer the fucking phone!"

Ty's façade finally broke. His lips parted, but Zane didn't let him speak.

"I told my mother to fuck off for you! I took off Becky's ring and put it away for you, you son of a bitch! And all you were doing was your job!"

"You know that's not true!"

"You were just following orders," Zane grumbled. He swayed as he took a careless step back, tired of trying to intimidate Ty into backing down. "Everything I know about you is based on lies. You're a caricature. Just a good little soldier."

Ty's voice broke. "You really believe that?"

Zane waved a hand at him. The warmth of the whiskey churned through him, leaving a cold outer shell that nothing would penetrate. "You make yourself whatever you need to be to get the job done, and then you move on to the next."

Ty's eyes flashed. "Bullshit."

"You made yourself perfect for me. But that's not the real you either, is it? I bet you don't even know who the real you is anymore."

Ty didn't move, but his breaths were harsh in the silence. Through the haze of anger, Zane could see the life seeping out of Ty's eyes, turning them hard and flat. A part of Zane screamed for him to stop—stop talking, stop being angry, stop going down this path. There was no coming back from this. But the part of Zane that was so hurt by Ty's betrayal, the part that had continued to drink downstairs, that couldn't get over the pain and anger, forced him to keep going.

He took a step toward Ty and jabbed a finger at his chest. "When this mess is settled and we get back to Baltimore? We're over. You and I. Done."

Ty grabbed his hand and shoved it away. "Right, Zane, that's great. Why wait until you're sober, right?"

Zane shoved him. "We're done!"

Ty slammed both forearms against Zane's arm and twisted, forcing Zane to contort with a howl of pain. Ty spun him and shoved him face first into the mattress. Furious, Zane flicked a wrist and one of his knives deployed. It nicked Ty, who cried out and let Zane go.

"Son of a bitch!" Ty shouted.

Zane rolled to his back and kicked at Ty's chest, sending him staggering as Zane stood.

"I'm trying not to hurt you, Garrett!" Ty shouted. He wiped blood from the cut on his forearm.

"Fuck that."

Zane grabbed for him, but Ty easily avoided his hand with a slap of one palm against Zane's forearm. Zane rounded with the other hand and Ty repeated the move, not dodging but merely redirecting the force of Zane's swings.

"Russian sambo, right?" Zane sneered as they circled each other. "Another secret I'll probably never have explained."

"Add that to the list, right behind sobriety."

Zane lunged and Ty went into a modified kick flip, only instead of kicking out, he rolled over Zane's back to land behind him. Zane shoved his shoulder back, catching Ty in the side and flinging him onto the bed. The springs complained and the headboard banged against the wall.

Zane climbed on top of him and grabbed both of Ty's wrists, holding him down before Ty had a chance to recover. Ty bucked under him, but he couldn't fight Zane's weight in that position, not unless he meant to do real harm. And if there was one thing Zane knew about Ty, it was that he would let himself be beaten to a pulp before he truly hurt Zane.

Zane could feel Ty's heart pounding, his breaths growing more difficult, his hard muscles working to free himself. Zane pressed down to keep him from getting loose and kissed him, hard and messy, forcing his tongue into Ty's mouth and not giving him a chance to say otherwise.

Ty fought his grip, bucking his hips. Zane was growing harder with every struggle. Just like the first time they'd fought in an alley in New York City and then fucked all night long, the violence fueled him. He thrust down, grinding his cock against Ty. Ty moaned into his mouth, but he still tried to pull his hands from Zane's grasp.

Zane let go of one wrist and grabbed a handful of Ty's hair instead, yanked Ty's head to the side, and bit at his neck. He let Ty's other wrist go and reached for his shirt, ripping it at the neck so he could taste the sweat along Ty's collarbone.

Ty's breathing was harsh and labored. He twisted, and his forearm caught Zane in the cheek. Zane grabbed his hand and yanked Ty's arm across his body, shoving it to the bed and pinning him. Ty tried to twist out of it, but Zane was too heavy.

"Asshole!" Ty snarled.

"I know you can throw me off," Zane grunted. "Go ahead, Ty. Do it."

Ty's eyes narrowed. His breaths were gusting across Zane's face. He didn't make a move to break Zane's grip, though.

Zane released his hand to see if Ty would struggle more. When he felt Ty's body relaxing under him, he kissed him again, pushing himself between Ty's legs, shoving his tongue between those sinful lips. He bit at Ty's lower lip. Bit hard.

Ty's fingers dragged down his shoulder and he let Ty's lip go. He thrust again, his cock growing painfully hard inside his jeans. He reached between their bodies to loosen his belt and pull the zipper, then pushed his jeans and boxers down.

Ty's eyes were dark and unreadable. "I thought we were done."

Zane smiled slowly. "As soon as you know what it feels like to be used. Then we're fucking done."

He grabbed Ty's shirt to rip it the rest of the way. Ty swatted at his fingers, but Zane knocked his hand away and instead reached to pull the straps on both his wrist sheaths. He tossed the knives away and hovered over Ty, pressing their bodies together.

"Where's your fucking kit?"

Ty licked his lips. "By the door."

Zane pushed off him and moved to rummage through Ty's toiletry bag. He finally dumped everything on the floor. Toothpaste and shaving cream and several EpiPens went rolling across the floor. Zane grabbed up the lubricant, but he stopped when he saw a small black jewelry box at his foot.

He picked it up and straightened. Ty had tossed his torn shirt to the floor and was shoving his pants to kick them off, his movements jerky and irritated.

"You don't have to order me around, you know," Ty told him. "As far as I'm concerned, I'm still yours."

Zane huffed, his stomach tumbling at Ty's words. The anger ebbed as he held the box up for Ty to see. "What is this?"

Zane watched sadness roll over Ty's face. "It was for you."

Zane was breathing hard, trying to fight the veil of whiskey to see through to the only man he'd thought he would ever love. Without asking for permission, he flipped the box open.

Inside was a rectangular silver token. A rough anchor had been etched into the face of it. Zane picked it up and dropped the box to the floor. He could feel something on the other side, but his eyes were fixed to the anchor.

"I had my ring from the cruise ship job melted down for it. It's a sobriety token."

Zane looked up. Ty was sitting on the edge of the bed, shoulders slumped, eyes on the floor.

"You told me one time that . . . I was your compass. I gave you direction when you were lost," Ty said, nearly choking on the words. He glanced up, eyes reflecting like liquid in the low light. "Well, you were my anchor. You were something solid for me to hold onto. I wanted you to remember that."

Zane stared at him for a solid minute, trying to feel something beyond the warmth of the whiskey, beyond the reach of the anger. He had convinced himself the Ty Grady he knew wasn't the real one.

But what if it was? What if Zane was the only one who'd seen the real man beneath all those layers?

He turned the token over in his hand. "I believe in you" was etched on the other side. He balled it in his fist and tossed it at the door with a mournful shout.

"You son of a bitch!" he shouted, stalking toward Ty. "I trusted you!"

Ty stood to meet the assault. Zane grabbed him and kissed him brutally, digging his fingers into Ty's hair, slamming him against the wall beside the bed. A moment later he shoved Ty onto the bed and climbed over him, continuing the kiss in all its angry glory.

"Zane," Ty said, breathless. Whether it was from the weight on top of him or the weight of his emotions, Zane didn't know and didn't care.

"Shut up, Ty. Don't fucking say my name." He reached between them, taking Ty in hand and squeezing. Ty gasped and closed his eyes. It made it easier for Zane, not being forced to look into Ty's eyes.

He filled his palm with lube and stroked himself, using his other hand to tug at Ty's thigh. He leaned over him, biting at his lip, yanking his leg higher, thrusting his hips, forcing Ty to lift his other leg and let Zane settle on top of him. Ty's entire body was trembling.

"For once in your life," he ground out against Ty's lips. "Be something honest for once in your life."

He pushed the head of his cock against Ty, waiting for the gasp he knew was coming. The gust of air came against his lips, the same one Ty always seemed to let out when Zane first entered him. Zane bit down on Ty's lip to turn that gasp into one of pain, then shoved harder, breaching, pushing past tight muscles.

He'd forgotten what it felt like to delve into the warmth of someone else when all he felt was the cold calm of the alcohol and the bite of unchecked anger. God, it was so good.

He gripped Ty's hair to hold him still beneath Zane's weight as he inched in. It was agonizing to go so slowly when all he wanted was to hear Ty cry out for mercy, to fuck him until he could feel nothing but the simplicity of emptying himself deep inside someone else, emptying all the pain and anger into someone who was begging for more.

He pushed until he was completely sheathed, until Ty was writhing beneath him, trembling against him. Ty's breath shivered over Zane's lips.

"Come on, then, Garrett," Ty whispered. "You want me to feel used?"

"Yes," Zane hissed. "I want you to hurt like I do."

"Then do it."

Zane smacked his hand over Ty's mouth. He pulled out and forced himself in again, lingering long enough to appreciate the slow slide of his cock as he delved deep, to feel Ty's body jerk beneath his. Ty gasped against his hand. His fingernails raked down Zane's back. Zane reached under Ty's hips and pulled him off the bed, shoving deeper, forcing Ty to contort.

Ty called out, the sound muffled by Zane's hand.

Zane started up a brutal rhythm, holding Ty down, the only sounds he heard were muffled and incoherent. His hips moved faster, harder, anger and anguish driving him, seeking pleasure that only his body registered and his mind refused to let him feel. He buried his face against Ty's chest, pushing harder, finally letting his hand fall away from Ty's mouth so he could lift Ty's hips higher.

Ty gasped his name. It was a pleading sound, filled with the same anguish Zane felt in every fiber of his being. Zane smacked his palm over Ty's mouth again.

"Don't you say it," he growled. "Don't you dare say it."

Ty's hands grasped at his back, dragging, clawing at him. His body writhed under Zane's as Zane came inside him. As Zane's movements slowed, his world came crashing back to him, everything black and white, everything made crystal clear and magnified to a pinpoint by the whiskey coursing through him. He moved his hand, and Ty gasped for air.

Zane pulled out of him, but he kissed him again, running his fingers down Ty's body to grip his cock. He was growing harder as Zane handled him, his moans vibrating against Zane's lips.

"You need to get off?" Zane asked, his voice surprisingly hoarse. Ty gasped. "Say it, say the words."

"Garrett," Ty tried.

Zane held him down and stroked him, riding out the rhythm of Ty's body seeking release. "Tell me what I want to hear, Grady."

Ty gripped Zane's shoulders, pushing his cock into Zane's hand. "I need you," he gasped.

The words tore through Zane with the precision of a scalpel. He kissed Ty greedily one last time, pumping him until Ty's entire body trembled with impending release. Then he let go and backed away from the bed, leaving Ty on the precipice without any stimulation to push him over. He nodded toward the door as he met Ty's eyes. "Go on. I'm betting Nick's fucking waiting for you with a nice warm bed."

Chapter 11

Zane woke with a splitting headache, cotton in his mouth, and a back that burned like he'd been dragged across gravel. He sat up carefully, waiting to see if his stomach would rebel. His head pounded, but thankfully nothing else protested.

He looked around the room with a growing frown. He didn't remember getting into bed. He didn't remember falling asleep. Pages and pages of old books were plastered to the walls of his room. The same room Ty had been in. The bed beside him was cold and obviously hadn't been slept in. His clothes were neatly folded and piled on the table, sitting beside a bottle of whiskey and an empty glass. Zane stared at the glass, a sinking feeling in the pit of his stomach finally making him nauseous.

The night came back to him in a jumble of words and smells, of demanding kisses and rough sex. The scratches on his back were from Ty. He remembered shouting at him. Telling him they were done. He remembered taking a swing at him. Had he thrown a chair at him? Oh Jesus, what else had he done? He knew he could be violent when he was drunk and angry. His only comfort was knowing Ty would have fought back, and from the bruise he could feel on his face, Ty had done just that.

He carefully got out of bed and shuffled to the table for his clothes. The glass wasn't empty after all. It was full of water, and two pills sat beside it. Zane's stomach lurched again. Ty had left ibuprofen for the hangover he knew Zane would have.

"Goddamn you, Ty."

He got dressed quickly, downed the pills, and very carefully avoided making eye contact with the label of that bottle. He could hear the murmur of voices downstairs, and he hustled to join them.

He stopped short at the head of the steps. He could hear Ava speaking, but she was speaking *over* the murmur of male voices.

She wasn't involved in the conversation the others were having. She sounded like she was on the phone. He strained to hear what she was saying, but he couldn't make out the words. She was speaking in hushed tones, and something about it pinged Zane's alarms. He searched all over the hallway, trying to figure out where her voice was coming from. He finally found a small air vent in the ceiling. Was she upstairs? Or was she down? Was there even an upstairs?

Zane waited a few more seconds, trying to make out anything she was saying. The conversation had stopped, though. Zane ran a hand through his messy hair and took a deep breath, trying to talk himself into going downstairs.

Flashes of last night were coming to him, and he wasn't sure he wanted to face Ty after what he'd said and done.

"We have to go on the offensive here," Nick said as Zane made his way down the steps. "It's the only thing they won't expect."

"How?" Owen asked.

"Ambush them," Ty said. His low growl sent shivers up Zane's spine. "Set up a meet with bait. Scout out a meeting place, take them out when they show themselves."

"Just like that?" Kelly asked.

"Just like that."

Zane moved around the table to one of the empty chairs. He sat opposite Ty and crossed his arms. Everyone was silent and tense, glancing at Zane as if they expected him to blow up like he had last night. Ty narrowed his eyes at him. Zane had to avert his gaze, examining the tabletop instead. In the periphery, he could see the remains of the barstool and table he had destroyed, neatly swept into a corner.

If Zane had to guess, Ty had stayed up all night cleaning up the mess.

Digger finally grunted to break the silence. "That's all great, in theory. But how do we contact them?"

Ty tore his attention away from Zane and gestured at Liam. "Can you get in touch with them?"

Liam gave a curt nod. "Sure, Grady. I'll just call them up and explain to them the situation. That I fucked off on their job because I found a pissed off Recon team instead of one easy target. And then

I'll ask them what hotel they're staying at. Just for shits and giggles. It's flawless."

"All right," Ty grunted.

"Flawless, I say."

"All right! Do you know how to get in touch with them or not?"

"You'll get yourselves killed."

"Do you really care if we do?" Nick asked.

"If you're going to bugger off and get yourselves killed, it might as well be me doing it so I can collect the bounties."

Zane snorted. "Maybe if you'd help us, we wouldn't be as likely to die."

"You're pretty, Garrett, but my heart ain't that soft. As soon as you lot are gone, I'm out the door."

"Always the hero," Ty muttered.

Ty and Liam shared a hateful glance before Ty pushed away from the table and stood.

"So, let me get this straight," Liam said, loud enough for his words to be aimed at Ty. "You want to call up the crew who wants you dead, tell them you're the man they're looking for, and then lure them into a kill zone?"

Ty met Liam's eyes. Then he sought out Zane for his opinion. Zane stared at him, feeling sick. Ty had looked to *him* still—not his former second-in-command, not one of the men he'd known and worked with for decades. Zane's mouth was too dry to even swallow.

"Yeah," Ty finally said.

"They think it's one man they're after. No way they'd expect six," Nick added.

"I have a bunch of ear buds, a few other things," Digger said. "Sniper rifle, a couple smoke canisters, Kevlar vest."

Kelly leaned forward. "A Kevlar vest?"

Digger nodded.

"You travel with full assault gear?" Ty asked.

"You don't?"

Everyone stared at him. Ty began to massage the bridge of his nose.

Liam stood and smoothed his hands over the front of his shirt, then walked away. "You're all criminally insane."

Nick rolled his head from side to side, working out the kinks. Then he rapped his knuckles on the table to draw everyone's attention. "If we're going to do this, we need to know how many they have and find a location good for the meet. And we need to do it fast. This place won't be safe for much longer."

Zane finally tore his eyes away from Ty. "Taking care of the cartel won't get us out of New Orleans any easier. It's the police we should really be worried about."

"What do you suggest?" Kelly asked.

"Call the local Bureau office. Tell them what's going on. Get backup. Get the cops off our asses. Make this something official instead of . . ." He waved at Digger. "Criminally insane."

"I'll lose my job," Ty said. He was pacing, head down and arms crossed.

Nick craned his head. "What? Why?"

"I'm not supposed to be here. I could compromise half a dozen cases just by showing my face."

"Why the hell didn't you say something before you came down here?"

"You told me you were in jail!"

Nick made a disgusted noise. He leaned his elbows on the table and began to massage his temples.

"Call Burns, he'll get you out of it," Zane said, surprised by the bitter sarcasm that came out.

Ty stared at him for a long moment, looking wounded, before he began to pace again. Zane forced himself to meet his eyes.

He was ashamed to admit he still wanted to see Ty burn. He'd hoped Ty would come at him again last night, that they'd go down swinging at each other. But he knew deep down that Ty wasn't that type of man. He wasn't going to chase Zane, or beg and plead with him. He wasn't going to hover over him and swat the drink from his hand every time he grasped it. He would let Zane walk away, he would let Zane self-destruct, he would internalize anything he was feeling, and become that same man he'd been the day they met. A hard, sarcastic shell. Zane could already see him building up those layers, and he hated Ty for it.

"So what'll it be, lads?" Liam asked. He winked at Zane.

Kelly and Digger both craned their heads to look at Ty as he paced. Owen was resting his head on the table.

Ty had his back to them, his head down. He really only had two choices. Get himself fired to keep everyone safe, or risk their lives, and a murder rap, to take down the cartel heavies.

"Hey, Six?" Digger said quietly.

"I'm not your goddamned Six anymore," Ty grunted. He began to pace again. "Call the Bureau," he finally said, his voice grim.

"Ty," Nick said carefully.

"My job or your lives? There's no choice there." Ty met Zane's eyes across the room. "Make the call. Tell them you're bringing in a Confidential Informant. That's what I was supposed to be if my cover was ever blown. Use the name Tyler Beaumont; that'll ping any dirty Feds, so we'll go in expecting a trap."

Zane didn't move. His heart was sinking and it was too painful to move right now, to look away from Ty's eyes. If Ty lost his job, what would they have between them? "You're willing to give it up?"

"It's not about being willing anymore, Garrett," Ty snarled. "Make the fucking call."

The curtain behind the bar wavered, and Ava pushed past it to lunge into the room. "They're coming!" she hissed. "My daddy and his boys. They're coming here. You have to leave!"

Chairs scraped on the wooden floors as everyone stood and scrambled toward the stairs to retrieve their gear.

"Are they coming for us?" Ty asked Ava.

She nodded. "Shine called me, told me they were on their way. They know you're here."

Ty cursed under his breath. He reached out and pulled her to him, hugging her tightly before he let her go and darted up the steps.

Only Zane remained, still sitting at the table, arms crossed. He stared at Ava until she turned to look at him.

"*You* called *him*. Didn't you?" Zane asked, voice pitched low so only she would hear it.

Her breath caught. She swallowed hard and inclined her head, squaring her shoulders. "Ty isn't the only one in town who's scared of that old bastard," she whispered. "But he's the only one I know who just might be able to kill him if he's given the chance."

"You're using him to get rid of your father. Risking his life."

"That's what men like him are for." She turned on her heel and ducked behind the curtain again.

Ty led them through the residential streets of Marigny, pushing them to reach the French Quarter, trying to stick to the Easter crowds, desperate to keep his mind on survival and off the fact that his heart was breaking every time he and Zane were close.

"If we can get to the cathedral, we can lose ourselves in the crowd until the parades start," he told them. Soon they neared Jackson Square and St. Louis Cathedral, one of the most recognizable landmarks in the French Quarter.

People milled around dressed in their Sunday best. Every woman wore a hat of some description, and many of the men did as well.

"Shit, you think we'll be killing people on Easter Sunday?" Nick muttered as they neared the cathedral.

Ty nodded and Nick cursed, then stopped briefly in front of the cathedral and made the sign of the cross as he faced the soaring spires. Kelly grabbed him by the arm and tugged him, peering up at the structure.

"Forgive him, baby Jesus, he knows not what he does," Kelly said, then pulled Nick with him.

"I'm going to Hell anyway, I don't know why I bother anymore."

Ty turned down Pirate's Alley, the narrow lane that skirted the cathedral, and then they cut through St. Anthony's garden, the tiny area behind the cathedral where four unmarked tombs rested. Ty leapt over one of the marble slabs. He could hear Nick complaining behind him.

"They're empty!" Ty called to him. All but one, but Ty didn't add that. He led them on through several turns until they reached Antoine's Restaurant. The place was obviously closed, but a crowd was building in the street.

"What is this?" Zane asked. He was a little out of breath, but then, so were the rest of them.

"The first parade starts here at nine or nine-thirty. We should be safe for a while."

"Despite the fact that the police station is two blocks that way?" Zane asked, pointing toward Royal Street.

"What are you, like a walking map?" Digger asked.

"Sort of, yeah," Zane answered.

"The station will be damn near empty right now," Ty told them. "There are three parades today, plus the Easter services. They're already out. The safest place is in a crowd, and this is all I got."

Nick patted him on the shoulder, nodding. "It'll do."

"Call the Feds," Owen said as they all parked themselves near the façade of the restaurant. They looked like wandering vagrants. Their clothes were unkempt, they were carrying bags on their backs, and Ty and Zane were both wearing hats they had taken from Murdoch's office before leaving.

Ty pulled out his phone and dialed the number for the local Bureau field office.

"Yes, I need to speak with Gregory Pike," Ty said as soon as the call was answered. He could feel the others forming a sort of barrier around him and Zane as they stood on the periphery of the parade crowd. He ducked his head to avoid being recognized or caught on any security feeds.

"I'm sorry, sir, Special Agent Pike no longer works here."

"Shit," Ty hissed. He put the phone to his chest and closed his eyes, trying to think. Pike had been the handler for all UC cases before Katrina hit. He'd been a solid, trustworthy local, one who'd proven impervious to bribes or scandal. His replacement could be anyone, and Ty didn't trust just anyone. He cleared his throat and brought the phone back up. "I need to speak with his replacement, then."

"One moment."

Nick shook his head urgently. "Replacement?"

"I know. I don't think we can trust him," Ty whispered.

Zane extended his hand. "How do you know?"

"This is New Orleans, Zane, you don't trust anyone. But if I hear his name, I might know him."

"Hang up," Nick hissed.

Kelly gripped Nick's shoulder and shook his head. "This is the only avenue that doesn't end bloody. We'll go in careful, bug out if he doesn't feel right."

Ty glanced around the faces staring at him and noticed one missing. "Where'd Liam go?"

The others searched around, but Liam Bell was nowhere to be found.

"He bailed," Zane said. He sounded surprised.

Ty gritted his teeth. "We consider him hostile now."

"Does that mean I get to shoot him?" Nick asked.

"Yes."

Owen cursed. "We can't fight a three-front war with a few of Digger's toys and four guns."

Zane shook his head. "We can't fight one front if we don't get help."

Saint Louis Cemetery #1 on Basin Street was the oldest cemetery in New Orleans. It wasn't far from where the parade started. The walk was excruciating for Zane. Ty wouldn't make eye contact with him, wouldn't even glance in his general direction. Zane wasn't sure which of them should be apologizing or if there was even anything left to say after last night. Ty had crossed a line, there was no question of that. But last night, Zane had crossed one too.

He trailed along, silent as Ty told them a little of the history of the cemetery so they'd be familiar with the terrain.

The raised tombs were due in part to the Spanish and French traditions of the original New Orleanians, but also served as a solution to the fact that New Orleans was below sea level. Solid land was at a premium even in the 1700s, and using it to bury the dead was just bad business. So the iconic aboveground cemeteries of New Orleans were pieced together over the centuries. Ty told them they would have lots of cover, but to be careful about taking blind turns, as they might wind up smacking straight into an abandoned vault that had sunk half into the ground.

There were three gated entrances into the cemetery, only one of which stayed open. It was otherwise surrounded by high walls. Not a fortress by any means, but an excellent place for such a meeting. The maze inside would offer cover, and the limited points of egress would make it easy to spot anyone who shouldn't be there.

As the parade inched down Bourbon, they began to split off. Ty was to double-time it to the north and circle back, heading down Rampart and then cutting through Louis Armstrong Park. He would approach Basin Street Station, a visitor center with a roof terrace that was the perfect place to put a sniper. He'd secure a position up there and remain until it was clear. He carried Liam's British-made AWS suppressed sniper rifle with folding action in a nondescript violin case he'd stolen from La Fée Verte.

Owen and Digger were to enter the cemetery and loiter on the south side to prevent entry, while Nick and Kelly were to guard the back gate from outside the cemetery.

Zane was left to head straight down St. Louis Street and approach the cemetery at its main entrance.

The ear buds Digger had provided were dependent on small wireless radios, and as long as the radio was within a few yards of the ear bud, they would work. Zane kept his in his pocket. They had a limited range, but Zane could still hear the others after they all went their separate ways. Ty remained silent for several minutes, his harsh breathing as he ran the only evidence that his ear bud worked at all. Then his breathing evened out and he began to whistle a tune. Zane slowed his pace, a feeling of dread coming over him. When Ty whistled, it never boded well.

The street in front of the cemetery's main entrance was crowded with parked cars and several horse-drawn carriages. Zane hung back, loitering and strolling up and down the street for nearly an hour as he observed the area. The others were doing the same, reporting in occasionally. Ty had made his way to his roost somehow, and since Zane hadn't heard him trying to charm any employees, his guess was Ty had just snuck up there.

"I got a Fed," Ty finally whispered in Zane's ear. "Coming up on Garrett now."

Zane watched a thin man in a dark suit step out of a black Tahoe that he'd parked illegally along the street, then head straight for the cemetery entrance as he buttoned his suit jacket.

"Got him," Zane said under his breath. "Anyone following?"

"It's clear back here," Nick said.

"Got a vehicle parked on this side," Owen reported. "Some sort of touring van."

"Go on your count, Garrett," Ty murmured.

Zane waited a few more minutes, then crossed the street at an angle, standing in the grassy median and shielding his eyes from the sun. The Basin Street Station building was to his right. It was pale yellow with black iron workings around the top terrace. That was where Ty had set up. It was impossible to see him, though; the sun sat right behind him. Behind the enclosed walls of the cemetery, Zane could see the uneven structures of tombs and tiny chapels. Stone angels wept. Brick faltered to the hands of time and unstable earth.

Zane took a moment to steady himself, and then crossed to the other side of the street. The agent saw him coming and nodded at him, then turned, following a small tour group into the cemetery and breaking off to the right. Ty had told the FBI contact to meet them in the front of the cemetery.

"He's heading in. It's a trap," Ty said in Zane's ear. "Everybody bug out."

"Negative," Zane said, and he followed the man into the cemetery.

"Dammit, Garrett, the others can't cover you in there!" Ty shouted.

Zane nodded. He'd spent most of his time undercover alone; he was more used to taking these types of risks than Ty was. And he had every confidence that Ty's sniper rifle would cover him just fine.

Zane trailed through the maze of tombs, following the directions Ty whispered in his ear. He headed to the back where Ty said the Protestant section would be. It was a grassy area, devoid of vaults and mostly clear. It took Zane many twists and turns, and several dead ends with Ty's voice in his ear telling him which way to go, before he found it.

The agent was sitting on an iron bench, waiting for him. He was possibly the most Federal-looking FBI agent Zane had ever seen:

black suit, loafers, sunglasses, and a thick black tie. He'd unbuttoned his jacket and his shoulder holster was partially visible, and his pants leg rode up to reveal his backup holster and weapon. A field agent he was not.

Zane sighed and stepped out of the row of tombs he'd cut through. The man straightened when he caught sight of Zane, and he stood, buttoning his jacket.

"Special Agent Howard?" Zane asked.

"That's right. Are you Garrett?"

Zane nodded.

"Where's your CI?"

"My CI?"

"You said you were bringing in a CI. A Tyler Beaumont."

"Oh, yeah. Yeah, he's the one with that little red dot on your chest," Zane said, pointing to Howard's tie.

Howard looked down and jerked when he saw the laser sight dancing on his tie. His eyes were wide and scared when they met Zane's. He reached for his gun, but his buttoned suit impeded him, so he brought his wrist to his mouth and ducked, as if that would save him from Ty's sniper rifle.

"They're onto us! They came armed!" he shouted to whoever was on the other end of his radio.

Zane cursed and turned to duck behind the nearest row of tombs. The telltale pops of a suppressed weapon echoed in the humidity. Marble chips flew as the rounds hit next to Zane's head. He ducked and weaved left, covering his head. He could hear the others in his ear bud. None of them sounded panicked. In fact, Ty's voice came over the frequency as calm as if he were ordering a sandwich at the local deli. Zane had heard more emotion from Ty as he watched a football game.

"Got five going over the northeast wall," Ty said in Zane's ear.

"Which one's northeast?" Owen shouted.

"Not yours. Garrett's hemmed in."

"Aye aye, we're going in," Nick growled. More suppressed pops came from the wall, followed by the boom of Nick's weapon.

"Five more through the main entrance," Ty murmured. "These aren't locals. Get out."

Shots fired from the roof. Zane peered around the tomb to see Special Agent Howard scrabbling for cover. Bullets hit at his feet, kicking up earth and grass, making him dance back and forth. Ty was playing with him, pinning him down.

Tourists screamed in the distance. Horses whinnied. Sirens began to blare from the traffic station down the street. Zane lunged from his hiding spot and ran low, angling toward Howard, where he was trapped in the open by Ty's covering fire. A bullet whizzed past his arm, so close it burned.

"Shit. Sorry," Ty said in his ear.

"Watch it!" Zane snarled. He reached Howard and grabbed him by the scruff of his neck, jerking him to his feet and pulling him toward the tombs. He saw Nick and Kelly scaling the gate on the back wall.

When he reached cover, Zane slammed Howard to the ground and held his gun to the man's nose. He patted him down, taking all his weapons, his badge, and his car keys.

"Six, you got cops on your position in three," Nick shouted.

Ty ignored the warning and fired more shots. Someone in the cemetery screamed.

"Two down. And a half. Seven live. Get your asses out of there!" Ty ordered. "Garrett, quit dancing with him and move!"

Zane didn't release the man, instead gripping him hard by his collar and forcing him along with him.

"It's too hot up here, I'm gone," Ty said. "Clear out!"

Shots continued to echo through the cemetery, but the sniper rifle fell silent.

Zane craned his head to look up at the roof as he dragged Howard through the maze of vaults and tombs. Ty had finally abandoned his post, but Zane didn't know how he planned to get out of that building now that all hell had broken loose.

There was more gunfire from the back of the cemetery. Zane couldn't tell if Sidewinder was chasing the unfriendlies or if they were now being chased. Agent Howard fell to his knees, whimpering and tugging at Zane's hand.

"Get up!" Zane shouted. He yanked him hard, slamming him against the crumbling exposed brick of an ancient vault. He shoved his gun under Howard's chin. "Who'd you call?"

Howard began blubbering. Zane could barely make out his words. He yanked the ear bud from his ear to be rid of the chatter and shoved the gun harder against Howard's neck. "Shut your damn mouth."

Howard's sniveling cut off with a gulp. "Please don't kill me," he whispered. "I have a family."

Zane bared his teeth. "I don't care. Who did you call?"

"Police commander. Gaudet."

"This isn't cop firepower; who else is involved?"

"He—he said he had help. Someone new in town."

"Names."

Howard jerked his head from side to side. He was trembling. "Spanish. I don't know."

"Colombian?"

"I don't know! Please God, don't hurt me."

Zane released him. He peered over the vault. The gunfire continued. He stuck the ear bud back in, only to be greeted by garbled shouts and echoes of shots.

He stepped away from Howard and pointed the gun at the man's leg.

"Oh, God no!"

"This is your final lesson in loyalty," Zane growled. He put a bullet in the man's kneecap and darted away.

"Where the hell did they get all this firepower?" Nick shouted as he and Kelly ducked behind a large marble vault. Bullets thwapped into the ground around them, ricocheting off marble and stone. Nick's face was bleeding and he could feel a shard of something stuck just below his eye. His sunglasses had probably saved his vision.

"Not cops!" Ty yelled through the static in Nick's ear. He was breathing hard, probably running.

"Cartel hitters," Zane hissed. "Howard said Gaudet called them in."

"So wait, the cartel and the cops are working together?" Owen asked. "How's that fair?"

"Does it matter?" Kelly shouted. "Sound the retreat, baby, let's get our happy asses out of here!" He reached to Nick's face and yanked the piece of shrapnel out. Nick cussed him up and down and held his hand to the wound.

Owen's voice came through. "Six?"

Ty's response was barely audible.

"Rabbit hole," Kelly muttered at Nick's side. He was reloading his gun, crouched as low as he could get. If Ty'd gone down the rabbit hole, there was no one to offer cover fire.

"Get the hell out of here," Zane ordered. "Everybody out!"

"Should've put a guard on the roost," Digger said. "Goddamn you Liam Bell!"

Nick couldn't make out where any of the others were. They'd been outnumbered and overpowered, chased into the maze of tombs within the cemetery. It encompassed an entire block, filled with crumbling sidewalks, winding alleyways too small to fit a grown man through, and towering stonework that abruptly cut off pathways and created kill boxes with no escape. Without Ty in the sniper's roost to cover them or give them enemy positions, they were in the dark.

"I'm almost at the front entrance," Zane said on the ear bud. "Make your way here, I'll cover you."

Nick patted Kelly's knee, pointing toward the direction of the main entrance. Kelly nodded and they both darted off down the closest lane.

Shots chased them.

"Free drinks! Fireworks!" Ty shouted at the top of his lungs. His signal was stronger, meaning he'd escaped the Basin Street building somehow. Nick snorted. Ty and the cockroaches. He could imagine him running into a crowd of Easter Sunday churchgoers, tourists, and parade marchers, trying to create a distraction and lure people out of harm's way. "Free drinks inside!"

Out of the corner of his eye, Nick saw a man climb on top of a touring van parked on a side street. He crouched on the roof and tossed something into the cemetery. An earsplitting boom and a flash followed. As he and Kelly darted between tombs and dodged bullets and shrapnel, Nick got a closer look at the man. Liam Bell.

"Oh shit," he hissed.

"Is he on our side?" Kelly called.

"I don't care! Run!"

Smoke began to billow from the back of the cemetery. Liam tossed two more canisters, closer to their own position. Nick and Kelly skidded to a stop. Nick covered his ears and squeezed his eyes closed as the flashbangs went off.

They wasted precious seconds trying to shake off the concussive blast. Nick could hear screams of pain and anger. He peeked around the corner of the tomb that shielded them, only to come face-to-face with a man who was doing the same thing. Nick rolled away as the man brought his gun up and fired.

"Go!" he yelled, pushing at Kelly's arm.

They sprinted down the lane, catching glimpses through the narrow alleys of two men racing down the opposite lane. When they reached a widened intersection, Nick raised his weapon, preparing to fire as their pursuers rounded the corner.

But Zane was there, flattened against the tomb wall, knives in his hands. When the two assassins reached the corner of the tomb, he stepped out and swept a hand across one man's neck. Blood spurted as Zane turned gracefully and shoved a knife into the other man's side. He jerked it up, under the body armor, under the ribs. He stepped back, covered in blood as both men fell to the ground, dead or dying.

Nick and Kelly gaped at him as he twirled both knives over his fingers and shoved them back into their sheaths.

"Nice," Kelly grunted.

Zane shrugged and bent to gather the weapons off the dead bodies. He pointed toward the entrance, a mere ten yards away.

Nick and Kelly stayed low and close, watching each other's backs as Zane brought up the rear, scurrying from tomb to tomb for cover. Owen and Digger appeared from the other side. The smoke bombs Liam had thrown seemed to have bought them enough time to clear the cemetery. Owen and Digger darted out, then took up posts behind the walls to cover their last few yards.

Nick was almost to the open gate when something thumped into him from behind. The report of the shot reached his ears a split-second later. He was thrown forward. More bullets hit the walls around him.

"He's hit, he's hit!" Owen cried, the voice coming both from nearby and inside Nick's ear. "Doc!"

"Who's hit?" Ty asked, voice suddenly panicked.

No one answered him.

Nick pushed at the ground, but the weight on top of him was too much. He turned his head. Kelly had fallen into him when the bullet hit. Owen fell to his knees beside Nick's face. They lifted Kelly off him and Nick pushed up, scrabbling the rest of the way out of the cemetery.

They hit open ground and ran, rushing into traffic on Rampart Street. Nick and Zane fell back to cover them as Owen and Digger carried Kelly between them. They faltered in the large grassy median and took cover behind a horse and carriage that had been abandoned by its driver.

Crowds of people were running to and fro, panicked and confused.

"Who's hit?" Ty demanded, his voice breaking.

"We're in the median," Zane said, breathless. "Kelly's down."

"Doc," Digger said as he put a hand on Kelly's face.

Kelly coughed and took in a loud, shivering breath. Owen knelt, cradling Kelly's head. Nick fell to his knees beside him and began trying to find the wound through all the blood.

Zane remained standing, keeping guard and watching out of the corner of his eye.

Mere seconds passed before Ty joined them. He dove to the ground beside Kelly, jostling Nick as he tried to cut away the bloody clothing. "Where's he hit?"

"I don't know, I can't find it," Nick stuttered.

"Doc, stay with me now," Digger pleaded. He patted Kelly's cheek. Kelly's eyes fluttered open. They all leaned over him. Digger sounded like a frightened child. "What do we do, Doc?"

Kelly tried to speak. Blood began to trickle out of the side of his mouth.

Ty grabbed Owen's shirt and shook him. "Get a car."

Owen nodded and pushed up, darting into traffic to commandeer a vehicle. They were mere blocks from the hospital. Zane fired into the cemetery, keeping their opponents at bay.

Kelly struggled to take another breath, but it only produced more blood. Digger held onto his hand. Nick's fingers trembled as he searched for an exit wound.

Ty leaned over and ran a bloody hand through Kelly's hair. "Steady now," he whispered.

Kelly nodded and closed his eyes.

Zane shot at the cemetery again. Return fire hit the carriage, and the horse panicked, pulling away and taking their cover with it.

Ty and Nick moved together, their backs to the cemetery so their bodies shielded Kelly's. Ty's voice shook as he whispered, "Yea, though I walk through the valley of the shadow of death, I will fear no evil—"

Kelly picked up when Ty's voice broke, his words a struggle. "For thou art with me. And thou carry a big-ass stick."

Ty hunched over him and winced as a bullet struck nearby. Tears trailed down his cheeks and he pressed his forehead to Kelly's. Nick realized he had tears streaming down his own face.

Screeching wheels and Owen's urgent shout forced Nick to tear his eyes away. He glanced over his shoulder to see Owen waving from the driver's side of a big yellow sedan.

"On three," Ty said. "Zane! Help us!"

Zane hustled over to help lift Kelly, and they carried him to the vehicle, still taking sporadic fire from the cemetery. Digger ducked into the backseat and pulled Kelly in by his shoulders. Nick spotted Liam, then, laying down covering fire with Zane to keep both the cartel thugs and the police at bay. Liam ducked into the front seat, still returning fire. Ty pushed Nick's shoulder, forcing him to get in next. Nick clambered into the back, kneeling on the floor between the front seats and holding Kelly's hand.

"Get in!" Ty shouted, shoving Zane by the shoulder.

Zane crawled in behind Nick, facing backward to keep from jostling Kelly's sprawled body. "What are you doing, Ty?"

"He's got to have time," Ty grunted as he slammed the door in Zane's face. "Go."

"No, wait! Ty!"

"Grady! Goddamnit!" Nick shouted.

Ty banged on the roof of the car and shouted at Owen. "Go!"

Owen gunned the engine and sped off. Nick and Zane watched through the window as Ty turned and fired a few shots over the heads of the police with his pistol, then sprinted off toward the French Quarter.

Chapter 12

Ty ran as fast as he could down the middle of the street, heading for Bourbon or Royal and what he prayed would be the parade crowd. He knew he had fifteen seconds, maybe thirty, before anyone pursued. They'd be too worried about him taking up a position somewhere and gunning them down. But that was all the leeway he'd have before he was caught, and he had to make it count.

He'd only managed one city block before someone shouted behind him. But they couldn't fire at him, not with the pedestrian traffic so close.

A bullet pinged off the road next to his feet.

Fuck! Ty covered his head and hunched his shoulders, but he kept running.

They were firing directly into the pedestrian areas of the French Quarter, directly into that parade crowd. The streets were lined with homes and businesses. People who'd been innocently strolling along were now screaming and taking cover wherever they could find it. These weren't local cops chasing him down. There would be no talking his way around an interrogation until the cavalry arrived. He was running for his life, not a few extra minutes.

He *had* to reach Canal Street, toward the business district and, if his luck held, Harrah's Casino.

The casino would have facial recognition software covering the floors, everyone knew that, and the cartel thugs wouldn't risk being identified by it. It was a solid mile away, though.

A chain-link fence appeared on his left, surrounding a rare outlying vacant lot, and he sprinted for it. More shots chased him, busting the rear window of a car parked along the road and pinging off a lamppost just inches from Ty's head.

"Son of a bitch!"

Ty vaulted the flimsy fence, catching the top of it and taking it down with him as he went over. He hit grass and gravel and rolled, regaining his feet but losing precious seconds. He dug for the other side of the lot where a higher, sturdier fence had been erected. He leapt at the brick wall and kicked off it to clear the fence like a high jumper, then hit the ground running. A bullet sprayed brick dust where his foot had been and men shouted in Spanish from the far corner of the building.

Ty found himself in the interior of a city block, weaving between trash bins, parked cars, bicycles, and buildings. He slowed at a small courtyard, his heart hammering as he realized he may have hemmed himself in. He could hear his pursuers clambering over the fence.

He looked up. He could use the iron stairs of the apartment building and maybe reach the roof with a short climb, but he'd be an easy target for far too long. And if he by some miracle made it up there without getting shot, he'd still have the dilemma of being stuck on a fucking roof.

There was nowhere to hide that he wouldn't be found eventually. He could kick down someone's door, hope they had windows or a door that faced the street, and risk whatever homeowner he barged in on being shot behind him. Or beating him with a curling iron.

He grabbed the gun at the small of his back. He had twelve shots left in the magazine, and a spare with fifteen more strapped to his ankle. If he had to make a last stand in this dead-end courtyard, he would make it a bloody one.

He ran for a large green dumpster in the far corner of the courtyard, intending to use it and the trash inside as cover. But as he rounded the dumpster, he found a gap between the buildings. It was narrow, hidden by the layout of the old structures, and it appeared to lead to a dead end. Ty headed down it anyway, praying the darkness was really another gap between buildings rather than mere shadow.

He heard angry voices behind him.

"¿Ha donde se fue este cabron?"

"No esta aqui."

"No le crecio alas. Buscale!"

Ty knew enough to understand the last word: Find him.

He moved faster, trying to stay silent as he reached the end of the alley. His gamble paid off, and he took a hard right down another tight alleyway that led to another seam between buildings. It went off to the left, even narrower than the first two. Ty had to turn sideways to get through it. It ended with a wooden fence, and after a few hard kicks, Ty broke through into a small, private courtyard filled with plants and garden decorations, colorful tile and antique string lights overhead. And on the far side was an alleyway to the street. Ty could see people walking past.

The alley was blocked at the street end by a tall iron gate topped with broken pieces of colored glass, glinting in the sunlight. But it sure as hell looked better than dying in a hail of bullets.

Ty tucked his gun back into his belt and darted across the courtyard.

He dodged creeping vines and salvaged antiques as he ran through the passage, and when he reached the end, he jumped for the gate, grabbing onto the iron with his hands and pushing with his feet. He scaled the gate as wide-eyed tourists and drunk college kids gaped at him from the other side. A frat boy handed his plastic cup to his friend and brought out a phone to begin recording. A horse and carriage clopped along with a young family in tow.

As Ty reached the top of the gate, where the shards of glass were his last obstacle to freedom, he heard shouting in the courtyard behind him.

He put a foot on the brick beside him and pressed his shoulder into the opposite wall, walking his feet up the side of the wall until he was high enough to simply twist his body into a flip and free-fall over the gate.

He landed too hard and rolled into the street, finding himself at the mercy of a very large white horse that tossed its head and snorted.

Ty scrambled to his feet, backing away from the animal as people broke into excited murmurs around him. He glanced back down the alleyway, edging out of sight behind the horse just as men appeared in the shadows through the wrecked wooden gate.

"That is so going on YouTube!" the guy with the phone cried.

Ty climbed onto the carriage.

"Hey!" the driver started, but Ty put a finger to his lips and showed the man his gun.

He snatched the man's top hat, then placed it on his head, slid off the carriage, and hustled to the intersection, hoping to blend in with the crowd.

As he rounded the corner, a large man stepped in front of him. Shine Gaudet. The man Ty suspected of killing Murdoch. The man who'd picked a girl out of a crowd and choked the life out of her because she resembled his sister. He was 6'8" with arms the size of river logs. Ty had once playfully sparred with him, and he'd been playfully tossed across the room and bruised three ribs in the process.

"Well if it ain't Tyler Beaumont," Shine drawled. He smirked.

Ty took a step back. "Let's be calm about this, bubba."

Shine raised his fist, displaying his knuckles to Ty. His attention shifted from Ty to his fist with a widening smile, then he opened his hand, turning his palm up to display a handful of gray dust. With one big puff, he blew the dust into Ty's face.

Ty held his breath and kept his eyes closed. He could hear Shine laughing, a deep rumbling sound that began to fade into the distance as Ty tried to wipe the dust away with his sleeve. His knees hit the pavement, and his world faded to nothing before the rest of his body could contact the ground.

Zane bulled his way through the electronic door almost before the nurse had it open. He didn't bother with appearances as he jogged down the hall.

Everyone had tumbled out of the stolen sedan at the emergency entrance, and Zane had rolled over the console to get to the front seat. He and Liam had then peeled away in the car, trying to lead any pursuers away from the others. They'd ditched the car several blocks away, and Zane had been hard-pressed to keep up with Liam as they'd raced back toward the hospital. They hadn't had a chance to speak a word, but Zane had infinite questions for the man.

When he rounded the corner, Zane saw their companions loitering around one of the emergency bays near a closed curtain. His heart sped up, making him dizzy as he neared them.

Digger was pacing in front of the curtain, fingers laced at the back of his head. The other two were sitting, both of them covering their faces with their hands. All three men were bloody. Bloody gauze littered the floors. Even the curtain had a bloody streak on the edge where someone had grabbed it.

Zane was nearly hyperventilating as he approached. Liam's breaths were harsh and loud behind him.

Nick looked up at the sound of their approach. His shirtfront was soaked red, his eyes gray, his face streaked with blood and tears. He had a butterfly bandage on his cheek.

Zane slowed, dreading what he might find.

"Kelly?" Zane asked hesitantly.

Nick shook his head, then lowered it again and covered his face in both hands.

"They took him into surgery," Owen managed to say. "We haven't heard anything."

Zane breathed a sigh of relief. Surgery at least meant he wasn't dead when they'd carried him in.

"Lads, I hate to be insensitive," Liam said, peering over his shoulder at the nurse's station. "But we have about five seconds to clear our arses out of here."

"Fuck you, I'm not leaving him," Digger growled.

"I know—"

"I said I'm not fucking leaving him!" Digger grabbed Liam by his leather jacket, shaking him. "Where the fuck were you when we needed you?"

"Take your hands off the coat," Liam said, voice calm. His eyes sparked, though, and even Zane recognized that he'd reached a dangerous point. He was no longer amused.

Digger sneered but released him with a final shove.

"I understand your desire to stay, I really do," Liam continued, his voice low and soothing. "But you've done all you can for the doc, you have to look now to the other team member we lost out there."

Owen stood and shook his head. "He's not any teammate of yours."

"Then why am I the only one wondering how long he'll survive without help?"

Zane swiped a hand over his face. "He got away from them."

"And you know that how?" Liam asked.

"Because I know Ty. You can't trap a cockroach."

Liam snorted. "But you can kill one if you stomp it hard enough."

"He got away. He'll go to ground," Zane insisted. "He won't let himself hang in the wind too long."

"Regardless of what Ty is doing or how capable he might be of slipping through the cracks, Liam's right," Nick said. "We need to clear out of here before we're found. All that blood . . . they'll know one of us was hit, they'll be here looking soon enough."

"What about Kelly? We can't leave him behind. Unprotected?" Owen asked.

"He's safer here than he was out there."

Nick stood, and Owen and Digger closed ranks behind him, facing Liam and Zane. Zane couldn't help but admire the way Sidewinder seemed to come together when they needed to. He had never worked as part of a team before Ty, preferring to go at things solo even when he'd been a child. Even Becky had been more of a confidante, a support system, something to fight *for* instead of with. She'd been a way to forget life's troubles rather than an ally to take them on, and Zane had been happy with that arrangement. She had been exactly what he'd needed at that point in his life. But he had changed. Life had changed. And he had never had someone to face the world beside him, not until Ty.

Zane's stomach lurched at the thought. Ty wasn't the happy escape Becky had been for him. He might never offer Zane the warmth and light Becky once had, but Zane knew Ty would be there in the dark. In the last twenty-four hours, Zane had lost sight of that, blinded by the anger.

"Where would he go?" Liam asked as he led them through the hallways, looking for a back exit.

"You're asking us to think like Ty?" Owen snorted. "I don't think that's possible; my brain isn't powered by squirrels on treadmills."

Nick shook his head, unbuttoning his bloody shirt as he walked. He shrugged out of it and dumped it into a hamper in the hallway. The others followed suit, discarding as much of their bloody clothes as they could in various nooks and crannies they passed on their way out.

"He'd go where they'd least expect," Nick said.

"Somewhere public?" Digger asked.

"The hotel, maybe. The rooms are still under your name, they can't be traced to Ty or Garrett," Owen said to Nick.

"That's how they found him to start with," Nick growled. "He's familiar with this city, there's no telling what kind of places he knows."

Zane inhaled sharply. "Ava."

Nick looked over his shoulder at Zane, eyebrows raised. "Maybe so. If he didn't go back there for help, maybe she'll know where he would go."

"He doesn't know Ava's the one who called her father."

Nick stopped short, and Zane almost barreled into him. "Wait, she what?"

Zane huffed. "She's the one who called her father. She hoped Ty would go up against him and take him out."

"That chick's all wrong, man," Digger whispered.

The change that came over Nick O'Flaherty was almost frightening. His face hardened, his eyes going a deep, striking green when he lowered his head. He glanced at Owen and Digger, and both men nodded at some unspoken communication.

Nick headed off toward the exit, Owen and Digger on his heels.

"Oh dear," Liam said with a sigh.

"What the hell just happened?" Zane asked.

"You flipped the wrong switch in that one. I think we've just landed the job of white knight," Liam grumbled. He started after them at a jog. "Let's go save the girl from the rabid Yank Marines."

They double-timed it from the hospital, skirting the edges of the confusion and panic that was now the French Quarter, and headed for Marigny and Frenchmen Street. Nick kept looking down each street as they ran by, both hoping to see signs of Ty's passing and praying he didn't. The chaos meant the pursuit had been hard and fast, and it seemed to have encompassed two or three blocks.

Ty had made a worthy chase of it, at least.

Nick hoped the calm of the latter regions meant that Ty had gotten away and blended into the scenery, rather than getting caught.

"What's the reach on these ear buds?" Zane asked. He refused to slow down, and for once Nick was glad for the man's stubbornness.

"You got to be in a mile range of the hand unit," Digger answered. "If Ty's got his unit on him, we should be able to hear him and he should be able to hear us."

"So we can't hear him, that means he dropped his radio?" Owen asked.

"Or his ear bud. Or he went into the drink. Or he's underground. Or he's behind lots of concrete. Or somewhere the signal's getting jacked."

"Digger!"

"What? They ain't military grade. Damn."

"Have any of you actually tried contacting him?" Liam asked.

They had to stop at Esplanade to wait for the heavy traffic. Nick put a finger to his ear and pulled the hand unit out, holding it up for the best reception he could give it. "Grady?"

They all waited, breathing shallowly to better hear.

All Nick received was the buzzing of radio silence in his ear.

"Maybe he's hiding," Zane said. "Maybe he can't talk."

"Yes, we'll go with that," Liam said, sarcasm dripping from his words.

Nick stared at him for a long moment, and when Liam met his eyes, Nick hit him. Liam tumbled to the sidewalk as everyone else watched impassively.

Digger patted Nick's shoulder. "Me too, brother."

Liam sat up and wiped a hand over his mouth. "Do you feel better?"

"A little," Nick said. The signal changed and they hustled across the street after Zane helped Liam to his feet.

When they reached La Fée Verte, the bar was closed down. Zane banged on the door and shouted for Ava to open it, but they got no response.

"The fucking place has no ground floor windows," Owen said as they all examined the façade of the building for any point of entry.

"It's all right, lads, daddy's here," Liam drawled. He stepped up to the door, digging in the backpack he was carrying.

"What are you doing?" Nick asked.

"Blowing your mind, love." Liam pulled out two small squares of off-white clay.

"Is that C4?" Zane asked.

"PE4, thank you very much." Liam molded the plastic explosive against the hinges of the door.

"You don't really understand going under the radar, do you?" Nick grumbled.

"You Recon boys sneak under the radar," Liam said as he set the charges. "The Special Air Service gets shit done."

Owen raised an eyebrow at Nick. "If you want to hit him again, I'll hold him down."

"Maybe later," Nick said. They all moved away and threw themselves against the wall.

Liam lit the charges and then hustled down the wall, flattening himself at Zane's side. The blast was small, and the sound was almost entirely covered by the racket of the Easter festivities and the live bands warming up nearby.

Zane was at the door before the smoke even cleared, kicking it off its destroyed hinges.

"You're welcome!" Liam called after him. "Good lord, to watch him you'd think Ty gave reward blowjobs for being rescued."

They streamed into the bar one after the other, clearing the room. Zane had already found Ava by the time Nick entered, grabbing her before she could barricade herself in the office. Zane held her around the waist as she struggled.

Nick stalked up to her and grabbed her chin, forcing her to look at him.

"Where are they?"

She was breathing hard, gritting her teeth. "I don't know."

"But you know they have him."

"I didn't want Ty hurt."

"That why you threw a butcher knife at him when he left before?" Zane growled in her ear.

"Says the man who threw him into a table," she snarled. She was still meeting Nick's eyes. "I didn't know Daddy had help. I swear. I thought you boys could take him."

"Doc's in the hospital dying," Nick sneered. "And you're sorry."

Her eyes widened.

Liam came up behind Nick and patted him on the shoulder, pulling at him gently. Nick released her and backed away before he was tempted to really hurt her. Then Liam reached out to pat Zane's arm. "Let her go," he said, his voice oddly soothing.

Zane lifted his chin stubbornly, but he did. Liam took her by the hand and led her to one of the barstools nearby. He sat her down and cupped her face.

"We need your help, dear, or Ty's days are up."

She glared at him for a few breathless seconds and then nodded.

"Where would he go if he was being chased?"

"Harrah's. He always told me, if I got in trouble, to get to the casino. Something about facial recognition. Every bad in town knows they have it, they won't risk getting swiped by it."

Liam nodded at Zane and Nick. That was a plan that sounded decidedly Ty-like.

"Now," Liam continued, his voice still low and almost seductive. "If your father were to get his hands on Tyler, where would he take him?"

"He wouldn't take him anywhere. He'd kill him right away."

Liam tutted, still looking her in the eye. "I don't believe so. Ty told us your father tried to set him up for murder first. He wanted him in his jail, not dead. He wanted to speak to him before he killed him. Think hard."

Ava shook her head almost defiantly.

"Somewhere underground maybe?" Owen asked.

"There's no underground in New Orleans," Zane growled. "It's all water."

"He'd take him somewhere no one would hear him scream," Liam whispered to Ava.

She nodded, closing her eyes. "The Lower Ninth Ward. He'd take him there."

Liam snapped his fingers at Digger. "You know where that is?"

"Yeah. Area got flooded by Katrina when the levees broke. There's whole blocks of wrecked houses just sitting there empty. It's not too far."

Liam nodded, then turned and backhanded Ava off the stool.

The others jumped, and Owen shouted in protest. Even Zane moved to intercede, but Ava remained on the floor, unconscious.

"What the hell?" Nick cried.

Liam shrugged and poked her with the toe of his boot. "Now we have leverage."

"What if Gaudet doesn't have him?" Nick gritted out.

Liam pursed his lips, then shrugged again. "Then that was for the doc."

Chapter 13

"You're either real stupid or real brave."

Ty shook his head. The world was spinning. He couldn't feel the ground under his feet.

"Why are you back in town, Tyler?"

Ty looked up at Commander Louis Gaudet. "Do you . . . do you ever become just very aware of your ears? They're . . . right there on your head."

"Is he high?"

"Probably," Shine answered.

Gaudet's voice came from right in front of Ty's face. "Is that some sort of code, boy? You took his little radio away, didn't you?"

"Yes, sir," Shine drawled. He pointed to a pile of Ty's effects in the corner of the room.

"Even so, check him for a wire."

The big man grabbed Ty's shirt and yanked it, pulling the buttons from their threads. Rough hands patted him down. Ty's head fell forward. He couldn't seem to make the spinning or the buzzing stop.

Fingers gripped his hair and yanked his head back. A callused hand smacked his face.

"Wake up, damn it!"

Ty forced his eyes open and inhaled noisily. Louis Gaudet peered at him. His face wobbled and Ty tried to blink the apparition away.

"What the hell is in that powder?" Ty asked.

"Couple things. Valerian root. Poppy dust. Bones of a pure white cat."

"That's messed up, man," Ty mumbled. "You're messed up."

He looked Shine up and down. The man had gained some muscle in the last five years, if that was possible. Ty's eyes landed on a cylinder shape in Shine's pocket. It was either a tube of his fucked-up hoodoo dust, or it was one of Ty's EpiPens from the room above the bar. Zane had dumped them out, and Ty hadn't been able to find them all in his haste to pack up that morning. That meant Shine had been in that room, which meant Ava had either given them up or been forced to talk.

Ty closed his eyes. "How much poppy dust?"

Shine laughed, and a moment later a bucket of water hit Ty's face. He gasped, trying not to hyperventilate as the icy water trailed down his arms to drip off the ropes that bound his hands.

"Why are you back in town, Tyler?" Gaudet asked.

Ty worked hard to swallow. He shook his head. "You wouldn't believe me."

"Try us, son. We got all day and all night to get the real story from you." He held up a syringe and waved it for Ty to see. "We can make it a quick overdose, or we can make it a painful one. Your choice."

Ty closed his eyes and nodded. "Okay. Okay." He licked his lips and began to flex his muscles, testing the ropes. His wrists were tied to the back legs of the chair, and his ankles were secured to the front legs. The water had given him a little leeway, but he still couldn't get free. "I . . . I'm here on a job."

"What sort of job?"

Ty opened his eyes as the buzzing in his ear continued. He was breathless, but that was good. It gave his words an element of truth, made it harder to detect a lie. "I hunt vampires."

Gaudet stared for a few seconds before straightening with a loud sigh. "Vampires."

"You have a very serious vampire problem here."

Gaudet rolled his eyes and scrubbed at one cheek. He looked at his son. "Shine? Make him sorry for pulling my leg."

The big man began to wrap a strip of cloth around his knuckles.

"No, Shine," Ty groaned. He shook his head. "Down boy."

Shine began to laugh. "Boy, you got bad gris-gris sticking to you. Almost like you're cursed."

"That was you, huh?" Shine nodded and Ty chuckled, even more breathless and hoarse than before. "Is this a bad time to talk about how I fucked your sister?"

Shine backhanded him hard enough to tilt the chair.

Gaudet sneered. "You got a smart mouth on you, boy. Always did. Shine'll fix that right up, though."

"He better hurry," Ty managed to say. He gulped for air, trying to force himself to hyperventilate. He had to be convincing.

Gaudet bent in front of him, narrowing his eyes. He waved at Shine. "He's having one of those damn allergy attacks," he said, disgusted. "I told you not to use that damn powder, boy, now he's gonna die before he can talk!"

"How in the hell are we supposed to search an entire neighborhood of ruined houses?" Owen hissed.

Zane pulled out a top shelf bottle of whiskey and didn't offer to share.

Nick sat beside him and leaned close so no one else would hear him. "You want to go easy on the hooch, Garrett?"

"What's it to you?" Zane whispered. He stared at the tabletop, unable to get Ty's face out of his mind.

"You're sitting here drinking when Ty's in trouble. That doesn't seem like the Zane Garrett I met."

"That man died last night."

"I get it," Nick said. "He lied to you."

Zane glanced at him then looked away quickly. The last person he wanted to talk to about this with was Nick O'Flaherty. Hell, the man was probably standing in line waiting for Ty to be single.

"You know what, Zane, he lied to us too. In fact, I don't know a single person Ty hasn't lied to, including himself."

Zane huffed and took another drink of whiskey. "You must be one hell of a loyal bastard."

"He's earned it."

"Has he? Has he really earned that from you, O'Flaherty? Because I thought he'd earned it from me too, and then I found out the truth. I found out he uses things like love and loyalty as tools."

"You have no idea what love and loyalty mean to him if that's what you really believe."

"No?" Zane took a gulp of whiskey. "Why don't you educate me then, O'Flaherty, because you know him so fucking well."

"I know Ty's not all there," Nick said, tapping his temple with a finger. "He has always been a step away from the wrong path. One screw comes loose, and he's gone. The only thing keeps him on the side of the righteous is his loyalty. His sense of purpose. You take that from him? And you're looking into the eyes of a monster."

Zane glanced at Nick, surprised by how hard the words hit him.

"So you question his motives. You question his tactics. But you be damn sure you know what you're doing before you question his loyalty."

"Two days ago, I was trying to decide how to ask him to marry me," Zane whispered. "Tonight I'm trying to figure out if I can even love someone like him."

Nick was silent for a long while, long enough for Zane to drain his glass. Then he leaned closer. "You ask yourself if you're in love. You're not asking the right question."

Zane laughed bitterly. "What's the right question?"

Nick pressed a finger onto the table. "Would you bust him out of prison?"

"No," Zane answered immediately.

Nick sat back, eyebrows climbing high. "No?"

"No," Zane said again. He poured another glass, gritting his teeth. "I wouldn't let him make it to a cell."

"How is that not enough?"

Zane glared. "Look, I know you're the team mother or whatever, but stop. I'm not part of your team."

Nick tilted his head. "You are now. And I know if Ty were here, he wouldn't want to see you like this."

Zane slammed a hand on the table and grabbed Nick's shirt collar. "Well Ty's not here!"

Nick didn't retaliate or try to break his hold. He just put a hand on Zane's shoulder. "So help me find him. And I'll help you break him out of jail."

Zane wanted to lash out, to shout again or to shove him away. But it was nearly impossible to remain angry and sullen under Nick's calming influence. Besides, Ty needed them. He let go of Nick's shirt and sat back. Nick reached slowly for the bottle, giving Zane a chance to stop him; Zane shook his head and stood up, running both hands through his hair. "Just put it where I can't find it."

Liam cleared his throat loudly. "Now that *that* crisis has passed, can we focus here?"

Zane glowered at him, but Liam merely leered in return.

"Okay, we can narrow it down," Digger said. He took out his combat knife and gouged a deep line across the table. "This is the canal. When the levees broke, the barges in the canal and the storm surge took out most of the houses alongside it. What's left in these first few blocks," he said, slashing the table into a grid, "is nothing but empty lots or rebuilt homes."

Zane studied the grid closer. "So we *can* narrow it down."

Digger nodded.

"It wouldn't be near the canal then, nor would it be near businesses or large thoroughfares," Zane said.

Digger scratched his cheek with the large knife, then marked the approximate areas Zane had mentioned. "Also, most of the houses with no one living in them will still have markings on the sides."

"What sort of markings?"

"A spray-painted X. Little markings in each quadrant. They were used when rescue crews went through the houses to show when they were there, which crew it was, what sort of dangers there were. And the body count."

Zane nodded, wincing. He remembered Ty talking about the rescue efforts he and others had been involved in after Hurricane Katrina hit. He couldn't quite wrap his mind around the horrors.

"Some of those houses still have their markings. Means the owners haven't been able to return to rebuild. Or they ain't coming back. We find a marked house with a vehicle near it, I guarandamntee you that's our spot."

"So we *can* find him," Owen said. He was standing behind Digger's chair, unable to sit still.

"We don't even know if they have him," Nick said. "If the Colombians got him first, he's dead."

"And if he got away, he's sitting in a casino, drinking a cocktail in front of a security camera," Zane said.

"In that case, our only avenue is to search for him here," Liam said, tapping the table. "If he's dead, we're no use to him. And if he's sitting somewhere safe, he's no use to us."

Nick tucked his gun into the back of his jeans. "So we go to the Lower Ninth Ward and split up."

"No, the hell we will," Owen growled. He pointed at Liam. "Last time we split up, this bastard ran away, Doc got shot, and Grady disappeared. We stay together."

Nick studied him for a long moment and finally nodded. "We need a plan if we find the place. How do we take it?"

Zane gripped the back of a chair. "Shock and awe."

"Care to explain?" Nick asked.

Zane nodded and locked eyes with Liam "I want it. Right now."

Liam raised both eyebrows and sat forward. "Pardon?"

"Your jacket is armored and your boots are for riding. Where's your bike?"

Ty worked the ropes at his wrists as Gaudet and his son argued, taking fast, shallow breaths, trying desperately to fake an allergic reaction.

"Hey!" he finally croaked. He shook his shoulders from side to side. "Get these ropes . . . off my chest . . . so I can fucking breathe!"

"The hell you say," Shine growled. "Let him die, what's the problem? We're going to kill him anyway!"

Gaudet smacked Shine on the side of the head. "I need information before I can let him kick off. Where's that doohickey Ava gave you?"

Ty groaned. A woman scorned was nothing to mess with. He'd remember that if he lived.

Shine began to dig in his pockets. "She found it in his room at the bar," he said, pulling out one of the EpiPens.

"Shoot him with it," Gaudet ordered.

"Oh hell no," Ty gasped. He shook his head violently as Shine turned the cylinder over and frowned at it. "Might as well . . . let him loose . . . with a Ginsu!"

"You're awfully particular for someone who's dying."

Shine put his hand on Ty's shoulder and flicked the cap off the EpiPen cylinder. He pulled it back, preparing to stab it right into Ty's chest.

"No, no, no!" Ty wheezed. "Jesus Christ!"

"What?"

"You can't inject ... adrenaline ... right into my heart. You dumb fuck!"

Shine turned it over in his hand and glanced at his father, who rolled his eyes. "Let me have it. You got to take it out of the case."

"I thought you just stab it in."

"But that's just the case, boy. Let me have it." Gaudet took it from Shine and slid the EpiPen from its case.

"Blue end," Ty told him.

"Shut up."

"It ain't a needle," Shine muttered. "Let's just give him a sack to breathe in."

"His throat's closing up."

"So we put a hole in his throat and he can breathe again."

"Instructions ... on it!" Ty managed. "Flip the blue ... jab the orange ... hold it—"

"Shut up!" Gaudet turned it over and tapped it.

Ty took a deep, rasping breath.

"Fuck it, untie one of his hands," Gaudet finally ordered.

"You sure about that?"

Gaudet nodded, and Shine pulled a large hunting knife from a sheath at his thigh. He waved the knife in Ty's face. "Try anything, I'll gut you."

Ty nodded jerkily. Shine cut through the rope around his left wrist and stepped back. Gaudet handed him the EpiPen. He flipped the end and gripped it tight, raising it above his thigh to jam it in. But instead of his own thigh, he swung his arm out and jabbed the injector into Gaudet's chest.

The man stumbled back, pawing at the EpiPen. Shine followed, taking his arm to steady him.

"Oh, that's gonna do so many bad things to your heart," Ty said as he began laughing. He reached across his lap to pull at the rope that bound his right hand.

Shine yanked the EpiPen out. He threw it to the ground and it shattered as it skidded across the floor. Gaudet grabbed at his chest, doubling over.

"He's having a heart attack, Shine," Ty said, his voice low and urgent. "Better get him out of here, Shine."

Shine rounded on him, the knife clutched in his huge hand. "I'm gonna make you bleed, Beaumont."

"They'll bury me right beside your daddy, bubba!"

Shine hesitated, and behind him, Gaudet was taking deep breaths and clutching at his chest. He waved his hand at Shine, as if telling him to go ahead and kill Ty. Shine held the knife close to his body and gripped Ty's shoulder, preparing to stick him, but Ty grabbed Shine's biceps, locking his elbow as Shine pushed forward. He gritted his teeth and put every ounce of strength he had into keeping that knife at bay, but he hadn't managed to loosen his other arm, his feet were still bound to the chair, and Shine was laughing at him, pushing the tip inexorably closer to Ty's chest.

He didn't have to push forward to hurt Ty. He could have sliced at Ty's forearm to loosen his grip. He could have wrenched away and come from behind to slit his throat. He could have easily killed him in so many ways, but Shine continued to push against him instead, forcing Ty to fight for his life. Ty's fingers worked frantically at the loose ropes on his other wrist. With his feet tied, he couldn't get any leverage. Shine laughed. He was enjoying the slow march of death as Ty lost the battle.

The knife touched the material of Ty's shirt and he shouted wordlessly, digging deep for more strength where he knew he would find none. Fighting for his life against a man who merely wanted to play with it.

The knife broke skin. Ty pushed back against the chair, desperate for more inches. His life didn't flash before his eyes. His evil deeds didn't come back to haunt him, nor did any of the good he'd done revisit him. He didn't find added strength in thoughts of the future or memories of the past. He didn't see his family, or his teammates, or the faces of men he'd comforted as they'd died. The only face he saw as the knife bit into him was Zane's.

"Ty?"

Ty cried out again. He didn't know where Zane's voice had come from, but he pushed harder against Shine's arm, desperate to hear it again.

"Zane!"

An engine revved somewhere close. Shine pulled back, his head shooting up at the sound.

Gaudet had finally recovered from the rush of epinephrine and adrenaline enough to hit Shine in the back. "Do him!"

The engine grew louder, drawing closer. Ty could hear it both outside the thin walls and in his ear. The ear bud Shine had missed was still there. It had been buzzing in Ty's ear all this time, and now it was picking up the roaring of an angry motorcycle.

Ty craned his head and saw the rider through the dirty front window, barreling toward the house through a field of weeds and brush. It was an off-white cruiser with a hulking rider sheathed in black leather and a skullcap-style helmet, face covered with a pair of sunglasses and a black bandana with a white skull printed on it.

Ty caught his breath, staring out the window as the rider pointed a gun toward the house. Gaudet and Shine seemed to be trying to decide between fight and flight. "Its rider was named Death," Ty told them, beginning to smile. Gunshots shattered the hinges and panels of the rickety front door and continued to rain down on the occupants of the room. "And Hell followed with him!" Ty shouted as both men dove to the floor, covering their heads.

Splinters and shards of bullets flew through the air. Shine and his father both scrambled to the corners of the room, covering themselves. Ty brought his hand up to shield his eyes as the motorcycle burst through the ruined door, screaming into the room and tearing up the floorboards and remnants of carpet as it went. The rider put a foot down and caused the back wheel of the motorcycle to slide around, chewing up the wood and shooting shrapnel at the men cowering on the floor.

Ty gaped at the reflective surface of the sunglasses. The rider tossed him a small knife—Zane, it was *Zane*—and Ty barely managed to overcome his shock to catch it. He sliced through his ropes and struggled out of the chair. Zane held his gun up and ejected the empty magazine onto the floor. He'd used all his ammunition busting through the door and had nothing left to finish the job.

Gaudet and Shine scrambled for their weapons. Ty lunged forward, taking Zane's hand and swinging onto the back of the bike.

He held on tight and pressed his face into the man's back as the motorcycle took off and darted out of the house.

Gunshots chased them, but the motorcycle was too fast for their pursuers. Ty's grip tightened, his hand clutching at the edges of the leather jacket, the same black leather jacket he'd given Zane years ago.

They took several twists and turns through the ruin of the neighborhood, then the bike slowed and Ty was able to lift his head. Soon they reached an empty intersection, and Ty saw the men of Sidewinder converging ahead.

The motorcycle pulled to a stop beside a nondescript gray van and an old Cutlass sedan, where the other men were gathered, armed and ready.

Ty rested his head against Zane's back, breathing hard and still shaking with adrenaline. He nodded at the others, who simply stood there and grinned.

Zane reached up and pulled the bandana down. Ty tilted sideways to pull Zane's sunglasses off, then patted his cheek. Zane nodded and turned his head away without saying a word.

The others came closer, all of them grinning like fools.

"Wicked jailbreak, Garrett," Nick said.

"That was some shit right there," Digger shouted, and he held his fist up for Zane to bump it. Even Owen offered him a slap on the shoulder.

Nick took Ty's arm and helped him off the back of the bike. "You okay?"

"Pretty much. Kelly?"

"In surgery. We don't know anything, we had to leave him."

Ty swallowed hard as relief flooded him. Behind Nick, Liam stood with Ava near the van. She was tied up, a bandana around her mouth to keep her quiet. Ty looked back at Nick.

"We were going to trade her for you if we had to. Zane was searching when he heard you."

Ty stepped away, turning to meet Zane's eyes. Zane stared at him, his face as impassive as the carved angels in St. Louis Cemetery. Ty wanted to say so many things to him, but they didn't have time. And from Zane's expression, he didn't want to hear them anyway.

Ty walked over to Liam and Ava instead. Ava flinched from him when he reached up to take the bandana out of her mouth, and Ty belatedly saw the bruise forming on her cheekbone. "It's okay," he said.

She glared at him as he pulled the bandana down.

"Did you call him?" Ty asked, voice pitched low.

She swallowed hard. "Yes."

Before she could explain, Ty stuffed the bandana back in. She thrashed her head, but Liam held her still as Ty tightened it and silenced her. Then he turned on Liam, who grinned and patted him on the shoulder.

"That bruise your handiwork?"

Liam rolled his eyes. "She grassed us out. And she may still have got the doc killed. So don't cry to me, Argentina, she got what she deserved."

He moved to pass Ty, but Ty stopped him with a hand on his chest. "We all get what we deserve," Ty whispered in his ear.

Liam cocked his head, mere inches from his face. Then he sniffed and pushed past him. Ty took Ava by the arm and pulled her with him, pointing in the direction of the house he'd been held at. "Your daddy is that way. Start walking."

Her dark eyes glared at him, but she jutted her chin out and started off down the crumbling road without looking back.

"You sure that's a good idea?" Nick asked.

Ty nodded. "Keeping her around would be like trying to keep a raccoon in a cage. You'll end up bloody. With rabies."

Nick chuckled and climbed into the van. Ty looked to Zane again, feeling his chest growing tighter. Liam stepped up to Zane, breaking the eye contact between them before Ty could say anything. He held up a hand, grasping Zane's and pulling in closer to hug him. "You'll do all right, mate! Bloody hell!"

Ty's attention was still on Zane when Liam turned back to him. Liam gave him a shove. "He deserves a bit more than your usual rescue blowjob, yeah?"

Ty tore his eyes away from Zane.

Liam grinned widely. "You don't give it to him, darling, I sure as hell will."

Ty swung at him before he'd thought it through, before it registered that Liam's words had made him angry. Possessive. Jealous as hell. His punch didn't land flush, though, because Liam leaned away and blocked Ty's hand. He wrapped Ty's arm up and twisted it, pulling Ty sideways toward him.

Ty grunted and arched his back as Liam torqued his arm and shoulder. Liam put his lips to Ty's ear, and when he spoke it was in whispered Russian. "Now, now, darling, wouldn't want you getting hurt in a fight for a man you've already lost."

Ty managed to land a jab to his midsection before Liam shoved him away as if Ty were some untrained drunken brawler.

Liam waved a hand at Zane. "Now give me back my motorbike before I knock you off it."

Zane sat in the passenger seat of the van as Digger drove. He didn't know where Sidewinder had found the various vehicles they'd driven to the Ninth Ward, only that Owen claimed they had "permanently borrowed" the van from the rental place near the French Quarter. He didn't care. His mind was roiling now that they'd pulled off the rescue.

He kept seeing Ty tied down to that chair, at the mercy of a large hunting knife wielded by an even larger man. He kept hearing Ty's desperate cry of "Zane!" ringing in his ears. He'd forgotten all the anger, all the hurt and humiliation, forgiven it in a heartbeat when he'd thought Ty might be taken from him.

But now it was all flooding back, and the way Ty stared at him, his eyes flat and lifeless, his jaw set in a hard line, made Zane cold all over. They couldn't even say they were back at square one, because now there was so much betrayal and anger between them, Zane could feel the chasm widening.

Nick's words echoed in Zane's ears. What the hell kind of person had Ty been that even Nick was afraid of him?

"Who's got a phone?" Ty asked. He was sitting in the middle of the bench seat, between Owen and Nick.

Zane shifted in his seat to look back at him. "Who are you calling?"

Ty cleared his throat, barely meeting Zane's eyes. "Burns. Even he can't save my job now, but at least he can get us out."

Zane locked eyes with him, knowing what that would mean, knowing that a life without his job, without a purpose, was one of Ty's biggest fears. Nick's warning echoed again. What would Ty turn into without a purpose, without that anchor? He nodded, though. It was their last resort.

"Are you sure you want to do that?" Nick asked.

Ty's jaw tightened. "This is out of hand."

"But—"

"They blew a cat at me!" Ty shouted. "Someone give me your phone!"

Zane handed his to Ty. "Put it on speaker," he requested.

"You promise you won't say anything to him?" Ty asked.

"Ty."

"Swear to me, Garrett."

"Fine, whatever, I pinky swear, just call him."

"I feel like I missed an episode of a television show here," Owen said.

"Blew a cat at you?" Nick asked, though he sounded like he didn't really want the answer.

Ty muttered that he'd explain later and dialed Richard Burns's number. He pressed the speaker button and held the phone out, leaning forward.

"Richard Burns."

"It's Grady."

"Happy Easter, kiddo. How's your dad?"

Ty closed his eyes. "I— I've gotten into something deep, I need help."

Burns was silent a few breaths. "Go on."

"I'm in New Orleans."

"What?"

"Garrett's with me. So are the Sidewinder boys."

"What the hell, Tyler?"

"It's worse. Liam Bell is here with a pink slip with our names on it. The Vega cartel has sniffed us both out, and someone somewhere told them we'd be here this weekend."

They heard him moving, closing a door and coughing. "How did anyone know you'd be there? Why *are* you there?"

"It was last minute, *we* didn't even know we'd be here."

"You have a mole, someone on you."

"Yes sir, but that's not my concern right now. The police commander here has me pegged as a CI that gave him fits five years ago; he's trying to kill me. He's got us locked down. The agent we tried to contact for extraction was dirty. I don't . . . we can't get out."

Burns didn't respond for a tense moment. Ty licked his lips, meeting Zane's eyes.

"I'm sorry, Grady," Burns finally said, his voice stern and professional. "I can't help you."

Ty stared at the phone, his mouth falling open. Zane's heart raced. Richard Burns was like a father to Ty. There were photos of the man holding Ty as a baby on Mara Grady's wall.

"Uncle Dick . . . we're going to die down here," Ty said, hoarse and pleading. "Please help me."

"I can't, Ty," Burns whispered. "You're too far out. Good luck, son."

He ended the call, leaving Ty holding the phone in a hand that had begun to tremble.

Ty hadn't said a word since his call with Burns, and Nick wasn't sure they were going to pull Ty back from the brink in time to save any of them.

Digger had taken them through several shortcuts and odd turns and finally back into the French Quarter. Road blocks had cropped up everywhere, and there was no way for the group to get out now. If they were going to escape New Orleans, they would have to split up to do so. And none of them were willing to do that.

They headed for the last place Ty knew to go. He said it was his former boss's home, the man who'd been murdered before they arrived in New Orleans. Arthur Murdoch had no family left, and his house would probably still be vacant. He had resided in the Tremé, a historical black neighborhood that bordered the other side of Rampart Street, across from the French Quarter.

They arrived at Murdoch's house and sat on it for an hour to watch it for surveillance. When they found it clear, they dumped the van nearby, where it was unlikely to be found any time soon. And if it was found, it would simply serve to point their pursuers away from the neighborhood. As they made their way back to Murdoch's house, Nick got the impression the area was usually a lively place, though it was run-down and in disrepair. It was also dead quiet after all the shooting on Rampart earlier.

They all crowded around Murdoch's living room, stretched out on the couch, hovering on the arms of the chairs, and sitting around the tiny dining table.

"He left you in the wind?" Liam asked in patent disbelief.

"What are you going to do?" Nick asked Ty.

Ty's jaw tightened and he stood, pacing away from the rest of them. Nick watched Zane and Liam, who were sitting at the table. Both men looked worried and defeated.

"Hey, this isn't the first time we've had to rely on our own devices, right?" Nick tried. He looked over at Ty, who still had his back to them, staring at a wall full of photographs and artwork. Ty was in several of those photos, arm around a grandfatherly black man in a Panama hat. "Ty?"

When Ty turned, he looked like a different person. His eyes had gone hard and flat, his mouth set in a thin line. All the humor and charisma that made Ty Grady who he was had disappeared, replaced by the soulless, lifeless person the military had battered them all into. They had been trained to morph into that person when they needed to act without emotion. Nick hadn't seen that look since they'd come home. It had always ended in blood. It sent a shiver down his spine.

"I need a few minutes," Ty said, then he stalked through the room and out the front door.

"Well, that's that," Liam sighed.

"What?" Zane asked.

Liam shook his head. "The only things Tyler's ever understood were loyalty, honor, and orders. His entire life has been devoted to them."

"I know," Zane growled.

"Do you really?" Liam shook his head. "Because I think if you did, you'd be a little more frightened right now. Do you know what happens to people like Ty when they realize everything they've been living for has been a con?"

Zane glanced at Nick quickly, then back at Liam. Nick lowered his head and closed his eyes.

"Have you ever seen a trained dog that's always been kept on a leash?" Liam asked after a few moments of tense silence. "Only released when the order to kill was given?"

Nick looked up. Zane was staring at Liam, grim.

No one answered. Liam sat straighter. "Have you ever seen what one of those dogs will do once no one's giving it orders?"

Zane sniffed and ran a hand over his face. He nodded, staring at the darkened window. "Not a goddamned thing."

"That's right," Liam said in disgust. "He won't even eat unless someone tells him to. He curls up and starves without his master." He stood and grabbed his jacket.

Nick scowled as Liam pulled on the coat. "What are you doing?"

"I'm leaving."

"What?"

"Leave. Ing. Leaving." He pointed toward the door. "That is not the man I knew ten years ago. He's not even half the man I knew. And now look at him. His heart's broken, Dick Burns has betrayed him, and he's getting his men shot left and right. He's done. And I for one don't intend to follow him into the hereafter."

Nick lunged to his feet, shaking with anger. If they knew half the things he and Ty had done, half the sacrifices Ty had made to see orders through, it wouldn't be so easy to sneer.

"Don't," Liam grunted. He waved a hand at Nick. "Don't defend him. Jesus, it was hard enough watching you two circle-jerk in service, I don't need to see it now."

He headed for the door, still shaking his head. When he yanked the door open, a hand reached out and grabbed him by the throat. Liam didn't have time to react or defend himself before Ty shoved him back into the room. Nick and Zane both lunged to their feet.

Liam kicked out, but instead of dropping back and defending like Ty often did, he attacked. He used Liam's leg and then shoulder for leverage, kicking up, wrapping a leg around Liam's neck and twisting and rolling to slam him to the floor. The entire house seemed to shake when they hit. Then Ty was on Liam, his knee in Liam's solar plexus, his hand on Liam's throat again in an iron grip. Liam kicked and flailed, grasping. Ty easily avoided every attempt he made to free himself.

"This trained dog's still got a few tricks up his sleeve," Ty snarled.

Liam made a gurgling noise and kicked his feet against the battered hardwood floor, trying to get leverage. He smacked at Ty's face. The veins in Ty's arm jumped as he squeezed Liam harder.

"Grady," Nick shouted, the same voice he'd used to relay orders. "Let him up."

Ty squeezed just long enough for Liam to start clawing at his head. Then he released him, grabbing him by his jacket collar and lifting his shoulders off the floor. "You're in this until the end," he hissed. "Is that understood?"

Liam grasped at Ty's wrists, gulping for air. He nodded. "As long as you can still do that to someone like me? I'm with you."

Ty released him and stood. They all stared at him with wide eyes. "Time to stop waiting for the cavalry."

A grin slowly overtook Nick, and he sat back down and put his hand over his mouth to hide it. That was the Ty Grady he remembered, the one a lost eighteen-year-old from Boston had fallen in awe of.

He wondered if Zane was seeing the same thing.

Zane's arms were crossed and his eyes narrowed. "Do you have a plan?" he asked Ty.

"No. But I'm in a room with some of the smartest, most devious assholes I've ever known. If we can't slither our way out of this, then we don't deserve our titles." Ty nodded at Owen and Digger, then at Nick. Nick smiled.

Liam began to sit up, but Ty put a foot on his shoulder and shoved him back to the floor. A ghost of a smile crossed Zane's lips.

"Right now we have two enemies, after two different things, who've joined forces," Liam rasped. He shoved at Ty's foot. "We need to pit them against one another. Will you get off me!"

Ty stepped away, smirking at Liam as he pushed himself off the floor and brushed himself off.

Owen stood from where he'd been lounging on the couch. "What if we give them what they want?"

Ty sat down hard in the chair Liam had vacated, across the table from Zane. "I'd rather not die in this plan."

Owen held up a hand. "They think you're Tyler Beaumont, right? Ex-military, wandering performer, hired henchman. CI important enough for the FBI to try to save." He shrugged. "Who's to say you weren't hired to off someone?"

Ty cut his eyes toward Nick, not yet willing to say he wasn't following but obviously not following any more than Nick was. Nick shrugged.

"And Garrett," Owen continued, "he could be a dirty Fed, still be part of the cartel crowd."

Ty and Zane shared a look over the table. Both men still seemed confused.

Digger leaned over and put both hands on his head. "Johns, I swear to baby Jesus, if you don't start making sense, I'm gonna kick you."

"Listen," Owen insisted. "Bell contacts the cartel, tells them Garrett, or whatever name you used, wants a meet with them. Follow?"

The room was silent.

"Oh my God!"

"Can you . . . draw it in a chart or something?" Nick asked.

"Look, Garrett's a dirty Fed. Liam's a hired gun. They're both after Ty, who is a dirty rat."

"Hey!"

Owen flopped his hands. "Well, you were!"

"Granted, but I am no longer after Ty," Liam added. "Turned the job down, remember?"

"Details. Garrett has Grady, wants to trade him in for safe passage to Miami, and Bell tells the cartel."

"Why didn't you just say that the first time?" Liam grumbled.

"I don't want safe passage to Miami," Zane said.

"He's not being literal, Garrett, Jesus Christ," Ty snapped.

"I'm sorry, Grady, I have a hard time thinking like an asshole!"

"He means getting back in good with the cartel. Or getting out clean, what the fuck ever. Would your cover still fly with them? Could you go in as a compromised agent?"

"Yeah," Zane said, nodding slowly. "I was there two years ago. The story was I got out of prison. When they pulled me, though, I just disappeared."

Ty tapped the table. "That was right around the same time de la Vega was killed."

"You would know," Zane mumbled.

"It's possible he found out you were a Fed, turned you, and gave you a job to do in the Bureau. You left to do it right before he was offed, and ever since, you've been looking for the man who killed him. Will that work?"

Zane stared at Ty for several seconds before nodding. "They'll be suspicious. Going in and admitting I'm a Fed, that . . . that might actually work. Yeah. Yeah, I can work with that."

"So Zane calls up the cartel boys," Nick drawled, "tells them he's their long lost buddy, and he's got the man who killed big papi?"

Digger made a clicking sound with his tongue. "So far, all I'm seeing is Garrett handing Grady over to the people who already want him dead and telling them more reasons why he should be dead."

"But they're not the *only* people who want him dead," Owen said.

"You want to play a fiddle game where Ty is the fiddle?" Liam asked.

"Fuck no." Ty shook his head. "The fiddle dies."

"I'm good with it," Liam said.

"The fiddle is usually an object," Digger said. "What the fuck kind of messed up fiddle game you been playing?"

"No, no," Owen said quickly. "We make the cartel believe Ty is the one they want, not Zane. And then we call up Papa Gaudet."

"Who obviously wants to talk to me before killing me," Ty added.

"Right. And we tell him when and where the cartel plans to acquire and kill Ty."

"So you've, in theory, pitted Gaudet against the cartel." Nick winced. "That's banking on Gaudet still wanting information from Ty badly enough to keep him alive. And hoping they'll fight over him instead of just teaming up to make him dead."

Owen's shoulders slumped and he sat back down. "True. I wouldn't want those odds if I was the fiddle."

"It's not the fiddle game!" Digger shouted.

Ty sat silent, resting his chin in his hand and scowling. His knee began to bounce as he examined the floor. Finally, he waved his hand and sat up straighter. "So we give them what they want."

"You? Dead?" Zane asked incredulously.

Ty nodded. "We don't need the two sides to wipe each other out, we don't need them to fight. We just need them to think they succeeded. So we get them both there. Zane brings me in, and he kills me in front of all of them. Their problem is gone so they'll clear out, and bonus points, they're no longer after Zane."

"How the hell is that a good plan when it involves me killing you?" Zane shouted.

Ty put a finger to his lips and shook his head. "There is a small glitch, I'll admit."

Nick rubbed at the stubble on his chin as the idea became clear. "We put you in Digger's vest."

"Fuck, that's risky," Digger whispered. "It's only NIJ II level protection. If Garrett's close enough to make sure someone doesn't take a head shot, he'd be too close for the vest; the bullet could go right through. And if it don't go through, it's definitely fucking him up. Broken ribs, sternum, maybe organ damage."

Nick shook his head. "Not if Zane's shooting a blank."

"There's no way that'd look real, there'd be no impact," Ty said, but he was sitting forward, warming to the idea. "But if the real shot is taken from further away..."

"A sniper?" Zane asked.

Ty gave him a curt nod. "It'd have to be a long-ass way. One, to make sure he's not spotted during the meet, and two, make sure it doesn't kill me. NIJ II is... 1,100 to 1,800 feet per second."

Nick groaned and ran a hand through his hair. "You're talking eight hundred, maybe a thousand yards before a sniper round drops to that velocity. Or more. I know I can't make that shot with enough accuracy to hit a vest with my best friend in it."

Ty met Nick's eyes and nodded. Nick's heart jumped into his throat. He gave a slight shake of his head, silently pleading with him not to ask. Ty smiled sadly, then met Liam's eyes. Liam began to grin.

"Oh fuck no," Zane blurted. "No way."

"He can make it," Ty assured him.

"Yeah, but *will* he, is the question."

Liam grinned wider. "Do you trust me not to hit your heart, Grady?"

"Ty," Zane hissed, reaching for his arm.

Ty tore his eyes away from Liam and met Zane's. "I swore to protect you from them," he whispered. "I was already willing to take a bullet to do that. After everything that's happened . . ." He shook his head, unable to finish.

Zane looked stricken, and he wasn't able to form words before Ty looked away.

Liam was rubbing his hands together. "Let's go practice!"

Nick slumped in his chair and rubbed his hands over his face. "This is a horrible plan."

"Before we get too excited, where the hell would we set up this meet?" Digger asked. "We'd need an open area free of bystanders, with somewhere high enough to clear a line of sight. There's nowhere in the city like that."

Liam thumped his back against the wall and sighed. "Damn."

The room fell silent.

"The river?" Owen suggested.

Liam made a derogatory noise. "With the wind and distance, there's no way in hell. And if you cut the distance and make it a ferry, that's even worse."

"The amusement park," Ty said suddenly.

"Are you shitting me?" Liam laughed. "There are way too many variables. Crowds, ride interference, not to mention security as you try to walk in with a very large weapon."

But Ty was shaking his head. "The Six Flags park was drowned by Katrina. They never reopened it. You can see the roller coaster from Interstate 510."

"The rides and stuff are still there?" Nick asked.

"For the most part, yeah. It's completely deserted, only patrolled by a private security company."

"That could work," Nick said. "Roller coasters in the air, wide thoroughfares laid out in a predictable fashion, no bystanders, and plenty of cover if things go to shit."

"Can you draw a map of it?" Liam asked Ty.

"What do I look like, an Etch A Sketch? I don't know the layout."

Zane stood and went to his suitcase, digging through it to bring out an iPad. "If it was ever on the internet, I'll find it."

Nick rested his elbows on his knees. "We're really doing this?"

"Unless you can see another way that doesn't involve a full-blown war," Ty said. "We've already lost Doc; we won't make it out alive if we go toe-to-toe."

Nick was silent, nodding.

Ty sucked in a shaky breath. "We're going to need some supplies. We might as well start now."

"We'll need fake blood," Nick said. "Lots of it."

"Oh, I can do that." Digger hopped to his feet and grinned, rubbing his hands together.

"There's a mom-and-pop store down on the corner," Ty said. "The back door only has bars for security."

"Got it."

"We'll need something for camouflage too," Nick told him.

"Got it!"

"No peppers!" Ty added urgently.

"All right with your damn peppers! One little anaphylactic episode and he's freaking out about the peppers."

Digger turned to get his jacket, and Owen began to gather his things as well.

"Owen," Ty said. Owen turned, and Ty shook his head. "He's got to go it alone."

"What? Why? No one should go anywhere alone right now."

Ty winced. "Quite frankly, he's the only one who can walk around in this neighborhood and not stand out."

Digger poked a finger in Ty's face. "That's racist." Ty rolled his eyes. Digger smacked his cheek gently. "That's okay. I still love you, hillbilly."

He turned to leave, a hop in his step. Nick didn't know if it was the prospect of action or of cooking up fake blood that made Digger so happy. And frankly, he didn't want to know.

Liam thumped his bag of supplies down on the coffee table, and everyone looked to the door, where Digger's canvas bag sat.

"Who wants to go through his fun bag?" Owen asked.

"Guarantee you he has it booby-trapped," Ty muttered.

Ty and Owen shared a glance. Nick held out his fist and the other two followed suit. "Two out of three."

Ty slapped Owen on the arm. "Close your eyes, man."

"Why?"

"You got a tell."

"I have a tell at Rock, Paper, Scissors?"

Ty and Nick both nodded.

"And you tell me ten years later? You're both assholes!"

Zane chuckled from across the room, but Liam walked away in disgust. "You're all bloody idiots."

Zane lay on one side of the full-sized guest bed, unable to sleep as the plans for the next day ran through his analytical mind. There was so much that could go wrong. Too much. People would probably die tomorrow. He might be one of them. Ty might be one of them.

Ty had set up a staggered watch so no one would be on together too long. He obviously didn't trust Liam, but with a man down, they had to use him. Zane could hear the occasional creak of steps as Digger and Liam moved about, taking their turns.

Owen and Nick had argued over going to the hospital to check on Kelly. Nick insisted there was no way to connect Kelly to them, and the best way to keep him safe was to stay away from him. Owen seemed almost desperate to get news, though, and Zane's heart went out to all of them. Not knowing if Kelly was alive or dead had to be driving them all crazy. Nick and Owen had moved to the larger bedroom, still arguing, leaving Ty and Zane to share this tiny bed in awkward, weighted silence. Ty had retreated to the shower with very little to say, and Zane had crawled into bed with a heavy heart and mind.

Now, Ty curled in the bed beside him. His back was to Zane and he had a pillow over his head so it was impossible to even see him. But Zane watched him anyway in the moonlight that filtered through the window.

He couldn't get over the fact that he'd met Ty years ago. An introduction so fleeting he hadn't even remembered what Ty looked like. When tragedy had struck Zane's life, that simple meeting had influenced him in ways he had never truly pondered. Ty had done that, touched his life even before he knew him.

Ty had said it was fate. But Zane didn't believe in fate.

Zane reached across the bed and poked him.

Ty jerked, and the pillow moved as he raised his head. "What?"

"How'd you know he was here?"

"What?" Ty asked. He rolled enough to be able to see Zane.

"Liam. You hallucinated him in the hospital *before* you found the note in my pocket. So how'd you know he was here?"

Ty settled onto his back, rubbing at his face. "I don't know. I hadn't thought about it."

"Yes you have, Ty. You think about everything."

Ty turned his head to look at Zane.

"How'd you know he was here?"

Ty's focus drifted until it was on the wall over Zane's shoulder.

"You think it was magic, don't you? Voodoo. Fate."

"I don't know." Ty sighed and pushed the pillow away. "You don't believe in any of it, so what does it matter?"

"I believe in you," Zane whispered. Ty looked at him sharply. "I believe you used to be one scary son of a bitch, Ty. Everything I've been told, the glimpses I've seen from you. What I've heard from Miami."

Ty was hoarse when he spoke. "What's your point, Zane?"

"I think you put that person behind you because you hated him. Because it scared you."

Ty swallowed hard and snorted.

"You're not a coward, Ty. I know what it takes to scare you. And I think the thing you're afraid of more than anything in the world is yourself. But when Richard Burns told you I was in trouble, you brought that man back out. For me."

Ty stared at the ceiling, unwilling or unable to meet Zane's eyes. He was holding his breath, and as Zane's eyes adjusted to the dark, he could see Ty trembling.

"I'd still do it again," Ty finally whispered.

Goose bumps rose all over Zane's body. He wondered what it would be like to see the man Ty was so frightened of showing him. He could see Ty closing off, so he switched directions. "When did you learn to speak Russian?"

"I can't."

"Liam said something to you today. He spoke in Russian."

Ty sighed. "I can understand it okay but I can't speak it. I could never get the hang of it. He tried to teach me."

"What did he say?"

Ty licked his lips, staring at the ceiling. "He told me there was no use in getting hurt in a fight for a man I'd lost."

Zane pushed onto his elbow, his eyes raking over the shadows that made up Ty's face. "He's you, isn't he?" A frown marred his features. "He's what you were like ten years ago."

Ty took a shaky breath. "Yes."

"What changed you?"

"Richard Burns gave me a cause." He closed his eyes and turned his head away.

Zane fell silent, trying to connect the new pieces of the man in front of him. Nick had said the only thing keeping Ty on the ground was a sense of purpose. A cause. Now that Burns had turned his back on him, what would happen to Ty when this was over? Would he spiral away? Zane remembered the piece of silver Ty had melted down for him, the anchor etched into it. Pain and fear flooded him, squeezing his chest.

The only thing he could make of it was that, tomorrow, Ty intended to risk a bullet to the chest for him. Zane wanted to shake him, to scream at him. As angry as he had been, as willing to walk away as he'd thought he was, the thought of never finding all these pieces to the puzzle, of losing Ty now, setting Ty adrift in that big sea of his mind, was terrifying.

Zane reached out, sliding his hand over Ty's waist beneath the covers. Ty tensed under his fingers, but Zane scooted into the neutral territory of the bed anyway, wrapping his arm over Ty's waist, pulling himself closer. He shoved his face against Ty's cheek and inhaled deeply. Ty's shoulder was rigid against him.

But then, Ty reached up for him. His fingers brushed through Zane's hair. His hand was cool against Zane's skin when he placed it on Zane's ribs.

He pushed his forehead against Zane's lips. Zane kissed his skin. "You're still," Zane whispered. "That means you're expending so much energy worrying, your body doesn't need to fidget."

Ty laughed, but it was a hollow sound. "I love that you know that about me," he said sadly. His fingers tightened against Zane's back. "I don't know how to make this better, Zane."

Zane closed his eyes. He didn't either. The words settled in the room like fog rolling in off the Mississippi. Zane's mouth went dry. "It can't be over," he whispered. "Right? Not when neither of us want it to be."

Ty lifted his head, and they lay facing each other in the dark.

"We've never made it simple," Zane finally said.

Ty laid his hand on Zane's cheek. "I swear to you, Zane. I thought what I was doing was right. I searched for you after I left New York. You were out of my reach. When Burns read me in, the only thing I could think of was that it was the only way of getting back to you. Being partnered with you full-time, being able . . . being able to see you every day, to have you in my life. When he said you might need protecting, it was the only thing I heard. I swear to you. All I wanted from the day I left you in that hospital was you. To be back there with you."

Zane throat tightened. The sincerity in Ty's eyes, the desperation in his voice, those weren't things he could fake, were they? "Ty . . ."

"What do you need me to do? I'll do it, Zane, whatever you need to save us."

Zane swore before he captured Ty's lips in a desperate kiss. When he pulled back, it was only barely, and their lips brushed as he said, "Goddamn you, Ty." By the time he got the last word out, Ty was pulling him closer by the back of the neck to kiss him again. "Feel like I've been on a goddamn seesaw," Zane growled, his fingers dragging over Ty's skin.

"I'm sorry," Ty breathed. His hand trailed along Zane's hip, fingers sliding under his boxers. He pulled away from the kiss and pressed his face against Zane's, sliding his nose against Zane's cheek.

A shiver ran through Zane. Ty's hands were warm against the goose bumps. Zane kissed him again, leaning back so Ty would have to roll on top of him to continue the kiss.

"You were worth it," Ty murmured.

That jolt of intense arousal and connection made its way through Zane's body. The effect Ty had on him was something he would never find anywhere else, he knew that much. He shivered again as Ty's fingers brushed his skin.

Ty slid his hands under Zane's shirt, pushing the material up. Zane sat to help him get the shirt off, wrapping his arms around Ty's waist lifting his head for a kiss. Ty's hands cupped his face. The kiss was gentle and tentative, so unlike what Zane was used to.

"You were right, you know," Ty whispered.

"About what?"

Ty swallowed hard. "I sold my soul a long time ago."

Ty gripped Zane's shoulder and pressed him down, laying him out again, then stretched out over Zane, his hand dragging down Zane's body to push at his boxers.

"Ty," Zane gasped.

Ty kissed him. Zane trailed the tips of his fingers down Ty's arm, sliding over the tattoo and the scars and the muscles.

"Do you really believe that?" Zane asked.

"I know it. I will never be the man you think I am."

Zane's breaths came harder. "We've both been trying so hard to be worthy of each other."

Ty nodded and pressed another kiss to Zane's lips, drawing it out, deepening it, putting some fire into it. He tossed Zane's boxers over the edge of the bed as soon as Zane shimmied out of them, then rested his weight over Zane, propping on his elbows and sliding both hands into Zane's hair. He dragged his body against Zane's and Zane spread his legs around him, squeezing his ribs with his knees. He slid his hands up Ty's back and hooked his arms under his, effectively latching onto him. Ty began to rock, his muscles twisting and bulging, the movement pushing their thickened cocks together.

Zane's entire body throbbed. He thought Ty would be able to feel his heart, it was beating so hard. Breathing was difficult as he inhaled Ty's familiar scent. They were on the eve of battle, making love in the calm before the storm, and it heightened Zane's senses to know this might be the last time Ty touched him.

He arched, feet sliding down the backs of Ty's legs, body writhing to increase the friction between them. He squeezed his thighs against Ty's hips, loving the way it felt when Ty thrust against him. He wasn't concerned with the endgame. He didn't care if either of them came. He didn't desperately need Ty inside him. He just wanted this feeling to last.

His hands found Ty's hair, tightening. Ty hitched against his body, continuing to rock and slide as he kissed him harder.

"I love you, Zane," Ty gasped. "Nothing I've done will ever change that."

Pleasure curled in Zane's groin, but it was joined by another curl, deep in his chest. He found Ty's eyes, gone dark with arousal. His body was hard and solid on top of Zane's, nothing wasted. The lines around his eyes and mouth bore witness to the trials he'd faced, and his skin was marred by years in the trenches of good and evil, battling back again and again to become the only person Zane had ever trusted with his life.

Zane ran his thumb over Ty's cheek, seeing him suddenly with new eyes. Ty had never tried to be something he wasn't. He'd never tried to hide what he was. Warrior. Weapon. Bad guy. Zane knew what he was. The pain and betrayal faded. The world faded.

Ty turned his face under Zane's thumb and kissed his palm. Zane raised his hips, pushing his cock against Ty's thigh.

"Zane," Ty moaned, lowering his forehead to Zane's shoulder and flexing his back and hips to keep the wildly arousing rhythm going. "I need you."

Zane didn't answer. He knew Ty needed him, could feel it in the very air they breathed. He pressed his nose and mouth against Ty's cheek, clenched hard at Ty's shoulder and hair, body writhing beneath Ty's. His cock slid against hard muscle and soft skin. Ty's cock drove against his hip and stomach, pressing against his.

Ty bit down on the curve of Zane's neck as he shoved a little harder against him, and a jolt went through Zane's body. Ty hummed against his skin until it degenerated into a low growl. The rocking stopped, shifting into a more sinuous, deliberate pressure.

"Oh Jesus, Ty," Zane gasped out.

Now he needed Ty inside him. It felt like he'd stuck his finger in a light socket, electricity zigzagging through him wherever Ty touched, settling deep in his belly, coiling. Ty knew exactly what he was doing to him and exploited it mercilessly, egging on the pleasure racking Zane's body with a violent kiss. Zane bucked his hips as Ty's tongue lapped at his. Ty grasped Zane's hands, lacing their fingers together, slid them under Zane's head until their chests touched, and pinned them to the mattress. Zane's body was completely at Ty's mercy.

Zane forced his eyes open and found Ty's as he surrendered all control to him. He trusted him, despite everything, despite trying to convince himself he couldn't. He trusted Ty with his body. He always had. He trusted Ty with his heart. It was his very soul that Ty had the power to break.

Ty captured Zane's mouth in a kiss.

Sensation overflowed for a brief, shining moment. Ty's lips against his. The warmth and weight of his body, the way he felt between Zane's thighs. The sensual rocking of his hips, their cocks sliding, leaking. Then it all came crashing down. He arched his back, squeezing Ty's hips, groaning Ty's name into their kiss, his entire body spasming and tightening as his orgasm crashed over him. Ty didn't let up, didn't pull away, still rubbing against him, sliding slick now between their bellies.

"Zane," Ty growled against his ear.

Zane was still gasping for breath, sensations and emotions washing over him in a jumble. He panted against the skin of Ty's neck, unable to do anything more than inhale his scent.

Ty released Zane's hands and pushed himself to his knees. Zane grabbed him by the shoulder. "You're not done."

Ty leaned over him to kiss him again. He reached between them, swiping one hand down Zane's slick abdomen and cock, stroking down to Zane's thighs and urging them apart.

Zane let his knees fall to the sides, spreading his legs wider. Ty kissed the inside of Zane's knee, then crawled backward. He left the bed and went in search of one of their bags, leaving Zane to try to regain his breath alone.

When Ty returned, he crawled between Zane's legs and ran his tongue along Zane's stomach. Zane lifted his head to watch, fascinated as Ty licked his cum from his abs.

"Ty," he gasped.

Ty knelt, running his hand through Zane's cum, spreading it across his stomach. Then he added a generous amount of lube to his palm and used that hand to grip his own straining cock. Zane pulled one leg up and rolled over onto his stomach, inviting Ty to take him. Ty gripped one of Zane's hips and moved in close, wasting no time pushing in.

Zane's fingers dragged across the sheets. Ty's hand found his and he laced their fingers together, clenching as he pushed in deeper. Once he was as far as he could get, he laid his body out over Zane's, kissing Zane's shoulder, enveloping him in strong arms. His breathing broke into sharp pants.

"Come on, Ty," Zane panted, rolling his hips just enough to spur Ty into action.

Ty pressed his face against Zane's back, groaning, kissing his skin. He pulled most of the way out before thrusting in again with a ragged curse. Zane gasped, arching. Ty tortured Zane with that incredible slow slide of his cock several more times, his breaths in Zane's ear, before he lost control and shoved in deeper.

Zane would never enjoy anything more than Ty taking him from behind. His chest pressed into the mattress, Ty's lips at his ear. The way Ty held him close, found his way into Zane's very soul.

Ty pulled Zane's hips up, curling until he could reach to tease at Zane's mouth with his tongue, trailing the taste of his cum along swollen lips. His hand slid over Zane's shoulder, closing over his chest, hugging him close.

There was nowhere to go, nowhere to run from the intimacy or the pleasure. And Zane didn't mind one bit.

When Ty moved again, it was a steady rolling of his hips, and he didn't relinquish Zane's mouth. More kisses, more intensity, faster rocking, harder thrusts . . . the thrill echoed through them as Ty held on tight. Zane managed to gasp out Ty's name through the kiss, urging him on, begging him. Ty never sped up his motions, though, just continued to thrust in, rocking in time with Zane's panting breaths.

Finally, he buried his face against Zane's shoulder and gasped, choking out Zane's name. His body locked up and he shoved in deep, shaking all over but still rocking as he climaxed.

Zane closed his eyes, drinking it in, sharing it with his lover. He shifted his hips and arched his back in an attempt to extend the pleasure.

Ty sagged over him, struggling for air, but each time he got half a breath, his chest caught and an aftershock tore through him. Zane could feel it echoing through Ty to himself.

After several long moments, Ty pulled out of him with a sound that was almost a sob and collapsed at his side.

Zane lay where he was, unable to move even if he'd wanted to. He snaked a hand across the short distance between them and slid his fingers into Ty's. Ty's hand closed around his with a gentle squeeze.

"I just need to be able to trust you, Ty," he whispered.

"You can. I swear you can. I'd die for you, Zane."

Zane's heart was in his throat as he studied Ty's profile. "I know."

Chapter 14

Ty had a handful of cartridges laid out in front of him, some the .40 caliber rounds for Zane's Glock, and some the high-powered, armor-piercing monstrosities that loaded Liam's sniper rifle. Ty wished they could have found less deadly ammunition, but this was all they had to work with.

He had converted three of Zane's shots to blanks, though having done it without the proper equipment they might still pack a little bit of a punch. He'd taken the bullet out, leaving nothing but the charge, and packed them with newspaper to seal the powder in the case.

That wad of newspaper would come out like any other projectile, and the muzzle blast would still be powerful. It wouldn't kill him, though.

He was just finishing the round that Liam would be firing at him, creating a makeshift hollow-point that should expand and break up when it hit the resistance of the vest. He cut the hollow of the jacket to weaken it so it would expand like a flower on impact, rather than penetrate deeply. Without the vest, the sharp petals of the flower would slice through flesh two to three times the size of the original bullet.

If Liam missed, it was going to be ugly.

He lifted his head as Liam stepped into the room. The man looked around at their preparations, an eyebrow raised.

He stopped in front of Digger and Owen. "What in God's name is that?"

"Ketchup. And some other stuff," Digger answered. He and Owen had spent all morning filling quart bags with the concoction. "Barbecue sauce, Crisco. Chocolate powder and water."

Ty's nose curled as the list went on. It sounded like something Digger would cook and serve at home.

They put enough of the sauce in each bag to let them remain slim when sealed and flattened. Then they duct-taped the bags to the outside of the Kevlar vest.

Liam picked up one of the bags and squished it. "Marines are disgusting."

"Hey," Owen grunted.

"I have to agree right now," Nick said. He had a quart tub of Crisco and had been mixing it with diaper cream and chocolate powder to make face paint. The diaper cream had an especially unpleasant smell. "We're putting this on our faces."

Liam shuddered and poked at the vest Ty would be wearing. "What about the back?"

Digger shrugged. "We got no way of doing that without wiring Ty with some small explosives."

"Fuck no," Ty said immediately.

Liam snorted. "It'll have to do."

The vest itself was white, made to look like a T-shirt beneath other clothing. It reduced one layer, but with the Kevlar and the slimy bags of fake blood, Ty's mobility would still be cut down. He wasn't meant to be mobile, though; he simply had to stand there and die.

His stomach tumbled with nerves and he wiped a hand over his face. "Did you scout the location?" he asked Liam.

Liam sauntered over and sat opposite him, nodding. "I have a nice little nest all set up on—"

"Don't tell me where," Ty interrupted. "If I get nervous, I'm afraid I'll look at you."

"Okay. There's graffiti everywhere, so I put a big black X on the pavement where you're meant to stand. Try to get as close as you can to it, yeah?"

Ty nodded. He picked up the bullet he'd just finished and held it up for Liam to see. "Hollow-point round." He held up another, one he hadn't messed with. "Armor-piercing round." He waved them together. "Do not get these mixed up."

Liam chuckled, then leaned closer, sighing heavily and meeting Ty's eyes. "Tyler, if I wanted you dead, I would have done when it was easy to kill you." He plucked the fragmenting round from Ty's fingers. "We have no way of marking it."

"No. Any etchings on the outside will fuck with the spin. Hell, I'm even afraid to mark it with a Sharpie."

Liam was humming, turning the bullet over. He clutched it in his hand, then patted the back of Ty's neck, pulling his head to press their foreheads together. Ty closed his eyes. Months of their time spent together in arid camps in Kabul and damp training installations in the south of England came back to him. He'd trusted this man.

"You did this for me once," Liam murmured. "It's time I return the favor."

Ty nodded, swallowing hard.

Liam's voice dropped lower. "And if you want to stay dead, I'll always be a call away." He released Ty and stood.

Ty sat back, eyes still closed as he fought for calm. He felt Liam moving away. The front door opened and snicked shut again, and just like that, Liam Bell was gone.

Ty took a deep, unsteady breath and glanced up.

Zane was standing in the bedroom door, watching him. "You okay?"

Ty nodded.

"I'm about to make the calls," Zane said. The activity in the room died down, everyone stopping to look at Zane. "Is everyone ready?"

Ty looked around, taking in the faces of the men he'd called his friends, the men he'd loved like brothers and spilled blood for. And then Zane. The only man Ty had ever truly given his heart to. If there was anyone to make a last stand with, it was the men in this room.

"We're ready."

Zane sat astride Liam's Honda Shadow, a bandana with a menacing skull printed on it pulled over his face. Ty sat behind him, his hands looped over Zane like a seatbelt, tied at the wrists. They had a pillowcase over his head, a large smiley face drawn on it.

"Trust me," Digger told him. "This is New Orleans. Nobody'll bat an eye."

"Let's kick it, Garrett," Ty said in Zane's ear.

Zane didn't waste more time with goodbyes. He gunned the bike away from the house, winding their way through the streets toward the hulking wasteland of Six Flags New Orleans.

The noise of the motorcycle signaled their arrival, and that was exactly how Zane had wanted it. All eyes on them. The front gate of the park had been cut and left ajar, and Zane used the bike to plow through it. He came to a halt in the park entrance, stunned by the shape of the place.

The map had shown a happy amusement park set up in a vague circle around a center pond. On the far side was a large body of water, abutted by an area of the park called Pontchartrain Beach. It was a long, wide thoroughfare, and that was where Zane had told Valencia and Gaudet to meet him.

But the map hadn't prepared him for the park itself: an urban badlands, left to hold its own against the elements and urban explorers with spray paint.

"Jesus, Ty, you know how to pick them," Zane muttered.

"Is it as creepy as it feels? 'Cause I can't see shit through this thing."

Zane nodded.

Main Street Square was built to mimic the architecture of the French Quarter. It boasted stunning colors and Creole townhouses with sweeping galleries, but it was all covered in graffiti and debris. Weeds encroached. Huge pots sprouted weeds and saplings, and many had "NOLA Rising" written on them. Zane couldn't take his eyes off the crumbling façades. Left to their own devices, the buildings had begun to tear themselves apart.

"Zane," Ty whispered. His arms tightened around Zane's chest. "We can't linger."

Zane gave a curt nod and maneuvered the bike through the trash and detritus along the causeways. Other parts of the park were in even worse shape, and Zane pushed the motorcycle faster, not liking the feeling the park gave him. When they reached the bend that began Pontchartrain Beach, Zane stopped the bike, and Ty pulled his hands over Zane's head so they could dismount. Zane grabbed the rope between Ty's hands and looked at him. The garish red smiley face grinned back.

He walked Ty ahead of him, jerking him by his arm, shoving him around debris in his path.

Five men in pristine suits stood to one side of Pontchartrain Beach, their backs to the swampland behind them. Under an awning on the other side of the wide causeway, Gaudet and his very large son stood with two men in uniform. And Ava. Her eyes were red and her face was puffy. She took an involuntary step toward them when they appeared. Her brother held her back.

Zane pulled Ty closer, standing just behind him, a gun jammed into his ribs. Faded blue waves were painted all over the pavement, as if he and Ty were submerged in some surreal river, and several feet away was the large X Liam had marked on the ground.

Zane stepped beside Ty and turned him, then swept the pillowcase off Ty's head. He met his eyes one last time, trying to memorize every fleck of gold, every imperfection and quirk. There was fear in Ty's eyes, and Zane's resolve almost left him. But he shoved him, making him stumble toward the X.

"Xander," Mateo Valencia said. He stepped forward, his arms spread wide. "Or should I say, Zane?"

"Call me whatever you want. I'm not here to chat. I'm here to end this."

"A position I share," Valencia said. He ran a hand along the scar on his cheek, the one Zane had given him years ago. "Tell me why I should not just kill everyone here and leave?"

Gaudet pulled his gun, and his men followed suit. "You can try it."

"That's exactly what I want to avoid," Zane shouted. "One death! That's all we need here. And I have just the man for it." He gave Ty another shove, closer to the X. "Commander Gaudet, you know this man as Tyler Beaumont. He has information you need, am I right?"

"That's right."

"And Mateo, the only thing you need is the man who killed Antonio. *Muerto. Si?*"

"*Claro que si.*"

"So what's the problem?" Zane asked.

"What is it you're getting out of this, cowboy?" Gaudet asked.

Zane opened his mouth to speak, but Valencia beat him to it. "He is one of ours. A thorn the FBI inserted into our paw. A thorn we removed and sent back to them with poison in him."

Zane hated the sound of that, but he kept a stony face.

"And I want out from under de la Vega. This is my ticket. Do we have a deal?"

"It is agreeable to me."

"And I'm guessing you want out of my city with a free pass, huh?" Gaudet asked.

Zane nodded.

"Fine."

"Let us get this done with," Valencia called.

Zane took a shaky breath. Nerves were building. "Gaudet, what is it you want to know?"

Gaudet stepped forward, but not too far from the protection of the others. "The information you gathered, Beaumont. What happened to it?"

Ty shook his head.

Gaudet gripped Ava by the arm, pulling her forward. "Talk some damn sense into him."

She took a ragged, unsteady breath. It was loud in the silence of the dead park. "Ty," she said with difficulty. "I'm sorry. I don't know what to do." She began walking toward him.

Zane saw her father raise his arm, his gun trained on her back. His body jerked, but thankfully Ty reacted before he could.

"No!" he called.

Ava startled and whirled to face her father. She stumbled back when she saw him lowering his gun. "Daddy?"

He shook his head. "I'm sorry, darlin'. Make that boy talk."

"Okay!" Ty shouted. His voice broke. "Okay. *Cher, viens à moi.*"

Zane had heard Ty whisper enough French to understand that order: Come to me. Ava didn't hesitate, and Ty caught her and stepped in front of her, shielding her. Tears were streaming down her face, but Zane saw her slip a small blade into Ty's palm. Zane shook his head. They hadn't anticipated this. Who the hell would've expected the man to threaten his own daughter? He licked his lips, glancing to the swamp. If this went to hell, that swamp was their only hope.

Liam made a low whistling sound through the device in Zane's ear. "Little touch and go there, lads. Who do I shoot first if things go to hell?"

Zane made a shushing sound.

"The information you gathered?" Gaudet demanded.

"Katrina wiped it out," Ty said quickly. "Everything I had, it's gone. There's nothing left on you."

Gaudet pursed his lips and nodded curtly. It seemed to Zane that Ty had merely confirmed what Gaudet already knew. "It'll do. Ava, girl, get back here."

"*Mais non*!" Ty cried.

"I think I'll be taking her with me," Zane growled. "Payment for services rendered."

She gulped air, trying not to cry as she gripped the back of Ty's shirt. Ty was covertly slicing through the ropes at his wrists with the knife she'd slipped him, preparing for everything to go to hell. Ava was made of tough stuff, Zane could say that about her. But she was about to fall apart.

"Shoot him now, Xander, or I will," Valencia called, obviously tiring of the family drama.

"Ava, run," Ty gasped. "Run!"

Ava backed away a few steps. Zane rounded on Ty, putting his back to the Colombians and raising his gun. He pointed it at Ty's chest. He met Ty's eyes, seeing the fear there, the uncertainty.

"One," Liam said in his ear. "Two."

"Zane," Ty whispered. Zane's world began to slow.

"Three."

Ava darted forward, grabbing Ty's shoulder and swinging around him. Zane pulled the trigger. The blast echoed through the park, two shots becoming one.

Ty's shout was lost in the sound of the shot. The bullet thumped into her back and threw her into Ty. He caught her around the waist as she fell, crying out, cradling her with a hand to her face as they both dropped to the ground.

"Shit!" Liam shouted. "Son of a bitch! Stupid fucking girl!"

Other shouts mingled with the hammering of Zane's heart in his ears. He took a step toward them, watching as Ty laid her lifeless body on the ground, his hands shaking and covered with blood.

"Oh God, Ty."

Zane could hear guns being drawn behind him. Ty grabbed Zane's hand and pulled himself to his feet. He shoved his shoulder into Zane's body, spinning them, forcing Zane to use him as a shield. He held Zane's hand behind his back, squeezing it hard, refusing to allow Zane to let go as Gaudet and his men opened fire on them.

Ty's body jerked against Zane's as the first bullet hit, then again and again, shoving Zane back, forcing him off-balance.

The Colombians opened fire on the crooked cops, offering Zane the covering fire they thought an informant of theirs deserved, mowing them down like ducks in a gallery with their high-powered weapons.

Zane's back hit the pavement, the weight of Ty's body pinning him. The back of Ty's head banged into Zane's lip and he tasted blood. More gunfire came from the swamp. Patches of swamp grass were rising from the mire. Sidewinder.

Mateo Valencia strolled toward them. He was shaking his head, reloading his gun.

"Ty, get off me, come on," Zane grunted. He pushed at Ty's shoulder, but Ty merely gasped a ragged breath in response. "Ty?"

"You think I forgive so easily?" Valencia asked Zane in Spanish. He ran a finger along the scar on his cheek as he loomed over Zane.

Zane freed his arm and fired before Valencia could finish his reload. It was a blank round, but he still staggered back, swiping at singed pieces of his suit and bleeding where the paper plug had embedded in his neck. He shouted, aiming his gun at Zane's head. But he never got to fire. One flick of Zane's wrist, and the Vega cartel's top enforcer fell to the ground with a knife in his heart, his gun sliding from his hand, useless.

Zane scrambled from under his partner's weight and knelt beside him, finally yanking the bandana off his face and tossing it aside. Ty was covered in blood from his chin to his knees, though what was real and what was fake, Zane couldn't tell. Ty blinked up at the gray sky, gasping for breath that wouldn't come. There were half a dozen bullet holes in his chest.

"Oh Jesus, Ty," Zane cried. He laid his gun aside and bent over Ty, grabbing his face with both hands. "Ty!"

Ty struggled to take in air to respond. He reached up to grab Zane's wrist instead, gripping it hard. He closed his eyes.

"Ty, please," Zane whispered. "Please don't leave me."

Ty opened his eyes again and met Zane's, gasping and making sounds like he was trying to form words. A bullet had grazed his neck. Another had grazed his arm. Zane had no idea how bad the rest of his wounds were. There was too much blood.

Tears blurred Zane's vision and he looked up, desperate for help. Sidewinder was sweeping in from the swamp like angels of death, clearing weapons from dying hands, putting bullets in the heads of anyone who remained alive.

Three helicopters thumped in the distance, coming closer.

"Take his vest off him, Zane," Liam said in Zane's ear.

Zane gasped and began pawing at Ty's shirt. He ripped it open, then used his knife to cut the straps of the vest away.

Ty gasped in air, his body arching off the ground as Zane freed him from the restrictive, mangled plates. He gasped again, pulling in air as hard as he could and beginning to shiver all over.

Zane patted at Ty chest, wiping away the blood. "You're not hit!" he cried, beginning to laugh hysterically. "Oh thank you, God." He used his bandana to wipe away the fake blood from Ty's neck, pressing it to the wound oozing real blood. He pulled Ty up to hug him and Ty groaned, but he wrapped his arms around Zane and dug his fingers into his shirt, hugging him fiercely. One hand came to tangle in Zane's hair.

"You're breaking my ribs, Zane," Ty managed to wheeze before a coughing fit overtook him.

Zane released him and helped him lie back down. Ty closed his eyes, taking in deep breaths, one hand pressing to Zane's against his neck, the other shaking as he rested it on his stomach. Zane used his sleeve to wipe the blood away from his own mouth and nose, and with his face clean of it, he could smell the fake blood on Ty, hints of tomato and chocolate and barbecue sauce. He collapsed beside Ty, relief overwhelming him as he rested his head on Ty's stomach.

"You're an utter asshole," Zane murmured against Ty's abs.

"You're welcome."

"Is he okay?" Nick shouted as he ran toward them.

Zane didn't move to answer. He felt Ty raise a hand, probably giving a thumbs-up.

The sound of the helicopters grew louder, and soon Zane could feel the wind of the rotor wash on his face. He finally realized a dozen men in SWAT gear were clearing the scene and trying to relieve Sidewinder of their weapons. Digger and Owen began to argue with two men who quickly pointed guns at their heads and made them get on their knees.

Zane sat up, confused by the appearance of another player. But then a familiar figure stepped out of the helicopter and began jogging toward them.

"Dick?" Ty croaked.

Richard Burns reached down to help Ty to his feet. He patted him on the shoulder, but then gave up on propriety and hugged him. "I got here as fast as I could."

"What are you doing here?" Zane demanded.

"When Ty called and said there was a mole relaying your movements, I ran a test and found a trace on your phone. I couldn't tell you I was coming in or the mole would have known."

"I... I thought you left us in the wind," Ty said, still breathless and holding his bleeding neck.

Burns patted his cheek. "I would never do that, Beaumont. You know that." He took a step back and surreptitiously wiped the disgusting blood concoction off his hand with a handkerchief as soon as Ty's attention was elsewhere.

Zane was still glowering at Burns when he realized Ty had stumbled away from them. He shed the remains of the vest and dropped to his knees at Ava's side. Blood had pooled under her and began to trail toward the center of the causeway. Her eyes stared into the sky.

Ty reached a shaking hand and set it over her forehead, closing her eyes. Zane could hear him murmuring a prayer in French through the ear bud in his ear.

Zane ran a hand through his hair, then yanked the ear bud out as he turned away from them. He met Burns's eyes. "Ty told me everything."

Burns stiffened, then nodded.

"You thought I was a traitor?" Zane asked through gritted teeth.

"Better safe than sorry, Zane. I knew as long as Ty trusted you, I could too."

Zane rushed forward and swung at him, knocking him to the ground with a shout. "You can't fuck with people's lives like that!" he barked as two men ran up to them, each grabbed an arm, and began pulling him back. "Can't you see what he would do for you? You can't use him like that, Dick! You can't!"

Burns sat up, jaw lax and nose bleeding. He clambered to his feet and waved the men off. Zane took short, quick breaths as Burns came closer and gripped both of his arms.

"Be calm, Zane. It's over. It's over."

Zane took deeper breaths, struggling to concentrate on the here and now and deal with the betrayal and anger later. Burns patted him on the cheek and then walked away. Zane watched him go, feeling the anger drain out of him, replaced with a wide swath of loss. Burns was the first person since Jack Tanner in the academy who Zane had really felt cared about him. What the hell was he supposed to do now?

Nick caught Zane's attention as he picked up the remains of Ty's Kevlar vest. The man looked from Ava's body to the vest, then peered into the distance, where the wooden rails of a roller coaster undulated like a felled dragon in the swamp.

Zane moved closer. "What's wrong?"

"Bullet went right through her. Ty's talon hollow-point would have torn her to shreds, but it wouldn't have gone through her." He shuffled guiltily when he realized Ty had trudged up to stand with them, but he held up the vest for them to see. Among the flattened pistol rounds was a larger one, embedded in the vest. Nick turned it over to show them the very tip, where it had penetrated almost through, right over Ty's heart. It had no petals from the grooves Ty had cut into it. It wasn't the same bullet.

"He mixed up the bullets. Used an armor-piercing round," Zane said, suddenly light-headed.

"That would have killed me," Ty said.

"She saved your life," Nick said. "Slowed it enough for the vest to stop it."

Ty nodded. They all turned toward the roller coaster in the distance, the only place the shot could have originated from.

"Why didn't he go for a head shot?" Nick asked.

"He knew you boys would catch him before he could get away. But if I went down like I was supposed to, no one's the wiser until he's long gone."

"You can't know it was on purpose," Zane tried. "The bullets looked alike."

Ty nodded, eyes still on the skeletal behemoth in the swamp. He finally lowered his head and walked away, following Burns toward the waiting helicopters.

"What happened out there?"

"He really shouldn't be speaking," the nurse told them.

"Honey, you get him to shut up long enough to heal, you let us know how you did it," Digger grumbled as he plucked a bit of saw grass from that morning off his face.

"We'll keep him quiet," Nick promised, giving her a charming smile. It was probably ruined by the homemade face paint he'd discovered wouldn't wash off. She nodded and left them, and Nick returned his attention to the man in the hospital bed.

Kelly grinned widely at them. "I know you all cried over me."

Nick laughed. "We did."

"Mainly because we knew we'd be the ones nursing you back to health," Owen added.

Kelly held up a fist, and Owen gently pressed their knuckles together.

"So how'd it go down?"

"Everyone died, pretty much," Digger answered. "Liam Bell was long gone by the time me and Irish climbed that death trap. Our names are being cleared by the FBI. Ty's been suspended until Hell freezes over."

Nick tore his eyes away from Kelly's face to study Ty, sitting in the reclining chair in the corner. His ribs were tightly wrapped, there was a bandage on his neck, and—perhaps the biggest tragedy of all—a bullet had sliced right through his bulldog tattoo. He had dark circles under his eyes. And he'd been holding that damn voodoo doll since he sat down.

"They're saying it'll be a few weeks, at least," Ty said. His voice was hoarse.

"So that's it?" Kelly asked. "We made it?"

They all laughed uncomfortably. For some reason, it didn't feel like they'd made it.

"What happened here?" Zane asked suddenly. He'd been sitting in the far corner, letting the rest of them visit.

Nick snorted, but Zane was frowning.

"I'm serious? What the fuck was that?"

"Liam Bell happened here," Ty said. His scratchy voice and hollow eyes and the way he was caressing that voodoo doll were eerie. Ty was starting to creep Nick out.

"What do you mean?" Zane demanded.

Ty turned the doll in his hand. "I didn't catch on fast enough."

"Ty," Nick said quietly. "None of what happened here is your fault."

"I know." Ty finally looked up. "It's his."

Nick said nothing. He wasn't going to touch that one.

"He outplayed me."

"This wasn't a game, Ty," Zane said.

"Sure it was. Liam wasn't freelancing here. He works for the NIA."

"How do you know?" Zane asked.

"Because I didn't miss. I don't miss. He was here as an NIA agent. And what is the NIA?"

"The brand new, ultra-militarized arm of the CIA," Kelly recited.

"With broad purpose but small, precious resources," Ty added.

"You're saying you think Liam and the NIA engineered all of this?" Zane asked. "Why?"

"To do exactly what we did."

"Clean out a rat's nest?" Nick asked.

"You're saying NIA pitted a retired Recon team against a Colombian cartel?" Owen asked. "On purpose?"

Ty shrugged. "It was a perfect storm. We cleared out a dozen of the cartel's men, plus a high-ranking dirty cop who controls a busy port city. They lose no assets. Don't take the heat."

"How do you figure?" Digger asked.

Ty held up his hand. He slowly extended his thumb. "He knew Sanchez. Knew he was dead, knew his birthday, knew we'd all gather. He knew Digger was confined to the state. That leaves one place and time we'd all be. And to know all that, he had to have CIA sources." He pointed his index finger, counting off his reasons. "The cartel came by boat, which means they left Miami before we did. He didn't see us and then call them. They knew to be here because he told them to be here." He flipped up another finger. "He knew my past here. You think it was coincidence I hit Gaudet's radar as soon as I landed? He effectively boxed us in, forced us to act."

"I don't know, Ty," Nick finally said. "I don't trust the bastard either, but . . . I'm just not comfortable thinking he's that many steps ahead."

Ty shrugged. "Neither am I."

"If that is what happened, why would he try to kill you?" Owen asked. "Do you really think he just mixed those bullets up?"

Ty stared at the voodoo doll, long enough the silence became uncomfortable. "He's a scorpion and I'm a turtle," Ty finally answered.

"Are you hallucinating again?" Zane asked.

Nick cleared his throat. "It's a fable. The scorpion asks the turtle to take him across the river. The turtle says no because he's afraid the scorpion will sting him. Scorpion tells Turtle he won't sting him because they'll both drown. But halfway across the river, the scorpion strikes. As they're sinking, Turtle asks him why, and Scorpion replies, 'It's just my nature.'"

Zane's worried eyes moved to Ty, who was studying the voodoo doll again. "That's not good enough."

"Maybe he knows Ty's the only one who can catch him," Kelly rasped.

Ty stood carefully without another word, then took a step toward Kelly. Kelly lifted a hand and Ty took it, squeezing it gently. "I'll be back, okay?"

"I'm not going anywhere."

Ty petted him on the head, then turned to shuffle out of the room.

The rest of them began to stand, giving Kelly their own goodbyes before they all filed out.

Nick stood at the doorway, watching the others walk away.

Digger put his arm over Owen's shoulders. "Care for a few cocktails?"

"It's barely noon, man."

"So? This is Nawlins!"

They laughed as they headed for the elevator. Ty and Zane followed, walking side by side but not saying anything. Nick shook his head as he watched them go.

"They gonna be okay?" Kelly asked from the bed.

Nick pondered them. "Oh, you know Ty," he finally said, injecting some cheer into his voice. "He can squirm out of anything."

Ty was silent as Zane hailed a cab for them. Digger and Owen had cavorted off into the French Quarter as if nothing had happened that morning, but Zane was finding it a bit more difficult to brush off.

He and Ty climbed into the cab, directing it to the Bourbon Orleans, where they still had a room under Nick's name. What remained of their belongings had been taken there earlier.

Zane glanced sideways at Ty. His neck was stained with remnants of Digger's fake blood and his real blood, and his face was ashen, but Zane had seen him look worse. "I can't believe we both came out of this without anything other than scratches," Zane tried.

Ty bobbed his head distractedly.

"Do you still have the gris-gris bag?"

That caused Ty to raise his head. He licked his lips. "Yeah. Gotta figure out how to cleanse it."

"How?"

"There used to be a priestess on Rampart. Probably still there."

Zane studied him, wishing the distance between them hadn't grown so full of thorns. He worked hard to swallow past the tightness in his throat.

The taxi came to a stop and Zane paid the driver as Ty trudged to the hotel entrance. Zane jogged to catch up with him. "Hey," he called, frustration growing as he followed Ty through the lobby. "Are we going to talk about . . . anything?"

Ty punched the button on the elevator. He nodded, not meeting Zane's eyes. The doors opened and Ty stepped in, turning to face Zane. "Do you love me, Zane?"

The simple question, asked with so little emotion in Ty's eyes, hit Zane like a hammer in the chest, stealing his breath, making his knees go weak. He stumbled into the elevator before the doors could close on them.

"Yes. Yes I do."

Ty nodded. "And I love you."

Zane released the breath he'd been holding. He was relieved to hear that confirmation after all that had happened, after all they'd said and done to each other. "So . . . what do we do?"

"Well." Ty swallowed, looking a little sick. "I can't . . . I can't sit on your pedestal."

"Ty."

"No. I'm not saying it's a bad thing, Zane. I'm not. We've both known from the start the only reason you got clean was because I begged you to. You hang on by your fingernails because I expect you to. It's not fair to you. It's not fair to me. I can't be the reason you're sober, Zane."

Zane's breath came out harsh and shaky.

"Because I'm not perfect, and the next time I let you down, it can't be me you're leaning on. You have to be strong enough to stay off the bottle. For you. Not me."

Zane couldn't meet Ty's eyes anymore and he averted his gaze to the floor. "I'm not proud of what I've done, Ty."

"Neither am I," Ty whispered. He reached out and put two fingers under Zane's chin, lifting his head to meet his eyes. "I'm sorry I let you down."

Zane moved closer, his eyes rapt on Ty's. Ty's hand moved from his chin to cup his cheek, and Zane leaned to kiss him carefully. The kiss demanded nothing. It was merely a sentiment of love and devotion from one man to another.

Zane's heart pounded with the acceptance. When he stepped back, they were still looking into each other's eyes. The elevator stopped and jolted them both. Zane took a deep, bracing breath. "Where does that leave us?"

Ty shook his head. "I love you. You love me. We know what we have can be strong. Stronger."

Zane lowered his head before he could see the pain that was about to pass over Ty's face. The elevator door opened and closed behind him. "But . . . the pieces have to be strong for the whole to be. Right?"

"Yes," Ty whispered. "And I'm not right now. I . . . I don't even know what I am anymore. I haven't for a long time."

"You're a good man," Zane said, vehement as he jerked his head up. "You're a brave man. And you're a man who loves with his whole heart and soul. That's who you are."

Ty pressed his lips together tightly. His eyes were glistening, and as Zane watched, a tear broke free and trailed down his face. Ty ducked his head and wiped it away with the heel of his hand. "That's who you think I am."

Zane swallowed hard.

"I'm an assassin," Ty said, his voice unsteady. "I'm a killer. I'm the tip of a spear."

The hair on Zane's arms rose. His stomach tumbled. Another tear followed the trail of the first down Ty's dirty face, but Ty didn't seem to notice.

"And you," Ty continued, his voice breaking. "You're a phoenix, Zane. Rising from the ashes. And all I do is make you burn."

Zane's throat was too tight to swallow past, and his next breath came out a choked sob. He had never imagined that was how Ty saw him, and hearing it now made him want to take back every harsh word they'd ever shared, every thrust and parry of their relationship. He reached for Ty's face, fingers trembling.

Ty hugged him, clinging to him, his breaths harsh in Zane's ear. "I'm going to stay here," Ty said shakily. Zane gasped, but Ty didn't let him pull away. He held to him tighter. "Until the suspension's over. I'm going to stay here with Kelly. I'll give you that time and space you said you need."

"Ty," Zane whispered.

Ty wrenched away and dug in his pocket for something, then shoved it into Zane's hand and hugged him again like he was afraid Zane might try to get away. When Zane looked at the object over Ty's shoulder, his chest fluttered at the sight of the silver anchor token Ty had made him. *I believe in you*, it read.

Zane wanted to argue, to beg Ty not to make him leave him here. But Ty was right. He had realized it himself, remembering the way he'd watched Becky, thinking her joy was shared. The way he observed Ty's vibrant lust for life and fooled himself into thinking he was living just by basking in that glow.

But he had no friends. He had no joys. He had nothing that wasn't about Ty or the job.

He had to learn to live. If he was a phoenix, he had to learn to fly on his own, or he'd keep smoldering in his own ashes.

He nodded against Ty's cheek. "Okay," he whispered. "Okay."

Chapter 15

Zane sat at his desk, finishing up paperwork from a racketeering case they had been building for the last four weeks. He'd been working without a partner, taking on more responsibilities as a team leader. Two weeks ago, the Assistant Special Agent in Charge had been promoted and transferred to a different post, and Zane had unofficially moved into the position, taking even more responsibility until it was filled.

It was a promotion in every sense of the word, and Dan McCoy had let Zane know the ASAIC was his if he decided to take it. It would mean no more field work.

No more partner.

Zane hadn't been able to say yes, but he hadn't refused it either. Candidates were being vetted and interviewed, and Zane had time to decide.

Until then, he concentrated on slowly but surely righting his ship. He'd begun his AA meetings again, keeping the anchor token with him at all times. He'd stopped going to the gym quite as often, trying to fill his free time with other, more varied things. He set up an easel and a massive drop cloth on the top floor of the row house and began painting again. He started talking out loud when the room was empty, like Ty sometimes did, and he found it made his thoughts clearer to send them into the air rather than keep them trapped in his mind to weigh him down. He reread the books he'd clung to all these years, reminding himself why he loved them the first time around. Then he went out and hunted down new ones.

With Ty's permission, he went through every nook and cranny in the row house. He looked through all of Ty's books, finding half a dozen with cutouts and things hidden in them: passports, lockbox keys, money from several different countries, a flash drive, the emblem from the grill of the Bronco, and one of Elias Sanchez's dog tags. He put it all back.

He finally looked under the kitchen sink, hunting through everything to find what it was Ty had hidden under there. He'd caught Ty once, when he'd lost his sight, rummaging through here. What he finally found made him grin from ear to ear: a box of Cuban cigars inside a fireproof, portable safe. He took one out and put the rest back where he'd found them.

The most shocking thing he found, though, was something he'd always known was there. In an armoire in the spare bedroom, Ty kept dozens of little boxes. Decorative boxes, old cigar boxes, leather jewelry cases. Zane had never asked about them, never looked in them. He'd always been just a little afraid to see what Ty kept in those boxes.

Ty managed to surprise him yet again. Inside he found trinkets Ty had collected over the years. Things he'd picked up and taken home for no apparent reason. Things from cases he'd worked. Things from people he'd known. In one box, Zane found a bottle cap from a Shiner beer, the kind he'd had in Texas. A poker chip. A purple crayon. A piece of the fake skin they'd used to cover his tattoo on the cruise ship. A dried flower.

Zane discovered that Ty was basically a squirrel.

After the initial shock of being alone, he started branching out further, trying to find out more about himself instead of Ty. He went to a few Orioles games alone, immersing himself in the intricacies and inches that had so fascinated him as a child. He started putting his knife skills and love of puzzles to good use and taught himself to cook.

He stood outside of a bar in Fell's Point with dozens of others and watched the news as it was announced that Osama bin Laden had been killed. For the first time in over a week, Ty called him. They watched the same newscast, sharing it together, neither saying more than ten words.

He escorted Clancy to her sister's wedding, pretending to be her very charming and wealthy boyfriend for her overly nosy mother in exchange for the honor of a few tangos. Clancy wasn't a half bad dancer.

He helped Alston move out of his girlfriend's condo, all the while dodging Alston's possessions being chucked at them from the top of the stairs. They bonded over hot wings, discussing all the ways the job fucked up their relationships.

Perrimore got engaged, and Zane was shocked and slightly panicked when he asked Zane to be his best man. He had never planned a bachelor party, but when his mind turned to Ty, to the obvious person to ask for help, Zane pushed it away. He could do this.

He'd driven to Philadelphia to see Deuce, Livi, and their baby girl. Amelia Rose Grady had been born a few weeks before Christmas, and at five months old, she was already pulling Deuce around like he was on roller skates. She had her mother's white-blonde hair, and her eyes appeared to be turning that particular Grady green that seemed to serve as nature's warning to other creatures.

He had spoken to Ty every week.

It had been a good month. A good start. Zane was proud of himself, and he realized that he hadn't been able to say that in a very long time.

He finished up his paperwork and packed it away. He was the last one in the office, and as he was walking to the elevator, he turned to look at the stairwell. He still wondered what the hell had happened a month ago. He believed Ty now when he said he hadn't known that Burns was in Baltimore the night of Zane's twenty-year party, but Zane knew he'd seen the man.

It frustrated him not to have all the answers.

His steps echoed in the empty parking garage. His leather jacket creaked as he slid his arms into it. It was times like this, times when he was alone, when the world was quiet, that he thought of Ty. It would be just like Ty to show up now, maybe sitting on his motorcycle with a smirk, reminding Zane that his birthday was in a few days. That was the type of entrance Ty would make.

Zane grinned at the thought. He found his bike sans Ty, but the thought still made the ride home a good one.

He parked in the backyard, behind the lovingly covered Mustang, and clomped up the steps to the door, humming to himself. When he stepped inside, he set his helmet down on the counter nearby and dumped his keys into the bowl next to it.

"Honey, I'm home," he said wryly to the empty row house.

"It's about damn time."

Zane's head shot up. Ty was sitting on the arm of the sofa, smiling. He was more tanned than he had been, and he certainly looked healthier. His hair was shorter, and the western style shirt he wore seemed to stretch across the taut muscles of his chest and arms.

"Ty," Zane breathed.

"You look good."

Zane took a few steps closer and Ty stood, his smile growing softer.

"You look really good, Zane."

Zane lunged for him and wrapped him up in a hug. The smell of Old Spice permeated Zane's senses for the first time in a month.

"How are you?" Ty asked as they hugged.

"I'm good," Zane managed. He pressed his nose to the scar on Ty's throat. "You?"

Ty nodded jerkily. He didn't let go of Zane. "Are you ready for me to come home?" he asked, voice breaking.

"Yes," Zane answered before Ty had even finished the question. He grabbed Ty's face in his hands and kissed him, over and over until Ty was laughing and trying to fend him off.

At last, Zane took a step back to examine him. "How have you been? How's Kelly doing?"

"He's good. They sent him home, and I think his ex-wife plans to take care of him, so he's desperate to get better so she'll leave. My suspension's been revoked. They're letting me come back next week."

Zane grinned. He grasped Ty's hand and moved around the sofa to pull him down with him. "Tell me everything."

Ty licked his lips, smirking.

Zane grinned widely. "And then I'll show you the new sheets I put on the bed."

Ty laughed and crawled onto the couch with him.

Zane wrapped his arms around him, pulling him into his lap instead. Ty straddled him, sitting back and cocking one eyebrow at Zane.

"What'd you do while you were down there?"

"I sang. I stayed with Kelly. With Ava gone, I was the closest thing to a relative Murdoch had left, so I took care of his estate."

Zane frowned. "The bar?"

Ty bit his lip and nodded. "It's mine. I uh... I closed it up. Looking into selling it. I'll donate whatever it makes to one of the groups trying to rebuild. There was a kid who used to bartend there, had real talent with the bottle juggling and mixing and stuff. I saw him at Murdoch's funeral. His boss is interested in buying it."

"You don't want to keep it?"

Ty shook his head. "It wouldn't last long as it is, not without Murdoch and Ava there. Her voice was what brought them in. He was what gave it life."

"I'm sorry."

Ty shrugged it off and nodded.

"Did you ever get the curse lifted?" Zane asked.

"Yes. Yes, I did," Ty drawled, but he frowned as he patted Zane's chest.

"What'd the priestess tell you?"

"She told me I had dark days ahead."

Zane didn't want to believe in any of it—the voodoo, the mysticism, the incredible coincidences Ty said were fate. But the words made his stomach flip. "Do you believe her?"

Ty met his eyes. "Do you believe we met in New Orleans because we were meant to?"

Zane's mouth went dry. "Yeah, I do," he whispered.

Ty nodded, looking grim. He leaned forward and brushed his lips over Zane's. "We'll be okay."

"More than okay," Zane said. "We'll be us."

Ty smiled against his lips. Zane chased him when he pulled back, kissing him again. It grew more heated, needier, devolving quickly into two men who hadn't seen each other in a month and desperately wanted to touch each other. Zane rolled Ty until they both tumbled off the couch and Ty was sprawled on the floor, Zane straddling him. "Have we caught up enough that I can start taking your clothes off?"

Ty laughed, a carefree, boyish sound, and glanced to his side, distracted by what he saw. "You moved the rug."

"I kitty-cornered it."

"Why would you do that?" Ty asked, aghast.

"To see you lose your shit when you got home." Zane leaned closer, grinning evilly. "There are other things out of order too. Books not alphabetized. Coffee mug handles facing different directions." He lowered his voice to a whisper as Ty's eyes widened in horror. "The closet isn't color coded."

"You're just watching the world burn, huh?"

Zane laughed.

"God I missed you," Ty said in a rush of breath.

Zane grabbed a handful of Ty's hair and tugged, and when Ty's head tipped back, Zane kissed him hungrily, not letting go of him. Ty's laugh turned into a growl, and suddenly there was no space between them. No tears or lonely days, no secrets and no lies. Just Ty and Zane. On the floor of their row house. On a crooked rug.

Zane reached between them to unzip Ty's jeans, and then began struggling with loosening his own belt.

Ty's growl became a groan as Zane rose up onto his knees. Ty jerked Zane's pants down to his thighs and sat up, kissing his stomach.

Zane's fingers tightened in his hair. He watched, inhaling sharply as Ty wrapped his hands around Zane's hips and dragged his teeth over Zane's hip bone. He tugged Zane's briefs down, grasping the back of one of Zane's thighs.

"Jesus, Ty," Zane managed. He wanted nothing more than to hold the back of Ty's head right there by his hair and shove himself down Ty's throat, but there was something else he'd been fantasizing about as he lay in bed alone, something he had to do now that Ty was back.

So he gripped Ty's hair harder and moved off him. "Get on the couch," he growled.

Zane grabbed the back couch cushions and tossed them to the floor. Ty began to laugh again, but he climbed onto the couch like he'd been told. He reached up to touch Zane, fingers digging into his hips. He thought Zane intended to fuck his mouth. He was ready for it, grinning.

Ty was too much to resist like that, and Zane leaned down to kiss him messily, settling between Ty's legs to let their bodies rub together as he moved.

Then he pushed back up and unzipped Ty's jeans the rest of the way, tugging at them. He didn't pull them off, though, instead standing to kick out of his suit pants. Ty sat up long enough to pull off his shoes and socks and toss them to the floor, then shimmy out of his jeans and boxers.

"You gonna do this wearing the jacket?" Ty asked.

Zane closed his eyes as that image flashed through him.

"You should have kept that skull bandana, Zane, it was the hottest thing I'd ever seen."

"Christ, Ty," Zane snarled. He yanked his battered leather jacket off and tossed it aside, struggling out of the rest of his clothes. Once naked, he knelt on the floor and bent over Ty's lap, taking him into his mouth to suck and tease, hands traveling up and down Ty's thighs and gripping his hips.

Ty breathed Zane's name as he arched his back. It was a sound Zane had sorely missed. He had missed everything about this: the easy teasing, the feel and smell of Ty's body against his, the sounds Ty made when Zane touched him. Zane's month alone had been a good one, but God was he glad to have Ty in his arms again.

Zane pushed off him and raised his head to kiss him again, tugging him close, wrapping him up. He stretched his hand down Ty's body, soaking in the warmth, re-familiarizing himself with the hard muscles and pulling at Ty's hip.

He wanted to maul him.

The muscles of Ty's shoulders and back bunched as he reached for Zane. He licked and kissed at Zane's ear. "What do you want?"

"I want you the other way," Zane commanded.

Ty raised one eyebrow. "You sure?"

Zane nodded and grinned, his hands sliding over Ty's skin. Ty kissed him one last time, then Zane was stretched out on the couch and Ty clambered carefully over him. Ty shifted back until his cock slid along Zane's cheek. With a groan, he dropped his head and licked along the side of Zane's cock.

Zane didn't waste any time. He wrapped his hands around Ty's hips and took Ty into his mouth, yanking so Ty would thrust down. He groaned appreciatively at the added stimulus of Ty's tongue. Very little could get Ty hotter faster than a hard cock between his lips, but it had taken Zane a few years to accept that the same might true of him. This was one of Ty's favorite things to do. Ty had told him that many times. So why the hell shouldn't Zane enjoy it to the fullest?

Ty started moving his hips, tentatively pushing down into Zane's mouth. Zane heard and felt Ty's groan.

Zane let his hands roam as he sucked, shifting to push up against Ty's tongue, pulling down to encourage Ty to thrust harder. It worked, and Ty finally gave him a firm thrust. He was supporting himself on one arm, the fingers of his other hand wrapped around the base of Zane's cock to squeeze.

Zane went into sensory overload. With Ty's mouth around his cock and his lips closed around the head of Ty's, his ears began buzzing and pleasure built in his groin. He dug his hands into Ty's hips, dragging his fingers along his skin, then raised one knee up and worked it under Ty's arm so he could wrap his legs around Ty's torso. Ty gasped, pulling his mouth off Zane to curse under his breath and moan desperately before sucking Zane onto his tongue again.

Even if Zane had wanted to say something, Ty was pressed too close for him to get his mouth free. Ty's measured strokes began to grow erratic as Ty sucked Zane harder. His fingers dragged along the crease of Zane's thigh and slide down to tease between his legs.

Zane hiked his leg up higher, writhing under Ty's body and moaning loudly as Ty thrust into his mouth. It was only a few more strokes before Ty groaned desperately and pushed himself up on both hands, coming almost free of Zane's mouth. "Zane," he gasped.

"No, come back," Zane breathed as he grasped Ty's hips and raised his head to take Ty back to his mouth. He licked him up and down, then ran his tongue over Ty's balls and sucked one of them into his mouth.

"Oh *fuck*." Ty huffed and reached for Zane's cock, wrapping his mouth around the leaking head and starting to suck again.

After giving each one of Ty's balls thorough attention, Zane let them roll off his tongue and guided Ty's cock back between his lips. Ty groaned and thrust down into Zane's mouth, harder and deeper than before, and he sucked Zane as his fingers massaged Zane's balls.

Zane couldn't stop the shout, but it came out muffled as Ty's cock filled his throat. He shoved his hips upward, knees squeezing at Ty's shoulders. Ty's needy noises came nonstop. Zane's cock brushed along the back of Ty's throat.

Zane reached down to drag his fingers over Ty's shoulder in warning. The muscles shifted under his touch as Ty bent his elbow and lowered himself further, still sucking and now sliding Zane's balls against his palm. Ty's thrusts into Zane's mouth turned short and quick and hard as he began to shudder.

Zane moaned nonstop, the stimulation coming from every possible direction. He dug his fingernails into Ty's thighs. He was going to come, and he was going to do it down Ty's throat. He wanted nothing more than for Ty to do the same to him.

Ty's hips stuttered to a stop before he arched his back and started to spill over Zane's tongue. Zane sucked and swallowed and moaned, burying his nose against Ty's balls, loving that Ty's cum was spurting down his throat and wondering how in the hell he had never tried this before. Ty slowly dragged his lips up, teeth grazing along the shaft of Zane's cock.

Zane sucked and swallowed as his body twisted and he shoved his hips up, chasing Ty's mouth, barely realizing he was doing it. His cock slid on Ty's tongue, and Ty jerked and inhaled in a rush before shuddering and starting to suck again.

Zane arched his back and threw his head to the side, releasing Ty's spent cock and dragging his teeth against the tender inside of Ty's thigh. Ty groaned appreciatively and Zane bit down as his orgasm washed over him, wishing like hell he could see what Ty was doing.

As the orgasm wound down, Zane's death grip on Ty's waist loosened, his teeth sliding against Ty's thigh, and his body began to relax beneath Ty's. His breaths were harsh and hard. After a long moment, Ty pushed himself to the side with a grunt and rolled off the couch to the floor. He sat with his back against it, his head coming to rest on Zane's thigh.

Zane settled his fingers in Ty's hair. "That was fun," he panted.

Ty couldn't comment. Zane's fingers tightened in Ty's hair.

"Why the hell couldn't you have tried that when I could watch?" Ty finally gasped.

Zane began to chuckle, low and dark. He wiped his mouth with the back of his hand. "Either get back up here with me or go get me a bottle of water," he muttered, still recovering from the full-body meltdown.

Ty's low laugh turned into a hum of approval. He knelt at Zane's side, leaning over to drop a kiss at Zane's hip before hovering over Zane again, this time face-to-face.

"Why the hell didn't you make me do that before?" Zane asked him. He claimed Ty's lips for a torrid kiss that prevented Ty from laughing. But Ty was grinning when he pulled back.

Zane shook his head minutely, clutching Ty to him and shifting his shoulders until they were both on their sides on the couch. Ty sighed and closed his arms around Zane. Zane raised his chin so Ty could fit his head against his chest, and he held him as close as he could get him.

His familiar smell permeated Zane's world.

"Who are you, Ty?"

Ty smiled against his cheek. "I was an assassin," he whispered. "I'm a Marine. I'm the man who doesn't miss. And I'm yours."

Zane bit his lip on a smile.

"Who are you, Zane?"

Zane cocked his head. "I'm an artist. I'm a geek." He felt Ty smile. "I am one badass motherfucker on a motorcycle."

Ty began to laugh.

Zane dipped his head until they were staring into each other's eyes. "And I'm yours."

※

The next day, Ty drove Zane to work and went up with him to say hello to everyone. A celebratory mood hung in the air. Zane wasn't the only one who had missed his partner.

Ty was wearing tattered jeans and a gray T-shirt with an angry elephant on it, holding a knife, that read "Elephants never forget, and they never forgive." It had made Zane laugh when Ty had pulled it out, and now Zane had a hard time keeping his eyes off Ty as he settled at his desk.

They weren't there for five minutes before McCoy called them into his office. Ty and Zane trudged along amidst the taunts and catcalls of their coworkers. Zane pulled the door shut behind him, and was shocked to see Richard Burns leaning against a file cabinet in the corner of the office.

"Glad to see you back, Grady," McCoy said to Ty. "Garrett, have a seat."

Zane sat, looking between McCoy and Burns apprehensively. McCoy got up and made his way out of the office, leaving them alone.

"I'll make this brief," Burns said as soon as the door shut. He moved toward the desk, bending and sliding his hand underneath it.

Ty and Zane shared a confused look.

Burns placed both hands on the desk. He waved Ty and Zane over, and after another moment of confusion, Ty got up to step around the other side of the desk. Zane followed. Burns spoke as they moved.

"Because of your recent exposure in the media, we're going to be taking you off undercover work permanently."

They'd already been warned of that much. They were in a fucking calendar, after all. Zane supposed they were just moving up the timeline after what had happened in New Orleans.

Burns pointed under the desk. Ty studied him cautiously, then knelt and peered underneath. When he looked back at Burns, his eyes had widened. Zane crouched to inspect the desk as well, and his heart stuttered when he saw a small microphone taped to the desk. A listening device.

"You'll both be strictly investigative agents from now on," Burns said. He laid a notecard on the desk.

Your mole is here.

Zane's heart stuttered again. Burns's hand came to rest on his shoulder, squeezing hard.

"Since you're both so good at closing cases," he said with special emphasis. "Carry on, gentlemen."

Ty took the card, crumpling it in his hand and turning away with a last glance at Burns. He nodded, his jaw tight and his eyes hard. Zane was numb, unable to process the information. One of their coworkers was spying on them. Trying to get them killed. How much did they know? How much had they seen? How were they getting their information?

They left Burns in the office, passing McCoy in the doorway. He patted Zane's back, giving him his usual friendly grin. Zane managed a smile and nod for his boss as they headed back to their desks.

Neither of them said a word. There was nothing to say, not here. Not now.

It barely registered when the elevator dinged, but when Ty straightened, Zane caught the movement. The look of concern on Ty's handsome face spurred Zane to turn.

Two men in Marine uniforms stood at the elevator, speaking with McCoy and displaying a packet of official looking papers. Burns joined the discussion when it got heated.

Alston sat on the edge of Zane's desk beside Ty to watch. "This is odd."

McCoy argued with the Marine, growing angrier until Burns finally sent him back to his office. Burns continued the discussion, but the stoic Marine merely answered with single words. Burns finally headed to McCoy's office too, pulling his cell phone out as he went.

Zane shared a glance with Ty, who shrugged.

One of the Marines took a few steps closer to the work groups and stood straight and tall. "Is there a B.T. Grady present?"

All eyes on the floor turned to Ty. Ty glanced around, his expression a mixture of confusion and trepidation. Then he stood, stepping away from Zane's desk. He matched the man's posture, a parody in his Converse sneakers and elephant T-shirt.

The Marine seemed startled, but he covered it quickly. "It's an honor to meet you, Staff Sergeant Grady."

"Special Agent Grady," Ty corrected.

The Marine gave a curt shake of his head and stepped forward, handing Ty a blue packet of papers. "I'm here to inform you that you have been recalled to active duty, Staff Sergeant, by special authority of the SOCOM initiative you agreed to when you were formerly released."

Ty reached out to take the orders, looking shell-shocked. He stared at the folded bunch of papers, then raised his head, meeting Zane's eyes briefly before looking back at the Marine. "And what if I refuse?"

"Then your team will be recalled without you, Staff Sergeant. And you and anyone else who refuses will spend up to three years in Leavenworth for dereliction of duty." There was no malice in the words, merely a Marine giving Ty the answer he had requested.

Ty was trying hard to keep his expression stony. "Thank you, Sergeant," he finally said, voice tight. The Marine turned on his heel and rejoined the other at the elevator, leaving with as little fanfare as they had arrived.

"Did you just get conscripted?" Lassiter asked.

Clancy stepped forward to look at the papers. "Jesus Christ, can they do that?"

Ty subtly turned the papers away from her and nodded.

"You're . . . you're going back to the Marines?" Alston stuttered. "I thought SOCOM was defunct."

"It's MARSOC now," Ty mumbled.

"But that's special operations. You don't have a choice?"

"No. I don't." He studied the orders. "I report in forty-eight hours. Immediate deployment."

Zane stood. His hands shook as he gripped the edge of the desk. Ty looked up, seeking Zane out. Zane could see it in Ty's eyes. There was no choice. No way to wriggle out of it. No way for anyone to save him.

"Oh God, Ty," Zane whispered.

Ty stared at him for a moment longer as the others broke into outraged babbling. Then Ty shook himself. He tossed the packet of orders onto the desk and stalked over to Zane.

He grabbed his face with both hands and kissed him.

The room spun to a halt. The babble ground to a stunned hush.

Ty's hands moved to the small of his back and he held him tight, bending him just enough for Zane to have to wrap his arms around him to keep from falling. He kissed him again. In front of their coworkers. In front of King and Country and anyone who would watch. It was the first purely honest kiss they'd ever shared.

And it was a kiss good-bye.

RP

ALSO BY
ABIGAIL ROUX

The Cut & Run Series

#1: Cut & Run (with Madeleine Urban)
#2: Sticks & Stones (with Madeleine Urban)
#3: Fish & Chips (with Madeleine Urban)
#4: Divide & Conquer (with Madeleine Urban)
#5: Armed & Dangerous
#6: Stars & Stripes

Novels

The Gravedigger's Brawl
According to Hoyle
Caught Running (with Madeleine Urban)
Love Ahead (with Madeleine Urban)
The Archer
Warrior's Cross (with Madeleine Urban)

Novellas

A Tale from de Rode
My Brother's Keeper
Seeing Is Believing
Unrequited

About the Author

Abigail Roux was born and raised in North Carolina. A past volleyball star who specializes in sarcasm and painful historical accuracy, she currently spends her time coaching high school volleyball and investigating the mysteries of single motherhood. Any spare time is spent living and dying with every Atlanta Braves and Carolina Panthers game of the year. Abigail has a daughter, Little Roux, who is the light of her life, a boxer, four rescued cats who play an ongoing live-action variation of Call of Duty throughout the house, one evil Ragdoll, a certifiable extended family down the road, and a cast of thousands in her head.

Enjoyed this book? Visit RiptidePublishing.com to find more romantic suspense!

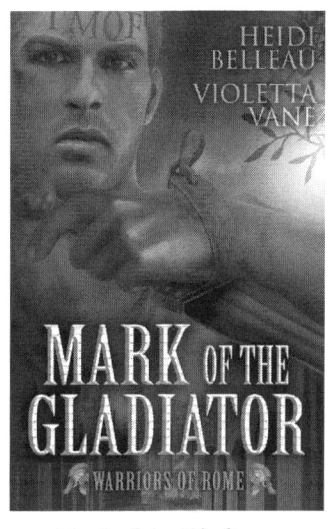

Mark of the Gladiator
ISBN: 978-1-937551-60-5

Santuario
ISBN: 978-1-937551-65-0

Earn Bonus Bucks!

Earn 1 Bonus Buck for each dollar you spend. Find out how at RiptidePublishing.com/news/bonus-bucks.

Win Free Ebooks for a Year!

Pre-order coming soon titles directly through our site and you'll receive one entry into a drawing to win free books for a year! Get the details at RiptidePublishing.com/contests.

RIPTIDE PUBLISHING

Printed in Great Britain
by Amazon.co.uk, Ltd.,
Marston Gate.